THE PENGU
FOUNDER EDITOR

GUY DE MAUPASSANT was born in Normandy in 1850. At his parents' separation he stayed with his mother, who was a friend of Flaubert. As a young man he was lively and athletic, but the first symptoms of syphilis appeared in the late 1870s. By this time Maupassant had become Flaubert's pupil in the art of prose. On the publication of the first short story to which he put his name, *Boule de Suif*, he left his job in the civil service and his temporary alliance with the disciples of Zola at Médan, and devoted all his energy to professional writing. In the next eleven years he published dozens of articles, nearly three hundred stories and six novels, the best known of which are *A Woman's Life*, *Bel-Ami* and *Pierre and Jean*. He led a hectic social life, lived up to his reputation for womanizing and fought his disease. By 1889 his friends saw that his mind was in danger, and in 1891 he attempted suicide and was committed to an asylum in Paris, where he died two years later.

ROGER COLET was educated in London, Paris and Grenoble. He lived for long periods in Normandy, where he first became interested in Maupassant's work. He now writes and paints in England, and is at work on a biography of Maupassant and a new translation of his *Bel-Ami*.

GUY DE MAUPASSANT

# SELECTED
# SHORT STORIES

TRANSLATED
WITH AN INTRODUCTION BY
ROGER COLET

PENGUIN BOOKS

Penguin Books Ltd, Harmondsworth, Middlesex, England
Penguin Books, 625 Madison Avenue, New York, New York 10022, U.S.A.
Penguin Books Australia Ltd, Ringwood, Victoria, Australia
Penguin Books Canada Ltd, 2801 John Street, Markham, Ontario, Canada L3R 1B4
Penguin Books (N.Z.) Ltd, 182–190 Wairau Road, Auckland 10, New Zealand

—

This translation first published 1971
Reprinted 1972, 1974, 1975, 1976, 1977, 1978, 1979

—

—

Made and printed in Great Britain by
Hazell Watson & Viney Ltd,
Aylesbury, Bucks
Set in Linotype Granjon

# CONTENTS

# CONTENTS

# INTRODUCTION

It is one of the ironies of literature that while Guy de Maupassant remains one of the most widely read of all authors in his own country and all over the world, the major critical studies of his work can be counted on the fingers of one hand. This gross neglect, and the contemptuous attitude which goes with it, cannot be ascribed to what was once considered the 'immorality' of his writings, for, in France at least, prudery long ago ceased to interfere with critical appreciation. A likelier cause may be seen in Maupassant's enormous popular success, both in his lifetime and since, for critics are notoriously reluctant to endorse judgments made by the public without their help and confirmed by generations of untutored readers. Worse still, they sometimes refuse even to read the work of any writer appreciated by the masses, and several sneering dismissals of Maupassant's talent by celebrated pundits in this century have clearly been based on the reading of only one or two stories, if that. And finally, those critics who have actually read Maupassant find him a difficult subject for exegesis: his stories are too intelligible to require learned elucidation, and his style too simple to give scope for scholarly commentary. He is the victim, in a sense, of his perfect art.

He was born on 5 August 1850 in Normandy, the province which he chose as the setting for many of his finest stories, though it is not known for certain exactly where. The register of births in the little village of Tourville-sur-Arques, five miles from Dieppe, gives his place of birth as the nearby Château de Miromesnil, but it is now believed that he was born in a humble house at Fécamp, and subsequently transferred to the imposing mansion which his parents were renting to give their first-born child a high-sounding birthplace.

His mother, Laure de Maupassant, was a neurotic, hysterical woman with a possessive passion for Guy and his younger brother Hervé, born six years later; while his father, Gustave de Maupassant, was an easy-going gentleman of leisure who made no secret of his preference for other women and was eventually persuaded to agree to a legal separation from his wife. Guy sided with his mother, and it has often been suggested that when he later portrayed countless cuckolded husbands in his stories he was taking revenge on the philandering Gustave on his mother's behalf. Another of his obsessive themes, that of the son fathered by a wife's lover, may also have been aimed at Gustave de Maupassant, for it is just possible that he was really the son of Laure's greatest friend, the novelist Gustave Flaubert, or at least suspected that to be the case.

Nothing in his early life gave any hint of the talent and creative energy he was to display in his maturity, although his unremarkable experiences in this period provided him with material for most of his later work. Thus scenes he witnessed as a young private in the retreating French army in 1870 reappeared in *Boule de Suif* and other stories of the Franco-Prussian War; the genteel poverty he saw at close quarters during the eighteen-seventies, when he was employed as a clerk in the Naval Ministry, furnished the background for tales such as *My Uncle Jules*; and his sporting activities – shooting in the autumn and rowing in the summer – gave rise to innumerable stories of field and river, from *Rust* to *Mouche*.

It is *Mouche*, indeed, which gives the real flavour of Maupassant's life in the seventies, hinting at the boredom of the weekday jobs of the five young friends, and evoking in vivid contrast the fun and camaraderie and sexual delights of Saturday night and Sunday. Written not long before the end of Maupassant's rational life, it conjures up as perfectly as the contemporary Renoir painting of a riverside restaurant a vanished world of mustachioed young men in boaters and striped jerseys and laughing girls in flowered bonnets. The details as well as the atmosphere of the story were largely accurate, according to the testimony given after Maupassant's death by Petit Bleu, a gentleman called Léon Fontaine, and La Tôque, *alias* Robert Pinchon, who at the end of the century was municipal librarian of Rouen. Fontaine wrote that N'a-qu'un-Oeil's name was Joinville, that the *Feuille-à-l'Envers* was really called the *Feuille-de-Rose* (the title of an obscene playlet written by Maupassant and Pinchon in 1875), and that Joseph Prunier was indeed the nickname of Maupassant himself, whom he described as 'a handsome, strapping fellow with an athlete's neck, body and biceps, enterprising, intrepid and exuberant, always gay and full of life'. Only two characters in the story have not been identified: Tomahawk and Mouche. But then, there were countless creatures like Mouche in Maupassant's life at that period, either casual companions like his delightful heroine, or actual prostitutes like the other occupants of a house in which he found himself the sole male lodger. And at some time in the seventies, in a riverside hotel or a Paris brothel, one of them infected Maupassant with the syphilis which was to destroy him.

In 1876 he complained of heart trouble, and two years later the same symptoms reappeared, accompanied by the loss of his hair and a skin disease. His condition was variously diagnosed as nicotine poisoning and rheumatism, and he was subjected to various treatments, from mineral waters to steam baths. At one point his doctors mentioned the possibility of a syphilitic infection, but, whatever their private opinion, they eventually convinced their patient that he was cured and that he had been suffering from nothing more serious than a nervous ailment inherited from his mother. In fact, however, as paralysis and later partial blindness of one eye indicated, the *spirocheta pallida* was firmly implanted, and in the absence of any effective cure Maupassant was doomed to madness and an early death.

Although Maupassant gave the impression of being simply a bull-necked oarsman and sexual athlete, he had begun writing poetry, with the encouragement of Flaubert's friend Louis Bouilhet and then of Flaubert himself. Gradually Flaubert and Maupassant had drawn together in an affectionate relationship, exchanging good-humoured and often obscene banter, and the master of Croisset had persuaded his young friend to try his hand at prose. Deciding that Maupassant was worthy of his tuition, he spent several years patiently coaching him in the art of writing, teaching him first of all the art of seeing. Reminding his pupil that 'talent is a long patience', he told him again and again: 'There is a part of everything which is unexplored, because we are accustomed to using our eyes only in association with the memory of what people before us have thought of the thing we are looking at. Even the smallest thing has something in it which is unknown. We must find it.' Having discovered what aspect of a person or object distinguished it from every other of the same race or species, Maupassant had then to describe it for his exacting mentor. 'Whatever you want to say,' he later quoted Flaubert as telling him, 'there is only one word to express it, only one verb to give it movement, only one adjective to qualify it. You must search for that word, that verb,

that adjective, and never be content with an approxima-
tion, never resort to tricks, even clever ones, and never
have recourse to verbal sleight-of-hand to avoid a difficulty.'

Year after year the disciple did his best to put the master's teaching into practice, sending him his literary exer-
cises every week and going to lunch with him the following
Sunday to hear his criticism. 'I wrote poetry,' he recalled
later, 'short stories, longer stories, even a detestable play.
Nothing of all this survives.' This was not strictly true.
Despite Flaubert's exhortations, he had been unable to
resist the temptation to publish a few of his efforts –
notably the macabre story entitled *The Hand* – in obscure
periodicals, but at least he had been careful to sign them
with a pseudonym. Not until 1880 did he feel sufficiently
confident to put his own name to a story, and when that
moment came Flaubert's counsels of patience were seen to
be fully justified. For the story in question was *Boule de
Suif*.

During the late seventies Maupassant had met four other
young men with literary ambitions who were united in
their admiration for Émile Zola, the most exciting and
controversial novelist of the decade. Of the four – Joris-
Karl Huysmans, Henry Céard, Paul Alexis and Léon
Hennique – only Huysmans had any real talent, and it is
difficult to avoid the suspicion that Maupassant joined up
with them simply to further his own ambitions. For a
while he reluctantly allowed himself to be classified as a
budding 'Naturalist' and a member of the so-called 'Médan
Group' – named after the country house at Médan, near
Paris, where Zola entertained the five young men he mis-
takenly considered his disciples; and when the Group decided to publish a collection of short stories, *Les Soirées
de Médan*, on the theme of the Franco-Prussian War, Mau-

passant contributed a tale about a Rouen prostitute inspired, it seems, by a woman called Adrienne Legay. His fellow authors, knowing nothing of the long apprenticeship he had served with Flaubert, were amazed at the revelation of his talent; Zola himself admitted that it outclassed his own story and was 'certainly the best of the six'; while Flaubert – who was to die less than a month after the book's appearance – proudly asserted that '*Boule de Suif*, the story by my disciple ... is a masterpiece of writing, comedy and observation'.

As if this success had been a signal to break with the past, Maupassant promptly left his post in the civil service, quietly dissociated himself from Zola and the other members of the Médan Group, and devoted all his energy and talent to his new career as a professional writer. In the next eleven years he published a vast body of work – dozens of articles, nearly three hundred stories, and six novels – almost all of a consistently high standard, while at the same time leading a hectic social life, living up to his reputation as a womanizer, and trying to combat the effects of his steadily encroaching disease. It is impossible to tell exactly when the first signs of insanity appeared, although most biographies point to 1887, when Maupassant published *The Horla*, one of the most terrifying stories of madness – or the supernatural – ever written. Admittedly the subjects of possession and dual personality were in fashion at the time, and the artistry of *The Horla* cannot be faulted; but then, the last stories Maupassant ever wrote, such as the light-hearted *Mouche*, were likewise impeccable works of art, and it is on record that he had earlier told Paul Bourget of having hallucinatory visions of his *alter ego*. In any case, by 1889 it had become obvious to Maupassant's friends that his mind was in danger, and when he saw his brother Hervé die that year of general paralysis of the insane, he must have realized that his turn could not be long delayed. At the end of 1891 he wrote to a friend that he was going mad and maintained that his brain was running out through his nose and mouth. A few days later he tried to commit suicide and was committed to Dr Blanche's asylum in Paris, where he died on 6 July 1893, aged forty-two.

Of the works he left behind, three of the novels – *A Woman's Life*, *Bel-Ami* and *Pierre and Jean* – still rank high in popular and critical esteem, but his greatest achievement is generally considered to lie in the short story, a *genre* which he revived and consecrated, and of which he became the supreme exponent in any literature. If the number of stories which he wrote during his brief career is a subject for astonishment, so is their infinite variety. In length they range from brief anecdote to miniature novel, in form from traditional narrative or reminiscence to dialogue or diary, in setting from elegant spa to peasant cottage, and in subject from murder and passion to an elderly sportsman's impotence. There are, admittedly, certain themes – adultery, prostitution, the Franco-Prussian War, the pleasures of river and countryside, and the cunning and avarice of the Norman peasantry – which recur frequently in Maupassant's stories; but they are always treated differently, and they serve, so to speak, as familiar landmarks to which the author turns repeatedly for support and inspiration. It is not insignificant that as insanity and death closed in on him, Maupassant nostalgically recalled his idyllic boating days in the story *Mouche*, and gave his last, unfinished novel, *The Angelus*, the same unforgettable wartime setting as his first literary success.

Maupassant's denigrators are fond of suggesting that he is an outdated writer, a *fin-de-siècle* fossil pathetically obsessed with old-fashioned national animosities and bour-

geois adulteries, whose stories have no relevance for us today. Nothing could be further from the truth. His characters have the same vices and virtues, the same passions and
obsessions as ourselves; but for generations the English
and American publics have been obliged to read Maupassant in expurgated or hideously emasculated translations,
because it was thought that they would be unable to accept
the realities of life which he depicts. The reader who dis-
misses Maupassant's war stories as the chauvinistic propa-
ganda of a nineteenth-century Prussophobe should ask himself whether *Mother Savage* might not just as well be the
tale of any modern martyr rebelling against an occupying
power, and note that the narrator also spares some pity for
the murdered soldiers of the occupation army and their
families. Likewise the reader who thinks, like many critics,
that Maupassant's attitude to sex is that of the dirty-
minded bar-room *raconteur* will be surprised to discover
him, in stories such as *In the Bedroom* and *Imprudence*,
ridiculing the notorious male 'double standard' more effec-
tively than any modern champion of sexual honesty and
sanity.

Possibly the most serious of all misconceptions about
Maupassant is the idea, held even by some of his admirers,
that he was nothing more than an observer, adept at de-
picting the surface of life but incapable of seeing the
hidden realities, supernatural or psychological. Yet surely
nobody who has read stories such as *The Horla* can fail
to realize that Maupassant was profoundly aware of the
existence of mysterious forces in the universe – forces of
which he was most conscious in holy places from Mont
Saint-Michel to Moslem shrines. As for the psychological
realities to which he is supposed to have been blind, he
was in fact obsessed with the idea of discovering and revealing the truth behind the façade of most human lives,

whether it was the old man's wrinkled face behind a mummer's youthful mask, the selfishness behind the smug respectability of a prostitute's companions, or the adulterous passion behind a doctor's subterfuge. However, where most writers would analyse their characters' thoughts and emotions, and perhaps even point a clumsy moral, Maupassant allows his characters' words and actions to express all that he has to say – a technique of deliberate restraint which simple-minded critics have inevitably mistaken for superficiality or incompetence.

The realities which Maupassant lays bare in his stories, with a zeal born perhaps of an anxious determination not to be deceived himself, are rarely pleasant. A pessimist by nature, a pessimist from the influence and example of his friend and mentor Flaubert, and a pessimist out of admiration for the great philosopher of his time, Arthur Schopenhauer, Maupassant saw avarice and lechery, cruelty and greed, selfishness and hatred at work wherever he turned.

In one of the most enthusiastic tributes ever paid to Schopenhauer, he declared that the German philosopher had 'stamped mankind with the seal of his disdain and disenchantment', and continued: 'He has upset belief, hope, poetry, fantasy, destroyed aspirations, ravaged confidence, killed love, overthrown the idealistic cult of womanhood, murdered the illusions of the heart, and altogether performed the most gigantic sceptical operation ever carried out. He has riddled everything with his mockery, and drained everything dry.' Maupassant himself was temperamentally incapable of going so far. His ridicule is never cruel, his sadness never quite despair. With his hatred of the world qualified by sensual love of the good things of life, with his suspicion of women lulled by sympathy for victims such as Boule de Suif or Mouche, and with his detestation of the rich and pretentious balanced by his pity for the poor and simple, he remains one of the sanest, kindest, most moving and heartwarming storytellers of all time.

ROGER COLET

## Translator's Note

THE stories in this selection have been arranged in the order of their publication under Maupassant's own name. Thus *The Hand*, which originally appeared under a pseudonym in 1875, is placed according to its publication under the author's real name in 1883. I make no apology for the omission of *The Necklace*, with its notorious trick ending so often regarded – quite unjustly – as typical of its author. In its place I have included *The Jewels*, a vastly superior story in which the reader guesses the truth long before the hero, and the ending of which is sad, but no surprise.

R.C.

# BOULE DE SUIF

FOR several days in succession remnants of a routed army had been passing through the town. They were not disciplined units but bands of stragglers. The men's beards were unkempt and dirty, their uniforms in rags, and they slouched along without colours or regiments. All of them seemed crushed and exhausted, incapable of thought or resolution, marching only out of force of habit and dropping with fatigue as soon as they stopped. Most of them were reservists, men of peace who had been quietly living on private means and who were staggering under the weight of their rifles, or lively little militiamen, as prone to panic as they were to enthusiasm and as ready to attack as they were to flee. Among them were a few regulars in red breeches, the remains of some division ground to powder in a big battle; sombrely clad gunners intermingled with all these different infantrymen; and here and there the shining helmet of a dragoon, whose heavy tread was making it difficult for him to keep up with the brisker pace of the soldiers of the line.

Detachments of *francs-tireurs* with high-sounding names – the Avengers of Defeat, the Citizens of the Grave, the Companions of Death – passed through in their turn, looking like bandits.

Their leaders, former drapers and corn-merchants or sometime dealers in soap and tallow, were only temporary warriors who had been elected officers by virtue of their money or the length of their moustaches. Armed to the teeth and covered with flannel and gold braid, they talked in loud voices, discussing plans of campaign and boastfully declaring that they alone were carrying their dying country on their shoulders. But they sometimes went in fear of their own men, thorough-going scoundrels who were often incredibly brave but given to looting and debauchery.

People were saying that the Prussians would soon be in Rouen.

The National Guard, who for the last two months had been cautiously reconnoitring the neighbouring woods, occasionally shooting their own sentries, and preparing for action every time a rabbit stirred in the undergrowth, had gone home. Their arms, their uniforms, all the apparatus of war which had previously made them the terror of the highroads for miles around, had suddenly disappeared.

The last French soldiers had finally just crossed the Seine, making for Pont-Audemer by way of Saint-Sever and Bourg-Achard. In their rear, walking between the two staff officers, came the general. In despair, unable to attempt anything with this disorganized rabble, he was bewildered himself by the disaster which had overwhelmed a people accustomed to victory and now, despite its legendary courage, utterly defeated.

Then a profound calm, an atmosphere of silent, terrified foreboding had descended upon the town. A great many pot-bellied citizens, emasculated by years of trade and commerce, waited anxiously for the arrival of the conquerors, terrified lest their roasting-spits or their long kitchen knives might be regarded as weapons.

Life seemed to have come to a standstill; the shops were closed, the streets deserted. Now and then some inhabitants, awed by this silence, would hurry along, keeping close to the walls.

The strain of waiting made everybody long for the enemy to arrive.

On the afternoon of the day following the departure of the French troops, a few Uhlans, appearing from heaven knows where, galloped through the town. Then, a little later, a dark mass of troops swept down St Catherine's hill, while two other invading torrents streamed in along the roads from Darnetal and Boisguillaume. The advance-guards of the three bodies, arriving at exactly the same moment, linked up on the Place de l'Hôtel-de-Ville; and the German army came pouring down all the nearby streets, the cobblestones ringing under the heavy, measured tread of its battalions.

Orders shouted in a strange guttural tongue resounded along the walls of the houses, which seemed dead and deserted, while behind the closed shutters eyes watched the conquerors, who by right of war were now masters of the city and of the lives and fortunes of its people. In their darkened rooms the inhabitants had given way to the same feeling of panic which is aroused by natural cataclysms, those devastating upheavals of the earth against which wisdom and strength alike are of no avail. For the same feeling is experienced whenever the established order of things is upset, when security ceases to exist, and when all that was previously protected by the laws of man or Nature is suddenly placed at the mercy of brutal, unreasoning force. The earthquake burying a whole people beneath the ruins of their houses; the river in spate sweeping away the bodies of drowned peasants together with the carcases of cattle and rafters torn from roofs; or the victorious army slaughtering all who resist, making prisoners of the rest, looting by right of the sword and thanking their god to the sound of cannon – all these are terrifying scourges which undermine all our belief in eternal justice and all the trust we have been taught to place in divine protection and human reason.

Small detachments of men were soon knocking at the door of every house and disappearing inside. Occupation was following invasion. The time had come for the vanquished to be obliging to the victors.

After a little while, once the first panic had subsided, a new sort of calm descended on the town. In many homes a Prussian officer took his meals with the family. Sometimes he was a man of breeding and out of politeness expressed sympathy with France, saying how much he disliked taking part in this war. His hosts were grateful to him for this sentiment; besides, some day they might need his protection. If they humoured him, they might perhaps have fewer men billeted on them. And why hurt somebody's feelings when you were entirely in his power? To do so would be to display foolhardiness rather than courage – and foolhardiness is no longer one of the failings of the burghers of Rouen, as it was in the days when the heroic defence of their city had brought them honour and glory. Finally, looking for their supreme justification in the French tradition of courtesy, they argued that it was perfectly permissible to treat the foreign soldiers politely inside their own homes provided that there was no fraternization in public. Outside they refused to recognize them, but indoors they were quite prepared to chat with them, and the Germans stayed longer with them every evening, warming themselves at the domestic hearth.

The town itself gradually began to assume its normal appearance. True, the French did not go out much as yet, but the streets swarmed with Prussian soldiers. What is more, the officers of the Blue Hussars, arrogantly trailing their great instruments of death along the pavement, did not seem to show much more contempt for ordinary civilians than had the French light infantry officers who the year before had sat drinking in the same cafés.

There was, however, something in the air, something subtle and mysterious, an unbearable alien atmosphere which hung about like a smell – the smell of invasion. It filled the town's houses and public places, changed the taste of foodstuffs, and made people feel as if they were in a foreign land, far from home, among dangerous savage tribes.

The conquerors demanded money, a great deal of money. The inhabitants went on paying up; after all, they were rich enough. But the wealthier a Norman business-man becomes, the more keenly he feels any sacrifice and the more he suffers at seeing any portion of his fortune pass into other hands.

In the meantime, five or six miles downstream from the city, in the vicinity of Croisset, Dieppedalle or Biessart, bargees or fishermen often used to bring up from the riverbed the bloated corpses of Germans in uniform, who had been stabbed or kicked to death, or had their heads smashed in with a stone, or been pushed over the parapet of a bridge. The river mud swallowed up the victims of these secret acts of vengeance, savage but legitimate, these unknown deeds of heroism, these silent attacks, more dangerous than battles fought in broad daylight and without the reward of fame.

For hatred of the foreigner always inspires a few brave men who are ready to die for an ideal.

At length, as the invaders, while subjecting the town to their inflexible discipline, had perpetrated none of the atrocities which rumour had attributed to them throughout the course of their triumphal progress, the inhabitants plucked up courage, and the urge to do business stirred again in the hearts of the local tradesmen. Some of them had considerable business interests at Le Havre, which was still in the hands of the French army, and they were anxious to try to reach that port by travelling overland to Dieppe and there taking ship.

Using the influence of German officers whose acquaintance they had made, they succeeded in obtaining a permit to leave Rouen from the general in command.

A large four-horse coach was accordingly hired for this journey, ten persons reserved seats in it, and it was decided to set off one Tuesday morning before daybreak to avoid any risk of drawing a crowd.

For some days now the ground had been frozen hard, and on the Monday, about three o'clock in the afternoon, great dark clouds from the north brought snow which fell continuously all that evening and throughout the night.

At half past four in the morning the travellers met in the courtyard of the Hôtel de Normandie, where they were to board the coach.

They were still half asleep, and shivering with cold under their wraps. They could scarcely see each other in the darkness and with all the heavy winter clothing they had put on they looked like portly priests in long cassocks. But two of the men recognized each other, a third joined them, and they got into conversation.

'I'm taking my wife away,' said one.

'So am I.'

'Me too.'

The first added: 'We're not coming back to Rouen, and if the Prussians advance on Le Havre, we're going to cross over to England.'

All three had the same intentions, being of the same ilk.

Meanwhile there was no sign of the horses. A small lantern carried by an ostler emerged now and then from one dark doorway, only to disappear straight away into another. The sound of horses' hoofs stamping on the ground could be heard, muffled by the manure in the litters, and the voice of a man talking to the animals and swearing came from the far end of the building. A faint tinkle of bells proclaimed that the harness was being put on; and this sound soon became a loud, continuous jingling, changing its rhythm with the horses' movements, stopping occasionally and then starting again with a sudden jerk accompanied by the dull thud of an iron-shod hoof on the ground.

Suddenly the door closed and all was silent. The frozen travellers had stopped talking and stood there stiff and motionless.

A curtain of glistening white flakes was falling ceaselessly towards the ground, blurring outlines and powdering every object with an icy coating. In the deep silence of the town, buried in a wintry calm, nothing could be heard but that vague, indefinable, rustling whisper, felt rather than heard, of the falling snow, a mingling of airy particles which seemed to be filling the sky and covering the world.

The man reappeared with his lantern, pulling along by a rope a miserable and reluctant horse. He made it stand by the pole and fastened the traces, spending a long time adjusting the harness, for he could use only one hand as the other was holding the lantern. As he was going back to fetch a second horse he noticed all the travellers standing there motionless, already white with snow.

'Why don't you get inside the coach?' he said. 'At least you'd be under cover.'

This idea had apparently not occurred to them, and they made a rush for the door. The three men installed their wives at the far end and got in themselves. Then the other vague, muffled figures took the remaining places without a word.

Their feet sank into the straw which covered the floor.

The ladies at the far end had brought with them some little copper foot-warmers heated by a chemical fuel, and they now lit these contraptions, extolling their advantages for some time in low voices, and repeating to one another facts of which they had long been aware.

At last the coach was ready, with six horses harnessed to it instead of four because of the extra effort required in the snow, and a voice outside asked: 'Is everybody in?' A voice from inside replied: 'Yes,' and they started off.

The coach moved slowly and laboriously. The wheels sank into the snow and the whole vehicle creaked and groaned. The horses slipped and panted and steamed and the driver's huge whip cracked incessantly, darting in every direction, tying itself into knots and then uncoiling like a slender snake, and suddenly stinging some rounded crupper, which promptly tensed into a greater effort.

Imperceptibly the darkness began to give place to light. The fall of feathery snowflakes which one of the travellers, a Rouen man born and bred, had compared to scraps of cottonwool, had stopped. A dingy light filtered through the huge, lowering clouds, whose leaden colour set off the dazzling whiteness of the countryside, against which there stood out, here a row of tall trees coated with frost, there a cottage under a cowl of snow.

Inside the coach the travellers inspected one another inquisitively in the melancholy light of dawn.

In the best places at the far end, Monsieur and Madame Loiseau, wholesale wine-merchants in the Rue Grand-Pont, sat dozing opposite each other.

Once the clerk to a wine-merchant who had gone bankrupt, Loiseau had bought the business and made a fortune. He sold very bad wine at very low prices to the small retailers in the country, and was regarded by his friends and acquaintances as a cunning scoundrel, a typical Norman full of guile and joviality.

His reputation as a crook was so well established that one evening at the Prefecture, a local celebrity called Monsieur Tournel, an author of songs and stories and a man of sharp and caustic wit, suggested to the ladies, who seemed a little drowsy, that they should ask Monsieur Loiseau to teach them Beggar-my-neighbour. The witticism had spread rapidly through the Prefect's drawing-rooms, and from there to the other drawing-rooms in the town, setting the whole province laughing for a month.

Loiseau himself was famous for practical jokes of all kinds, good and bad, and nobody could mention his name without adding immediately: 'Loiseau's a real card.'

He was a small man with a large pot-belly and a red face framed in grizzled sidewhiskers.

His wife, a tall, stout, strong-minded woman, shrill-voiced and quick to make decisions, ran the firm and did the book-keeping, while he kept the business alive with his jovial vitality.

Next to them, and more dignified, as befitted a member of a superior social class, sat Monsieur Carré-Lamadon, a man of substance with a solid position in the cotton business, the owner of three spinning-mills, an officer of the Legion of Honour, and a member of the General Council. Throughout the period of the Empire he had remained the leader of the benevolent opposition, simply in order to extract a higher price for his support of a policy which he fought with what he called 'gentlemanly weapons'. Madame Carré-Lamadon, who was much younger than her husband, had been a constant comfort to those officers of good family who were quartered in Rouen.

She sat facing her husband, a dainty, pretty little thing

muffled up in her furs, gazing disconsolately at the depressing interior of the coach.

Her neighbours, the Comte and Comtesse Hubert de Bréville, bore one of the oldest and noblest names in Normandy. The Comte, an elderly nobleman of distinguished appearance, did all he could to accentuate by the artifices of dress his natural resemblance to King Henri IV, who, according to a legend of which the family was very proud, had got a Madame de Bréville with child, rewarding her husband by making him a count and the governor of a province.

Comte Hubert served with Monsieur Carré-Lamadon on the General Council, where he represented the Orleanist party in the Department. The story of his marriage to the daughter of a small Nantes ship-owner had always remained a mystery. But as the Comtesse had a distinguished manner, was an incomparable hostess, and was said to have been the mistress of one of Louis-Philippe's sons, the local aristocracy all paid court to her, and her *salon* was the most exclusive in the region, the only one where old-world courtesy survived and to which access was difficult.

The Brévilles' fortune, which was all in landed property, was said to produce an annual income of half a million francs.

These six persons occupied the far end of the coach, representing the moneyed, self-assured, solid element of society, the respectable, privileged folk with a proper respect for religion and morality.

By a strange coincidence all the women were seated on the same side, and next to the Comtesse were two nuns telling their beads and muttering *paternosters* and *aves*. One of them was an old woman whose skin was pitted with smallpox as if she had received a charge of grapeshot full in the face at point-blank range. The other was a puny creature with a pretty, sickly-looking face and the narrow chest of a consumptive, eaten up by that devouring faith which makes martyrs and visionaries.

Opposite the two nuns were a man and a woman who attracted everybody's interest.

The man, a well-known figure, was Cornudet, the democrat, the terror of all respectable people. For twenty years he had been dipping his long red beard in mugs of beer in all the democratic cafés. With the help of his friends and comrades he had squandered a sizeable fortune inherited from his father, a retired confectioner, and he was waiting impatiently for the coming of the Republic to obtain at long last the official position he had earned with so many revolutionary potations. On the Fourth of September, possibly as the result of a practical joke, he had got the idea that he had been appointed Prefect, but when he had tried to take up his duties the office messengers, left in sole charge of the Prefecture, had refused to recognize him and he had been forced to beat a retreat. A good-natured fellow, though, inoffensive and obliging, he had devoted himself with incomparable enthusiasm to organizing the defence of the town. He had had pits dug in the open country, all the young trees in the nearby forests felled, and booby-traps scattered over all the roads. Satisfied with his preparations, he had hurriedly withdrawn into the town on the approach of the enemy. Now he thought that he could be more useful at Le Havre, where new defensive positions would have to be established.

The woman, one of those who are generally known as of easy virtue, was famous for her premature corpulence, which had earned her the nickname of Boule de Suif, or Suet Dumpling. Short, completely round, fat as a pig, with puffy fingers constricted at the joints like strings of tiny sausages, taut shiny skin, and huge breasts swelling underneath her dress, her freshness was so attractive that she nonetheless remained desirable and much sought after. Her face was like a ruddy apple, or a peony bud about to burst into flower; and out of it looked two splendid black eyes shaded and deepened by thick lashes. Beneath them was a charming little mouth with moist, inviting lips and tiny, gleaming teeth.

She was also said to possess many other inestimable qualities.

As soon as she was recognized the respectable women began to whisper among themselves, and the words 'prostitute' and 'absolute scandal' were whispered loudly enough to make her raise her eyes. The look she gave her neighbours was so bold and challenging that there was a sudden silence, and everybody dropped their eyes except for Loiseau, who fixed a lecherous gaze on her.

But conversation was soon resumed between the three ladies, whom the prostitute's presence had suddenly made friends, almost intimates. It was their duty, they felt, to confront this shameless whore with their united marital dignity, for legalized love always looks down on its free colleague.

The three men too, drawn together by a conservative instinct at the sight of Cornudet, started discussing money matters in a tone which showed a certain contempt for the poor. Comte Hubert spoke of the damage the Prussians had caused him, the losses he had suffered in stolen cattle and ruined crops, with the assurance of a great landowner, a millionaire ten times over, who would recoup all these losses in less than a year. Monsieur Carré-Lamadon, who had been hard hit in the cotton business, had taken the precaution of sending six hundred thousand francs to England, so as to have something stored away for a rainy day.

As for Loiseau, he had arranged to sell the French Commissariat all the cheap wine he had left in his cellars, so that the State owed him a large sum of money which he hoped to collect at Le Havre.

All three exchanged quick, friendly glances. Although they belonged to different social classes, they were conscious of being brothers in wealth, members of that great freemasonry of the well-to-do, who can always be sure of having money to jingle in their trouser pockets.

The coach moved so slowly that by ten o'clock in the morning they had covered less than ten miles. The men got out three times to walk up hills. They were beginning to get worried, for they had intended to lunch at Tôtes, and now there seemed little hope of their arriving there before nightfall. Everybody was keeping a look-out for a wayside inn when the coach got stuck in a snowdrift, and it took two hours to pull it out.

Increasing hunger began to affect the company's spirits, but there was no sign of an eating-house or a tavern, since the approach of the Prussians and the passage of the starving French troops had scared away all trade.

The gentlemen tried to get food from the farms by the roadside, but they could not even obtain any bread, for the suspicious peasants had hidden their stocks away for fear of being robbed by the soldiers who, with nothing to eat, were taking by force anything they found.

About one o'clock in the afternoon, Loiseau announced that there was no doubt about it, he had an aching void in his stomach. Everybody had been suffering in the same way for a long time; and the craving for food, becoming steadily more acute, had killed all conversation.

From time to time somebody yawned, and almost at once somebody else would follow suit. Each person in turn, according to his character, breeding and social position, opened his mouth noisily, or politely put his hand in front of the gaping, steaming orifice.

Several times Boule de Suif bent down as if she were looking for something under her petticoats. She would hesitate for a moment, glance at her neighbours, and then quietly straighten up again. Every face was pale and drawn. Loiseau declared that he would give a thousand francs for a knuckle of ham. His wife made as if to protest, but then subsided. It was always painful to her to hear anybody talk about throwing money away, and she could not even understand jokes on the subject.

'I must admit I don't feel at all well,' said the Comte. 'Why on earth didn't I think of bringing some provisions?'

Everybody was blaming himself for the same omission.

Cornudet, however, had a flask of rum; he offered it round, but met with a cold refusal. Loiseau alone accepted a drop, and, when he handed back the flask expressed his thanks: 'That's good stuff, all the same. It warms you up and takes the edge off your hunger.'

The alcohol put him in a good humour and he suggested imitating the sailors in the song about the little boat and eating the fattest of the passengers. This indirect allusion to Boule de Suif shocked his more refined companions. Nobody said a word; only Cornudet smiled. The two nuns had stopped mumbling over their rosaries and were now sitting motionless, their hands thrust into their long sleeves and their eyes stubbornly downcast, no doubt offering up to Heaven the suffering it was inflicting on them.

At last, at three o'clock, when they were in the middle of an endless plain without a single village in sight, Boule de Suif bent down quickly and brought out from under her seat a large basket covered with a white napkin.

From it she took, first a small china plate and a dainty

silver drinking-cup, and then a huge pie-dish containing two whole chickens carved up and embedded in aspic. Other good things could be seen carefully wrapped up in the basket – *pâtés*, fruit and other delicacies – for she had packed enough food for a three days' journey, so as not to have to touch the fare provided in inns. The necks of four bottles protruded from among the packets of eatables. She took the wing of a chicken and began eating it daintily with one of those small rolls of bread which are called Regency rolls in Normandy.

Every eye was fixed on her. Then the smell of the food spread through the coach, making nostrils distend, mouths water, and jaw muscles twitch painfully under ears. The ladies' contempt for the hussy grew into a ferocious longing to kill her or throw her out into the snow with her drinking-cup, her basket, and all her provisions.

But Loiseau was devouring the pie-dish and its contents with his eyes.

'Well,' he said, 'there's no denying Madame had more foresight than the rest of us. Some people think of everything.'

She looked at him.

'Would you like some, Monsieur?' she asked. 'It's no fun going without food all day.'

He bowed.

'Frankly, I can't refuse; I'm at the end of my tether. But you've got to rough it in wartime, eh, Madame?' And, glancing round the coach, he added: 'At times like these it's good to meet somebody who'll give you a helping hand.'

He had a newspaper, which he spread over his knees so as not to dirty his trousers, and with the point of a knife which he always carried in his pocket he speared a leg of chicken thickly coated with jelly, tore at it with his teeth, and munched away with such obvious relish that a great sigh of distress went up from his companions.

In a low, respectful voice Boule de Suif invited the nuns to share her meal. They both accepted immediately, and, without raising their eyes, began eating very quickly after stammering their thanks. Cornudet did not refuse his neighbour's offer either, and the four of them made a sort of table by spreading newspapers over their knees.

Mouths opened and shut without pause, swallowing, chewing and gulping ravenously. Loiseau, eating away in his corner, urged his wife in a low voice to follow his example. She held out for a long time, but after a pang of hunger which went right through her vitals, gave in. Then her husband, in a well-turned phrase, asked their 'charming companion' if he might offer Madame Loiseau a small portion.

'Why, certainly, Monsieur,' she replied with a pleasant smile, and handed him the dish.

A difficulty arose when the first bottle of claret was opened; there was only one drinking-cup. They passed it round, each person wiping it in turn. Cornudet alone, presumably out of gallantry, put his mouth to the rim where it was still moist from his neighbour's lips.

Surrounded by people eating and drinking, and half choked by the smell of the food, the Comte and Comtesse de Bréville and Monsieur and Madame Carré-Lamadon suffered the agonies of that hideous torment associated with the name of Tantalus. All of a sudden the manufacturer's young wife heaved a sigh which attracted everybody's attention. She was as white as the snow outside; her eyes closed, her head fell forward: she had lost consciousness. Her distracted husband appealed for help. Everybody was at a loss except for the elder of the two nuns, who, supporting the young lady's head, forced the rim of Boule de

Suif's drinking-cup between her lips and made her swallow a few drops of wine. The lady stirred, opened her eyes, smiled, and declared in a faint voice that she felt quite well again. But to prevent a repetition of what had happened the nun made her drink a whole cupful of claret, saying as she did so: 'It's nothing but hunger.'

Then Boule de Suif, blushing in confusion, looked at the four travellers who were still fasting, and stammered: 'Heavens, if only I dared to offer these ladies and gentlemen . . .' She broke off, fearing a rebuff.

Loiseau came to her rescue.

'Dammit all,' he said, 'in a case like this we're all brothers in adversity and ought to help one another. Come, ladies, don't stand on ceremony: accept her offer! Why, we can't even be sure that we'll find a place to sleep tonight. At this rate, we shan't get to Tôtes before midday tomorrow.'

There was a pause, nobody wanting to take the responsibility of saying 'yes'.

It was the Comte who settled the question. Turning to the fat, shy woman, and assuming his lordliest air, he said to her: 'Madame, we gratefully accept your offer.'

The first step was the only difficulty. Once the Rubicon had been crossed they set to with a will, emptying the basket. It still contained a *pâté de foie gras*, a lark *pâté*, a piece of smoked tongue, some Crassane pears, a slab of Pont-l'Évêque cheese, some fancy biscuits, and a jar of gherkins and pickled onions, for Boule de Suif, like all women, loved sharp flavours.

It was impossible to eat the woman's food without talking to her. So talk to her they did, at first with a certain reserve, then, as her manners seemed very good, with greater freedom. Madame de Bréville and Madame Carré-Lamadon, who were women of the world, were gracious and tactful. The Comtesse in particular showed the kindly condescension of the great lady whom no contact can possibly smirch and was very charming. But stout Madame Loiseau, who had the soul of a gendarme, remained surly, saying little and eating a lot.

The conversation naturally turned on the war, the atrocities perpetrated by the Prussians and the gallant deeds of the French. All these people who were fleeing for their lives paid tribute to the courage of those who were staying behind. Before long they got on to personal experiences and Boule de Suif, with genuine emotion and that vigorous language which women of her profession sometimes employ to express their feelings, told how she had come to leave Rouen.

'I thought at first that I'd be able to stay,' she said. 'My house was full of food, and I preferred feeding a few soldiers to going off heaven knows where. But when I saw those Prussians, it was more than I could stand. They made my blood boil, and I cried with shame all day. Oh, if only I were a man! I used to look at them out of the window, those fat swine with their spiked helmets, and my maid had to hold my hands to keep me from throwing the furniture out on to their heads. Then some of them were billeted on me. Well, I went for the throat of the first who arrived – they're no harder to strangle than anybody else. I'd have done for him too, if they hadn't dragged me off by the hair. After that I had to go in hiding. Finally I got a chance to leave the town, and here I am.'

She was warmly congratulated. She had risen in the esteem of her companions, who had been far less courageous. Cornudet smiled as he listened to her with the benevolent approval of an apostle, like a priest hearing a devout member of his flock praising God, for bearded democrats think they have the monopoly of patriotism, just as the men in cassocks do of religion. He spoke in his turn, laying down the law with a pomposity learnt from the proclamations posted up on the walls every day, and he wound up with a peroration in which he gave a verbal trouncing to 'that scoundrel Badinguet', as he called Napoleon III.

But Boule de Suif immediately flared up, for she was a Bonapartist. Turning as red as a turkey-cock, and stammering with indignation, she cried: 'I'd like to have seen you lot in his place. A nice mess you'd have made of it! It's folk like you that have let him down! If France was governed by blackguards like you, there'd be nothing for it but to clear out.'

Cornudet was unmoved and continued to smile his superior, disdainful smile, but it was obvious that high words were soon going to be exchanged. However, the Comte intervened and, not without difficulty, pacified the exasperated young woman, declaring authoritatively that all opinions sincerely held were entitled to respect. Nonetheless, the Comtesse and the manufacturer's wife, who nurtured in their hearts the irrational hatred felt by all respectable people for the Republic, and that instinctive admiration all women have for flamboyant and despotic governments, were drawn in spite of themselves to this dignified prostitute whose convictions were so similar to their own.

The basket was empty. The ten travellers had made short work of its contents, their only regret being that it was not larger. Conversation continued for a while, but in a somewhat chillier atmosphere after the end of the meal.

Night was falling. The darkness gradually grew denser and the cold, which is always felt more keenly during the process of digestion, made Boule de Suif shiver in spite of her fat. Madame de Bréville offered her the use of her foot-warmer, in which the fuel had been renewed several times since the morning, and Boule de Suif accepted with alacrity, for her feet were freezing. Madame Carré-Lamadon and Madame Loiseau gave their foot-warmers to the nuns.

The driver had lit his lamps. They shed a vivid glare on the cloud of steam rising from the cruppers of the two wheelers, and on the snow on both sides of the road, which seemed to be unrolling under the moving beams of light.

It was no longer possible to make out anything inside the coach, but suddenly there was a movement between Boule de Suif and Cornudet; and Loiseau, peering through the darkness, thought he saw the bearded man start back as if he had received a sharp but silent blow.

Some little points of light appeared on the road ahead. It was Tôtes. They had been travelling for eleven hours, and the four halts of half an hour each, to allow the horses to eat their oats and recover their wind, made thirteen hours in all. They entered the village and drew up in front of the Hôtel du Commerce.

The door opened. A familiar sound made all the travellers start: it was the clanking of a scabbard on the ground. Immediately afterwards something was shouted out in a German voice.

Although the coach was stationary, nobody got out. It was as if they all expected to be murdered as soon as they emerged. Then the driver appeared, holding one of his lanterns, which cast a sudden beam of light all the way down the coach, revealing two rows of frightened faces with mouths open and eyes bulging with terror and surprise.

Standing beside the driver in the full glare of the lantern was a German officer, a tall young man, incredibly slim and fair, in a uniform as tight-fitting as a woman's corset, and wearing on one side of his head a flat, shiny cap which made him look like a page-boy in an English hotel. His huge moustache, with its long, straight hairs tapering off imperceptibly and finishing on each side in a single fair hair so fine that the end was invisible, seemed to weigh down the corners of his mouth, and, by dragging down his cheeks, to give his lips a drooping appearance.

Speaking in French with an Alsatian accent, he invited the passengers to alight, saying curtly: 'Please get out, ladies and gentlemen.'

The two nuns were the first to obey, with the meekness of pious women accustomed to absolute submission. Then the Comte and Comtesse emerged, followed by the manufacturer and his wife. Next came Loiseau, pushing his better and larger half before him, and saying: 'Good evening, Monsieur' to the officer as he set foot on the ground, more out of prudence than politeness. The German, with the insolence of those who wield complete authority, looked at him without replying.

Boule de Suif and Cornudet, although they had been sitting nearest to the door, were the last to get out, facing the enemy with a grave and haughty air. The fat young woman was trying to keep her self-control and remain calm, while the democrat was tugging angrily at his long red beard with a hand which trembled slightly. They were anxious to preserve their dignity, conscious that in encounters of this kind everybody is to some extent the representative of his country, and both were disgusted at their companions' obsequiousness. Boule de Suif wanted to show greater self-respect than her fellow-travellers, the respectable women, while Cornudet, realizing that it behoved him to set an example, continued in his whole attitude the task of resistance which he had begun by blocking the roads.

They all went into the great kitchen of the inn where

the German demanded to see the permit to leave Rouen signed by the general in command, which gave the name, description and occupation of each passenger. He spent some time scrutinizing them all carefully and comparing their appearance with the information contained in the document.

Then he said curtly: 'All right,' and disappeared.

They breathed again. They were still hungry, and supper was ordered. It was promised in half an hour, and while two maids bustled about, apparently making preparations for the meal, the travellers went to look at their rooms, which were all off a long corridor ending in a glazed door marked with a number indicating its function.

At last they were about to sit down to supper when the landlord appeared. He was a former horse-dealer, a fat asthmatic man with a wheezy, husky voice full of phlegm. His father had saddled him with the name of Follenvie.

'Mademoiselle Élisabeth Rousset?' he asked.

Boule de Suif gave a start and turned round.

'That's me.'

'Mademoiselle, the Prussian officer wants to speak to you at once.'

'To me?'

'Yes, if you are Mademoiselle Élisabeth Rousset.'

She hesitated, thought for a moment, and then said roundly: 'Maybe he does, but I'm not going.'

There was a general stir as everybody started talking and trying to guess the reason for the summons. The Comte went up to Boule de Suif and said: 'You are wrong to take that attitude, Madame, for your refusal may have serious consequences, not only for yourself, but for all your companions. One should never resist people who have the upper hand. I am sure there can be no danger in your obeying this summons; it is probably to do with some formality that has been overlooked.'

Everybody backed him up. They begged, urged and lectured Boule de Suif until she finally gave way, for they all dreaded the complications which might ensue from an impulsive refusal.

'All right,' she said at last, 'but I'm only doing it for your sakes.'

The Comtesse took her hand.

'And we are very grateful to you,' she said.

She left the room, and the others waited for her to come back before sitting down to supper.

Everybody regretted not having been sent for instead of that headstrong, quick-tempered girl, and each began silently rehearsing suitable platitudes in case he should be summoned in his turn.

But ten minutes later she reappeared, breathing hard, red in the face, and choking with rage.

'The swine!' she stammered. 'The filthy swine!'

Everybody wanted to know what had happened, but she would not say a word. When the Comte insisted she replied with great dignity: 'No, it's nothing to do with you. I can't tell you.'

They sat down round a large soup-tureen from which there rose a smell of cabbage. In spite of the recent incident it was a cheerful meal. The cider was good, and Monsieur and Madame Loiseau and the two nuns drank it for the sake of economy. The others ordered wine, except for Cornudet, who demanded beer. He had his own special way of opening the bottle, giving the liquid a good head, and examining it, first tilting the glass and then holding it up between the lamp and his eyes to appreciate the colour. When he drank, his great beard, which was the colour of his favourite beverage, seemed to quiver with emotion, and he squinted so as not to lose sight of his mug; he looked as if he were performing the one function for which he had been born. It was as though he were establishing in his mind a connexion, or even an affinity, between the two ruling passions of his life – Pale Ale and Revolution – and he certainly never drank the one without thinking of the other.

Monsieur and Madame Follenvie had their supper at the far end of the table. The man, wheezing like a broken-down locomotive, had too much congestion in his lungs to be able to talk while he ate, but the woman never stopped chattering. She recounted all her impressions of the arrival of the Prussians, what they did and what they said, cursing them, first because they cost her money, and secondly because she had two sons in the army. She addressed her remarks chiefly to the Comtesse, flattered at the thought that she was speaking to a lady of quality.

Then she lowered her voice as she broached more delicate topics. Her husband interrupted her from time to time, saying: 'You'd do better to keep your mouth shut, Madame Follenvie,' but she took no notice and went on: 'Yes, Madame, those folk do nothing but eat potatoes and pork, and then pork and potatoes. And don't you go thinking they're clean! Oh, no! They do their business everywhere, if you'll pardon me saying so. And you ought to see them drilling, hour after hour, day after day! They all get out there in a field, marching backwards and forwards and turning this way and that. It wouldn't be so bad if they worked on the land or mended the roads in their own country. But no, Madame, them soldiers are no good to nobody! And us poor folk have to feed them, so they can learn all about killing! I know I'm just an old woman without no education, but when I see them wearing themselves out tramping about from morning till night, I says to myself: "When there's folk finding out useful things, what's the point in others working so hard to be hurtful?" Because isn't it a shame to kill people, whether they're Prussians, or Englishmen, or Poles, or even Frenchmen? If you get your own back on somebody who's done you wrong, that's bad, because you get punished for it; but when you shoot our boys down like game, that's good, because those as kill most get medals for it. I tell you, try as I might, I'll never understand it!'

Cornudet raised his voice to say: 'War is barbarous when it's an attack on a peaceful neighbour, but a sacred duty when it's in defence of one's country.'

The old woman bowed her head.

'Yes,' she said, 'it's different when you're defending yourself. But wouldn't it be better to kill all the kings as make war for their pleasure?'

Cornudet's eyes flashed.

'Bravo, citizen!' he cried.

Monsieur Carré-Lamadon was deep in thought. Although he had a fanatical admiration for great soldiers, this old peasant woman's common sense made him think of all the wealth that could be created in a country if so many idle and therefore costly hands and so much unproductive strength were employed on great industrial enterprises it would take centuries to complete.

Loiseau, however, left his seat to go and have a whispered conversation with the innkeeper. The fat man laughed, coughed and spat. His huge belly heaved with laughter at his neighbour's jokes, and he ordered six casks of claret from him, to be delivered in the spring after the Prussians had gone.

Supper was scarcely over when the travellers, who were tired out, went to bed.

But Loiseau had been taking everything in, and after getting his wife into bed, he put first his ear and then his eye to the keyhole, with a view to discovering what he called the 'secrets of the corridor'.

After about an hour he heard a rustling sound, peered out quickly, and saw Boule de Suif, looking fatter than ever in a blue cashmere dressing-gown edged with white lace. She had a candle in her hand and was making for the door with the number on it at the end of the corridor. Another door opened a little way, and when she returned a few minutes later, Cornudet came out in his shirtsleeves and followed her. There was a whispered conversation, and then they stopped. Boule de Suif seemed to be trying hard to keep him from entering her room. Loiseau was unfortunately unable to hear what they were saying, but after a while they raised their voices and he caught a few words. Cornudet was being very insistent.

'Come, now, don't be silly, what difference does it make?'

She seemed to be indignant and replied: 'No, there are times when you just can't do that sort of thing. Besides, here it would be shameful!'

He apparently failed to understand, and asked why. At that she lost her temper and raised her voice still more.

'Why? You mean to say you don't see why? When there are Prussians in the house, perhaps even in the next room?'

He said no more. This patriotic modesty on the part of a whore who refused to allow a man to make love to her with the enemy in the house must have revived something of his flagging sense of dignity, for after merely giving her a kiss, he tiptoed back to his room.

Loiseau, excited by what he had just seen, left the keyhole, skipped across the room, put on his nightcap, pulled back the sheet covering his wife's gaunt frame, and, waking her with a kiss, murmured: 'Do you love me, darling?'

Silence then fell upon the house. But soon, from some unidentifiable spot which might have been the cellar or the attic, there came the sound of a powerful, monotonous regular snore, a long-drawn, muffled noise, with vibrations like those of a boiler at high pressure. Monsieur Follenvie was asleep.

As it had been decided to start at eight o'clock the next morning, the party assembled in the kitchen at an early hour; but the coach, its roof covered with snow, stood forlornly in the middle of the yard, without horses or driver. They looked in vain for the latter in the stables, the hay-lofts and the coach-house. The men then decided to go out and search the town for him. They found themselves in the market-place, with the church at one end, and on either side a row of low-roofed houses in which Prussian soldiers could be seen. The first one they saw was peeling potatoes. The second, farther on, was scrubbing out the barber's shop. Another, bearded up to his eyes, was kissing a crying baby, dandling it on his knees and trying to calm it down. Buxom peasant women whose men were 'away at the war' were indicating by signs to their obedient conquerors the jobs which had to be done – the wood to be chopped, the soup to be ladled out, the coffee to be ground. One of them was even doing the washing for his hostess, a helpless old woman.

The Comte, surprised by what he saw, questioned the verger, who was coming out of the presbytery. The old man replied: 'Oh, this lot aren't so bad. They aren't Prussians, so they tell me. They come from some place farther off, though I don't know exactly where. They've all left a wife and kids at home, and the war's not much fun for them. I bet their women are crying for their men just like ours, and there's hard times coming for them as well as us. Though things aren't too bad here for the moment, because they don't do no harm and they give us a hand just like they were back home. You see, Monsieur, poor folk have got to help each other.... It's the rich as make wars.'

Cornudet, shocked at the friendly relations which had been established between victors and vanquished, turned back, preferring to shut himself up at the inn.

Loiseau had to make a joke: 'Repopulation – that's the job they're doing.'

'Reparation, you mean,' Monsieur Carré-Lamadon retorted solemnly.

But there was no sign of their driver. Finally they ran him to earth in the village café, sitting in friendly fashion at the same table as the officer's orderly. The Comte asked him: 'Weren't you told to have the horses put in by eight o'clock?'

'That's right, but later on I was told different.'

'What do you mean?'

'I was told not to put them in at all.'

'Who gave you that order?'

'Why, the Prussian commandant, of course.'

'Why?'

'I don't know. Go and ask him if you like. I'm told not to put the horses in, so I don't put the horses in, and that's that.'

'Did he give you the order himself?'

'No, Monsieur, the innkeeper passed it on.'

'When?'

'Last night, just as I was going to bed.'

The three men returned to the inn, feeling very uneasy.

They asked to see Monsieur Follenvie, but the maid replied that the master never got up before ten, on account of his asthma. He had even given strict instructions that he was never to be called earlier, except in case of fire.

They then asked if they might see the officer, but that was entirely out of the question, even though he was billeted at the inn. Monsieur Follenvie alone was authorized to speak to him on civilian matters. So they had to wait. The women went back to their rooms and busied themselves with trifling odds and ends.

Cornudet settled down in the chimney corner in the kitchen, where a huge fire was blazing. He had one of the little tables brought in from the café, ordered a mug of beer, and took out his pipe, which in democratic circles enjoyed a prestige almost equal to his own, as if in serving Cornudet it was serving the country. It was a superb meerschaum, beautifully seasoned, as black as its owner's teeth, but fragrant, curved and shining, fitting comfortably in his hand and forming an attractive adjunct to his face. He sat motionless, his eyes fixed now on the fire in the hearth, now on the froth crowning his mug of beer; and after each drink he ran his long, thin fingers through his lank, greasy hair with an air of satisfaction, while he sucked at the foam fringing his moustache.

Loiseau, on the pretext of stretching his legs, went out to sell some wine to the local retailers. The Comte and the manufacturer started talking politics and forecasting the future of France. The one believed in the Orléans family, the other in some unknown saviour, a hero who would appear when all seemed lost: a Du Guesclin, or perhaps a Joan of Arc, or even another Napoleon I. Oh, if only the Prince Imperial were not so young! Listening to them, Cornudet smiled like a man who knows the secrets of destiny. His pipe filled the kitchen with its aroma.

On the stroke of ten Monsieur Follenvie appeared. He

was questioned immediately, but he had only one reply which he repeated verbatim two or three times: 'The officer says to me, he says: "Monsieur Follenvie, you will give orders not to get the coach ready for those travellers tomorrow. I do not wish them to leave without orders from me. You understand? That is all."'

They then tried to obtain an interview with the officer. The Comte sent in his card, on which Monsieur Carré-Lamadon added his name and all his distinctions. The Prussian sent word that he would see the two men after he had had his lunch, that was to say, about one o'clock.

The ladies reappeared, and they all ate a little in spite of their uneasiness. Boule de Suif seemed out of sorts and extremely worried.

They were finishing their coffee when the orderly came to fetch the gentlemen.

Loiseau joined the original pair; but when they tried to persuade Cornudet to accompany them to add weight to the deputation, he proudly declared that he would never have anything to do with the Germans; and he returned to his chimney-corner, calling for another bottle of beer.

The three men went upstairs and were shown into the best room in the inn. The officer received them there stretched out in an armchair with his feet on the mantel-piece, smoking a long porcelain pipe, and wrapped in a gaudy dressing-gown which had probably been filched from the abandoned house of some middle-class citizen of appalling taste. He did not get up, did not greet them, did not even look at them. He was a perfect specimen of the boorishness which comes naturally to the soldiers of a victorious army.

After a few moments he finally asked: 'What do you want?'

The Comte acted as spokesman: 'We wish to continue our journey, Monsieur.'

'No.'

'May I venture to ask the reason for this refusal?'

'Because I say so.'

'I would respectfully point out to you, Monsieur, that your commanding officer gave us a permit to travel to Dieppe, and I do not think we have done anything to deserve this prohibition.'

'I say no. . . . That is all. . . . You can go now.'

The three men bowed and withdrew.

The whole party spent a wretched afternoon. They could not understand the German's capricious refusal, and the most fantastic explanations occurred to them. Everybody stayed in the kitchen, engaging in endless discussions and putting forward the unlikeliest theories. Perhaps it was intended to hold them as hostages – but what for? Or to take them away as prisoners? Or, more likely, to hold them to ransom? At this possibility they were stricken with panic. The richer members of the party were the most terrified, already seeing themselves forced to pour sackfuls of gold into the hands of that insolent soldier in order to save their lives. They racked their brains for plausible lies to conceal their wealth and enable them to pass themselves off as the poorest of the poor. Loiseau took off his watch chain and hid it in his pocket. The gathering dusk added to their fears. The lamp was lit, and as there were still two hours to go until dinner, Madame Loiseau suggested a game of *trente-et-un* to pass the time. Everybody agreed and even Cornudet joined in after politely putting out his pipe.

The Comte shuffled the cards and dealt. Boule de Suif got thirty-one straight away, and soon the excitement of the game made the players forget their fears. But Cornudet noticed that the Loiseaus were helping each other to cheat.

Just as they were sitting down to dinner Monsieur Follenvie reappeared and said in his husky voice: 'The Prussian officer wishes to know if Mademoiselle Élisabeth Rousset has changed her mind yet.'

Boule de Suif remained standing. She was very pale, but suddenly she flushed crimson, choking with rage and unable to say a word. Finally she burst out: 'Tell that blackguard, that scoundrel, that swine of a Prussian that I'll never do it. Have you got that clear? Never, never, never!'

The fat innkeeper left the room. Boule de Suif was immediately surrounded, questioned, and begged to reveal the secret of her visit. At first she refused, but soon she was carried away by her rage.

'What does he want?... What does he want? He wants to go to bed with me!'

The general indignation was so keen that nobody was shocked at the crudity of her language. Cornudet slammed his mug down on the table so violently that he broke it. There was a chorus of reprobation against the despicable soldier, a storm of anger which brought them all together in a common feeling of resistance, as if each had been asked to share in the sacrifice demanded of her. The Comte declared in a tone of disgust that those Prussians were no better than the barbarians of old. The women in particular lavished intense and affectionate sympathy on Boule de Suif. The nuns, who appeared only at meal times, bowed their heads and said nothing.

All the same, once the first outburst of indignation had subsided, they had their dinner, but there was little conversation: everybody was thinking.

The ladies retired early, leaving the men to smoke and get up a game of *écarté*. Monsieur Follenvie was invited to join in, as the others intended to question him tactfully as to the best way of overcoming the officer's resistance. But he was so absorbed in his hand that he listened to no questions and gave no answers, simply repeating continually: 'Play, gentlemen, play!'

His concentration on the game was so intense that he actually forgot to spit, an omission which occasionally produced organ notes in his chest. His wheezing lungs ran the whole asthmatic gamut, from deep bass notes to the husky squawks of a cockerel trying to crow.

He even refused to go upstairs when his wife, who was dropping with sleep, came to fetch him. So she went off alone, for she was an 'early bird', always up with the sun, while her husband was a 'late bird', always ready to sit up all night with his friends. He called out to her: 'Put my egg-flip in front of the fire,' and went on with the game. When it was clear that there was nothing to be got out of him, they declared that it was time for bed and all retired for the night.

They got up early again the next morning, filled with a vague hope, an increasing desire to get away, and a dread of the prospect of spending another day in that horrible little inn.

Alas, the horses remained in the stable and the driver was still invisible. For want of anything better to do they hung about the coach.

Lunch was a melancholy meal. A certain coolness was noticeable in the general attitude to Boule de Suif, for sleeping on the problem had somewhat modified her companions' views. They now almost felt annoyed with the prostitute for not having gone to the Prussian on the sly so as to provide her fellow travellers with a pleasant surprise in the morning. What could have been simpler? Besides, who would have been any the wiser? She could have saved her face by sending word to the officer that she felt sorry for the others. After all, it was such a trivial thing for her.

But nobody as yet was prepared to put these thoughts into words.

In the afternoon, as they were bored stiff, the Comte suggested a stroll around the village. Everybody wrapped up warmly and the little party set off, with the exception of Cornudet, who preferred to stay by the fire, and the nuns, who were spending their days in the church or with the parish priest.

The cold, which was becoming more intense every day, nipped their noses and ears cruelly; their feet hurt so badly that every step was agony; and when the country came into sight it looked so dreadfully bleak under its unbroken pall of snow that they all turned back immediately, their spirits chilled and their hearts numbed.

The four women walked in front, with the three men not far behind.

Loiseau, who understood the situation perfectly, suddenly asked how much longer 'that tart' was going to keep them hanging about in this God-forsaken place. The Comte, as chivalrous as ever, said that no woman could be called upon to make such a painful sacrifice, and that the offer must come from herself. Monsieur Carré-Lamadon observed that if, as was considered likely, the French launched a counter-attack by way of Dieppe, the only place where the two armies could meet was Tôtes. This remark made the other two uneasy.

'How about trying to get away on foot?' said Loiseau.

The Comte shrugged his shoulders.

'Out of the question,' he said, 'in all this snow, and with our wives as well. Besides, we would be pursued straight away, caught within ten minutes, and brought back as prisoners at the mercy of the soldiers.'

This was obviously true and nothing more was said.

The ladies were talking about clothes, but a certain constraint seemed to have shattered the harmony between them.

All of a sudden the officer appeared at the end of the street. His tall, wasp-waisted, uniformed figure stood out sharply against the snow; and he was walking with his knees wide apart, with the gait peculiar to military men who are trying not to dirty their carefully polished boots.

He bowed as he passed the ladies but glanced contemptuously at the men, who, for their part, had sufficient dignity not to raise their hats, although Loiseau made as if to do so.

Boule de Suif had blushed to the roots of her hair; and the three married women felt deeply humiliated at being seen by the officer in the company of this prostitute whom he had treated in such a cavalier fashion.

They began talking about him, discussing his looks and his general appearance. Madame Carré-Lamadon, who had known a great many officers and could judge them with an expert eye, declared that this one was quite presentable. She even expressed regret that he was not a Frenchman, because he would have made a very good-looking Hussar every woman would have fallen madly in love with.

When they got back to the inn they did not know what to do with themselves. Sharp words were even exchanged over trivial matters. Dinner was a short and silent meal, and everybody went to bed, hoping to kill time by sleeping.

The next morning they came downstairs with tired faces and frayed tempers. The women scarcely spoke to Boule de Suif.

The church bell started ringing for a christening. The fat young woman had a child who was being brought up in a peasant family at Yvetot. She saw it once a year at the most and never bothered her head about it; but the thought of the baby about to be christened filled her heart with a sudden, overpowering feeling of affection for her own offspring, and she decided that she simply had to attend the ceremony.

As soon as she had gone they all looked at one another and pulled their chairs together, for everybody realized that it was time they came to some decision. Loiseau had an inspiration; he proposed suggesting to the officer that he should keep Boule de Suif and let the others go.

Monsieur Follenvie once again agreed to act as intermediary, but he came back almost at once. The German, who knew what human nature was like, had shown him the door. He intended to detain the whole party until his demand had been satisfied.

At that, Madame Loiseau's plebeian nature broke out. 'But we can't stay here to die of old age!' she cried. 'Seeing that it's that slut's job to go with any man who wants her, I don't think she's any right to refuse one man rather than another. Why she took everybody who came along in Rouen, even coachmen! Yes, Madame, she's even been with the Prefect's coachman! I know all about it because he buys his wine from us. And now, when it's a question of getting us out of a hole, the hussy starts putting on airs! Personally, I think that officer is behaving very well. He may have had to go without for a long time, and he'd probably have preferred one of us three. But no, he makes do with a common prostitute. He shows a proper respect for married women. Just think, he's the master here. He had only to give his men the order, and he could have taken us by force.'

The two women gave a little shudder. Pretty little Madame Carré-Lamadon's eyes were shining, and she looked rather pale, as if she could already feel herself being raped by the officer.

The men, who had been conferring privately, now joined the ladies. Loiseau was in a fury and wanted to hand 'the wretched woman' over to the enemy bound hand and foot. But the Comte, who was sprung from three generations of ambassadors and looked like a diplomat himself, advocated a more subtle approach.

'We have to persuade her to do it,' he said.

So they set about hatching a plot.

The women huddled together, voices were lowered, and the discussion became general, each person expressing an opinion. But it was all perfectly respectable. The ladies in particular found delicate turns of phrase and charming euphemisms to express the coarsest ideas. The conventions of polite conversation were so scrupulously observed that a stranger would have understood nothing of what they were saying. But as the thin veneer of modesty displayed by every woman of the world is only skin-deep, they revelled in this unsavoury business, enjoying it tremendously and feeling in their element as they laid their plans with the sensual enjoyment of an epicurean chef cooking somebody else's dinner.

The whole affair struck them as so amusing after a while that their spirits rose again. The Comte ventured a few jokes which were rather risky but so well told that they made everybody smile. Loiseau in his turn made some cruder remarks, and even these failed to give offence. Everybody was thinking of Madame Loiseau's brutal observation: 'Seeing that it's that slut's job to go with any man who wants her, I don't think she's any right to refuse one man rather than another.' Indeed, pretty Madame Carré-Lamadon seemed to think that if she had been in Boule de Suif's place she would have been less likely to refuse this particular man than most.

Elaborate plans were laid for the blockade, as though for

the siege of a fortress. It was agreed what part each person should play, what arguments he should put forward and what tactics he should use. The plan of attack was decided on, together with the stratagems to be employed and the surprise assaults to be delivered in order to force a citadel of flesh and blood to yield admittance to the enemy.

Cornudet, however, remained aloof, refusing to have anything to do with the affair.

They were so absorbed in their plotting that they did not hear Boule de Suif return. But the Comte's whispered 'shh!' made them all look up. There she was. A sudden silence fell, and at first a feeling of embarrassment prevented them from speaking to her. At last, however, the Comtesse, more of an adept than the rest in social duplicity, asked her: 'Did you enjoy the christening?'

The fat young woman, still under the influence of the ceremony she had just attended, gave them all the details, how everybody had looked, how everybody had behaved, and even what the church had looked like. She added: 'It does you good to pray now and then.'

Until it was time for lunch, the ladies contented themselves with being pleasant to her, in order to gain her confidence and make her more amenable to their advice.

As soon as they were seated at table, however, the first moves were made. To begin with there was a vague conversation about self-sacrifice. Examples were quoted from ancient history: first Judith and Holofernes, next, for no particular reason, Lucretia and Sextus, and then Cleopatra taking all the enemy generals into her bed and reducing them to slavish obedience. These examples were followed by a fantastic story, hatched in the imagination of these ignorant plutocrats, telling how the women of Rome had gone to Capua in order to rock Hannibal to sleep in their arms, and with him his lieutenants and his phalanxes of mercenaries. Then they cited all the women who had halted conquerors by turning their bodies into battlefields, into instruments of domination, into weapons; women who by means of their heroic caresses had overcome hideous or hated creatures and sacrificed their chastity on the altar of revenge and devotion.

They even referred in veiled terms to a certain English lady of good family who had had herself inoculated with a horrible contagious disease in order to transmit it to Bonaparte, who had been miraculously saved by a sudden indisposition at the moment of the fateful meeting.

All these stories were told in a decent and decorous manner, with occasional outbursts of a deliberate enthusiasm calculated to inspire emulation.

By the time they had finished, anybody might have thought that woman's only duty on earth was the perpetual sacrifice of her person, a continual surrender of her body to the lustful caprices of military men.

The two nuns gave the impression of hearing nothing of all this, they were so absorbed in profound meditation, while Boule de Suif remained silent.

All afternoon she was left to her own reflections. But instead of calling her 'Madame', as they had done so far, they addressed her simply as 'Mademoiselle', nobody quite knew why, as if they wanted to take her down a peg from the position of respect to which she had attained and make her conscious of her shameful situation.

Just as the soup was being served Monsieur Follenvie reappeared with the same question as on the previous day: 'The Prussian officer wishes to know if Mademoiselle Élisabeth Rousset has changed her mind yet.'

Boule de Suif replied curtly: 'No, Monsieur.'

Over dinner the coalition weakened. Loiseau made three

unfortunate remarks. Everybody was racking his brains for fresh examples, but without success, when the Comtesse, possibly without deliberate intent and simply from a vague desire to pay homage to religion, questioned the elder of the nuns about the great events in the lives of the saints. Many of them had done things which we would regard as crimes; but the Church makes no difficulties about granting absolution for such offences when they are committed for the glory of God or the benefit of one's neighbour. This was a powerful argument and the Comtesse made the most of it. Then, either by one of those tacit understandings, those veiled complicities, in which all who wear ecclesiastical dress excel, or simply as the result of a fortunate lack of intelligence, an opportune stupidity, the old nun gave tremendous support to the conspiracy. They had thought that she was shy, but she now showed herself to be bold, garrulous and violent. She was not worried by the fumbling arguments of casuistry; her doctrine seemed to be as firm as an iron bar; her faith never faltered; and her conscience knew no scruples. She regarded Abraham's sacrifice as perfectly natural, for she would have killed her father and mother without a qualm on an order from on high; and nothing, in her opinion, could be displeasing to the Lord if the intention was praiseworthy. The Comtesse, taking advantage of the sacred authority of her unexpected ally, egged her on to deliver an edifying paraphrase of the moral axiom: 'The end justifies the means.'

'So, Sister,' she said, 'you think that all means are acceptable to God and that he pardons any act when the motive is pure?'

'Who could doubt it, Madame? An action which is blameworthy in itself often becomes meritorious by virtue of the idea which inspires it.'

And so they went on, interpreting the will of God, predicting his decisions, and attributing to him an interest in things which were really no concern of his.

All this was said in allusive, subtle, discreet language. But every word spoken by the holy woman in the coif made a breach in the prostitute's indignant resistance. Then the conversation took a different turn as the woman with the rosary spoke of the houses of her order, of her Mother Superior, of herself, and of her sweet companion, dear Sister Saint-Nicéphore. They had been summoned to Le Havre to nurse the hundreds of smallpox cases in the hospitals there. She painted a picture of those poor men, describing their disease in detail; and while they were being held up on the way by the caprice of this Prussian, scores of Frenchmen might die whose lives they could perhaps have saved. Nursing soldiers was her speciality. She had been in the Crimea, in Italy, and in Austria; and in telling the story of her campaigns, she suddenly revealed herself as one of those drum and fife nuns who seem to have been born to follow armies and pick up wounded in the wake of battle, and who are better than any officer at quelling tough, undisciplined soldiers with a single word. She was, in fact, a typical army sister, whose ravaged face, scarred and pitted with countless pockmarks, was like a symbol of the devastation of war.

Her words seemed to have made such an impression that after she had finished nobody added anything.

As soon as the meal was over they all went straight to their rooms and did not come down again until late next morning.

Lunch was a quiet meal. The seed sown the previous evening was being given time to germinate and bear fruit.

In the afternoon the Comtesse suggested a walk. The Comte gave his arm to Boule de Suif, as had been arranged beforehand, and lingered with her behind the others.

He spoke to her in that familiar, paternal, slightly supercilious tone which staid elderly gentlemen adopt in conversation with women of her profession, calling her 'my dear child', and talking down to her from the height of his exalted social rank and his undisputed respectability.

He went straight to the heart of the matter:

'So you prefer to keep us here, exposed like yourself to all the outrages which would ensue if the Prussian troops suffered a reverse, rather than grant one of those favours which you have bestowed so often in the course of your life?'

Boule de Suif made no reply.

He tried gentleness on her, then argument, then appeals to her feelings. He managed to remain 'Monsieur le Comte' all the time, although he could play the ladies' man when necessary, paying compliments and generally making himself agreeable. He emphasized the service she would be rendering them and spoke of their gratitude. Then, suddenly addressing her with gay familiarity, he exclaimed: 'And you know, my dear, he'd be able to boast of having enjoyed a prettier girl than he's likely to find in his own country.'

Boule de Suif made no reply and caught up with the others.

As soon as they got back to the inn, she went up to her room and did not reappear. The suspense was acute. What was she going to do? How awkward it would be if she continued to hold out!

Dinner-time arrived; they waited for her in vain. Then Monsieur Follenvie came in and announced that Mademoiselle Rousset was indisposed and that they might start dinner without her. They all pricked up their ears. The Comte went over to the innkeeper and whispered: 'Is everything all right?'

'Yes.'

Out of a sense of propriety he refrained from saying anything to his companions, but he gave them a slight nod. Immediately everybody heaved a great sigh of relief and every face lit up.

'Hurray!' shouted Loiseau. 'I'll stand champagne all round if there's any to be had in this place.'

To Madame Loiseau's horror, the landlord came back with four bottles. Everybody had suddenly become voluble and noisy, full of ribald merriment. The Comte seemed to notice Madame Carré-Lamadon's charms for the first time, and the manufacturer complimented the Comtesse on her beauty. The conversation became lively, gay and racy.

All of a sudden Loiseau assumed a worried expression, raised his arms, and called for silence. Everybody stopped talking, taken by surprise, and almost frightened. Then, cocking his head and motioning to them to keep quiet, he looked up at the ceiling, listened once again, and said in his ordinary voice: 'Don't worry: everything's going well.'

They took some time to grasp his meaning, but then a smile went round the table.

A quarter of an hour later he went through the same performance again, repeating it several times in the course of the evening. He pretended to be questioning somebody on the floor above, and giving ambiguous advice fished up from the depths of his commercial-traveller's mind. From time to time he put on a sorrowful expression and sighed: 'Poor girl!' or muttered angrily between his teeth: 'Oh, you Prussian swine, you!' Sometimes, when everybody least expected it, he would repeat several times in a voice vibrant with emotion: 'Stop it, stop it!' adding, as if to himself: 'I only hope we see her again, and the bastard doesn't kill her!'

Although these jokes were in deplorable taste everybody

enjoyed them and nobody was shocked, for indignation, like anything else, is the product of environment, and the atmosphere which had gradually been created around them was charged with salacious thoughts.

Over dessert even the women made discreetly witty allusions. Eyes were sparkling, for everybody had drunk a good deal. The Comte, who even in his cups preserved his air of noble gravity, drew a comparison, which was greatly appreciated, between their situation and that of shipwrecked sailors at the Pole, rejoicing when winter comes to an end and a way to the south opens up before them.

Loiseau, who was now in very high spirits, stood up with a glass of champagne in his hand, and cried: 'I drink to our deliverance!'

Everybody rose and applauded. Even the two nuns, egged on by the ladies, agreed to take a sip of the sparkling wine, which they had never tasted before. They said it was like fizzy lemonade, but with a more delicate flavour.

Loiseau gave expression to the general feeling when he said: 'What a pity we haven't got a piano. We might have had a bit of dancing.'

Cornudet had not uttered a single word or made a single gesture. Indeed, he seemed too deep in serious thought, and tugged angrily at his great beard now and then, as if he wanted to make it even longer than it was. At last, towards midnight, when the party was on the point of breaking up, Loiseau walked unsteadily over to him, dug him in the ribs, and said in a thick voice: 'You're not much fun tonight, are you? Cat got your tongue, citizen?'

Cornudet raised his head sharply, and glaring at the company with flashing eyes, said: 'I tell you, you've all done a shameful thing tonight.'

He stood up and made his way to the door.

'A shameful thing,' he repeated, and disappeared.

This damped their spirits for a moment. Loiseau, utterly taken aback, stood there gaping; but he soon recovered his composure and suddenly burst out laughing.

'Sour grapes!' he exclaimed. 'Sour grapes!'

As nobody understood what he meant, he told them about 'the secrets of the corridor'. There was a fresh outburst of merriment. The ladies were tremendously amused, while the Comte and Monsieur Carré-Lamadon laughed until they cried. They could not believe their ears.

'Really? Are you sure? He wanted to ...'

'I tell you I saw him.'

'And she refused?'

'Because the Prussian was in the next room.'

'I don't believe it!'

'I swear it's true.'

The Comte was choking with laughter, and the manufacturer holding his sides. Loiseau went on: 'And now you understand why he didn't see the joke tonight.'

And the three of them started off again, laughing until they were gasping for breath.

Then the party broke up. But Madame Loiseau, who had a temperament like a stinging-nettle, remarked to her husband as they were getting into bed that 'that little sour-puss Madame Carré-Lamadon' had been looking peeved all evening: 'You know, when a woman's mad about a uniform it doesn't matter to her whether it's a Frenchman or a Prussian inside it. It makes you sick, it really does!'

All night long the dark corridor was full of rustling sounds, faint, barely audible noises, like the patter of bare feet, the imperceptible creaking of boards. From the thin lines of light showing under the doors, it was clear that nobody went to sleep until very late. Champagne has that effect; it is said to keep people awake.

The next morning the snow was a dazzling white in the

bright winter sun. The coach, ready at long last, was standing at the door, while an army of white pigeons with pink eyes and black pupils were preening themselves in their thick plumage and strutting about between the legs of the six horses, pecking for food in the steaming dung.

The driver, wrapped in his sheepskin coat, was puffing at his pipe on the box, and the delighted travellers were all hurriedly packing provisions for the rest of the journey.

Only Boule de Suif was missing. At last she appeared.

She seemed a little ill at ease and shamefaced; and as she walked shyly towards her companions they turned away with one accord, as if they had not seen her. The Comte took his wife's arm with a dignified air and drew her out of range of that impure contact.

The fat young woman stopped short in amazement; then, summoning up all her courage, she greeted the manufacturer's wife with a humble 'Good morning, Madame'. The other woman merely returned a supercilious nod, accompanied by a glare of outraged virtue. Everybody seemed very busy and gave her a wide berth, as if she were carrying some infection in her skirts. Then they made a dash for the coach. She was the last to reach it, and silently took the seat she had occupied during the first part of the journey.

They did not seem to see her or recognize her; but Madame Loiseau, gazing at her indignantly from a distance, said in a low voice to her husband: 'I'm glad I'm not sitting next to her.'

The heavy coach moved off, and the second part of the journey started.

At first nobody said a word. Boule de Suif did not dare to raise her eyes. She felt angry with all her neighbours, ashamed of having given way to their pleas, and defiled by

the kisses of the Prussian into whose arms they had hypo-
critically thrown her.

After a while the Comtesse turned to Madame Carré-
Lamadon and broke the awkward silence.

'I believe you know Madame d'Étrelles?'

'Yes, she's a friend of mine.'

'What a charming woman she is!'

'Delightful! A quite exceptional person, well educated
too, and an artist to her fingertips. She sings divinely and
draws beautifully.'

The manufacturer started talking to the Comte, and
above the rattle of the windows a few words were audible:
'Dividend ... fall due ... option ... mature.'

Loiseau, who had filched the inn's old pack of cards,
greasy from five years' contact with filthy tables, embarked
on a game of bezique with his wife.

The nuns, taking the long rosaries hanging from their
belts, crossed themselves simultaneously, and all of a sudden their lips started moving, the speed of their murmured
prayers increasing as if they were engaged in a race. From
time to time they would kiss a medal, cross themselves
again, and then resume their rapid, endless mumbling.

Cornudet sat motionless, deep in thought.

After three hours' travelling, Loiseau gathered up his
cards, and said: 'I'm hungry.'

His wife reached for a packet done up with string, from
which she took a piece of cold veal. She cut this into neat,
thin slices and they both started eating.

'Why don't we follow suit?' said the Comtesse. There
was a chorus of approval and she set about unpacking the
food which had been prepared for the two couples. In one
of those long receptacles with a china hare on the lid to
indicate the contents there was a *lièvre en pâté*, a succulent

cold dish in which the hare's dark flesh, mixed with other finely chopped meat, was streaked with white rivulets of bacon fat. There was also a fine slab of Gruyère which bore the words 'News in brief' on its sticky surface, for it had been wrapped in a piece of newspaper.

The two nuns unwrapped a hunk of sausage which smelt of garlic; and Cornudet, plunging both hands at the same time into the capacious pockets of his loose-fitting overcoat, took four hard-boiled eggs out of one and the crusty end of a loaf from the other. Shelling the first egg, and dropping the pieces of shell in the straw on the floor, he bit into it, scattering his great beard with fragments of yellow yolk which shone in it like stars.

Boule de Suif, in the hurry and confusion of getting up, had not had time to think of anything; and now, as she watched all her neighbours placidly eating, she found herself choking with rage and indignation. In the first flush of anger she opened her mouth to tell them what she thought of them, and a flood of abuse rose to her lips; but her exasperation was so violent that she could not utter a word.

Nobody looked at her: nobody gave her a thought. She felt overwhelmed by the contempt of these respectable boors who had first sacrificed her, and then cast her aside like an unclean object for which they had no further use. Then she remembered her big basket, full of good things which they had guzzled – her two chickens in aspic, her *pâtés*, her pears, her four bottles of claret. Her anger suddenly collapsed like a cord snapping when it has been stretched too tight, and she felt on the verge of tears. She made a tremendous effort to control her feelings, bracing herself and swallowing her sobs like a little child, but her tears welled up, glistening on her eyelids, and soon two great drops brimmed over and rolled slowly down her cheeks.

Others followed more rapidly, flowing like drops of water trickling from a rock and falling at regular intervals on to her bosom's swelling curve. She sat erect, staring straight in front of her, her face pale and set, hoping that nobody would notice.

But the Comtesse saw her distress and drew her husband's attention to it with a gesture. He shrugged his shoulders as if to say: 'Well, what of it? It isn't my fault.'

Madame Loiseau gave a silent laugh and whispered triumphantly: 'She's crying because she's ashamed of herself.'

The two nuns had returned to their prayers after wrapping up what was left of their sausage in a piece of paper.

Then Cornudet, who was digesting his eggs, stretched his long legs under the opposite seat, leant back, folded his arms, smiled like a man who has just thought of a good joke, and started whistling the *'Marseillaise'*.

A shadow fell across every face. The song of the Republic was obviously not to his neighbours' liking. They fidgeted irritably and looked as if they were ready to howl like dogs hearing the sound of a barrel-organ. He noticed this and went on whistling. Now and then he even hummed the words:

> Amour sacré de la patrie,
> Conduis, soutiens nos bras vengeurs,
> Liberté, liberté chérie,
> Combats avec les défenseurs!

They were moving faster now, for the snow was harder; and all the way to Dieppe, through the long, tedious hours of the journey along the bumpy roads, in the gathering dusk and later in the darkness which filled the coach, he kept up his monotonous, vengeful whistling with savage obstinacy, forcing his tired, exasperated listeners to follow the song from beginning to end, and to fit the appropriate word to every note.

Boule de Suif went on crying; and now and then, in the pause between two verses, a sob which she had been unable to hold back could be heard in the darkness.

# IN THE SPRING

When the first fine days arrive, when the earth awakens and clothes itself in green, when the warm, scented air caresses your skin, fills your lungs and seems to reach your very heart, you feel a vague yearning for an unknown happiness, an urge to run about, to wander at random, to look for adventure and gulp down deep draughts of spring.

As the winter which had just finished had been very hard, this longing overwhelmed me in the month of May like an intoxicating wine or a surge of rising sap. Waking up one morning, I saw from my window, above the neighbouring houses, the great blue expanse of the sky ablaze with sunshine. The canaries in their cages hanging in the windows were twittering away, the maids on every floor were singing, a cheerful noise was rising from the street, and I went out in a holiday mood, without caring where I was going.

The passers-by were all smiling: spring had returned, the light was warm and bright, and happiness was in the air. It was as if a breeze of love were blowing through the city, and the young women I saw in the streets in their morning frocks had a hidden tenderness in their eyes and a languid grace in their movements which filled my heart with agitation.

Without knowing how or why I found myself on the banks of the Seine. Steamers were going past on their way to Suresnes and I was suddenly seized by an indescribable longing to go running through the woods.

The deck of the *Mouche* was crowded with passengers, for the first sunny day draws you out of doors in spite of yourself, and everyone is on the move, coming and going, and chattering with his neighbour.

My neighbour was a girl – a little working-girl no doubt – with a charm that was entirely Parisian. She had a sweet little face with a fair complexion and golden hair clustering round her temples like curls of light. Dancing in the breeze, her hair rippled down to her ears and the nape of her neck, and then, lower still, turned into down so fine and light that I could scarcely see it but felt an irresistible longing to cover it with kisses.

I stared at her so intently that she turned her head towards me and then suddenly lowered her eyes, while a tiny crease, like the beginning of a smile, puckered one corner of her mouth, revealing there the same fine, pale, silky down which the sun was faintly touching with gold.

The smooth-flowing river grew wider. The atmosphere was warm and still and the air seemed full of a living murmur. My neighbour raised her eyes again, and this time, as I was still looking at her, she gave an unmistakable smile. She looked charming when she smiled and in her fleeting glance I saw a thousand things I had never suspected before – unknown depths, all the charm of tender affection, all the poetry we dream of, all the happiness we look for all our lives. I felt a mad longing to clasp her in my arms and carry her away somewhere to whisper in her ears the sweet music of words of love.

I was just about to speak to her when somebody touched me on the shoulder. I turned round in surprise and saw an ordinary-looking man, neither young nor old, who was gazing at me sadly.

'I should like to have a word with you,' he said.

I pulled a face, and no doubt he noticed, for he added: 'It's a matter of importance.'

I got up and followed him to the other end of the boat.

'Monsieur,' he continued, 'when winter comes with cold and rain and snow, your doctor says to you whenever he sees you: "Keep your feet warm, and beware of chills, colds, bronchitis and pleurisy." So you take all sorts of precautions: you wear flannel underwear, thick overcoats and heavy shoes. And even then you sometimes find yourself bed-ridden for a couple of months. But when spring returns with its leaves and flowers, its warm relaxing breezes, and its country scents which fill you with a vague disquiet and inexplicable emotions, there is nobody to say to you: "Monsieur, beware of love! It is lurking everywhere, lying in wait for you at every corner. All its snares are set, all its weapons are sharpened, all its treacherous wiles are prepared! Beware of love! It is more dangerous than colds, bronchitis or pleurisy. It shows no mercy and it drives us all to commit irreparable acts of folly." Yes, Monsieur, I tell you the Government ought to put up huge posters on the walls every year saying: "Spring is here again. Frenchmen, beware of love," just as people chalk "Wet Paint" on house doors. However, as the Government fails to perform this duty, I make a point of acting in its place, and I say to you: "Beware of love, for it is on the point of catching you, and it is my duty to warn you of the danger, just as in Russia people warn a passer-by that his nose is getting frost-bitten."'

I was astounded by this odd individual, and, assuming a dignified expression, I said: 'It seems to me, Monsieur, that you are meddling in a matter which is no concern of yours.'

He made an impatient gesture and replied: 'Oh, Monsieur, if I see a man in danger of drowning, am I supposed to leave him to perish? Just listen to my story and then you will understand why I have ventured to speak to you like this.

'It all happened this time last year. I should tell you first

71

that I am a clerk in the Admiralty, where our superiors take their pen-pushing commissions seriously and treat us like ordinary seamen. Well, from my office window I could see a little patch of blue sky with swallows flying across it, and it made me feel like dancing a jig among my black filing-cases.

'My longing for liberty became so fierce that I stifled my repugnance and went to see my chief. He was a peevish little man and always in a bad temper. I told him I was feeling ill. He looked me in the eye and said: "I don't believe a word of it, Monsieur. Still, off you go! How do you expect me to run an office with clerks like you?"

'I left straight away and went down to the Seine. It was a day like today and I boarded the *Mouche* to go to Saint-Cloud.

'Oh, Monsieur, if only my chief had refused me permission to leave the office!

'I felt as if I were expanding in the sunshine. I was in love with everything: the boat, the river, the trees, the houses, my fellow passengers, everything. I wanted to kiss something, no matter what: this was Love setting its trap for me.

'All of a sudden, at the Trocadéro, a young woman came on board carrying a small parcel, and sat down facing me. She was a pretty girl, Monsieur – I admit that – but it is surprising how much more attractive women look on a fine day in early spring. They have a heady charm, a very special appeal. It's just like the wine you drink after cheese.

'I looked at her and she looked at me, but only now and then, like that girl next to you just now. After we had exchanged glances for some time I felt that we knew each other well enough to start a conversation. So I spoke to her and she replied. She was a sweet girl, there was no doubt about that, and she went straight to my head.

'At Saint-Cloud she got off the boat and I followed her. She had an order to deliver and when she reappeared the boat had just left. I started walking beside her and the balmy softness of the air made us both sigh.

'"It would be nice in the woods," I said.

'"Yes, it would," she agreed.

'"Would you care to take a stroll with me, Mademoiselle?"

'She gave me a quick sidelong glance, as if to size me up, and then, after hesitating for a moment, agreed. Soon we were walking side by side among the trees. Under the foliage, which was still rather sparse, the tall, thick, bright green grass was drenched in sunshine and full of tiny creatures making love. We could hear birds singing everywhere. My companion began running and skipping, intoxicated by the fresh air and the country smells. And I ran after her, skipping and jumping in the same way. How silly we can be at times, Monsieur!

'Then she gaily sang a thousand things, operatic airs and Musetta's Song. Musetta's Song! How poetic it seemed to me then! It almost moved me to tears! That's the sort of rubbish that turns our heads. Believe me, never marry a woman who sings in the country, especially if she sings Musetta's Song.

'Soon she grew tired and sat down on a grassy bank. I sat down at her feet and seized her hands, her little hands all speckled with needle pricks. The sight stirred my heart and I said to myself: "These are the sacred marks of toil." Oh, Monsieur, do you know what they really mean, those sacred marks of toil? They stand for the tittle-tattle of the workroom, for whispered smut, for minds polluted by dirty stories; they stand for lost chastity, for foolish chatter, for all the wretched chores of everyday life, for all the narrow ideas found in all working-class women, but particularly in those whose fingertips bear the sacred marks of toil.

'Then we gazed into each other's eyes for a long time.

'Oh, what power there is in a woman's eyes! How they disturb us, overwhelm us, take possession of us, dominate us! How deep they seem, how full of infinite promise! People call that looking into each other's souls. What nonsense, Monsieur! If we could really see into each other's souls we'd be much wiser than we are!

'To cut a long story short, I was swept off my feet, mad with love. I tried to take her in my arms, but she cried: "Hands off!" So then I knelt down beside her and opened my heart to her, pouring out all the tenderness which was choking me. She seemed astonished at my change of manner and gave me a sidelong glance as if she were saying to herself: "So that's his little game, is it? Well, we shall see!"

'In love, Monsieur, we men are always the innocents and women the tricksters.

'I could probably have taken her there and then, and later on I realized my stupidity. But what I was looking for was not a body but an ideal love. I sentimentalized over her when I should have made better use of my time.

'As soon as she had had enough of my declarations of love, she got up, and we returned to Saint-Cloud. I stayed with her until we reached Paris and she looked so sad on the way home that I asked her what the matter was. She replied: "I was thinking that we don't have many days like this in a lifetime."

'My heart beat fit to burst.

'I saw her again the following Sunday, and the next Sunday, and every Sunday after that. I took her to Bougival, Saint-Germain, Maisons-Laffitte, Poissy – to every haunt of suburban love.

'The little hussy, for her part, led me on with a pretence of passionate ardour. Finally I lost my head completely, and three months later I married her.

'What can you expect, Monsieur, when a man is a clerk, living alone, without any relatives or anybody to advise him? You say to yourself how happy life would be with a woman, and off you go and marry her.

'And then she calls you names from morning till night, understands nothing, knows nothing, chatters endlessly, sings Musetta's Song at the top of her voice (oh, how tired you get of Musetta's Song!), squabbles with the coalman, tells the concierge all your domestic secrets, confides all your bedroom intimacies to the maid next door, sneers at you to the tradespeople, and has her head stuffed with such stupid stories, such idiotic superstitions, such ludicrous opinions and such monstrous prejudices that I for one cry from sheer discouragement, Monsieur, every time I talk to my wife.'

He stopped speaking, a little out of breath and extremely agitated. I looked at him, feeling sorry for the poor, simple-minded fellow, and I was trying to think of something to say when the boat stopped. We had reached Saint-Cloud.

The girl who had caught my fancy got up to go ashore. She passed close to me and gave me a sidelong glance and a furtive smile, one of those smiles that drive a man mad. Then she jumped down on to the landing-stage.

I sprang to my feet to follow her, but my neighbour caught hold of my sleeve. I shook myself free, but then he grabbed the tails of my coat and pulled me back.

'You shan't go! You shan't go!' he cried in such a loud voice that everybody turned round.

A ripple of laughter ran round the crowd, and I stood there motionless, furiously angry, but without the courage to brave further ridicule and scandal.

And the steamer moved off again.

The girl remained standing on the landing-stage, watching me disappear with an air of disappointment, while my persecutor rubbed his hands and whispered in my ear: 'I've done you a good turn there, and no mistake.'

# THE GRAVEYARD SISTERHOOD

THE five friends had nearly finished their dinner. They were all rich, middle-aged men of the world, two of them bachelors, three married men. They met like this once a month, in memory of their younger days, and after dinner chatted together until two in the morning. These evenings were some of the happiest in their lives, for they had remained close friends and enjoyed one another's company. Their conversation was about anything and everything that interests and amuses Parisians; as in most drawing-rooms, it was a sort of spoken recapitulation of the morning papers.

One of the gayest of the five, Joseph de Bardon, was a bachelor. He lived the Parisian life in the most thorough and whimsical fashion, without being either debauched or depraved. It interested him, and as he was still young, being scarcely forty, he enjoyed it to the full. A man of the world in the widest and best sense of the word, he possessed a great deal of wit without much depth, varied knowledge without real erudition, and quick understanding without serious penetration; and his observations and adventures, his experiences and encounters furnished him with amusing anecdotes of a comical and philosophical nature which earned him a considerable reputation in society as an intelligent man.

He was the after-dinner speaker of the group, always having a story to tell which the others looked forward to hearing. He began telling one now without being asked.

Smoking a cigar, with his elbows on the table and a half-full glass of liqueur brandy in front of his plate, lulled by the smoky atmosphere filled with the fragrance of hot coffee, he seemed completely at ease, just as certain beings are perfectly at ease in certain places and at certain times – a nun in a chapel, for instance, or a goldfish in its bowl.

Between two puffs of his cigar, he said: 'I had a strange adventure a little while ago.'

The others said with almost a single voice: 'Tell us about it.'

'Gladly,' he replied. 'You know that I love wandering round Paris, like a collector peering into shop windows. I for my part enjoy watching people and things, everything that's happening and everything that's passing by.

'Well, about the middle of September, when we were having a spell of very fine weather, I went out one afternoon without knowing where I was going. We men always have a vague desire to call on some pretty woman. We review our gallery of acquaintances, we compare them in our mind, we gauge their relative charms and the interest they arouse in us, and we finally choose the one who attracts us most. But when the sun is shining brightly and the air is warm, we often lose all desire to pay calls.

'That day the sun was shining brightly and the air was warm, so I just lit a cigar and went for a stroll along the outer boulevard. Then, as I was sauntering along, the idea occurred to me of going to have a look round the Montmartre Cemetery.

'I like cemeteries, you know. They sadden me and soothe my nerves, and I need something to do that. Besides, there are some good friends of mine there, friends nobody goes to see any more, so I go to see them now and then.

'As it happens, in that very cemetery, I once buried an old romance, a mistress of mine to whom I was greatly attached, a charming little woman whose memory not only grieves me deeply but awakens regrets in my heart ... all kinds of regrets. . . . I go and dream beside her grave. . . . It's all over for her.

'I like cemeteries too because they are huge, densely populated cities. Just think of all the bodies in that small space, of all the generations of Parisians lodged there for ever, troglodytes eternally imprisoned in their little vaults, in little holes covered with a stone or marked by a cross, while the living, fools that they are, take up so much room and make so much noise.

'Again, in cemeteries you can find monuments that are almost as interesting as those you find in museums. Though I wouldn't compare the two works, Cavaignac's tomb reminded me of that masterpiece of Jean Goujon's, the statue of Louis de Brézé in the underground chapel in Rouen Cathedral. Gentlemen, all so-called modern, realistic art started there. That statue of the dead Louis de Brézé is more convincing, more terrible, more suggestive of inanimate flesh still convulsed by the death-agony, than any of the tortured corpses you see on modern tombs.

'But in the Montmartre Cemetery you can still admire the monument to Baudin, which is quite impressive, Gautier's tomb, and Murger's – where the other day I saw a poor, solitary wreath of yellow immortelles. Who do you think laid it there? Perhaps the last of the *grisettes*, an old woman who has become a concierge in the neighbourhood. It's a pretty little statue by Millet, but spoilt by dirt and neglect. Sing the joys of youth, Murger!

'So there I was, going into the Montmartre Cemetery, and suddenly filled with sadness, a sadness which didn't hurt too much, as it happened, the sort of sadness which makes a healthy man think: This isn't a very cheerful place, but at least it isn't time yet for me to come here . . .

'The feeling of autumn, that warm dampness which evokes the idea of dead leaves and tired, anaemic sunshine, intensified and poeticized the sense of solitude and finality surrounding that place, which evokes the idea of dead men.

'I wandered slowly along those streets of tombs where the neighbours never call on each other, no longer sleep together, and don't read the papers. And I started reading the epitaphs. Let me assure you that nothing in the whole world could be more amusing. Labiche and Meilhac have never made me laugh as much as that tombstone prose. Those crosses and marble slabs on which the relatives of the dead have poured out their grief, their wishes for the happiness of the departed in the next world, and their longing to rejoin their loved one – the hypocrites! – make funnier reading than any book by Paul de Kock.

'But what I love most of all in that cemetery is the deserted, lonely part planted with great yew trees and cypresses, the old district inhabited by those who died long ago. For soon it will once again become a new district, and the green trees nourished by human corpses will be felled to make room for the recently departed to be lined up under little marble slabs.

'After I had wandered about long enough to refresh my mind I realized that I was in danger of getting bored and that it was time for me to go to the last bed of my sometime mistress and pay her the faithful tribute of my memory. My heart was heavy as I reached her grave. The poor darling was so sweet and loving, so fair and lovely ... and now ... if her grave were opened. ...

'Bending over the iron railing I whispered a few sorrowful words to her which she probably never heard, and I was about to walk away when I saw a woman in deep mourning kneeling down in front of the next grave. Her crape veil had been thrown back to reveal a pretty head of fair hair which looked like a bright dawn under the dark night of her head-dress. I stayed where I was.

'She was obviously in the grip of profound sorrow. She had buried her face in her hands and was deep in meditation, holding herself as rigid as a statue. Absorbed in her grief, and telling the painful beads of memory behind her closed and hidden eyes, she seemed herself like a corpse mourning a corpse. Then, all of a sudden, from a slight movement of her back like a willow stirring in the wind, I guessed that she was going to cry. She wept gently at first, then more violently, her neck and shoulders shaking. Suddenly she uncovered her eyes. They were full of tears and quite charming. She looked around her frantically, as if awakening from a nightmare. She saw me gazing at her, looked embarrassed, and hid her face again in her hands. Then she burst into convulsive sobs and her head slowly bent towards the marble tombstone. She rested her forehead on it and her veil, falling around her, covered the white corners of the beloved sepulchre like a new mourning-cloth. I heard her moan, and then she collapsed with her cheek against the tombstone and lay there motionless and unconscious.

'I rushed over to her, slapped her hands and breathed on her eyelids, at the same time reading the simple epitaph on the tombstone:

HERE LIES LOUIS-THÉODORE CARREL,
*Captain in the Marine Light Infantry,*
*killed by the enemy in Tonkin.*
PRAY FOR HIS SOUL.

This death had occurred only a few months earlier. I was moved to tears, and I redoubled my efforts to revive her. At last they succeeded and she came to. I am not a bad-looking fellow – I'm not forty yet – and at that moment I looked extremely upset. I realized from her first glance that she was likely to be polite and grateful. I was not disappointed, and between further tears and sobs she told me about the officer who had been killed in Tonkin after they had been married only a year. He had married her for love, as she was an orphan and possessed nothing but her dowry.

'I consoled her, comforted her, lifted her up, and helped her to her feet. Then I said: "You can't stay here. Come along."

'"I'm incapable of walking," she murmured.

'"Let me help you."

'"Thank you, Monsieur, you are very kind. Did you come here to mourn someone?"

'"Yes, Madame."

'"Your wife?"

'"A mistress."

'"A man may love a mistress as much as a wife, for passion knows no law."

'"Yes, Madame," I replied.

'And we walked away together, she leaning on me and I almost carrying her along the alleys. As we left the cemetery she murmured: "I think I'm going to faint."

'"Would you like to go somewhere and take something to revive you?"

'"Yes, Monsieur."

'I noticed a restaurant nearby, one of those restaurants where the friends of the dead go to celebrate the end of their mournful duty. We went in and I made her drink a cup of hot tea which seemed to restore her strength. A faint smile came to her lips, and she started telling me about herself. It was so sad, she said, to be all alone in the world, to be alone at home day and night, to have nobody any more to whom she could give her love, trust and intimacy.

'This all seemed sincere and sounded well on her lips. I felt my heart softening. She was very young, perhaps twenty. I paid her a few compliments which she accepted gracefully. Then, as it was getting late, I offered to take her home in a cab. She accepted. In the cab we were so close to each other that we could feel the warmth of our bodies through our clothes, which is really the most disturbing thing in the world.

'When the cab drew up in front of her house she murmured: "I don't feel capable of walking upstairs by myself, for I live on the fourth floor. You have already been so kind to me: will you give me your arm as far as my apartment?"

'I gladly agreed. She walked up slowly, breathing hard. Then, outside her door, she added: "Do come in for a few minutes so that I can thank you."

'And I went in.

'Her apartment was modest, even rather poor, but simply and tastefully furnished.

'We sat down side by side on a little sofa, and she began talking to me again about her loneliness.

'She rang for her maid, to offer me a drink, but the girl didn't come. I was delighted, concluding that this maid probably came only in the morning and was really just a cleaning-woman.

'She had taken off her hat. She was so charming with her limpid eyes fixed upon me, so clear and steady, that I was seized by a terrible temptation to which I succumbed. I clasped her in my arms and kissed her again and again on her eyelids, which she had promptly lowered.

'She struggled to free herself, pushing me away and repeating: "Please . . . please . . . please . . ."

'What did she mean by that word? In such circumstances "please" could have at least two meanings. To silence her I passed from her eyes to her lips and gave the word "please" the conclusion I preferred. She didn't resist overmuch, and when we looked at each other again after this insult to the memory of the captain killed in Tonkin, she had a languorous expression of tender resignation which dispelled my misgivings.

'I showed my gratitude by being gallant and attentive. After further conversation lasting about an hour I asked her: "Where do you usually dine?"

'"In a little restaurant near here."

'"All alone?"

'"Why, yes."

'"Will you have dinner with me?"

'"Where?"

'"In a good restaurant on the boulevard."

'She demurred, but I insisted, and she finally gave way, consoling herself with the argument that she was bored and lonely. Then she added: "I must put on a dress that isn't so dark."

'She went into her bedroom, and when she came out she was in half-mourning, wearing a very simple grey dress which made her look slim and charming. She obviously had different outfits for town and cemetery.

'Dinner was very pleasant. She drank some champagne and became very animated and lively. I went back to her apartment with her.

'This liaison begun among the tombstones lasted about three weeks. But men grow tired of everything, and especially of women. I left her on the pretext of an unavoidable journey. I was very generous when we parted, and she was very grateful. She made me promise and even

84

swear that I would come back on my return to Paris, for she really seemed to care for me a little.

'I lost no time in forming other attachments and about a month went by without the temptation to resume that funereal affair becoming strong enough for me to yield to it. However, I had not forgotten her. The memory of her haunted me like a mystery, a psychological problem, one of those inexplicable questions which nag at you for an answer.

'I don't know why, but one day it occurred to me that I might find her in the Montmartre Cemetery, so I went back there.

'I walked around for a long time without meeting anyone but the usual visitors to the place, mourners who had not yet broken off all relations with their dead. The tomb of the captain killed in Tonkin had no weeping woman kneeling beside it and no flowers or wreaths on the marble slab.

'But as I was walking through another district of that great city of the dead I suddenly saw a couple in deep mourning coming towards me down a narrow avenue lined with crosses. To my amazement, when they drew near, I recognized . . . her!

'She saw me and blushed. As I brushed past her she gave me a little signal, a little glance which meant: "Don't recognize me," but which also seemed to say: "Come back and see me, darling."

'The man with her was about fifty years old, distinguished and well-dressed, with the rosette of an officer of the Legion of Honour. And he was supporting her, just as I had supported her when we had left the cemetery together.

'I went off dumbfounded, puzzling over what I had just

seen, and wondering to what race of creatures that grave-yard huntress belonged. Was she just an ordinary whore, an inspired prostitute who visited graveyards to pick up unhappy men haunted by the loss of a wife or mistress and troubled by the memory of past caresses? Was she unique? Or were there several like her? Was it a profession – a graveyard sisterhood who walked the cemeteries as others walk the streets? Or had she alone hit upon that admirable idea, that profoundly philosophical notion, of exploiting the amorous regrets awakened in those mournful places?

'I would have dearly loved to know whose widow she had chosen to be that day . . .'

# MADAME TELLIER'S
# ESTABLISHMENT

## I

THEY went there every night, about eleven o'clock, just as naturally as they would drop into a café.

There were seven or eight of them, always the same, not a fast set but respectable citizens, tradesmen and young men of the town; and they would drink their chartreuse and tease the girls a little, or else have a serious conversation with Madame, whom everybody treated with respect.

Then they would go home to bed before midnight, except for the young men, who sometimes stayed on.

It was a homely-looking house, quite small, with yellow walls, standing at the corner of a street behind the church of Saint-Étienne; and the windows looked out on the dock, full of ships unloading, the great salt marsh known as La Retenue, and, in the background, the Virgin's hill with its old grey chapel.

Madame, who came from a respectable peasant family in the department of the Eure, had adopted her present profession just as she might have become a milliner or a draper. The stigma attached to prostitution, so deep and inveterate in big towns, does not exist in the Normandy countryside. The peasant says: 'It's a good trade,' and sends his daughter off to keep a harem of prostitutes just as he would send her off to run a boarding-school for young ladies.

In any case, this establishment had been left to her by its former owner, an old uncle of hers. Monsieur and Madame, who had previously kept an inn near Yvetot, had promptly sold out, considering that the business at Fécamp would be more profitable; and they had arrived one fine morning to take over the management of the concern, which had been getting into a bad way in the absence of its owner.

They were an excellent couple who immediately won the affections of their employees and the neighbours.

Monsieur died of a stroke two years later. His new profession had maintained him in such comfort and immobility that he had grown very stout and his good health had killed him.

Since she had become a widow, all the clients of the establishment had hankered after Madame's favours, but in vain; she was said to be above suspicion, and even her young women had never managed to discover anything against her.

She was tall, plump and prepossessing. Her complexion, which had grown pale in the twilight of this house whose shutters were always closed, shone as if it were coated with varnish. Her forehead was framed in a thin, fluffy fringe of false hair which gave her a youthful look at variance with the mature curves of her figure. She was always cheerful, had a frank and open face, and enjoyed a joke, though with a hint of reserve which her new occupation had not yet succeeded in removing. Coarse language always shocked her slightly; and whenever some ill-bred young fellow called her establishment by its proper name she was angry and indignant. In short, she had a natural delicacy, and although she treated her girls as friends she was fond of observing that they were 'not her sort'.

Sometimes, on a week-day, she would go for a drive in a hired carriage with some of her flock; and they would go and romp about on the grassy banks of the little river which flows through the Valmont meadows. They would behave like schoolgirls let out for the day, racing madly about and playing childish games with all the high spirits of recluses intoxicated by the fresh air. Sitting on the grass, they would picnic off cold meat washed down with cider, and they would return home at nightfall deliciously tired and sweetly sentimental; in the carriage they would hug and kiss Madame as if she were the best of mothers, full of kindness and understanding.

The house had two entrances. On the corner there was a sort of shady café which was open in the evening to workmen and sailors. Two of the young women engaged in the principal occupation of the establishment were detailed to minister to the needs of this section of the clientele. With the help of a waiter called Frédéric – a fair-haired, smooth-faced little fellow who was as strong as an ox – they brought jugs of wine and pots of beer to the rickety marble-topped tables, and, sitting on the customers' knees with their arms round their necks, encouraged them to drink.

The other three ladies (there were only five in all) formed a sort of aristocracy and were reserved for the company on the first floor, except when the first-floor room was deserted and they were needed downstairs.

The Jupiter Room, where the respectable citizens of the town forgathered, was papered in blue and decorated with a large drawing showing Leda stretched out under a swan. This room was reached by means of a spiral staircase with a narrow, unpretentious door at the bottom, opening on to the street; all night long, behind a grille above this door, there burned a little lantern of the kind still lighted in certain cities at the feet of madonnas in wall niches.

The building was old and damp and had a slightly musty smell. Now and then a whiff of eau-de-Cologne was wafted along the corridors; or through a half-open door downstairs the coarse shouts of the men sitting at the tables in the café would echo through the whole building like a clap of thunder, bringing an expression of uneasiness and disgust to the faces of the gentlemen on the first floor.

Madame, who was on familiar terms with those clients whom she regarded as her friends, never left the drawing-room, but took a lively interest in the local gossip which they retailed to her. Her serious remarks made a change from the inconsequential chatter of the three girls; they were like a restful pause among the suggestive jokes bandied about by the portly citizens who indulged every evening in this harmless, unremarkable dissipation of taking a glass of liqueur in the company of prostitutes.

The names of the three first-floor ladies were Fernande, Raphaële and Rosa la Rosse.

As the staff was limited in number, Madame had tried to see that each girl should be as it were a sample or epitome of one female type, so that every client of the establishment might find there at least something approximating to his ideal.

Fernande was the typical blonde. She was very tall and flabby, almost obese, a country girl whose freckles refused to disappear and whose short-cropped fair hair, pale and colourless like combed flax, scarcely covered her head.

Raphaële, a Marseilles girl and a typical waterfront tart, was cast for the indispensable role of the lovely Jewess. She was a thin creature with prominent cheekbones plastered with rouge. Her black hair, greased with marrow-fat, hung over her temples in kiss-curls. Her eyes would have been considered beautiful if the right one had not been disfigured with a white speck. Her aquiline nose jutted out above a powerful jaw in which two false teeth in the upper row formed a marked contrast with the lower ones, which with age had taken on the dark colour of old wood.

Rosa la Rosse was a little ball of flesh, all belly with tiny legs. She had a husky voice and from morning till night sang ditties which were alternately smutty and sentimental, told interminable stories without any point to them, never stopped talking except to eat, and never stopped eating except to talk. She was always on the go, as nimble as a squirrel in spite of her fat body and diminutive legs. Her laughter, a cascade of shrill shrieks, was forever bursting out here, there and everywhere, in bedroom, attic or café, all over the house, and for no reason in particular.

The two ground-floor women were Louise, nicknamed Cocote, and Flora, known as Balançoire because she had a slight limp. The former always dressed like Liberty, with a tricolour sash, and the latter like a comic-opera Spanish woman, with copper sequins dancing in her carroty hair at every uneven step she took; they looked like a couple of kitchen-maids dolled up for a carnival. No uglier and no prettier than any other lower-class girls, they were typical barmaids, and they were known on the waterfront as the Two Beer-Pulls.

An uneasy but rarely troubled peace reigned among these five women, thanks to Madame's conciliatory tact and unfailing good humour.

The establishment, the only one of its kind in the little town, was very well frequented. Madame had given it such a respectable tone, was so amiable and obliging to everybody, and was so well known for her kindness of heart, that she was treated with a certain respect. The regular clients put themselves out to please her and were delighted when she showed them any special mark of friendship. Whenever they met on business during the day they would say to each other: 'See you this evening, you know where,' just as one might say: 'See you in the café after dinner.'

In short, Madame Tellier's establishment was a convenient meeting-place and it was unusual for anybody to miss the daily reunion.

One evening, towards the end of May, the first arrival, Monsieur Poulin, the timber merchant and a former mayor, found the door locked. The little lantern behind the grille was not alight and there was no sound coming from the house, which seemed completely dead. He knocked on the door, first softly, then louder; there was no answer. Then he went slowly back up the street, and when he got to the market square he met Monsieur Duvert, the ship-owner, who was on his way to the same place. They returned there together but with no more success. Then a tremendous up-roar suddenly broke out quite close to them, and walking round the corner they saw a crowd of English and French sailors hammering with their fists on the closed shutters of the café.

The two worthy citizens promptly took to their heels to avoid being involved, but a faint 'psst' stopped them; it was Monsieur Tournevau, the fish-curer, who had recognized them and was hailing them. They explained the situation, which was all the more upsetting for him in that, as a married man with a family who was closely watched, he came only on Saturdays, *securitas causa*, as he put it, referring to the weekly medical inspection of which his friend Doctor Borde had told him. This happened to be his evening, so that he was going to suffer deprivation for a whole week.

The three men made a wide detour as far as the quay-side and on the way met young Monsieur Philippe, the banker's son, a regular client, and Monsieur Pimpesse, the tax-collector. All of them then returned together by way of the Rue aux Juifs to make a last attempt. But the in-furiated sailors were besieging the house, throwing stones and shouting, so that the five first-floor clients beat a hasty retreat and started roaming the streets.

They then encountered the insurance agent, Monsieur

Dupuis, and Monsieur Vasse, the judge of the commercial court, and a long walk began which took them first of all to the jetty. There they sat down in a row on the granite parapet and looked at the white horses. The foam on the crest of the waves made bright patches of white in the darkness which disappeared as quickly as they came, and the monotonous sound of the sea breaking on the rocks echoed through the night all along the cliffs. After the melancholy party had stayed there for some time, Monsieur Tournevau remarked: 'This isn't very cheerful, is it?'

'It certainly isn't!' replied Monsieur Pimpesse, and they slowly set off again.

After going along the street known as Sous-le-Bois which dominates the coast, they returned across the wooden bridge over La Retenue, passed close to the railway line, and came out again on to the market square. There a quarrel suddenly flared up between the tax-collector, Monsieur Pimpesse, and the fish-curer, Monsieur Tournevau, about an edible mushroom which one of them claimed to have found in the neighbourhood.

Boredom had made them so irritable that they might have come to blows if the others had not intervened. Monsieur Pimpesse went off in a fury, and immediately a fresh dispute arose between the former mayor, Monsieur Poulin, and the insurance agent, Monsieur Dupuis, on the subject of the tax-collector's salary and the extra money he could probably make on the side. Insults were flying thick and fast when a storm of shouting broke out and the crowd of sailors, tired of waiting in vain outside the closed house, poured on to the square. They were walking in twos, arm in arm, in a long procession, and yelling at the tops of their voices.

The local worthies took refuge in a doorway, and the howling mob disappeared in the direction of the abbey.

The din could be heard for a long time, growing fainter like a storm moving away, and then silence returned.

Monsieur Poulin and Monsieur Dupuis, both still furious with each other, went off in different directions without saying good night.

The other four set off again, instinctively making their way downhill towards Madame Tellier's establishment. It was still shut up, silent, impenetrable. A drunkard was quietly but stubbornly tapping on the café shutters, then stopping to call Frédéric, the waiter, in a low voice. Getting no answer, he decided to sit down on the doorstep and await developments.

The regulars were on the point of going home when the noisy band of seamen appeared at the end of the street. The French sailors were bawling the '*Marseillaise*' and the English 'Rule Britannia'. There was a general rush at the walls of the house, and then the torrent of brutish humanity surged away in the direction of the quay, where a fight broke out between the sailors of the two nations. In the course of the brawl an Englishman had an arm broken and a Frenchman his nose split open.

The drunkard, who had remained on the doorstep, was crying now as topers cry, or children who cannot get their way.

The party of good citizens finally broke up.

Calm gradually returned to the troubled town. Here and there the sound of voices could occasionally be heard again, but then faded away in the distance.

One man alone was still wandering about. Monsieur Tournevau, the fish-curer, miserable at the thought of having to wait until the following Saturday, and unable to understand what had happened, was hoping against hope that something might turn up. He was furious with the police for allowing an establishment of public utility, which was under their supervision and control, to be closed in this way.

He came back to the house, prowling round the walls and trying to find an explanation of the mystery. Suddenly he spotted a notice stuck on the door. He quickly struck a wax-vesta and read these words written in a large uneven hand: 'Closed for a First Communion.'

Then he walked away, realizing that there was no point in staying any longer.

The drunkard was asleep by now, stretched out at full length across the inhospitable threshold.

The next day all the regulars, one after the other, contrived to walk along the street, each with a bundle of papers under his arm to provide him with a pretext. And with a furtive glance each of them read the mysterious notice: 'Closed for a First Communion.'

II

The fact of the matter was that Madame had a brother who had set up as a carpenter in their native village of Virville in the department of the Eure. At the time when she was still keeping the inn at Yvetot, she had stood godmother to that brother's daughter, to whom she had given the name of Constance – Constance Rivet, she herself being a Rivet by birth. The carpenter, who knew that his sister was comfortably off, had been careful not to lose touch with her, although they rarely met, both being fully occupied with their businesses and also living a long way from each other. But now, as the little girl was nearly twelve and due to make her First Communion that year, he seized the opportunity for a meeting and wrote to his sister that he was counting on her to be present at the ceremony. She could not refuse this favour to her goddaughter, whose grandparents were dead, so she accepted. Her brother, whose name was Joseph, hoped that if he showered sufficient attentions on her he might induce her to make a will in his daughter's favour, as she had no children of her own.

His sister's profession caused him no embarrassment at all, and besides, nobody in his district knew anything about it. Whenever people mentioned her they simply said: 'Madame Tellier has a house at Fécamp,' which suggested that she was living on a private income. Fécamp is at least fifty miles from Virville, and for a peasant a fifty-mile journey across country is more daunting than an ocean voyage for an educated person. The people of Virville had never been further afield than Rouen, and there was nothing to attract the people of Fécamp to a little village of five hundred houses lost in the middle of a plain and belonging to a different department. As a result nobody knew anything about her business.

But as the date of the ceremony drew nearer Madame found herself in a difficult position. She had no assistant to take her place and had no desire to leave her establishment without supervision, even for a day. All the rivalries between the ladies upstairs and those downstairs would be sure to break out; moreover, Frédéric would probably get drunk, and when he was drunk he would knock people down for no reason at all. Finally she decided to take the whole of her staff with her, except for the waiter, to whom she gave two days off.

When she asked her brother he raised no objection and undertook to put up the whole party for the night. Accordingly, on the Saturday morning, the eight o'clock express carried off Madame and her companions in a second-class carriage.

As far as Beuzeville they had the carriage to themselves and chattered away like magpies, but at that station a couple got in. The man, an old peasant, was wearing a blue smock with a pleated collar and wide sleeves caught in at the wrists and decorated with a small pattern in white embroidery. On his head he had an old-fashioned top hat, the reddish nap of which looked as if it had been brushed the wrong way. In one hand he was carrying a huge green umbrella, and in the other a large basket from which the heads of three frightened ducks protruded. The woman, holding herself stiffly in her country clothes, had a face like a hen, with a nose as pointed as a beak. She sat down opposite her husband and stayed completely motionless, embarrassed at finding herself in such smart company.

The carriage did in fact offer a dazzling assortment of vivid colours. Madame was all in blue, blue silk from head to foot, with a red shawl in imitation French cashmere over her dress which was blinding in its brightness. Fernande was gasping for breath in a tartan dress, the bodice of which had been tightly laced by her companions so that it forced up her sagging breasts, which looked like two balls of jelly heaving up and down under the material.

Raphaële, in a feathered hat which looked like a nestful of birds, was wearing a lilac dress spangled with gold, a vaguely oriental outfit which suited her Jewish features. Rosa la Rosse wore a pink skirt with wide flounces which gave her the appearance of a podgy child or a fat dwarf, while the Two Beer-Pulls looked as if they had made their dresses out of those old-fashioned curtains with a floral pattern which date back to the Restoration.

As soon as they were no longer alone in the carriage the ladies put on solemn expressions and began talking about serious topics in order to create a good impression. But at Bolbec a gentleman with fair side-whiskers, rings on his fingers and a gold watch-chain got in and put several parcels wrapped in oilcloth into the rack over his head. He seemed a good-natured fellow and a bit of a wag. He bowed to all the company and asked smoothly: 'Are you ladies moving to a new garrison?'

This question plunged the party into acute embarrassment. Eventually Madame recovered herself and replied curtly, to avenge the honour of the troop: 'There's no call to be rude!'

'I beg your pardon,' he said apologetically. 'I should have said to a new convent.'

Madame, unable to think of a suitable retort, or perhaps considering the correction adequate, gave a dignified nod of her head and pursed her lips.

Then the gentleman, who was sitting between Rosa la Rosse and the old peasant, began winking at the three ducks whose heads were poking out of the big basket. As soon as he felt that he had attracted sufficient attention, he started tickling the birds under their beaks and making facetious remarks to them to make everybody laugh: 'So we've left our little pond, have we – quack, quack, quack – to go and try a little spit – quack, quack, quack!'

The unfortunate birds kept twisting their necks away to avoid his fingers and made frantic efforts to get out of their wickerwork prison. Then suddenly all three in unison uttered a mournful complaint: 'Quack, quack, quack!' This produced an explosion of laughter among the women. They leaned forward, pushing each other aside to get a better view; they had begun to take a passionate interest in the ducks, and the gentleman surpassed himself in his display of fun, wit and charm.

Then Rosa joined in, and, leaning over her neighbour's legs, kissed the three birds on the beak. All the others promptly wanted to kiss them too, and the gentleman sat the ladies on his knee, bouncing them up and down and pinching them. All of a sudden he began using the familiar form of address with them.

The two peasants, who were even more scared than their ducks, rolled their eyes as if they were possessed. They did not dare to move a muscle and not a smile or a tremor appeared on their wrinkled old faces.

Next, the gentleman, who was a commercial traveller, offered the ladies some braces as a joke and taking down one of his parcels opened it. He had been pulling their legs: the parcel contained nothing but garters.

They were in every possible shade of silk – blue, pink, purple, mauve, and flaming red – with metal clasps in the form of gilt cupids embracing. The ladies uttered shrieks of joy, and then examined the samples with that seriousness which comes naturally to women as soon as they lay their hands on an article of clothing. They consulted one another with glances or whispers, while Madame longingly handled a pair of orange garters, broader and more imposing than the rest and just the thing for the mistress of an establishment such as hers.

The gentleman sat waiting, turning over an idea in his head.

'Come along, my loves,' he said, 'you must try them on!'

There was a storm of protests, and the women gripped their skirts between their legs as if they were afraid of being raped. He quietly bided his time.

'If you don't want them, I'll pack them up again,' he declared. Then he added slyly: 'Any lady who tries them on can have the pair she likes for nothing!'

But they refused, sitting very erect and dignified. The Two Beer-Pulls, however, looked so unhappy that he repeated his offer. Flora Balançoire in particular, tortured by longing, was visibly weakening. He pressed her hard: 'Come on, dear, don't be frightened. Look – this lilac pair will match your dress perfectly.'

That decided her, and, pulling up her dress, she revealed a powerful milkmaid's leg in a coarse, badly fitting stocking. Bending down, the gentleman fastened the garter, first below the knee, then above it; and he tickled the girl to make her squeal and wriggle. When he had finished he gave her the lilac pair and asked: 'Who's next?'

'Me! Me!' they all cried together.

He began with Rosa la Rosse, who disclosed a shapeless object, round all the way down, without any ankle, 'a regular sausage of a leg', as Raphaële used to say. Fernande was complimented by the commercial traveller, who waxed eloquent over her massive columns. The spindly shanks of the lovely Jewess evoked less enthusiasm. Louise Cocote draped her skirts over the gentleman's head as a joke, and Madame felt obliged to intervene to put a stop to such unseemly behaviour. Finally Madame herself stretched out her leg, a fine Norman leg, plump and muscular; and the commercial traveller, surprised and impressed, gallantly took his hat off to salute this superb calf with proper French courtesy.

The two peasants, rooted to their seats with amazement, kept stealing sidelong glances at these goings-on; and they looked so exactly like a couple of chickens that when the man with the fair side-whiskers stood up, he let off a cockle-doodle-do right in their faces. This set off another storm of merriment.

The old couple got out at Motteville with their basket, their ducks and their umbrella; and as they walked away the woman could be heard saying to her husband: 'A lot of sluts, they be, on their way to that wicked place, Paris.'

The amusing pedlar got out himself at Rouen, after

behaving so grossly that Madame had felt it incumbent upon her to put him sharply in his place. She added by way of a moral: 'This will teach us not to talk to any Tom, Dick or Harry!'

They changed at Oisel, and at a station not much farther on they found Monsieur Joseph Rivet waiting for them with a large farm-cart filled with chairs and drawn by a white horse.

The carpenter politely kissed all the ladies and helped them into his cart. Three of them sat on the three chairs at the back; Raphaële, Madame and her brother on the three chairs in front; and Rosa, not having a seat, perched as best she could on big Fernande's knees. Then they set off.

However, right from the start, the horse's jerky trot shook the cart so violently that the chairs started dancing about, throwing the passengers up into the air and to right and left, as if they were puppets. Their faces were contorted with fright and they uttered shrieks of terror which were suddenly cut short by some more than usually violent jolt. They clung to the sides of the vehicle, their hats falling backwards, over their noses or on to their shoulders, while the white horse kept jogging along, straining its head forward and holding its tail out straight, a hairless little rat's tail with which it flicked its haunches every now and then. Joseph Rivet, with one foot braced against the shaft and the other leg doubled up under him, held the reins with his elbows up in the air, emitting a clucking sound from time to time which made the nag prick up its ears and quicken its pace.

The green countryside stretched out on both sides of the road. Here and there fields of rape in flower formed waving expanses of yellow giving off a strong wholesome smell, a sweet, penetrating smell which was carried a long way by the wind. In the rye, which was already tall, cornflowers were showing their little sky-blue heads, and the women wanted to pick them, but Monsieur Rivet refused to stop. Now and then they saw a field invaded by so many poppies that it seemed to be spattered with blood. Through this plain coloured by the flowers of the field, the cart, which itself looked as if it were carrying a bouquet of even brighter-coloured flowers, moved behind the trotting white horse, disappeared behind the tall trees surrounding a farmstead only to reappear beyond the foliage, and continued on its sunlit way between the green and gold crops, speckled with red and blue, carrying its dazzling load of women into the distance.

One o'clock was striking when they reached the carpenter's house.

They were tired out and pale with hunger as they had had nothing to eat since they had set off from Fécamp. Madame Rivet came running out and helped them down one after another, giving each one a kiss as soon as she set foot on the ground. She was so eager to make a good impression on her sister-in-law that it seemed as if she would never stop kissing her. The company then sat down to a meal in the workshop which had been cleared of its benches in readiness for the dinner to be held there next day.

A tasty omelette, followed by grilled sausages washed down with good sharp cider, restored everybody's spirits. Rivet had taken a glass to drink with his guests, while his wife did the cooking and serving, bringing in the dishes, clearing them away, and whispering in each person's ear: 'Are you sure you've got enough?' Rows of planks leaning against the walls and piles of shavings swept into the corners gave off a smell of planed wood, that resinous smell of a carpenter's shop which penetrates right into the lungs.

Everybody wanted to see the little girl, but she was at the church and would not be back till the evening.

Then the company went out for a stroll.

It was a small village with a main road running through it. About a dozen houses bordering this single thoroughfare housed the local tradesmen – the butcher, the grocer, the carpenter, the café-proprietor, the cobbler and the baker. The church stood at the end of this sort of street, surrounded by a small graveyard and completely overshadowed by four enormous lime-trees in front of the door. It was built of chipped flints, in no particular style, and was crowned by a slate-roofed belfry. Beyond it the open country began again, broken here and there by a clump of trees concealing a farmstead.

Although he was in his working clothes Rivet had politely taken his sister's arm and was escorting her with solemn dignity. His wife, overwhelmed by Raphaële's gold-spangled dress, walked between her and Fernande. Plump Rosa trotted along behind with Louise Cocote and Flora Balançoire, who was so tired that she was limping more than usual.

The villagers came to their doors, the children stopped their games, and a curtain drawn to one side revealed a glimpse of a head in a muslin cap. An old woman with a crutch, who was almost blind, crossed herself as if a religious procession were passing; and for a long time everybody's eyes followed the fine city ladies who had come so far to attend the First Communion of Joseph Rivet's little girl. The carpenter basked in a glow of reflected glory.

As they passed the church they heard some children singing, their shrill little voices sending up a song of praise to Heaven. But Madame would not let anybody go in, for fear of disturbing the little angels.

After a short walk in the countryside, in the course of which Joseph Rivet listed all the principal farms and gave details of their yield in crops and livestock, he brought his party home and settled the women in.

As the accommodation was extremely limited it had been decided that they should be split up, two to a room.

Rivet, for this once, was to sleep in the workshop, on the shavings; his wife would share her bed with her sister-in-law; and Fernande and Raphaële would sleep together in the room next door. Louise and Flora found themselves installed in the kitchen on a mattress on the floor, and Rosa was given a little dark cupboard to herself at the top of the stairs, next to the narrow garret where the young communicant was to spend the night.

When the little girl came home she was greeted with a shower of kisses; all the women wanted to fondle her, with that instinctive need to demonstrate affection and that habit of professional cajolery which had led them all to kiss the ducks on the train. All of them in turn sat her on their knees, stroked her fair silky hair and hugged her tight in an ecstasy of spontaneous tenderness. The child, well-behaved, filled with pious thoughts, and as it were spellbound by the absolution she had just received, submitted to these effusions with patient resignation.

It had been a tiring day for everybody and they went to bed very soon after dinner. The village was wrapped in that boundless silence of the fields which seems almost religious in character, a peaceful, penetrating silence which reaches to the stars, The women, accustomed to the noisy evenings at Madame Tellier's establishment, were deeply affected by the absolute quiet of the sleeping countryside. They shivered, not with cold, but with the loneliness of uneasy, troubled hearts.

As soon as they were in bed, two by two, they put their

arms round each other as if to ward off the pervading influence of the earth's profound and peaceful slumber. But Rosa la Rosse, alone in her dark cupboard and unused to sleeping with nobody in her arms, was overcome by a vague feeling of disquiet. She was tossing about in bed, unable to get to sleep, when she heard faint sobs like those of a crying child coming from behind the wooden partition by her head. Frightened, she called out quietly, and a little voice broken with sobs answered. It was the little girl, who had always slept in her mother's room and was afraid in her tiny garret.

A delighted Rosa got out of bed, and quietly, so as not to wake anybody up, went and fetched the child. She took her into her own warm bed, hugged her, kissed her, cuddled her, treated her to an extravagant show of affection, and finally, feeling calmer herself, fell asleep. And till daybreak the little communicant slept with her head on the prostitute's naked bosom.

At five o'clock the little church bell, ringing the Angelus at full peal, woke the ladies, who usually slept all morning, that being the only time they had to recover from their nocturnal labours. The villagers were already up, the women bustling from door to door, chatting eagerly, and carefully carrying short muslin dresses starched as stiff as cardboard, or huge candles with gold-fringed silk bows round the middle and grooves cut in the wax to show where they should be held. The sun was already high in the clear blue sky, although a faint trace of dawn remained in a rosy flush along the horizon. Families of hens were strutting about in front of their houses and here and there a black rooster with a gleaming neck lifted its crimson-crested head, flapping its wings, and flung its brazen call to the winds, to be echoed by all the other cocks.

Carts were coming in from the neighbouring villages,

discharging on the various doorsteps tall Norman women in dark dresses with fichus crossed over their breasts and fastened with silver brooches of great age. The men had put on blue smocks over new frock-coats or old-fashioned green broadcloth tail-coats, the skirts of which hung down underneath.

When the horses had been stabled the whole length of the main road was lined with a double row of ramshackle country conveyances – carts, traps, gigs, waggons, and other vehicles of every shape and age, tilted forward or sitting on the ground with their shafts in the air.

The carpenter's house was as busy as a beehive. The ladies, in dressing-jackets and petticoats, with their sparse short hair which looked as if it had been faded and worn with use hanging down their backs, were engaged in dressing the child.

The little girl was standing motionless on the table while Madame Tellier directed the operations of her flying squad. They washed her face, combed her hair, put on her veil and her dress, and then with the help of a host of pins arranged the pleats of her skirt, took in the waist which was too large, and generally made sure that she looked just right. When they had finished they made the long-suffering child sit down, telling her not to move, and the excited bunch of women ran off to get ready themselves.

The bell of the little church began ringing again. Its faint tinkle rose into the air until it was lost, like a feeble voice, in the immensity of the blue sky.

The communicants started coming out of their houses and making their way towards the village hall, which housed the two schools and the mayor's office, and which stood at the opposite end of the village from the 'house of God'.

The parents, looking self-conscious in their Sunday best,

and walking with the awkward movements of people whose bodies are forever bent in toil, followed their children. The little girls were lost in a cloud of snowy tulle like whipped cream, while the little men, like embryonic waiters with their hair plastered down with grease, walked with their legs apart so as not to dirty their black trousers.

It was a cause of pride to a family when a great many relatives came a long way to attend a child's First Communion, so the carpenter's triumph was complete. Constance was followed by the entire Tellier contingent, led by Madame, with her father arm in arm with his sister, her mother walking beside Raphaële, Fernande with Rosa, and the Two Beer-Pulls side by side. The company marched along majestically with all the dignity of a General Staff in full dress.

The effect on the village was overwhelming.

At the school the girls fell in under the coif of the good Sister, the boys under the hat of the village schoolmaster, a handsome man of presence, and they all moved off, singing a hymn.

The boys at the head of the procession walked in double file between the two rows of unharnessed vehicles, with the girls following in the same formation, and as all the villagers had respectfully yielded pride of place to the ladies from the town the latter came immediately behind the little girls, prolonging the double line of the procession even further, three on the left and three on the right, and looking like a firework display in their dazzling dresses.

Their entry into the church dumbfounded the locals who jostled and turned round and pushed one another to see them. The more pious women in the church almost spoke in raised voices, they were so amazed at the sight of these ladies who were more splendidly garbed than the cantors in their chasubles. The mayor offered them his pew, the first pew on the right near the choir, and Madame Tellier took her seat in it with her sister-in-law, Fernande and Raphaële. Rosa la Rosse and the Two Beer-Pulls occupied the second pew with the carpenter.

The choir of the church was full of kneeling children, girls on one side, boys on the other, and the long candles in their hands looked like lances tilted in every direction.

In front of the lectern stood three men singing at the tops of their voices. They prolonged the sonorous Latin syllables indefinitely, lengthening the '*a-a*' of the '*Amens*' as if they would never stop, supported by a long-drawn monotonous note from the serpent, bellowed from that instrument's wide brass gullet. A child's shrill voice gave the responses, and now and then a priest sitting in one of the stalls and wearing a square biretta got to his feet, mumbled a few words, and sat down again, while the three cantors started off once more, their eyes fixed on the great book of plain-song which lay open in front of them on the outspread wings of a wooden eagle mounted on a pivot.

Then silence fell. The whole congregation knelt down as one man, and the celebrant entered, a venerable, white-haired old man, his head bent over the chalice he carried in his left hand. In front of him walked the two servers in red cassocks and behind him came a crowd of choristers in heavy boots who lined up on either side of the choir.

A little bell tinkled in the dead silence and the Mass began. The priest moved slowly about in front of the golden tabernacle, genuflecting from time to time, and in a cracked voice quavering with age intoned the preliminary prayers. As soon as he stopped all the cantors and the serpent came in together, and some men in the body of the church joined in, though less loudly and more humbly, as befits the ordinary members of a congregation.

Suddenly the *Kyrie eleison* burst heavenwards from every

breast and every heart. Particles of dust and fragments of worm-eaten wood actually fell from the old vaulted ceiling, shaken by this explosion of sound. The sun beating on the slate roof was turning the little church into an oven; and as the moment of ineffable mystery drew near a wave of emotion, a feeling of anxious expectation gripped the children's hearts and produced a tightening of their mothers' throats.

The priest, who had been seated for some time, went back up the steps to the altar, and with his silvery head uncovered and his hands trembling, made ready for the supernatural act.

He turned towards the congregation, and, stretching out his hands, said: '*Orate, fratres*: brethren, let us pray.' As everybody prayed the old priest murmured the words of the supreme mystery, the bell tinkled three times, the congregation, their heads bowed low, called upon the name of God, and the children felt faint with unbearable anticipation.

It was then that Rosa, her face buried in her hands, suddenly remembered her mother, the church in her village, and her own First Communion. She felt as if she were living that day again when she had been such a little girl, lost in her white dress, and she started to cry. At first she wept quietly, the tears welling slowly from her eyes, but then, as her memories crowded in on her and her emotion grew, she burst out sobbing, her throat swelling and her bosom heaving. She took out her handkerchief, wiped her eyes, dabbed at her nose and mouth to stifle her cries, but all in vain; a sort of groan came from her throat, answered by two other deep, heartrending sighs, for her two neighbours, Louise and Flora, overcome by similar memories of a distant past, were also moaning and weeping floods of tears.

As tears are contagious, it was not long before Madame in her turn felt her eyelids growing moist, and, turning towards her sister-in-law, she saw the whole of her pew was weeping too.

The priest was turning the bread and wine into the body and blood of God. The children were past thinking, bent double on the stone flags in a sort of pious awe; and here and there in the church a woman, a mother, a sister, caught up in the mysterious sympathy of strong emotions, and also affected by the sight of the fine ladies shaking and sobbing as they knelt in their pews, wept into her checked cotton handkerchief and pressed her left hand against her pounding heart.

Like a spark which sets fire to a whole field of ripe corn, the tears of Rosa and her companions swept through the whole congregation in a flash. Soon men, women, old people and young lads in new smocks were all sobbing helplessly, and something superhuman seemed to be hovering over their heads, an all-embracing spirit, the miraculous breath of an invisible omnipotent being.

Then, from the choir of the church, there came a short, sharp sound. The good Sister had rapped on her missal to give the signal for Communion, and the children, shaking with a divine fever, approached the holy table.

A whole row of them knelt down. The old priest, holding the silver-gilt ciborium in one hand, passed down the line, offering each child, between his finger and thumb, the sacred host, the body of Christ, the redemption of the world. They opened their mouths with their eyes tight shut, their deathly white faces twitching convulsively; and the long white cloth spread underneath their chins rippled like running water.

Suddenly a kind of madness seemed to sweep the church, a noise like that of a frenzied crowd, a storm of sobs and muffled cries. It passed like one of those gusts of wind which bend the trees in a forest, and the priest, standing motionless with a wafer in his hand, paralysed by emotion, said to himself: 'This is God in our midst, manifesting his presence, descending upon his kneeling people in answer to my voice.' And he stammered frantic prayers, forgetting the words, the prayers of a soul straining fervently towards heaven.

He finished administering Communion in such an ecstasy of faith that his legs almost gave way under him, and when he had drunk his Saviour's blood he prostrated himself in an act of ardent thanksgiving.

Behind him the congregation was gradually recovering its composure. The cantors, sustained by the dignity of their white surplices, resumed their singing, though with un-steady voices still full of tears, and the serpent too sounded hoarse, as if the instrument itself had been weeping.

Then the priest raised his hands and motioned to them to be silent; and, making his way between the two rows of communicants lost in an ecstasy of joy, he came down to the choir screen.

'My dear brethren, my dear sisters, my dear children,' he said, 'I thank you from the bottom of my heart; you have just given me the greatest joy I have known in all my life. For just now I felt God descending upon us in answer to my prayer. He came; he was here among us, filling your souls and bringing tears to your eyes. I am the oldest priest in this diocese and today I am also the happiest. A miracle has taken place in our midst, a true miracle, a great miracle, a sublime miracle. While Jesus Christ was entering for the first time into the bodies of these little ones, the Holy Ghost, the Heavenly Dove, the Breath of God came down upon you, possessed you and took hold of you, so that you were bent like reeds in the wind.'

Then, in a clearer voice, turning towards the two pews occupied by the carpenter's guests, he went on: 'My thanks are due above all to you, my dear sisters, who have come such a long way to be with us. Your presence among us, your manifest faith and your lively piety have been a salutary example to us all. You have been a source of edification for my parish; your emotion has warmed our hearts; without you, perhaps this great day would not have had such a truly divine character. Sometimes the presence of only a single chosen lamb is enough to persuade Our Lord to visit his flock.'

His voice faltered, and he concluded: 'May the Grace of God be with you. Amen.'

Then he went back up the steps to the altar to bring the Mass to a close.

Now everybody was in a hurry to go. Even the children were fidgeting, exhausted by such a long emotional strain. They were hungry too, and one after another their parents went off without waiting for the last Gospel, to finish getting everything ready for the meal.

Outside the church there was a noisy crush, a medley of shrill voices speaking in the sing-song Normandy accent. The villagers all formed up in two rows and when the children came out each family pounced upon its own.

Constance found herself seized upon, surrounded and kissed by the whole houseful of women. It seemed as though Rosa in particular would go on hugging her for ever. Finally, however, she took one hand and Madame Tellier grabbed the other; Raphaële and Fernande picked up the long muslin train to keep it from trailing in the dust; Louise and Flora brought up the rear with Madame Rivet; and the child, still in a daze at the thought of the God she carried within her, set off surrounded by this guard of honour.

The dinner was served in the workshop on long trestle-tables.

The door to the street had been left open, letting in all the sounds and sights of the village's merrymaking. Everybody was having a good time. Tables surrounded by people in their Sunday best could be seen through every window and shouts of gaiety came from every house. The peasants in their shirt-sleeves were drinking brimming mugs of undiluted cider, and in the midst of each group could be seen a couple of children, here two girls, there two boys, having dinner with one of their respective families.

Now and then, in the sultry midday heat, a cart would pass through the village drawn by an old nag at an ambling trot and the driver in his smock would throw an envious glance at all the revelry that met his eyes.

In the carpenter's house the gaiety was rather subdued, for something of the morning's emotion still lingered on. Rivet alone was in a festive mood and drinking hard. Madame Tellier kept looking at the clock, for if they were not to lose two successive working-days, they would have to catch the 3.55 train which would get them back to Fécamp by the evening.

The carpenter did everything he could to divert her attention in the hope of keeping his guests till the next day, but Madame would not allow herself to be distracted: business was a serious matter.

As soon as they had finished coffee she ordered her staff to get ready as quickly as possible. Then, turning to her brother, she said: 'Now you go and harness the horse straight away,' and went upstairs to finish her own preparations. When she came down again her sister-in-law was waiting to have a word with her about the little girl and a long conversation ensued in which nothing was decided. The peasant woman used all her cunning and put on a great show of affection, but Madame Tellier, who had the child on her lap, refused to commit herself and only made vague promises: she would not forget the little girl, there was plenty of time, and besides they would be seeing each other again.

Meanwhile there was no sign of the cart, and the women had not come down. Indeed, roars of laughter could be heard upstairs, together with scuffling, screams and the clapping of hands. Accordingly, while the carpenter's wife went round to the stable to see if the cart was ready, Madame finally went upstairs herself.

Rivet, very drunk and half undressed, was making vain attempts to rape Rosa, who was helpless with laughter. The Two Beer-Pulls were holding him back by the arms and trying to calm him down, shocked at such a scene after the morning's ceremony; but Raphaële and Fernande were egging him on, convulsed with merriment and holding their sides. They uttered shrill screams at every one of the drunkard's unsuccessful efforts. The man, red-faced and furious, with all his buttons undone, was trying to shake off the two women clinging to him and tugging with all his might at Rosa's skirt, mumbling: 'So you won't, eh, you slut?' Madame rushed at her brother in a rage, seized him by the shoulders, and flung him out of the room with such force that he hit the wall on the landing.

A minute later they heard him in the yard pumping water over his head; and when he reappeared with the cart he had sobered up completely.

They took the road again as they had done the day before, and the little white horse set off once more at its brisk dancing trot.

Under the blazing sun the gaiety which had been held in check during the meal broke out. This time the women were amused by the jolting of the cart; they even pushed their neighbours' chairs about and kept bursting out laughing, for they had been put in a merry mood by Rivet's unsuccessful assault.

A shimmering haze hung over the fields, dazzling the eye, and the wheels raised two trails of dust which swirled above the road long after the cart had passed.

Suddenly Fernande, who loved music, begged Rosa for a song, and she boldly plunged into 'The Fat Curé of Meudon'. But Madame stopped her straight away, considering that particular song unseemly on such a day. 'Sing us something of Béranger's instead,' she added. After a few moments' hesitation, Rosa made her choice and struck up 'Grandma' in her husky voice:

> 'My Grandma, on her birthday night,
> Took a few sips of heady wine,
> And told us when a little tight:
> "How many lovers once were mine!
>  Oh, how they loved to see
>  My pretty dimpled arms,
>  A trim and shapely knee,
>  And all my other charms." '

And the other women, led by Madame herself, took up the refrain:

> ' "Oh, how they loved to see
>  My pretty dimpled arms,
>  A trim and shapely knee,
>  And all my other charms!" '

'That's the stuff!' declared Rivet, carried away by the rhythm, and Rosa went on at once:

> ' "What, Grandma, weren't you good?" we said.
> "Why, no! At fifteen my delights
> I learnt to use alone in bed,
> When I couldn't sleep at nights." '

They all shouted the refrain together, and Rivet tapped with his foot on the shaft and beat time with the reins on the back of the white horse, which broke into a mad gallop, as if it too were excited by the rhythm, flinging the ladies in a heap on top of one another at the bottom of the cart.

They picked themselves up, roaring with laughter, and the song went on, bawled at the tops of their voices across the countryside under the burning sky, in the midst of the ripening crops, as the little horse sped along, breaking into a gallop for a hundred yards every time the refrain was repeated, to the huge delight of the passengers.

Here and there a stonebreaker straightened up and through his wire mask watched the yelling cartload speeding madly past him in a cloud of dust.

When they got down at the station the carpenter waxed sentimental.

'It's a shame you're going,' he said. 'We could have had a grand time together.'

Madame answered soberly: 'There's a time for everything. People can't have fun every day of the week.'

Then Rivet had a sudden inspiration.

'Tell you what,' he said. 'I'll come and see you at Fécamp next month.' And he gave Rosa a knowing look out of his bright, roguish eyes.

'Now then,' said Madame, 'don't be silly. You can come if you like, but I don't want any nonsense.'

He made no reply, and, hearing the whistle of the train, promptly started kissing everybody. When it came to Rosa's turn he tried hard to get at her mouth, but she, laughing with her lips tight closed, turned her head away every time with a quick sideways movement. He held her in his arms but could not succeed in his object, being impeded by the long whip which he had kept in his hand and was waving about behind the woman's back in his desperate efforts.

'Passengers for Rouen, take your seats!' shouted the guard, and they all got in.

There was a shrill blast from the guard's whistle, followed by a louder one from the engine, which noisily spat out its first jet of steam while the wheels began turning slightly with an obvious effort.

Leaving the platform Rivet ran to the level-crossing gates to catch a last glimpse of Rosa; and as the carriage with its load of human merchandise passed him he started dancing about, cracking his whip and singing at the top of his voice:

> ' "Oh, how they loved to see
> My pretty dimpled arms,
> A trim and shapely knee,
> And all my other charms!" '

Then he fixed his eyes on a white handkerchief which somebody was waving, until it disappeared from sight.

### III

They slept all the way to Fécamp, with the sound sleep of easy consciences; and when they reached home, refreshed and rested in readiness for the night's work, Madame could not help remarking: 'You can say what you like, it's good to be back.'

They had supper quickly and then, when they had changed into battle order, sat down to wait for their regular clients. The little Madonna lantern had been lit again, and passers-by could see that the sheep had returned to the fold.

The news spread in a twinkling, nobody knew how, nobody knew through whom. Monsieur Philippe, the banker's son, even carried kindness so far as to send an express letter to Monsieur Tournevau who was imprisoned in the bosom of his family.

The fish-curer had several cousins to dinner every Sunday, and they were having their coffee when a man called with a letter in his hand. In a state of great excitement, Monsieur Tournevau tore open the envelope and turned pale. All it contained was the following message written in pencil: 'Cargo of cod traced; ship back in port; chance of a good deal for you; come quick.'

He rummaged in his pockets, gave the messenger a twenty-centime tip and, blushing to the tips of his ears, said: 'I've got to go out.' And he handed his wife the brief, mysterious note. He rang the bell and when the maid appeared said: 'Quick, my hat and coat!' He was no sooner out in the street than he broke into a run, whistling a tune, and he was so impatient that the distance seemed twice as long as usual.

Madame Tellier's establishment had a festive air about it. On the ground floor the loud voices of the men from the harbour were making a deafening din. Louise and Flora did not know which way to turn, but drank first with one and then with another, justifying more than ever their nickname of the Two Beer-Pulls. Everybody was calling for them at once; there was already more work than they could cope with and it looked as if they had an exhausting night ahead of them.

The company in the upstairs room was at full strength by nine o'clock. Monsieur Vasse, the commercial-court judge, and Madame's acknowledged but platonic suitor, was chatting quietly with her in a corner; and they were both smiling as if some agreement was about to be reached. Monsieur Poulin, the former mayor, had Rosa sitting astride his legs and she was pressing her nose against his and running her little chubby hands through the old fellow's white side-whiskers. She had hitched up her yellow silk skirt, so that a patch of bare thigh showed white against the dark cloth of his trousers, and her red stockings were held in place by the blue garters the commercial traveller had given her.

Tall Fernande was stretched out on the sofa with her feet on the stomach of Monsieur Pimpesse, the tax-collector, and the upper part of her body resting on young Monsieur Philippe's waistcoat. She had her right hand round his neck, while in her left she held a cigarette.

Raphaële seemed to be conducting negotiations with Monsieur Dupuis, the insurance agent, and she brought the conversation to an end by saying: 'Yes, darling, tonight's all right.' Then, doing a quick waltz by herself across the room, she shouted: 'Tonight everything's all right!'

At that moment the door was flung open and Monsieur Tournevau appeared. There were enthusiastic shouts of 'Good old Tournevau!' and Raphaële, who was still waltzing around, threw herself into his arms. He clasped her in a tight embrace, and, without a word, lifting her off the ground as if she were a feather, he crossed the room to the door at the far end and disappeared with his living burden up the stairs leading to the bedrooms, to the accompaniment of loud applause.

Rosa, who was doing her best to excite the former mayor, kissing him repeatedly and pulling both his whiskers at the same time to keep his head straight, decided to take advantage of the example which had just been given them. 'Come on, do the same!' she said, whereupon the old man got up, straightened his waistcoat, and followed her out of the room, rummaging in the pocket where he kept his money.

Fernande and Madame were left alone with the four men, and Monsieur Philippe suddenly exclaimed: 'I'm standing champagne all round: Madame Tellier, send for three bottles.'

Putting her arms round him, Fernande whispered in his ear: 'Do play us something to dance to, will you?'

He got to his feet, sat down at the ancient spinet sleeping in a corner, and coaxed a husky, sentimental waltz out of its wheezy belly. The tall girl put her arms round the tax collector, Madame abandoned herself to the embrace of Monsieur Vasse, and the two couples began waltzing about, kissing as they danced. Monsieur Vasse, who in the past had danced at society balls, moved with such elegance that Madame gazed at him in fascination, with that look which says 'yes' more discreetly and deliciously than any spoken word.

Frédéric brought the champagne. The first cork popped, and Monsieur Philippe played the first bars of a quadrille.

The four dancers trod it with fashionable decorum, in a stately, dignified fashion, with all the proper bows and curtseys. After which they started drinking.

Then Monsieur Tournevau reappeared, satisfied, relieved and radiant. 'I don't know what's happened to Raphaële,' he exclaimed, 'but she's wonderful tonight.' He was handed a glass, which he emptied at one draught, murmuring: 'Dammit, there's nothing like champagne for a celebration.'

Monsieur Philippe promptly struck up a lively polka and Monsieur Tournevau plunged into the dance with the lovely Jewess, whom he held in the air so that her feet never touched the floor. Monsieur Pimpesse and Monsieur Vasse started off again with renewed vigour. Every now and then one of the couples stopped at the mantelpiece to toss off a glass of the sparkling wine; and it was beginning to look as if this dance would go on for ever when Rosa opened the door a little way, with a candlestick in her hand. She was in a nightdress and bedroom slippers with her hair down, very excited and flushed.

'I want to dance!' she cried.

'What about your old man?' asked Raphaële.

'Him?' Rosa said with a laugh. 'He's asleep already. He goes to sleep straight away.'

She seized hold of Monsieur Dupuis, who was sitting on the sofa without a partner, and the polka began again.

But the bottles were empty. 'I'll stand another,' declared Monsieur Tournevau.

'So will I,' announced Monsieur Vasse.

'Me too,' said Monsieur Dupuis.

And everybody clapped.

The party soon became a regular ball. From time to time even Louise and Flora dashed upstairs, had a quick waltz while their customers kicked their heels below, and then ran down to the café again with heavy hearts.

At midnight the dancing was still going on. Now and then one of the women disappeared and when she was wanted as a partner it was suddenly discovered that one of the men was missing too.

'Where on earth have you been?' Monsieur Philippe asked playfully when Monsieur Pimpesse came back into the room with Fernande.

'Looking at Monsieur Poulin sleeping,' replied the tax collector.

The witticism was a huge success, and all the gentlemen in turn went upstairs 'to look at Monsieur Poulin sleeping', accompanied by one or other of the young ladies, who were amazingly obliging that night. Madame turned a blind eye to what was going on; and she had a number of private conversations with Monsieur Vasse, as if she were settling the final details of an arrangement which had already been decided between them.

Finally, at one o'clock, the two married men, Monsieur Tournevau and Monsieur Pimpesse, declared that they must be getting home and asked for their bills. Only the champagne was charged for, and that at only six francs a bottle instead of the usual ten. And when they expressed astonishment at this generosity, Madame replied with a radiant smile: 'It isn't every day we've something to celebrate.'

# A RUSE

THE old doctor and his young patient were chatting by the fire. She was not really ill, but merely suffering from one of those feminine ailments which often afflict pretty women: a touch of nerves, a little anaemia, and a hint of fatigue, that fatigue which a newly married couple normally experience at the end of their first month of married life, when they have made a love match.

She was lying on her couch and talking.

'No, Doctor,' she said, 'I shall never be able to understand a woman deceiving her husband. Even supposing that she doesn't love him, that she takes no notice of her promises and vows, how can she bear to give herself to another man? How can she conceal what she is doing from other people's eyes? How can she find it possible to love in the midst of lies and treachery?'

The doctor smiled.

'Oh, that's easy. I can assure you that a woman doesn't think about all those little niceties when she takes it into her head to stray off the straight and narrow path. I would go further and say that no woman is ripe for true love until she has gone through all the promiscuities and disappointments of married life, which, according to a famous man, is nothing but an exchange of bad tempers during the day and bad smells during the night. Nobody ever spoke a truer word, for no woman can love passionately until she has been married. If I might compare her to a house, she's uninhabitable until a husband has dried out the plaster.

'As for dissimulation, every woman can provide plenty

of that on such occasions. The simplest of women are wonderful liars and can extricate themselves from the most difficult dilemmas with a skill bordering on genius.'

The young woman seemed reluctant to believe him.

'No, Doctor,' she said, 'nobody ever thinks of what he ought to have done in a dangerous situation until after it is over, and women are certainly more liable than men to lose their heads in such circumstances.'

The doctor threw up his hands.

'After it is over, you say! We men only get our inspirations after the event, that's true. But you women!... Look here, let me tell you something that happened to one of my patients whom I had always regarded as a woman of unimpeachable virtue.

'It happened in a provincial town. One night when I was fast asleep, in that deep first sleep which it is so difficult to disturb, I had the impression, in my dreams, that all the bells in the town were sounding the fire alarm. Suddenly I woke up: it was my own door-bell which was ringing wildly. As my manservant didn't seem to be answering it, I in my turn pulled the bell at the head of my bed, and soon the sound of banging doors and hurrying footsteps disturbed the silence of the sleeping house. Then Jean appeared and handed me a letter which said: "Madame Lelièvre begs Doctor Siméon to come to her house at once."

'I thought for a few moments, and then said to myself: "Nerves, a fit of hysterics, something of that sort: I'm too tired." So I replied: "Doctor Siméon is ill and asks Madame Lelièvre to be good enough to send for his colleague Monsieur Bonnet."

'I sent this note off in an envelope and went back to sleep. Half an hour later the doorbell went again and Jean came to tell me: "There is somebody downstairs – I don't know whether it's a man or a woman, he's so well wrapped up – who would like to see you straight away. He says it's a matter of life and death for two people."

'I sat up in bed, told Jean to show the caller in, and waited.

'A sort of black phantom appeared who raised her veil as soon as Jean had left the room. It was Madame Berthe Lelièvre, a young woman who had been married for three years to a large shopkeeper in the town and was considered the prettiest girl in the province.

'She was terribly pale, her face twitching with panic and her hands trembling violently. Twice she tried to speak without being able to utter a sound. At last she managed to stammer: "Quick ... quick ... quick, Doctor. ... Come quick. My ... my lover has just died in my bedroom." She stopped, choking with emotion, then went on: "My husband will be ... will be coming home from the club soon ..."

'I jumped out of bed without even thinking that I was in my nightshirt and got dressed in a few seconds. Then I said: "Was it you who came a little while ago?"

'"No," she murmured, standing there like a statue, petrified with fear. "That was my maid. ... She knows ..." Then after a pause she went on: "I stayed ... by his side." A sort of terrible cry of horror came from her lips and after a fit of choking which made her gasp for breath she burst into tears, weeping helplessly and shaking with sobs for a minute or two. Then her tears suddenly stopped, as if dried up by an inner fire, and resuming her air of tragic calm she said: "Let's hurry."

'I was ready, but I exclaimed: "Heavens, I forgot to order my carriage!"

'"I have one," she said; "it's his carriage, which was waiting for him."

'She wrapped herself up, covering her face completely, and we set off.

'When she was beside me in the darkness of the carriage she suddenly seized my hand and crushing it in her delicate fingers she said quaveringly in a voice which came from a broken heart: "Oh, if you only knew, if you only knew how I'm suffering! I've been in love with him, madly in love with him, for the past six months."

'"Is anybody up at your house?" I asked.

' "No," she replied. "Nobody except Rose, who knows everything."

'We stopped in front of the door. As she had said, everybody was obviously asleep. We let ourselves in with a latchkey without making any noise and tiptoed upstairs. The frightened maid was sitting on the floor at the top of the stairs with a lighted candle beside her, as she had not dared to stay with the dead man.

'I went into the bedroom which was turned upside down as if there had been a struggle in it. The bed was crumpled and open and seemed to be waiting for somebody. One of the sheets was hanging down to the carpet and wet towels with which they had bathed the young man's temples were lying on the floor beside a basin and a glass. A peculiar smell of kitchen vinegar mingled with whiffs of perfume filled the room.

'The corpse was lying full length on its back in the middle of the room. I went up to it, looked at it, touched it. I opened the eyes and felt the hands, and then, turning to the two women who were shivering as if they were freezing, I said: "Help me to lift him on to the bed." After we had laid him out gently, I listened to his heart and held a mirror to his lips. Then I murmured: "It's all over; let's dress him quickly."

'It was a terrible business. I took his limbs one by one,

like those of an enormous doll, and held them out to the clothes the women brought. Like that we put on his socks, underpants, trousers and waistcoat; and finally we managed to put on his coat, although we had a great deal of trouble getting his arms into the sleeves.

'When it came to buttoning his boots, the two women knelt down, while I held the light. His feet were slightly swollen, so this was extremely difficult; and as they were unable to find a buttonhook they had to use their hairpins.

'As soon as the horrible business of dressing the corpse was over, I inspected our handiwork and said: "You ought to tidy up his hair." The maid went and fetched her mistress's brush and comb, but as she was trembling and kept pulling out the long, tangled hairs without meaning to, Madame Lelièvre snatched the comb out of her hand and arranged the dead man's hair as if she were caressing it. She made a fresh parting, brushed the beard, and slowly rolled the ends of the moustache round her fingers, as she had probably been used to doing in the familiarities of love.

'All of a sudden, letting go of his hair, she grasped her lover's inert head and gazed for a long time in despair at the dead face which could no longer smile at her. Then throwing herself on to him she clasped him in her arms and kissed him passionately. Her kisses fell like blows on the closed lips, on the dead eyes, on the temples and the forehead. And then, putting her lips to his ear, as if he could still hear her and she were about to whisper something to make their embraces still more ardent, she repeated several times in a heartrending voice: "Good-bye darling."

'Just then the clock struck midnight and I gave a start. "Good Lord," I said, "twelve o'clock. That's the time the club closes. Come, Madame, we've no time to lose!"

'She got to her feet, and I said: "Let's carry him into the drawing-room." The three of us carried him there and I sat him on a sofa and lit the candelabra.

'The front door opened and shut with a bang. The husband was already back. I said: "Rose, quick, bring me the towels and basin and tidy up the bedroom. Hurry, for God's sake! Monsieur Lelièvre has just come home."

'I heard his steps coming upstairs and along the corridor. His hands were feeling the walls in the dark. "Come in here, my dear fellow," I called out; "we have had an accident."

'And the astonished husband appeared in the doorway with a cigar in his mouth. "What's the matter?" he asked. "What's the meaning of this?"

' "My dear chap," I said, going up to him, "you find us in something of a spot. I had stayed here late, chatting with your wife and our friend, who had brought me in his carriage. All of a sudden he collapsed, and in spite of all our efforts he has remained unconscious for the last two hours. I didn't want to call in any strangers, and if you'll help me to get him downstairs I'll be able to attend to him better in his own house."

'The husband, who was surprised but completely unsuspecting, took off his hat. Then he took hold of his henceforth inoffensive rival under the armpits, I got between the legs like a horse between the shafts, and we went downstairs, with the wife now holding the light.

'When we got outside I held the corpse up and spoke to it encouragingly so as to deceive the coachman. "Come now, old fellow," I said, "it's nothing; you feel better already, don't you? Buck up, now, and make an effort, and it'll soon be over."

'As I could feel that the body was on the point of collapsing and slipping out of my hands, I gave it a shove which sent it tumbling into the carriage. Then I got in after it.

'Monsieur Lelièvre asked me anxiously: "Do you think it's anything serious?" I replied: "No," with a smile, and looked at his wife. She had put her arm into that of her lawful husband and was staring into the dark interior of the carriage.

'I shook hands with them and told the coachman to start. During the whole journey the dead man kept falling against my right side. When we got to his house I said that he had lost consciousness on the way and helped to carry him upstairs. There I certified that he was dead and acted another comedy for the benefit of the distracted family. At last I got back to bed, not without cursing all lovers.'

The doctor stopped, still smiling, and the young woman asked him with a shudder: 'Why did you tell me that horrible story?'

He gave her a gallant bow and answered: 'So as to offer you my services in case of need.'

# AN OLD MAN

ALL the newspapers had carried this advertisement:

The new spa at Rondelis offers all the advantages desirable for a lengthy stay or even for permanent residence. Its ferruginous waters, recognized as the best in the world for countering all impurities of the blood, also seem to possess special qualities calculated to prolong human life. This remarkable circumstance may be due in part to the exceptional situation of the little town, which lies in a mountainous region, in the middle of a forest of firs. The fact remains that for several centuries it has been noted for cases of extraordinary longevity.

And the public came along in droves.

One morning the doctor in charge of the springs was asked to call on a newcomer, Monsieur Daron, who had arrived a few days before and had rented a charming villa on the edge of the forest. He was a little old man of eighty-six, still quite sprightly, wiry, healthy and active, who went to infinite pains to conceal his age.

He offered the doctor a seat and started questioning him straight away.

'Doctor,' he said, 'if I am in good health, it is thanks to careful living. Though not very old, I have already attained a respectable age, yet I keep free of all illnesses and indispositions, even the slightest malaises, by means of careful living. It is said that the climate here is very good for the health. I am perfectly prepared to believe it, but before settling down here I want proof. I am therefore going to ask you to come and see me once a week to give me the following information in detail.

'First of all I wish to have a complete, absolutely complete, list of all the inhabitants of the town and the surrounding area who are over eighty years old. I also need a few physical and physiological details regarding each of them. I wish to know their professions, their way of life, their habits. Every time one of those people dies you will be good enough to inform me, giving me the precise cause of death and describing the circumstances.'

Then he added graciously: 'I hope, Doctor, that we shall become good friends,' and held out his wrinkled little hand. The doctor shook it, promising him his devoted co-operation.

Monsieur Daron had always had an obsessive fear of death. He had deprived himself of nearly all the pleasures of this world because they were dangerous, and whenever anyone expressed surprise that he should not drink wine – wine, that purveyor of dreams and gaiety – he would reply in a voice in which a note of fear could be detected: 'I value my life.' And he stressed the word *my*, as if that life, *his* life, possessed some special distinction. He put into that *my* such a difference between his life and other people's lives that any rejoinder was out of the question.

For that matter he had a very special way of stressing the possessive pronouns designating parts of his person and even things which belonged to him. When he said 'my eyes, my legs, my arms, my hands', it was quite obvious that there must be no mistake about this: those organs were not at all like other people's. But where this distinction was particularly noticeable was in his references to his doctor. When he said 'my doctor', one would have thought that that doctor belonged to him and nobody else, destined for him alone, to attend to his illnesses and to nothing else, and that he was superior to all the other doctors in the world, without exception.

He had never regarded other men as anything but puppets of a sort, created to fill up an empty world. He divided them into two classes: those he greeted because some chance had put him in contact with them, and those he did not greet. But both these categories of individuals were equally insignificant in his eyes.

However, beginning with the day when the Rondelis doctor brought him the list of the seventeen inhabitants of the town who were over eighty, he felt a new interest awaken in his heart, an unfamiliar solicitude for these old people whom he was going to see fall by the wayside one by one. He had no desire to make their acquaintance, but he formed a very clear idea of their persons, and when the doctor dined with him, every Thursday, he spoke only of them. 'Well, doctor,' he would say, 'and how is Joseph Poinçot today? We left him feeling a little ill last week.' And when the doctor had given him the patient's bill of health, Monsieur Daron would suggest changes in his diet, experiments, methods of treatment which he might later apply to himself if they had succeeded with the others. Those seventeen old people provided him with an experimental field from which he learnt many a lesson.

One evening the doctor announced as he came in: 'Rosalie Tournel has died.'

Monsieur Daron gave a start and immediately asked: 'What of?'

'Of a chill.'

The little old man gave a sigh of relief. Then he said: 'She was too fat, too heavy; she must have eaten too much. When I get to her age I'll be more careful about my weight.' (He was two years older than Rosalie Tournel, but he claimed to be only seventy.)

A few months later it was the turn of Henri Brissot. Monsieur Daron was very upset. This time it was a man, and a thin man at that, within three months of his own age, and careful about his health. He did not dare to ask any questions, but waited anxiously for the doctor to give him some details.

'Oh, so he died just like that, all of a sudden,' he said. 'But he was perfectly all right last week. He must have done something silly, I suppose, Doctor?'

The doctor, who was enjoying himself, replied: 'I don't think so. His children told me he had been very careful.'

Then, unable to contain himself any longer, and filled with fear, Monsieur Daron asked: 'But...but...what did he die of, then?'

'Of pleurisy.'

The little old man clapped his dry hands in sheer joy.

'I told you so! I told you he had done something silly. You don't get pleurisy for nothing. He must have gone out for a breath of air after his dinner and the cold must have gone to his chest. Pleurisy! Why, that's an accident, not an illness. Only fools die of pleurisy.'

And he ate his dinner in high spirits, talking about those who were left.

'There are only fifteen of them now, but they are all hale and hearty, aren't they? The whole of life is like that: the weakest go first; people who live beyond thirty have a good chance of reaching sixty; those who pass sixty often get to eighty; and those who pass eighty nearly always live to be a hundred, because they are the fittest, toughest and most sensible of all.'

Another two disappeared during the year, one of dysentery and the other of a choking fit. Monsieur Daron was highly amused by the death of the former and concluded that he must have eaten something stimulating the day before.

'Dysentery is the disease of careless people. Dammit all, Doctor, you ought to have watched over his diet.'

As for the man who had been carried off by a choking fit, his death could only be due to a heart condition which had hitherto gone unnoticed.

But one evening the doctor announced the decease of Paul Timonet, a sort of mummy of whom it had been hoped to make a centenarian and an advertisement for the spa.

When Monsieur Daron asked, as usual: 'What did he die of?' the doctor replied: 'Bless me, I really don't know.'

'What do you mean, you don't know. A doctor always knows. Hadn't he some organic lesion?'

The doctor shook his head.

'No, none.'

'Possibly some infection of the liver or the kidneys?'

'No, they were quite sound.'

'Did you check whether the stomach was functioning properly? A stroke is often caused by poor digestion.'

'There was no stroke.'

Monsieur Daron, very perplexed, said excitedly: 'Look, he must have died of something! What do you think it was?'

The doctor threw up his hands.

'I've no idea, no idea at all. He died because he died, that's all.'

Then Monsieur Daron, in a voice full of emotion, asked: 'Exactly how old was that one? I can't remember.'

'Eighty-nine.'

And the little old man, at once incredulous and re-assured, exclaimed:

'Eighty-nine! So whatever it was, it wasn't old age...'

# RUST

ALL his life he had only one insatiable passion, hunting. He hunted every day, from morning till night, with incredible fervour. He hunted winter and summer alike, in the spring as well as the autumn, in the marshes when it was the close season for the woods and the plains. He hunted, he shot, he coursed and he ferreted. He spoke of nothing else, dreamt of nothing else, and was forever saying: 'I pity the man who doesn't like hunting.'

He was now in his fifties, still robust, healthy and vigorous, though bald and rather stout; and he kept his moustache cut short so that it did not cover his lips and interfere with his horn-blowing.

Everyone in his part of the country called him by his Christian name, Monsieur Hector, but his full name was Baron Hector Gontran de Coutelier.

He lived deep in the woods in a small manor house which he had inherited; and although he knew all the local nobility and met all its male representatives when hunting or shooting, he visited only one family regularly, the Courvilles, who were pleasant neighbours and had been related to his family for centuries.

In their house he was coddled, fussed over, and spoilt, and he used to say: 'If I weren't so fond of hunting, I'd like to spend all my time here.' Monsieur de Courville had been his friend and companion since childhood. He was a gentleman farmer who lived quietly with his wife, his daughter, and his son-in-law, Monsieur de Darnetot, who did nothing, under the pretext of carrying out historical research.

Baron de Coutelier often went to dinner at his friends' house, chiefly in order to tell them his hunting exploits. He had some long-drawn stories about dogs and ferrets, of which he spoke as if they were people in the public eye whom he knew very well. He explained their thoughts and intentions, analysing and explaining them: 'When Médor saw that the corncrake was leading him quite a dance, he said to himself: "Just you wait, old chap, and we'll have a bit of fun." Then, with a jerk of his head in my direction to tell me to go into the corner of the clover field, he began quartering obliquely, pushing through the clover noisily to drive the bird into a corner from which it could not escape. Everything happened as Médor had foreseen, and the corncrake suddenly found itself at the edge of the field. It could not go any further without breaking cover. It said to itself: "Dammit, I'm caught," and lay low. Médor then stood and pointed, looking at me. I signalled to him and he ran at it. Brrroo! The corncrake flew into the air. I raised my gun. Bang! Down it came. And Médor, as he brought it to me, wagged his tail to say: "That went well, didn't it, Monsieur Hector?"'

Courville, Darnetot and the two women used to laugh uproariously at these picturesque stories into which the baron put all his heart and soul. He got excited, waved his arms about, gesticulated with his whole body, and gave a roar of laughter whenever he came to the kill. And at the end of a story he always said: 'That was a good one, wasn't it?'

As soon as the conversation turned to some other subject he stopped listening and started humming hunting calls to himself. So whenever there was a pause between two sentences, one of those moments of abrupt silence which interrupt the noisy flow of words, they would suddenly hear a hunting tune – 'Ta, ra, ra, ta, ra, ra, ta, ra, ra' –

which the baron was humming, puffing his cheeks out as if he were blowing his horn.

He had lived for nothing but hunting and shooting, and was growing old without realizing it or noticing it. Suddenly he had an attack of rheumatism and had to stay in bed for two months. He nearly died of boredom and vexation. As he had no housekeeper, for an old manservant did all his cooking, he got no hot poultices, no little attentions, and none of the other things a sick person needs. His gamekeeper was his nurse, and this servant, who was every bit as bored as his master, slept day and night in an armchair, while the baron tossed and turned impatiently between the sheets.

The ladies of the Courville family came to see him occasionally; and these visits were welcome periods of calm and luxury. They made his tea for him, attended to the fire, and served his lunch daintily at his bedside. When they left he used to murmur: 'Darn it, you ought to stay here all the time,' which made them laugh uproariously.

When he was getting better and beginning to go shooting in the marshes again, he came to dinner with his friends every evening; but he had lost all his old verve and gaiety. He was tormented all the time by a single thought, the fear that he might have another attack before the season opened. As he was taking his leave, while the women were wrapping him in a shawl and tying a scarf round his neck, and he was submitting to these attentions for the first time in his life, he murmured disconsolately: 'If it starts all over again, I'm done for.'

When he had left, Madame de Darnetot said to her mother: 'We ought to find a wife for the baron.'

They all raised their hands in the air. Why hadn't they thought of that before? They spent all the rest of the evening discussing the various widows they knew, and their choice fell on a woman of forty who was still pretty, fairly rich, good-tempered and in excellent health, whose name was Madame Berthe Vilers.

She was invited to spend a month at the château, and as she was bored at home she accepted. She was gay and lively, and Monsieur de Coutelier took her fancy straight away. She amused herself with him as if he had been a living toy and spent hours on end slyly questioning him about rabbits' feelings and foxes' machinations, while he solemnly drew distinctions between the various points of view of different animals, attributing subtle schemes and ideas to them as he did to men of his acquaintance.

The attention she paid him delighted him; and one evening, to show the esteem he felt for her, he asked her to go shooting with him, something he had never done to any woman before. The invitation struck her as so amusing that she accepted. Fitting her out was tremendous fun; everybody joined in, offering her something; and eventually she appeared dressed as a sort of Amazon, wearing boots, a pair of men's breeches, a short skirt, a velvet jacket which was rather tight across the chest, and a huntsman's cap.

The baron seemed as excited as if he were going to fire his first shot. He explained to her in detail the direction of the wind, the different positions the dogs adopted, and the way to flush game. Then he took her into a field, following her step by step as anxiously as a nursemaid watching her charge walk for the first time.

Médor found some game, crawled towards it, stopped and raised one paw. The baron, standing behind his pupil, was shaking like a leaf. He stammered: 'Careful, careful, it's some par . . . par . . . partridges.'

Before he had finished, there was a loud noise – brr, brr,

brr – and a covey of large birds rose into the air, beating their wings.

Startled out of her wits, Madame Vilers shut her eyes, fired off both barrels, and staggered backwards under the recoil of the gun; then, when she recovered her composure, she saw the baron dancing about like a madman, and Médor bringing back two partridges in his mouth.

That very day Monsieur de Coutelier fell in love with her.

He used to raise his eyes to heaven, saying: 'What a woman!' and he came round every evening now to talk about shooting.

One day Monsieur de Courville, who was walking him part of the way home and listening to him singing the praises of his new friend, suddenly asked him: 'Why don't you marry her?'

The baron was taken by surprise.

'Me? Me? Marry her? ... Why ... well ...'

And he fell silent. Then, abruptly shaking hands with his companion, he murmured: 'Good night, old chap,' and strode away into the darkness.

He did not show up again for three days. When he reappeared he was pale from the effect of solitary reflection and more serious than usual. Taking Monsieur de Courville aside, he said: 'That was a splendid idea of yours. Try to get her ready to accept me. Dammit all, a woman like that might have been made for me. We'll go hunting together all the year round.'

Monsieur de Courville, convinced that the baron would not meet with a refusal, replied: 'Propose to her straight away, old chap. Would you like me to do it for you?'

But the baron suddenly hesitated and stammered: 'No. ... No.... I have to go to Paris first for ... for a short trip. As soon as I get back I'll give you a definite answer.'

It proved impossible to get any further explanation from him, and he left the next day.

The short trip lasted a long time. One week, two weeks, three weeks went by. Monsieur de Coutelier did not re-appear. Surprised and uneasy, the Courvilles did not know what to say to their friend, whom they had informed of the baron's intentions. Every other day they sent to his house for news of him, but none of his servants had heard from him.

Then one evening, while Madame Vilers was singing for her friends and accompanying herself on the piano, a maidservant came in looking very mysterious and whis-pered to Monsieur de Courville that a gentleman was ask-ing to see him. It was the baron, dressed in his travelling clothes, and looking older and greatly altered. As soon as he saw his old friend, he seized both his hands and said in a rather tired voice: 'I've only just got back, old chap, and I hurried over to see you at once. I'm all in.'

Then he hesitated in visible embarrassment, before going on: 'I wanted to tell you ... straight away ... that that ... that affair ... you know what I mean ... is all over.'

Monsieur de Courville looked at him in astonishment.

'What do you mean, all over? And why?'

'Oh, please don't ask any questions. It would be too painful to explain. But you may rest assured that I am ... acting honourably. I cannot ... I have no right, you understand, no right to marry the lady in question. I'll wait until she has left before I come back here; it would be too painful for me to see her again. Good-bye.'

And he fled.

The whole family deliberated and discussed the matter, imagining countless hypotheses. They finally decided that the baron's life concealed a great mystery, that perhaps he had some natural children or a long-standing liaison. At any rate there appeared to be a serious obstacle in the way of his marriage; and to avoid any difficult complications they tactfully explained the situation to Madame Vilers, who returned home just as much of a widow as she had come.

Another three months went by. One evening, when he had dined rather too well and was a little unsteady on his legs, Monsieur de Coutelier, smoking his pipe with Monsieur de Courville, said to him: 'You'd really feel sorry for me if you knew how often I keep thinking about your friend.'

The other, who had been rather vexed by the baron's behaviour in this affair, retorted sharply: 'Dammit all, old chap, when a fellow has some secret in his life he doesn't make advances to a woman as you did; because after all, you must have foreseen the reason why you'd have to pull back.'

The baron looked embarrassed and stopped smoking.

'Yes, and no. In any case, I couldn't have imagined what happened.'

Monsieur de Courville replied impatiently: 'A fellow ought to foresee everything.'

But Monsieur de Coutelier, peering into the darkness to make sure that nobody was listening to them, answered in a low voice: 'I can see that I've hurt your feelings, and I'm going to tell you everything in the hope that you'll forgive me. For twenty years, old chap, I've lived only for hunting and shooting. As you know, that's all I care about, all I think about. Consequently, when I was on the point of entering into certain obligations towards the lady in question, I felt a conscientious scruple. Since I'd got out of the habit of ... of ... of love, well, I didn't know whether I'd still be capable of ... of ... you know what I mean. ... Just think, it's exactly sixteen years since ...

since . . . since . . . the last time, you understand. In this part of the world it isn't easy to . . . to . . . you know. Besides, I had other things to do. I'd rather have a good day's shooting any time. To cut a long story short, just as I was getting ready to promise in front of the mayor and the priest to . . . you know what, I felt scared. I said to myself: Dammit all, what if . . . what if I misfired? A decent fellow never breaks a promise, and there I was, about to make a solemn promise to that lady. So to make absolutely sure I decided to go and spend a week in Paris.

'By the end of a week nothing had happened, absolutely nothing. And it wasn't for want of trying. I picked the best there was of every variety and they did everything they could. . . . Yes . . . they did their best, and no mistake. . . . But whatever they did they had nothing to show for it . . . nothing . . . nothing.

'So then I waited for two weeks, three weeks, hoping against hope. In every restaurant I went to I ate lots of spicy dishes which ruined my stomach . . . but . . . but still there was nothing . . . absolutely nothing.

'You'll understand that in those circumstances, faced with that state of affairs, the only decent thing I could do was . . . was to withdraw. And that's what I did.'

Monsieur de Courville had to make a tremendous effort to keep a straight face. He solemnly shook hands with the baron, saying: 'I'm very sorry for you.'

Then he walked half way home with him.

When he got back and was alone with his wife he told her the whole story, practically choking with merriment. But Madame de Courville didn't laugh. She listened very attentively and when her husband had finished she replied very seriously: 'The baron's a fool, dear. He was scared, that's all. I'm going to write to Berthe asking her to come back here as soon as possible.'

And when Monsieur de Courville referred to the lengthy and futile efforts their friend had made, she retorted: 'Nonsense! When a man's in love with his wife, well ... that sort of thing always comes back.'

And Monsieur de Courville made no reply, feeling a little embarrassed himself.

# TWO FRIENDS

PARIS was under siege, starving and at her last gasp. The sparrows were disappearing from the roofs, and the city's sewers were being depopulated. People were eating anything they could find.

One bright morning in January Monsieur Morissot, a watchmaker by trade but an idler by necessity, was walking sadly along the outer boulevard with an empty stomach and his hands in the pockets of his uniform trousers when he came face to face with a comrade in arms whom he recognized as an old friend. It was Monsieur Sauvage, a riverside acquaintance.

Every Sunday before the war Morissot used to leave home at dawn with a bamboo rod in his hand and a tin box on his back. He took the Argenteuil train, got out at Colombes, and walked to Marante Island. As soon as he reached this place of his dreams he started fishing and he went on fishing till nightfall.

There, every Sunday, he used to meet another fanatical angler, a stout, jolly little man called Monsieur Sauvage, a haberdasher from the Rue Notre-Dame-de-Lorette. They often spent half the day sitting side by side with their rods in their hands and their feet dangling over the water; and they had become firm friends.

Some days they never said a word; sometimes they chatted. But they understood each other perfectly without any need for words, having similar tastes and identical feelings.

On spring mornings, about ten o'clock, when a faint mist was rising from the smooth surface of the river and drifting along with the current, and the two enthusiastic anglers could feel the pleasant warmth of the spring sun on their backs, Morissot would say to his neighbour: 'This is the life, eh?'

And Monsieur Sauvage would reply: 'This is the life all right.'

That was all that was necessary for them to understand and respect one another.

In the autumn, towards the end of the day, when the setting sun reddened the sky and stained the river crimson, when the horizon was ablaze and the water reflected the shapes of scarlet clouds, and when the trees between the two friends, already russet-coloured and shivering with the foretaste of winter, turned fiery red and gold, Monsieur Sauvage would look at Morissot with a smile and say: 'What a picture!'

And Morissot, struck by the beauty of the scene but keeping his eyes fixed on his float, would reply: 'Better than the boulevard, isn't it?'

They had no sooner recognized each other than they shook hands warmly, struck by the changed circumstances in which they had met. Monsieur Sauvage heaved a sigh and murmured: 'What a mess we're in!'

Morissot answered gloomily: 'And what weather we're having! This is the first fine day we've had this year.'

The sky was indeed a bright unclouded blue.

They walked on together, side by side, sad and thoughtful.

'Remember our fishing?' Morissot went on. 'Those were the days!'

'I wonder when we'll go fishing again,' said Monsieur Sauvage.

They went into a little café and had an absinthe together. Then they resumed their stroll along the pavement.

Suddenly Morissot stopped short.

'What about another?'

'I won't say no,' replied Monsieur Sauvage, and they went into another café.

When they came out they were rather fuddled, as people are when they have been drinking spirits on an empty stomach. It was a mild day and a gentle breeze fanned their faces.

The warm air made Monsieur Sauvage, already intoxicated by the absinthe, quite tipsy. He stopped and said: 'Let's go.'

'Where?'

'Fishing of course.'

'But where?'

'Why, our usual island. The French outposts aren't far from Colombes. I know Colonel Dumoulin: they'll let us through without any trouble.'

Quivering with excitement, Morissot replied: 'Right, I'm with you.'

And they separated to go and get their fishing tackle.

An hour later they were walking side by side along the main road. Eventually they reached the villa which the colonel was using as his headquarters. He smiled at their whimsical request and gave his consent. They set off again, armed with a pass.

Before long they had crossed the line of outposts, passed through the deserted village of Colombes, and found themselves on the edge of the little vineyards which sloped down to the Seine. It was about eleven o'clock.

Across the river, the village of Argenteuil looked dead. The heights of Orgemont and Sannois dominated the whole countryside. The great plain which stretches as far as Nanterre was empty, completely empty, with its bare cherry trees and its grey fields.

Pointing to the high ground, Monsieur Sauvage murmured: 'The Prussians are up there.'

And a paralysing sense of anxiety took hold of the two friends as they looked at this deserted scene.

The Prussians! They had never seen any of them, but for months they had been aware of their presence around Paris, bringing ruin on France, looting, murdering, starving, invisible and irresistible. And a sort of superstitious terror was added to the hatred they felt for that unknown, victorious people.

'Suppose we met some of them,' stammered Morissot, 'what would we do?'

With that mocking Parisian humour which had survived in spite of everything, Monsieur Sauvage replied: 'We'd offer them some fish to fry.'

But they hesitated about venturing into the open country, intimidated by the silence all around them.

At last Monsieur Sauvage made up his mind.

'Come on, let's go,' he said, 'but keep your eyes skinned!'

And they went down into a vineyard, bent double or crawling along, their ears cocked and their eyes darting about nervously.

They still had a strip of open ground to cross to reach the river bank. They broke into a run, and as soon as they got to the bank they crouched down among the dry rushes.

Morissot put his ear to the ground to listen for the sound of footsteps in their vicinity. He heard nothing. They were alone, absolutely alone.

Feeling reassured, they started to fish.

In front of them Marante Island, now deserted, hid them from the opposite bank. The little restaurant was closed and looked as if it had been abandoned for years.

Monsieur Sauvage caught the first gudgeon, Morissot the second, and after that they kept lifting their rods every other moment with little silver creatures wriggling at the end of the lines—a miraculous draught of fishes!

They carefully slipped the fish into a fine-meshed net bag dangling in the water at their feet, and a feeling of joy took hold of them, that delicious joy one feels at rediscovering a pleasure after being deprived of it for months.

The kindly sun warmed their backs; they heard nothing and thought of nothing; the rest of the world no longer existed for them; they simply fished.

But suddenly a dull roar which seemed to come from under the ground made the earth tremble. The big guns were opening up again.

Morissot turned his head, and above the bank, away to the left, he saw the great bulk of Mont-Valérien, its summit sporting a white plume, a puff of smoke it had just spat out.

The next moment a second puff of smoke came from the top of the fort, and a few seconds later the boom of another detonation reached their ears.

Others followed, as in quick succession the hill sent out its deadly breath, emitting clouds of milky vapour which rose slowly into the peaceful sky to form a cloud above the fort.

Monsieur Sauvage shrugged his shoulders.

'There they go, at it again!' he said.

Morissot, who was anxiously watching the feather on his float bobbing up and down, was suddenly filled with a peace-loving man's anger at these madmen who insisted on fighting one another, and he growled: 'They must be fools, killing each other like that.'

'They're worse than wild beasts,' said Monsieur Sauvage.

And Morissot, who had just hooked a bleak, declared: 'To think that it'll always be like that as long as we have governments!'

Monsieur Sauvage corrected him: 'The Republic would never have declared war. . . .'

'With kings,' Morissot broke in, 'you have war abroad; with republics, you have war at home.'

They started a friendly argument, discussing the great political problems with the sweet reasonableness of peaceful men of limited intelligence, and agreeing on one point: that men would never be free. And all the time Mont-Valérien went on thundering, destroying French houses with its shells, pulverizing human lives, crushing bodies, putting an end to countless dreams, countless expectations, countless hopes of happiness, and inflicting wounds that would never heal on the hearts of girls, wives and mothers in other lands.

'Such is life,' said Monsieur Sauvage.

'Or rather, such is death,' retorted Morissot with a laugh.

Then they gave a start of terror as they became aware that somebody was moving behind them. Looking round they saw four armed men standing right behind them – four big, bearded men, dressed like liveried servants with flat caps on their heads, covering them with rifles.

The two rods dropped from their hands and floated away down the river.

In a matter of seconds they were seized, bound, marched off, thrown into a boat, and ferried across to the island.

Behind the house they had thought to be deserted they saw a score of German soldiers.

A hairy giant of a man, sitting astride a chair and smoking a large porcelain pipe, asked them in excellent French: 'Well, gentlemen, have you had a good day's fishing?'

Just then one of the soldiers deposited at his feet the net bag full of fish, which he had taken care to bring along.

The Prussian officer smiled: 'Ah, I see you weren't doing so badly. But that's not what I want to talk to you about. Listen to me and don't get alarmed.

'As far as I'm concerned, you are a couple of spies sent to keep an eye on me. I capture you and shoot you. You pretend to be fishing to conceal your real intentions. You have fallen into my hands: so much the worse for you. War is war.

'But as you came out here through your own lines, I presume you have a password in order to get back. Give me that password and I'll spare your lives.'

The two friends were standing side by side, ashen-faced. Their hands were trembling slightly, but they said nothing.

The officer went on: 'Nobody will be any the wiser. You will go back as if nothing had happened, and the secret will go with you. If you refuse, you die – you die on the spot. Now choose.'

They remained motionless and made no reply.

The Prussian pointed to the water and calmly continued: 'Five minutes from now you will be at the bottom of that river. Five minutes! You've got relatives waiting for you, I presume?'

Mont-Valérien was still firing.

The two anglers stood there silent. The German gave an order in his own language. Then he moved his chair so as not to be too close to the prisoners; and twelve men took up a position at a distance of twenty paces, their rifles at the order.

'I give you one minute,' said the officer, 'not a second more.'

Then he suddenly got to his feet, went over to the two Frenchmen, took Morissot by the arm, and led him to one side.

'Quick, the password,' he whispered. 'Your friend will never know. I'll pretend I've relented.'

Morissot made no reply.

The Prussian then took Monsieur Sauvage aside and made the same suggestion to him.

Monsieur Sauvage said nothing.

They found themselves together again, side by side.

The officer gave an order. The soldiers raised their rifles.

Just then Morissot's eye fell on the net bag full of gudgeon lying on the grass a few feet away. The pile of fish, which were still wriggling, glistened in a ray of sunshine. He felt a momentary weakness. Try as he might to hold them back, tears came into his eyes.

'Good-bye, Monsieur Sauvage,' he stammered.

'Good-bye, Monsieur Morissot,' said his friend.

They shook hands, trembling uncontrollably from head to foot.

'Fire!' shouted the officer.

The twelve shots rang out together.

Monsieur Sauvage fell forward like a log. Morissot, being taller, swayed, spun round, and fell across his friend's body. He lay there with his face to the sky while blood gushed out of the holes in the front of his tunic.

The German gave another order.

His men dispersed and came back with some lengths of rope and some stones which they fastened to the feet of the two dead men; then they carried them to the bank.

Mont-Valérien was firing all the time, capped now by a huge cloud of smoke.

Two soldiers took Morissot by the head and feet. Two others picked up Monsieur Sauvage in the same way. They swung them backwards and forwards and threw them as far as they could. The bodies described a curve in the air, then, weighted by the stones, plunged feet-first into the river.

The water splashed, bubbled and quivered, then became calm again. A few tiny waves spread to each bank.

A little blood was floating on the surface.

Still perfectly calm, the officer murmured to himself: 'Now it's the fishes' turn.'

And he set off back to the house.

Suddenly he noticed the bag of gudgeon on the grass. He picked it up, examined it, smiled, and shouted: 'Wilhelm!'

A soldier in a white apron came running up. Throwing him the two dead men's haul, the officer said: 'Fry these little things for me straight away while they are still alive. They'll be delicious.'

Then he lit his pipe again.

# THE JEWELS

MONSIEUR LANTIN had met the girl at a party given one evening by his office superior and love had caught him in its net.

She was the daughter of a country tax-collector who had died a few years before. She had come to Paris then with her mother, who struck up acquaintance with a few middle-class families in her district in the hope of marrying her off. They were poor and decent, quiet and gentle. The girl seemed the perfect example of the virtuous woman to whom every sensible young man dreams of entrusting his life. Her simple beauty had a modest, angelic charm and the imperceptible smile which always hovered about her lips seemed to be a reflection of her heart.

Everybody sang her praises and people who knew her never tired of saying: 'Happy the man who marries her. Nobody could find a better wife.'

Monsieur Lantin, who was then a senior clerk at the Ministry of the Interior with a salary of three thousand five hundred francs a year, proposed to her and married her.

He was incredibly happy with her. She ran his household so skilfully and economically that they gave the impression of living in luxury. She lavished attention on her husband, spoiling and coddling him, and the charm of her person was so great that six years after their first meeting he loved her even more than in the early days.

He found fault with only two of her tastes: her love for the theatre and her passion for imitation jewellery.

Her friends (she knew the wives of a few petty officials) often obtained a box at the theatre for her for popular plays, and even for first nights; and she dragged her husband along willy-nilly to these entertainments, which he found terribly tiring after a day's work at the office. He therefore begged her to go to the theatre with some lady of her acquaintance who would bring her home afterwards. It was a long time before she gave in, as she thought that this arrangement was not quite respectable. But finally, just to please him, she agreed, and he was terribly grateful to her.

Now this love for the theatre soon aroused in her a desire to adorn her person. True, her dresses remained very simple, always in good taste, but unpretentious; and her gentle grace, her irresistible, humble, smiling charm seemed to be enhanced by the simplicity of her gowns. But she took to wearing two big rhinestone earrings which sparkled like diamonds, and she also wore necklaces of fake pearls, bracelets of imitation gold, and combs set with coloured glass cut to look like real stones.

Her husband, who was rather shocked by this love of show, often used to say: 'My dear, when a woman can't afford to buy real jewels, she ought to appear adorned with her beauty and grace alone: those are still the rarest of gems.'

But she would smile sweetly and reply: 'I can't help it. I like imitation jewellery. It's my only vice. I know you're right, but people can't change their natures. I would have loved to own some real jewels.'

Then she would run the pearl necklaces through her fingers and make the cut-glass gems flash in the light, saying: 'Look! Aren't they beautifully made? Anyone would swear they were real.'

He would smile and say: 'You have the taste of a gipsy.'

Sometimes, in the evening, when they were sitting together by the fireside, she would place on the tea-table the leather box in which she kept her 'trash', as Monsieur Lantin called it. Then she would start examining these imitation jewels with passionate attention, as if she were enjoying some deep and secret pleasure; and she would insist on hanging a necklace around her husband's neck, laughing uproariously and crying: 'How funny you look!' And then she would throw herself into his arms and kiss him passionately.

One night in winter when she had been to the Opera, she came home shivering with cold. The next morning she had a cough, and a week later she died of pneumonia.

Lantin very nearly followed her to the grave. His despair was so terrible that his hair turned white within a month. He wept from morning to night, his heart ravaged by unbearable grief, haunted by the memory, the smile, the voice, the every charm of his dead wife.

Time did nothing to assuage his grief. Often during office hours, when his colleagues came along to chat about the topics of the day, his cheeks would suddenly puff out, his nose wrinkle up, his eyes fill with tears, and with a terrible grimace he would burst out sobbing.

He had left his wife's room untouched, and every day would shut himself in it and think about her. All the furniture and even her clothes remained exactly where they had been on the day she had died.

But life soon became a struggle for him. His income, which in his wife's hands had covered all their expenses, was now no longer sufficient for him on his own; and he wondered in amazement how she had managed to provide him with excellent wines and rare delicacies which he could no longer afford on his modest salary.

He incurred a few debts and ran after money in the way people do when they are reduced to desperate shifts. Finally, one morning, finding himself without a sou a whole week before the end of the month, he decided to sell something; and immediately the idea occurred to him of disposing of his wife's 'trash'. He still harboured a sort of secret grudge against those false gems which had irritated him in the past, and indeed the sight of them every day somewhat spoiled the memory of his beloved.

He rummaged for a long time among the heap of gawdy trinkets she had left behind, for she had stubbornly gone on buying jewellery until the last days of her life, bringing home a new piece almost every evening. At last he decided on the large necklace which she had seemed to like best, and which, he thought, might well be worth six or seven francs, for it was beautifully made for a piece of paste.

He put it in his pocket and set off for his Ministry, following the boulevards and looking for a jeweller's shop which inspired confidence.

At last he spotted one and went in, feeling a little ashamed of exposing his poverty in this way, and of trying to sell such a worthless article.

'Monsieur,' he said to the jeweller, 'I would like to know what you think this piece is worth.'

The man took the necklace, examined it, turned it over, weighed it, inspected it with a magnifying glass, called his assistant, made a few remarks to him in an undertone, placed the necklace on the counter and looked at it from a distance to gauge the effect.

Monsieur Lantin, embarrassed by all this ritual, was opening his mouth to say: 'Oh, I know perfectly well that it isn't worth anything,' when the jeweller said: 'Monsieur, this necklace is worth between twelve and fifteen thousand francs; but I couldn't buy it unless you told me where it came from.'

The widower opened his eyes wide and stood there gaping, unable to understand what the jeweller had said.

Finally he stammered: 'What was that you said?... Are you sure?'

The other misunderstood his astonishment and said curtly: 'You can go somewhere else and see if they'll offer you more. In my opinion it's worth fifteen thousand at the most. Come back and see me if you can't find a better price.'

Completely dumbfounded, Monsieur Lantin took back his necklace and left the shop, in obedience to a vague desire to be alone and to think.

Once outside, however, he felt an impulse to laugh, and he thought: 'The fool! Oh, the fool! But what if I'd taken him at his word? There's a jeweller who can't tell real diamonds from paste!'

And he went into another jeweller's shop at the beginning of the Rue de la Paix. As soon as he saw the necklace, the jeweller exclaimed: 'Why, I know that necklace well: it was bought here.'

Monsieur Lantin asked in amazement: 'How much is it worth?'

'Monsieur, I sold it for twenty-five thousand. I am prepared to buy it back for eighteen thousand once you have told me, in accordance with the legal requirements, how you came to be in possession of it.'

This time Monsieur Lantin was dumbfounded. He sat down and said: 'But ... but ... examine it carefully, Monsieur. Until now I thought it was paste.'

'Will you give me your name, Monsieur?' said the jeweller.

'Certainly. My name's Lantin. I'm an official at the Ministry of the Interior, and I live at No. 16, Rue des Martyrs.'

The jeweller opened his books, looked for the entry, and said: 'Yes, this necklace was sent to Madame Lantin's address, No. 16, Rue des Martyrs, on the 20th of July 1876.'

The two men looked into each other's eyes, the clerk speechless with astonishment, the jeweller scenting a thief. Finally the latter said: 'Will you leave the necklace with me for twenty-four hours? I'll give you a receipt.'

'Why, certainly,' stammered Monsieur Lantin. And he went out folding the piece of paper, which he put in his pocket.

Then he crossed the street, walked up it again, noticed that he was going the wrong way, went back as far as the Tuileries, crossed the Seine, realized that he had gone wrong again, and returned to the Champs-Élysées, his mind a complete blank. He tried to think it out, to understand. His wife couldn't have afforded to buy something so valuable – that was certain. But in that case it was a present! A present! But a present from whom? And why was it given her?

He halted in his tracks and remained standing in the middle of the avenue. A horrible doubt crossed his mind. Her? But in that case all the other jewels were presents too! The earth seemed to be trembling under his feet and a tree in front of him to be falling; he threw up his arms and fell to the ground unconscious.

He came to his senses in a chemist's shop into which the passers-by had carried him. He took a cab home and shut himself up.

He wept bitterly until nightfall, biting on a handkerchief so as not to cry out. Then he went to bed worn out with grief and fatigue and slept like a log.

A ray of sunlight awoke him and he slowly got up to go to his Ministry. It was hard to think of working after such a series of shocks. It occurred to him that he could ask to be excused and he wrote a letter to his superior. Then he remembered that he had to go back to the jeweller's and he blushed with shame. He spent a long time thinking it over, but decided that he could not leave the necklace with that man. So he dressed and went out.

It was a fine day and the city seemed to be smiling under the clear blue sky. People were strolling about the streets with their hands in their pockets.

Watching them, Lantin said to himself: 'How lucky rich people are! With money you can forget even the deepest of sorrows. You can go where you like, travel, enjoy yourself. Oh, if only I were rich!'

He began to feel hungry, for he had eaten nothing for two days, but his pocket was empty. Then he remembered the necklace. Eighteen thousand francs! Eighteen thousand francs! That was a tidy sum, and no mistake!

When he reached the Rue de la Paix he started walking up and down the pavement opposite the jeweller's shop. Eighteen thousand francs! A score of times he almost went in, but every time shame held him back.

He was hungry, though, very hungry, and he had no money at all. He quickly made up his mind, ran across the street so as not to have any time to think, and rushed into the shop.

As soon as he saw him the jeweller came forward and offered him a chair with smiling politeness. His assistants came into the shop, too, and glanced surreptitiously at Lantin with laughter in their eyes and on their lips.

'I have made inquiries, Monsieur,' said the jeweller, 'and if you still wish to sell the necklace, I am prepared to pay you the price I offered you.'

'Why, certainly,' stammered the clerk.

The jeweller took eighteen large banknotes out of a drawer, counted them and handed them to Lantin, who signed a little receipt and with a trembling hand put the money in his pocket.

Then, as he was about to leave the shop, he turned towards the jeweller, who was still smiling, and lowering his eyes said: 'I have ... I have some other jewels which have come to me from ... from the same legacy. Would you care to buy them from me too?'

The jeweller bowed.

'Certainly, Monsieur.'

One of the assistants went out, unable to contain his laughter; another blew his nose loudly.

Lantin, red-faced and solemn, remained unmoved.

'I will bring them to you,' he said.

And he took a cab to go and fetch the jewels.

When he returned to the shop an hour later he still had had nothing to eat. The jeweller and his assistants began examining the jewels one by one, estimating the value of each piece. Almost all of them had been bought at that shop.

Lantin now began arguing about the valuations, lost his temper, insisted on seeing the sales registers, and spoke more and more loudly as the sum increased.

The large diamond earrings were worth twenty thousand francs, the bracelets thirty-five thousand, the brooches, rings and lockets sixteen thousand, a set of emeralds and sapphires fourteen thousand, and a solitaire pendant on a gold chain forty thousand – making a total sum of one hundred and ninety-six thousand francs.

The jeweller remarked jokingly: 'These obviously belonged to a lady who invested all her savings in jewellery.'

Lantin replied seriously: 'It's as good a way as any of investing one's money.'

And he went off after arranging with the jeweller to have a second expert valuation the next day.

Out in the street he looked at the Vendôme column and felt tempted to climb up it as if it were a greasy pole. He felt light enough to play leap-frog with the statue of the Emperor perched up there in the sky.

He went to Voisin's for lunch and ordered wine with his meal at twenty francs a bottle.

Then he took a cab and went for a drive in the Bois. He looked at the other carriages with a slightly contemptuous air, longing to call out to the passers-by: 'I'm a rich man too! I'm worth two hundred thousand francs!'

Suddenly he remembered his Ministry. He drove there at once, strode into his superior's office, and said: 'Monsieur, I have come to resign my post. I have just been left three hundred thousand francs.'

He shook hands with his former colleagues and told them some of his plans for the future; then he went off to dine at the Café Anglais.

Finding himself next to a distinguished-looking gentleman, he was unable to refrain from informing him, with a certain coyness, that he had just inherited four hundred thousand francs.

For the first time in his life he was not bored at the theatre, and he spent the night with some prostitutes.

Six months later he married again. His second wife was a very virtuous woman, but extremely bad-tempered. She made him very unhappy.

# THE CONSERVATORY

MONSIEUR and Madame Lerebour were the same age, but Monsieur looked younger than his wife, although he was the less robust of the two. They lived near Mantes in a pretty country house which they had built after making their fortune selling printed cottons.

The house was surrounded by a beautiful garden containing a poultry-yard, a Chinese pavilion and a little conservatory at the far end of the property. Monsieur Lerebour was short, round and jovial, with the joviality of a shopkeeper who liked to do himself well. His wife, who was thin, selfwilled and perpetually discontented, had still not succeeded in overcoming her husband's good humour. She dyed her hair and occasionally read novels which set her dreaming, although she affected to despise that sort of literature. She was said to be a woman of passionate temperament, without ever having done anything to deserve that reputation. But her husband sometimes said: 'My wife is quite a woman!' with a knowing air which aroused certain suppositions.

For some years, however, she had been somewhat aggressive towards Monsieur Lerebour, always behaving in a harsh, irritable manner, as if she were tormented by some secret and unspeakable sorrow. The result was a sort of misunderstanding. They scarcely spoke to each other any more, and Madame, whose name was Palmyre, was forever plying Monsieur, whose name was Gustave, with unkind compliments, wounding allusions and bitter remarks, for no apparent reason.

He bowed his head to the storm, vexed but goodhumoured in spite of everything, and endowed with such a fund of contentment that he put up with this private bickering. All the same he wondered what unknown cause could be embittering his wife more and more like this, for he felt sure that her irritability had a hidden reason, but one so difficult to discover that all his attempts to do so were in vain.

He often asked her: 'Look here, my dear, tell me what you've got against me. I can feel that you're hiding something.'

She invariably replied: 'But there's nothing the matter with me, absolutely nothing! Besides, if I had some reason for discontent, it would be up to you to guess what it was. I don't like men who understand nothing, who are so soft and incapable that you have to help them to grasp the slightest thing.'

He would murmur disconsolately: 'I can see that you don't want to say anything.'

And he would walk away trying to fathom the mystery.

The nights in particular had become very painful for him, for they still shared the same bed, as husbands and wives do in good, simple households. At night there was no form of vexation she failed to use against him. She chose the time when they were lying side by side to shoot her sharpest barbs at him. Her chief reproach against him was that he was putting on weight: 'You take up all the room, you're getting so fat. And you sweat against my back like melting lard. If you think that's nice for me, you can think again!'

She forced him to get up on the slightest pretext, sending him downstairs to fetch a newspaper she had forgotten, or a bottle of orange-flower water which he couldn't find, for she had hidden it away. And she would exclaim in a fierce, sarcastic voice: 'You ought to know where it is, you great booby!' When, after searching all over the sleeping house for a whole hour, he returned to the bedroom empty-handed, the only thanks she gave him was to say: 'All right, get back into bed; it will make you thinner to walk about a bit; you're getting as flabby as a sponge.'

She woke him up constantly to say that she was suffering from stomach cramps and to insist on his rubbing her belly with a piece of flannel soaked in eau-de-Cologne. He would try to make her better, upset at seeing her ill, and would suggest going to wake Céleste, their maid. Then she would get really angry, shouting: 'What a fool you are! There, it's all over, I feel better now. Go back to sleep, you big ninny.'

'Are you quite sure you feel better?' he would ask.

She would reply brutally: 'Of course I'm sure. Now shut up and let me get some sleep. Stop pestering me like that. You're incapable of doing anything, even of giving a woman a rub-down.'

'But darling,' he would protest sadly.

'I want none of your buts,' she would snap. 'That's enough now. Leave me alone...'

And she would turn her face to the wall.

Now one night she shook him so abruptly that he gave a frightened start and sat up with an agility which was unusual for him. He stammered: 'What is it?... What's the matter?'

She gripped his arm, pinching him till he cried out, and whispered in his ear: 'I heard a noise in the house.'

Accustomed to Madame Lerebour's frequent alarms, he did not get unduly excited, and asked calmly: 'What sort of noise, darling?'

Shaking with terror, she replied: 'What sort of noise?... Why, a noise.... A noise of footsteps.... There's somebody in the house.'

He remained incredulous.

'Somebody in the house? You really think so? Why no, you must be mistaken. Who do you think it could be, anyway?'

She gave a shudder.

'Who? Who? Why, burglars, you fool!'

He snuggled down gently between the sheets.

'No, darling, there's nobody. You must have dreamt it.'

She flung back the blankets and jumped out of bed in a rage.

'Why, you're a coward as well as a fool! Well, I'm not going to let myself be murdered just because you've no courage.'

And snatching up the tongs in the fireplace she stationed herself in a fighting posture in front of the bolted door.

Impressed by his wife's courageous example and perhaps feeling a little ashamed, Monsieur Lerebour got up too, grumbling to himself, and, without taking off his nightcap, picked up the shovel and stationed himself opposite his better half.

They waited for twenty minutes in dead silence.

No fresh noise disturbed the peace of the house. Then Madame went back to bed in a fury, declaring: 'All the same, I'm sure there *was* somebody.'

To avoid any possibility of a quarrel, he made no mention of this false alarm next day. But during the following night Madame Lerebour woke up her husband even more violently than the night before, and, gasping for breath, stammered: 'Gustave, Gustave, somebody has just opened the back door.'

Astonished at this persistence, he thought that his wife might be suffering from somnambulism, and he was about to make an attempt to rouse her from this dangerous sleep when he himself fancied he heard a slight noise under the walls of the house.

He got up, rushed to the window, and, sure enough, saw a white figure darting across one of the paths.

He murmured weakly: 'Yes, there *is* somebody there!'

Then he collected his wits, plucked up his courage, and, suddenly carried away by the fearful wrath of a householder whose property has been broken into, muttered: 'Just you wait! Just you wait!'

He rushed over to the writing-desk, opened it, took his revolver, and dashed out of the room.

His wife ran after him in a panic, shouting: 'Gustave, Gustave, stay with me! Don't leave me alone! Gustave! Gustave!'

But he was not listening to her; he was already opening the back door.

So she hurried back upstairs and barricaded herself in the conjugal bedroom.

She waited five minutes, ten minutes, a quarter of an hour. A mad panic took hold of her. They had probably killed him, seized him, garrotted him, strangled him. She would have preferred to hear the six revolver shots, to know that he was putting up a fight, that he was defending himself. But this utter silence, this frightening silence of the countryside, terrified her.

She rang for Céleste. Céleste did not come, gave no sign of life. She rang again, faint with fear, on the point of swooning away. The whole house remained silent.

Pressing her burning forehead against the window, she tried to penetrate the darkness outside. She could make out nothing but the grey lines of the paths and the darker shadows of the trees.

The clock struck half past twelve. Her husband had been away three quarters of an hour. She would never see him again! And she fell on her knees, sobbing.

Two light taps on the bedroom door made her jump to

her feet. Monsieur Lerebour called out: 'Open the door, Palmyre. It's me.'

She rushed over to the door, flung it open, and standing in front of him, her hands on her hips and her eyes still full of tears, she cried: 'Where have you been, you beast? Leaving me here all alone to die of fright! I might never exist for all you care about me!'

He had shut the door and was shaking with laughter, tears of mirth in his eyes, grinning from ear to ear and holding his belly with both hands.

Madame Lerebour was so astonished that she stopped speaking.

He stammered: 'It was.... It was ... Céleste with a young man in the conservatory.... If you only knew what ... what ... what ... I've seen ...'

She had turned pale with indignation.

'What's that you say?... Céleste?... In my house?... In my ... my conservatory? And you didn't kill the man, the accomplice? You had a revolver and you didn't kill him?... In my house!... In my house!'

She sat down, overcome with emotion.

He danced a pirouette, snapped his fingers, clicked his tongue, and, still laughing, said: 'If you only knew.... If you only knew ...'

Suddenly he kissed her.

She pulled away from him and in a voice choking with anger said: 'I don't want that girl to stay another day in my house, do you hear? Not another day.... Not another hour! When she comes back, we'll throw her out ...'

Monsieur Lerebour had seized his wife by the waist and was planting rows of kisses on her neck, noisy kisses such as he used to give her in the old days. She fell silent once more, too astonished to speak. And holding her in his arms he drew her gently towards the bed ...

About half past nine in the morning, Céleste, surprised to see no sign of her master and mistress, who were always up early, came and knocked gently on their door.

They were in bed, chatting gaily together side by side. She stood there in astonishment and said: 'Madame, it's about the coffee.'

Madame Lerebour said in a very sweet voice: 'Bring it here, my dear. We are rather tired: we have slept very badly.'

The maid had scarcely left the room before Monsieur Lerebour burst out laughing again, tickling his wife and repeating: 'If you only knew! Oh, if you only knew!'

But she caught hold of his hands and said: 'Come now, darling, lie still. If you laugh like that, you'll make yourself ill.'

And she kissed him gently on the eyes.

Madame Lerebour is never sour or irritable nowadays. Sometimes, on moonlit nights, husband and wife tiptoe past the trees and flowerbeds, down to the conservatory at the bottom of the garden. And they stay there side by side with their faces pressed against the glass, as if they were looking at something strange and interesting going on inside.

They have increased Céleste's wages.

Now Monsieur Lerebour has lost weight.

# THE MATTER WITH ANDRÉ

The notary's house faced on to the square. Behind it there was a pleasant, well-kept garden stretching as far as the Passage des Piques, an alley which was always deserted and from which it was separated by a wall.

It was at the bottom of this garden that Maître Moreau's wife had given a rendezvous, for the first time, to Captain Sommerive, who had been paying attentions to her for a long time.

Her husband had gone to Paris for a week, so she was free for the whole of that time. The captain had pressed her so hard, had implored her with such persuasive words; she was so convinced that he was passionately in love with her; and she felt so isolated, so misunderstood, so neglected in the midst of all the contracts which seemed to be her husband's only interest, that she had given away her heart without asking herself whether she would give anything more one day.

Then, after months of platonic love, of squeezed hands, of brief kisses stolen behind doors, the captain had declared that he would leave town straight away and apply for a posting unless she gave him a rendezvous, a real rendezvous under the trees, during her husband's absence.

She had given way; she had promised a meeting.

Now she was waiting for him, huddled against the wall, her heart pounding wildly, and starting at the slightest sound.

Suddenly she heard somebody clambering over the wall and she nearly ran away. What if it weren't the captain? What if it were a thief? But no – a voice called out softly:

'Mathilde!' She replied: 'Étienne!' And a man dropped on to the path with a clatter of metal.

It was he! And what a kiss they exchanged!

For a long time they remained clasped in each other's arms, their lips pressed together. But suddenly a fine drizzle began to fall and the raindrops dripping from one leaf to another produced a rippling sound of water in the darkness. She gave a start as the first drop fell on her neck.

'Mathilde,' he said, 'my darling, my love, my sweet, my angel, let's go indoors. It's midnight; we have nothing to fear. Let's go inside, please.'

'No, dearest,' she replied. 'I'm frightened. Who knows what might happen?'

But he held her tight in his arms and whispered in her ear: 'Your servants' rooms are on the third floor, overlooking the square. Your room is on the first floor, looking on to the garden. Nobody will hear us. I love you, and I want to love you freely and completely, from head to foot.' And he embraced her passionately, covering her face with kisses.

She still resisted him, frightened and even ashamed. But he put his arm round her waist, picked her up, and carried her off through the rain which was now pouring down.

The door was open; they groped their way upstairs, and, as soon as they were in the bedroom, she bolted the door while he struck a match.

Then she fell half-fainting into an armchair. He knelt down and slowly began undressing her, taking off her boots and stockings and kissing her feet.

'No, Étienne,' she gasped, 'please let me keep my virtue! I'd hate you for it afterwards! Besides, it's so crude and ugly! Why can't we love each other with just our souls?... Étienne!'

With the skill of a chambermaid and the urgency of a

man in a hurry he was busily undoing buttons, knots, hooks and laces. And when she tried to stand up to escape from his attacks she suddenly emerged from her dress, her skirts and her lingerie as naked as a hand emerging from a muff.

She ran in a panic towards the bed to hide behind the curtains. It was a dangerous refuge and he followed her. But in his haste to join her he took off his sword too quickly and it fell on the floor with a crash.

Immediately a prolonged wail, a shrill, continuous cry came from the next room, the door of which had been left open.

'Oh!' she murmured. 'You've woken up André. He won't be able to go back to sleep.'

Her son was fifteen months old and slept in the room adjoining hers so that she could keep an eye on him.

The captain, mad with excitement, was not listening.

'What does it matter?' he said. 'I love you; You're mine, Mathilde!'

But she pushed him away, frightened and upset.

'No, no! Listen to him crying; he'll wake up the nurse. What would we do if she came down? We'd be done for! Étienne, listen: when he cries like that at night his father brings him into our bed to calm him down and he stops crying straight away. It's the only way. Let me go and fetch him, Étienne.'

The child was howling away, giving the sort of shrill scream which pierces the thickest walls and can be heard by passers-by in the streets.

The captain got up in consternation and Mathilde rushed into the next room to get the child, whom she put into bed. He fell silent.

Étienne sat down astride a chair and started rolling a cigarette. Within less than five minutes André was asleep.

'I'll take him back,' murmured his mother, and she put him back in his cot with infinite precautions.

When she returned the captain was waiting for her with open arms.

Mad with love, he clasped her in his arms, and she, surrendering at last, hugged him tight and stammered: 'Étienne!... Étienne, my love! Oh, if you only knew how ... how ...'

André started crying again. The captain flew into a rage. 'Hell and damnation!' he exclaimed. 'Won't the little beast shut up?'

No, the little beast wouldn't. He was bellowing at the top of his voice.

Mathilde thought she could hear somebody moving about upstairs. It was probably the nurse coming to see what was wrong. She jumped up and went to fetch the child. As soon as she put him in her bed he stopped crying.

Three times in succession he was put back in his cot. Three times in succession he had to be taken out again.

Captain Sommerive left the house an hour before dawn, swearing like a trooper.

However, to calm his impatience Mathilde had promised to let him come back that very evening.

He came as he had done the night before, but more ardent and impatient, excited by the delay.

He took care to put his sword down very quietly, across the arms of a chair; he took his boots off like a thief and spoke so quietly that Mathilde could scarcely hear him. At last he was on the point of achieving happiness, complete happiness, when the floor, or a piece of furniture, or perhaps the bed itself, creaked. It was a sharp sound, as if a support had snapped, and it was promptly answered by a cry, faint at first, but then growing shriller. André had woken up.

Soon he was yelping like a fox. If he went on like that the whole household was going to get up.

The frantic mother rushed to get him and put him in her own bed. The captain, fuming with anger, did not get up. Very gently he stretched out his hand, took a small piece of the child's flesh, on his thighs or his buttocks, between two fingers, and pinched it. The child struggled and uttered deafening screams. Then the captain, losing patience, pinched him harder all over his body. Gripping a fold of flesh, he squeezed it hard and twisted it, then let it go to take another fold next to it, then another further on, then yet another.

The child screamed like a pig being stuck or a dog being beaten. His weeping mother kissed him and caressed him, trying to calm him down and stifle his cries with kisses. But André turned purple, as if he were about to go into convulsions, and waved his little hands and feet about in a frightening, pitiful way.

The captain said quietly: 'Now try taking him back to his cot; he may quieten down.'

And Mathilde went off towards the other room with her child in her arms.

As soon as he was out of his mother's bed his cries died down, and as soon as he was back in his own he fell completely silent apart from a few sobs now and then. The rest of the night was quiet; and the captain achieved the happiness he desired.

The next night he came again. At one point, as he was talking rather loudly, André woke up once more and started crying. His mother went and fetched him straight away; but the captain pinched him so hard, so violently and for such a long time that the child nearly choked, rolling his eyes and foaming at the mouth.

He was taken back to his cot and quietened down at once.

After four days he had stopped crying to come to his mother's bed.

The notary came back on Saturday night to resume his place at the domestic hearth and in the marriage chamber.

As he was tired from his journey, he went to bed early; then, as soon as he had settled down to his old routine and done his duty with the scrupulous attention of a good husband, he remarked in surprise: 'That's funny; André isn't crying tonight. Do go and fetch him for a little while, Mathilde; I like feeling him here between us.'

His wife got up at once and went to fetch the child; but as soon as he found himself in the bed where he had been so fond of going to sleep a few days before he writhed in terror and screamed so loudly that he had to be taken back to his cot.

Maître Moreau could not get over his surprise.

'What a funny thing!' he said. 'What's the matter with him tonight? Perhaps he's sleepy.'

'He's been like that all the time you've been away,' replied his wife. 'I haven't been able to have him in bed with me once.'

In the morning, when he woke up, the child started playing and laughing and waving his hands about.

The lawyer was touched, and ran to kiss his offspring. Then he picked him up to take him to his parents' bed. André was laughing with the vacant laughter of little creatures whose minds are still unformed. Suddenly he caught sight of the bed with his mother in it and his happy little face puckered up, while shrill cries came from his throat and he struggled as if he were being tortured.

'There's something wrong with the child,' the father murmured in astonishment; and he automatically pulled up his little nightshirt.

He gave a gasp of amazement. The child's calves, thighs, back and buttocks were covered with huge blue spots.

'Look at this, Mathilde!' shouted Maître Moreau. 'It's horrible!'

The child's mother came running in a panic. The middle of each spot was crossed by a purple line where the blood seemed to have died. It was obviously some strange and horrible disease, the beginning of a sort of leprosy, one of those peculiar ailments in which the skin comes out in warts like a toad's back or in scales like a crocodile's.

The parents looked at each other in consternation. Maître Moreau cried: 'We must send for the doctor!'

Mathilde, deathly pale, was staring at her son, who was as spotted as a leopard. And suddenly, giving a shrill, unthinking cry, as if she had caught sight of somebody who filled her with horror, she exclaimed: 'Oh, the wretch!'

Maître Moreau asked in surprise: 'Who do you mean? What wretch?'

She blushed to the roots of her hair and stammered: 'Nothing. . . . It's just. . . . You see. . . . I think I can guess. . . . There's no need to send for the doctor. . . . It must be that wretch of a nurse who's been pinching the child to make him keep quiet when he cries.'

The angry notary went to fetch the nurse and nearly beat her. She had the effrontery to deny everything, but was promptly dismissed.

Her behaviour was reported to the town council, and she found it impossible to find another situation.

# MY UNCLE JULES

A POOR old man with a white beard asked us for some money. My friend Joseph Davranche gave him five francs. Noticing that I looked surprised, he said: 'That poor old fellow reminded me of a story I'm going to tell you which I can never forget. Here it is:

'My parents, who came from Le Havre, weren't well off. They just managed to make both ends meet and that was all. My father worked for his living, came home late from the office, and earned very little. I had two sisters.

'My mother suffered a great deal from our straitened circumstances and she often thought up bitter things to say to her husband, sly, veiled reproaches. The poor man would react with a gesture which used to break my heart. He would pass his open hand across his forehead as if to wipe away perspiration which didn't exist and say nothing in reply. I could feel his helpless suffering. We economized on everything; we never accepted an invitation to dinner, so as not to have to return it; and we bought everything we needed at reduced prices, as oddments or leftovers. My sisters made their own dresses and had long discussions about the price of braid which cost fifteen centimes a yard. Our meals generally consisted of meat soup and beef served up with every kind of sauce. That's good wholesome food, they say, but I'd have preferred a change now and then.

'My mother used to make terrible scenes over buttons that got lost or trousers that got torn.

'Every Sunday, though, we used to go for a walk along the jetty in our best clothes. My father, in a frock coat, top hat and gloves, would offer his arm to my mother, who was decked out like a ship on a holiday. My sisters, who were always ready first, would wait for the signal to leave; but at the last minute somebody always found a forgotten stain on my father's frock coat and it had to be removed straight away with a rag moistened with benzine.

'My father, in his shirt-sleeves, but keeping his top hat on, would wait for the operation to be completed, while my mother would hurry as fast as she could, putting on her spectacles and taking off her gloves so as not to spoil them.

'We set off very ceremoniously. My sisters led the way, walking arm in arm. They were of marriageable age and had to be shown off in the town. I walked on my mother's left and my father on her right, and I remember the pompous attitude my poor parents adopted on those Sunday walks, their stern expressions and their rigid bearing. They walked along at a solemn pace, their bodies erect, their legs stiff, as if a matter of extreme importance depended on their appearance.

'And every Sunday, seeing the big ships coming into port from far-off, unknown countries, my father would invariably utter the same words: "Wouldn't it be a surprise if Jules were on that one, eh?"

'My Uncle Jules, my father's brother, was my family's only hope, after being the bane of its existence. I had heard about him since early childhood and the thought of him had become so familiar that it seemed to me that if I met him I would recognize him immediately. I knew every detail of his life up to the day he set off for America, although this period of his life was spoken of only in hushed tones.

'It seems that he had led an evil life, in other words he had squandered a little money, which is easily the worst of crimes for a poor family. Among the rich, a man who leads a gay life "sows his wild oats". He is what people smilingly call a gay dog. But among the poor a young fellow who forces his parents to break into their capital is a good-for-nothing, a scoundrel, a wastrel. And that distinction is a fair one, even though the man's behaviour in each case is identical, for the consequences alone determine the gravity of the act.

'At any rate Uncle Jules had seriously reduced the inheritance on which my father had been counting, after spending his own down to the last penny.

'Following the practice prevalent in those days, he had been shipped off to America on a cargo-boat going from Le Havre to New York.

'Once he had arrived there, my Uncle Jules set up as a dealer in something or other, and soon he wrote to say that he was making a little money and that he hoped to be able to indemnify my father for the wrong he had done him. This letter caused something of a sensation in our family. Jules, who till then hadn't been worth a tinker's cuss, suddenly became a decent fellow, a man who had his heart in the right place, a real Davranche, as trustworthy and reliable as all the Davranches.

'The captain of one ship told us that he had rented a large shop and was doing very good business.

'Two years later a second letter came which said: "My dear Philippe, I am writing to tell you not to worry about my health which is very good. Business is good too. I am leaving tomorrow for a long trip to South America. I may be away for several years without sending you any news. If I don't write to you, don't worry. Once I have made my fortune I shall come back to Le Havre. I hope that that won't be too long from now, and that we shall all live happily together . . ."

'This letter had become the family gospel. It was read at the slightest provocation and was shown to all and sundry.

'For ten years nothing more was heard from Uncle Jules; but as time went by my father's hopes grew stronger, and my mother too was often heard to say: "When Jules comes home, our position will be different. Now *there's* a man who knew how to get on in life!"

'And every Sunday, watching the big black steamers approaching from the horizon and pouring out long trails of smoke into the sky, my father would repeat his perpetual comment: "Wouldn't it be a surprise if Jules were on that one, eh?"

'And we almost expected to see him waving a handkerchief and shouting: "Hey there, Philippe!"

'Countless schemes had been worked out on the strength of this guaranteed homecoming; we were even going to buy a little place in the country with my uncle's money, a house near Ingouville. Indeed, I wouldn't be prepared to swear that my father hadn't already begun negotiations to buy the property.

'The elder of my sisters was twenty-eight at the time, the other twenty-six. Neither of them had found a husband, and that was a source of distress to everybody.

'Finally a suitor turned up for the younger one. He was a clerk, not well off, but presentable. I have always been convinced that Uncle Jules's letter, which was brought out and shown to him one evening, had swept away the young man's hesitations and made up his mind for him.

'He was eagerly accepted, and it was decided that after the wedding the whole family should go on a trip to Jersey.

'Jersey is the ideal holiday spot for poor people. It isn't far away, yet a short sea journey takes you to foreign soil, for the island belongs to the English. Consequently, for the price of a couple of hours at sea, a Frenchman can treat himself to the sight of a neighbouring people at home and study the customs – which, incidentally, are quite deplorable – of an island which lives, as the saying goes, under the protection of the Union Jack.

'This trip to Jersey became our only preoccupation, our sole expectation, the all-absorbing subject of our thoughts and dreams.

'At long last we set off. I can see it all as clearly as if it had happened only yesterday: the boat getting up steam beside the quay at Granville; my father nervously supervising the loading of our three pieces of luggage; my mother anxiously taking the arm of her unmarried daughter, who seemed quite lost since her sister's departure, like a chicken left behind by the rest of a brood; and, bringing up the rear, the bride and groom, who always hung back, a habit which kept making me turn round to look at them.

'The whistle blew. By now we were on board, and the ship left the jetty, setting off across a sea as flat as a green marble table. We watched the coast fading into the distance, feeling proud and happy, like all those who don't travel much.

'My father stuck out his belly under his frock coat, which had been carefully cleaned that morning, spreading all around him that smell of benzine by which I always recognized a Sunday.

'All of a sudden he noticed two elegantly dressed ladies whom two gentlemen were treating to oysters. An old sailor in rags was opening the shells with a knife and passing them to the gentlemen, who then handed them to the ladies. They were eating them very daintily, holding the shell in a fine handkerchief and bending their heads forward so as not to stain their dresses. Then they would drink the liquid with a little rapid movement and throw the shell into the sea.

'My father was probably impressed by the very idea of eating oysters on a ship at sea. He considered the practice good form, refined, upper-class, and going over to my mother and my sisters, he asked: "Would you like me to treat you to some oysters?"

'My mother hesitated, on account of the expense; but my sisters accepted straight away. My mother said in a vexed tone of voice: "I'm afraid of upsetting my stomach. Just get some for the children, but not too many, or you'll make them sick."

'Then, turning towards me, she added: "As for Joseph, he can do without. Boys shouldn't be spoiled."

'So I stayed with my mother, though I regarded this distinction as most unfair. I watched my father pompously taking his two daughters and his son-in-law towards the ragged old sailor.

'The two ladies had just moved away, and my father started telling my sisters how to eat the oysters without spilling the liquid. He even decided to give them a demonstration and seized an oyster. Trying to imitate the ladies, he promptly spilt the liquid over his frock coat, and I heard my mother murmur: "He'd do better not to show off like that."

'But all of a sudden my father looked worried; he stepped back a few paces, stared hard at his family gathered around the shell-opener, and suddenly came towards us. He seemed very pale, with a strange look in his eyes. In a low voice he said to my mother: "It's extraordinary how much that man looks like Jules."

'My mother asked in bewilderment: "What Jules?"

'My father went on: "Why . . . my brother of course. . . . If I didn't know that he was doing well in America, I'd think it was him."

'Taken aback, my mother stammered: "You're crazy!

Seeing that you know it can't be him, why do you say such silly things?"

'But my father insisted: "Do go and have a look at him, Clarisse. I'd rather you made sure for yourself."

'She stood up and went over to her daughters. I too examined the man. He was old and dirty, with a wrinkled face, and didn't raise his eyes from his work.

'My mother came back. I noticed that she was trembling. She said very quickly: "I think it's him all right. Go and ask the captain about him. But be careful what you say! We don't want that scoundrel on our hands again!"

'My father walked away, but this time I followed him. I felt strangely moved.

'The captain, a tall thin man with fair side-whiskers, was walking up and down the bridge with a self-important air, as if he were in command of the mail-boat to India.

'My father approached him ceremoniously, asking him about his profession and interspersing his questions with compliments.

'How big was Jersey? What did it produce? What was its population? What were the local customs? What was the nature of the soil? And so on, and so forth.

'Anybody would have thought he was asking about the United States of America at the very least.

'Then the conversation turned to the boat we were travelling on, the *Express,* and after that to her crew. Finally, in a nervous voice my father said: "You have an old man over there opening shells who looks rather interesting. Do you know anything about the fellow?"

'The captain, who was beginning to find this conversation wearisome, replied curtly: "He's an old French tramp I found last year in America and brought back to this country. I gather he has some relatives in Le Havre, but he doesn't want to go back to them because he owes them money. His name is Jules ... Jules Darmanche or Dar-vanche or something like that. It seems he was very well off for a while over there, but you can see what he's come down to now."

'My father had turned pale and haggard, and muttered in a choking voice: "Ah! Yes, of course ... I see. ... I'm not in the least surprised. ... Thank you very much, Captain."

'And he walked away, while the astonished sailor followed him with his eyes.

'He came back to my mother looking so upset that she said to him: "Sit down, or people will notice that there's something wrong."

'He collapsed on to the bench, stammering: "It's him! It's him all right!"

'Then he asked: "What are we going to do?"

'She replied sharply: "We must get the children out of the way. Seeing that Joseph knows all about it he can go and fetch them. Whatever happens, we must make sure our son-in-law doesn't suspect anything."

'My father seemed absolutely dumbfounded. He murmured: "What a catastrophe!"

'My mother, losing her temper all of a sudden, exclaimed: "I always thought that that thief would never come to any good! I knew that he'd start battening on us again! As if you could expect anything from a Davranche!"

'And my father passed his hand over his forehead, as he always did when his wife started scolding him. She added: "Give Joseph some money so that he can go and pay for the oysters. All we need now is to be recognized by that beggar. That would make a wonderful impression. Let's go to the other end of the boat and take care that the old man doesn't come near us!"

'She stood up, and they walked away after giving me a five-franc piece.

'My sisters had been expecting their father and were surprised to see me. I said that the sea had made Mother feel a little queasy, and I asked the shell-opener: "How much do we owe you, Monsieur?"

'I felt like saying: "Uncle".

'He replied: "Two francs fifty."

'I held out my five francs and he gave me the change.

'I looked at his hand, a poor, gnarled, sailor's hand, and I looked at his face, an unhappy old face, sad and careworn. And I said to myself: "This is my uncle, my father's brother, my uncle!"

'I gave him ten sous as a tip. He said: "God bless you, young sir!"

'He spoke like a poor man who had been given alms. I couldn't help thinking that he must have begged over there.

'My sisters stared at me, amazed by my generosity.

'When I returned the two francs to my father, my mother asked in surprise: "Was there three francs' worth? . . . That's impossible!"

'I replied in a firm voice: "I gave ten sous as a tip."

'My mother gave a start, and looking me in the eyes she said: "You're crazy! Giving ten sous to that man, that tramp!"

'She stopped at a glance from my father who nodded towards his son-in-law. Then everybody was silent.

'In front of us, on the horizon, a purple shadow seemed to be rising out of the sea. It was Jersey.

'As we approached the jetties I was seized by a violent longing to see my Uncle Jules once more, to go up to him and say something affectionate and consoling to him.

'But as nobody was eating oysters any more he had disappeared, probably down below to the foul hold where the poor wretch lived.

'We came back by the Saint-Malo boat so as not to run into him again. My mother was eaten up with worry.

'I never saw my father's brother again.

'And that's why you'll sometimes see me give five francs to a tramp.'

# A DUEL

THE war was over. The Germans had occupied France, and the country lay quivering like a defeated wrestler under his opponent's knee.

The first trains from the famished, suffering, despairing capital were making their way to the new frontiers, crawling across the countryside and through the villages. The first travellers were looking out of the windows at the ravaged plains and burnt-out hamlets. At the door of every house that was still standing Prussian soldiers in black helmets with brass spikes were sitting astride chairs, smoking their pipes. Others were chatting or doing odd jobs as if they were members of the family. Whenever a train passed through a town the passengers could see whole regiments drilling in the main square, and in spite of the rumble of the wheels hoarse words of command could be heard now and then.

Monsieur Dubuis, who had served in the National Guard throughout the siege of Paris, was on his way to Switzerland to join his wife and daughter, whom he had prudently sent abroad before the invasion.

Neither hunger nor hardship had reduced his pot belly, the belly of a well-to-do, peace-loving tradesman. He had endured the terrible events of the past few months with sorrowful resignation and bitter comments on the inhumanity of man. Although he had done his duty on the ramparts and had mounted guard on many a cold night, it was only now, when the war was over and he was approaching the frontier, that he caught his first sight of some Prussians.

He stared with mingled fear and irritation at these armed and bearded foreigners who had made themselves at home on the soil of France, and he felt in his heart a sort of fever of helpless patriotism and at the same time that instinct of self-preservation, that newly acquired sense of prudence which has never left us since.

In the same compartment were two Englishmen who had come to France as sightseers, and who looked at everything with calm, inquisitive eyes. They were both very stout too, and chatted together in their own language, occasionally referring to their guidebook and reading out extracts aloud while trying to identify the places mentioned.

The train stopped at the station of a little town and suddenly a Prussian officer climbed the two steps into the carriage, with a great clanking of his sword. He was a tall man, dressed in a tight-fitting uniform, with a flaming red beard up to his eyes. His face was cut in half by a pair of long moustachioes, paler in colour, which stuck out on either side.

The Englishmen promptly began examining him with smiles of gratified curiosity, while Monsieur Dubuis pretended to be reading a newspaper. He sat huddled in his corner, like a thief faced with a policeman.

The train moved off again. The Englishmen went on chatting and looking for the exact positions of different battles. All of a sudden, as one of them was pointing to a village on the horizon, the Prussian officer stretched out his long legs, leaned back in his seat, and said in very Teutonic French: 'I killed twelve Frenchmen in that village. I took over one hundred prisoners.'

The Englishmen's interest was immediately aroused, and they asked: 'Oh, really? What was the name of the village?'

'Pharsbourg,' replied the Prussian.

He went on: 'I took those French rogues by the ears.'

And he looked at Monsieur Dubuis, laughing proudly in his whiskers.

The train crawled on, passing through more and more occupied hamlets. German soldiers could be seen on the roads, on the outskirts of meadows, standing by gates or chatting outside cafés. They covered the earth like African locusts.

The officer stretched out his hand.

'If I had been in command, I would have taken Paris, burned everything, killed everybody. No more France!'

Out of politeness the Englishmen replied simply: 'Oh, really?'

He went on: 'In another twenty years the whole of Europe, every bit of it, will belong to us. Prussia is stronger than all the rest.'

The Englishmen, feeling a little uneasy, made no further reply. Their faces had become expressionless and looked like wax masks between their long sidewhiskers. Then the Prussian officer burst out laughing. Still lying back in his seat, he sneered at France, insulted the prostrate foe. He sneered at Austria, defeated a few years before. He sneered at the fierce but futile defence put up by the provinces, at the French militia, at the ineffectual artillery. He declared that Bismarck was going to build a city of iron with the captured guns. And suddenly he pushed his boots up against the thigh of Monsieur Dubuis, who flushed to the roots of his hair and looked away.

The Englishmen seemed to have become oblivious to everything, as if they had suddenly found themselves shut up within the confines of their island, far from the din and clamour of the world.

The officer took out his pipe, and, looking straight at the Frenchman, said: 'Have you any tobacco on you?'

'No, Monsieur,' replied Monsieur Dubuis.

The German went on: 'Then go and buy some when the train stops.'

He added with a laugh: 'I'll give you a tip.'

The train whistled and slowed down. It passed the burnt-out buildings of a station and came to a stop.

The German opened the door and took Monsieur Dubuis by the arm.

'Go and do what I told you,' he said, 'and be quick about it.'

The station was occupied by a detachment of Prussian troops. More soldiers were standing behind the wooden barriers looking on. Monsieur Dubuis jumped down on the platform, and, despite the gesticulations of the station-master, clambered into the next compartment.

He was alone! His heart was pounding so wildly that he had to unbutton his waistcoat. He mopped his forehead, panting for breath. The train stopped again at another station. Suddenly the officer appeared at the door and entered the compartment, followed by the two Englishmen, who were actuated by curiosity. The German sat down opposite the Frenchman and, still laughing, said: 'So you refused to do as I told you?'

'Yes, Monsieur,' replied Monsieur Dubuis.

The train moved off again.

'I'll cut off your moustache,' said the officer, 'to fill my pipe.'

And he stretched out his hand towards the Frenchman's face.

The Englishmen, as impassive as ever, watched intently.

The German had already caught hold of the moustache and was pulling at it when Monsieur Dubuis struck up his arm with the back of his hand and, seizing him by the collar, flung him down on the seat. Then, mad with rage, his temples swollen and his eyes suffused with blood, throttling the Prussian with one hand, he started punching him furiously in the face with the other. The Prussian struggled wildly, trying to draw his sword and to get a grip on his adversary, who was lying right on top of him. But Monsieur Dubuis pinned him down with the huge bulk of his belly and went on punching him, without pausing to draw breath and without knowing where his blows were falling. Blood flowed freely while the German, choking and gasping for breath, spat out broken teeth and struggled in vain to shake off the infuriated fat man who was pummelling him.

The Englishmen had stood up and drawn nearer to get a better view. They stood watching, full of delighted curiosity, ready to lay a bet on one or other of the combatants.

Then, all of a sudden, exhausted by his exertions, Monsieur Dubuis stood up and resumed his seat without saying a word.

The Prussian was too astounded, too numb with astonishment and pain, to fling himself upon his adversary. When he had got his breath back he said: 'Either you give me satisfaction in a pistol duel or I shall kill you.'

Monsieur Dubuis replied: 'Whenever you wish.'

'We are just coming into Strasbourg,' the German continued. 'I will find two other officers to be my seconds. There will be just enough time before the train leaves again.'

Monsieur Dubuis, who was puffing as hard as the engine, said to the Englishmen: 'Will you act as my seconds?'

They both replied at the same time: 'Oh, yes!'

And the train stopped.

In less than a minute the Prussian had found two brother

officers who fetched a pair of pistols, and they all set off for the ramparts.

The Englishmen, worried in case they should miss the train, kept pulling out their watches, quickening their pace, speeding up the preparations.

Monsieur Dubuis had never held a pistol in his life. He was positioned twenty paces from his opponent. Then he was asked: 'Are you ready?'

As he was replying: 'Yes, Monsieur,' he noticed that one of the Englishmen had opened his umbrella to protect himself from the sun.

A voice gave the word of command.

'Fire!'

Monsieur Dubuis fired straight away, without waiting to take aim, and was amazed to see the Prussian standing in front of him stagger, throw up his arms, and fall forward on his face. He had killed him.

'Oh, I say!' exclaimed one of the Englishmen, in a voice quivering with delight, gratified curiosity and joyful impatience. His companion, who still had his watch in his hand, seized Monsieur Dubuis by the arm and hurried him off at a run in the direction of the station.

The first Englishman marked time as he ran along, his fists clenched and his elbows tucked into his sides.

'One, two, one two.'

All three trotted along in line, regardless of their paunches, like three grotesque figures in a comic paper.

The train was just moving off. They jumped into their carriage. The Englishmen took off their travelling-caps, waved them in the air, and shouted three times: 'Hip, hip, hooray!'

Then, one after the other, they solemnly shook hands with Monsieur Dubuis and sat down again side by side in their corner of the compartment.

# THE CONVERT

WHENEVER Sabot came into the Martinville inn everybody laughed in anticipation. What a card the fellow was! You couldn't say he was fond of priests, either – there was no doubt about that! He used to eat them for breakfast.

Sabot (Théodule), master carpenter, represented the radical party in Martinville. He was a tall, thin man with sly grey eyes, hair stuck down on his temples, and thin lips. When he said: 'Our holy father the pap' in a certain way, everybody doubled up with laughter. He made a point of working on Sunday during Mass. Every year he killed his pig on the Monday of Holy Week, so as to have a supply of black pudding till Easter, and when the parish priest went by he always said jokingly: 'There goes a fellow who's just swallowed his God at the bar.'

The priest, a fat man who was also very tall, feared him for his wit, which won him a good many supporters. The Abbé Maritime was a diplomatist and favoured subtle methods. The struggle between the two had been going on for ten years, a secret, bitter, continuous struggle. Sabot was on the town council and it was thought that he was going to be made mayor, which would mean a resounding defeat for the Church.

The elections were about to take place, and the religious party in Martinville shook in its shoes. Then, one morning, the priest set off for Rouen, telling his housekeeper that he was going to see the Archbishop.

He came back two days later looking joyful and triumphant. The next day everybody knew that the choir of the church was going to be restored. His Grace had contributed six hundred francs towards the cost out of his own pocket.

All the old deal stalls were to be taken out and replaced with new stalls made of oak. It was a big carpentry job, and that evening everybody was talking about it.

Théodule Sabot was not amused.

When he left his house the next day to walk through the village, his neighbours, friends and enemies alike, all asked him teasingly: 'Is it you who's going to do the church choir?'

He could think of nothing to say in reply, but he fumed with anger.

'It's a big job,' the unkind ones added, 'worth at least two or three hundred clear profit.'

Two days later it was known that the restoration work was to be entrusted to Célestin Chambrelan, the carpenter at Percheville. Then the news was denied, and then it was announced that all the pews in the church were to be replaced as well. This would cost a good two thousand francs and the Ministry had been asked to provide the money. There was considerable excitement at the news.

Théodule Sabot could no longer sleep at nights. Never in living memory had a local carpenter carried out such a commission. Then a rumour started going around that the priest was heartbroken at giving this job to a carpenter outside the village, but that Sabot's opinions made it impossible to entrust the work to him.

Sabot heard this. At nightfall he betook himself to the presbytery. The housekeeper told him that the priest was in church. He went over there.

Two sour old maids, members of the Legion of Mary, were decorating the altar for Our Lady's month under the direction of the priest. He was standing in the middle of the choir, pushing out his huge belly, and supervising the work of the two women, who were perched on chairs arranging flowers around the tabernacle.

Sabot felt awkward there in the church, as if he had entered the house of his deadliest enemy, but the desire for profit spurred him on. He walked forward, cap in hand, taking no notice of the two members of the Legion of Mary, who remained motionless on their chairs, dumbfounded with amazement.

'Good evening, curé,' he stammered.

The priest, preoccupied with his altar, replied without looking at him: 'Good evening, carpenter.'

Sabot, who was rather at a loss, could think of nothing more to say. However, after a pause, he asked: 'You're getting things ready?'

The Abbé Maritime replied: 'Yes, we're getting near to Our Lady's month.'

'That's right,' said Sabot, and then fell silent.

By now he was tempted to leave without saying anything, but a glance at the choir held him back. He counted sixteen stalls to be replaced, six on the right and eight on the left, the sacristy door taking up two places. Sixteen stalls in oak would cost three hundred francs at the most, and with a little fiddling he should easily be able to make two hundred francs on the job.

He stammered: 'I've come for the work.'

The priest looked surprised.

'What work?' he asked.

Sabot murmured in desperation: 'The work to be done.' At that the priest turned and looked him in the eyes.

'Do you mean the restoration of the choir of my church?'

The tone of the Abbé Maritime's voice sent a cold shiver down Théodule Sabot's spine, and once more he felt a violent longing to run away. However, he answered meekly: 'Yes, Father.'

The priest folded his arms across his broad paunch and said, as if overcome with amazement: 'And you ... you ... you, Sabot ... come here and ask me for that. ... You ... the only unbeliever in my parish. ... Why, it would be a scandal, a public scandal! His Grace would reprimand me. He might even move me to another parish.'

He breathed hard for a few seconds, then went on in a calmer voice: 'I quite understand how painful it must be for you to see a task of this magnitude entrusted to a carpenter from a neighbouring parish. But I cannot do otherwise, unless ... but no ... that's impossible. You'd never agree to it, and without that it's out of the question.'

Sabot was now looking at the rows of pews running all the way to the door. Heavens above ... if all that was to be replaced!

'What would you need?' he asked. 'There's no harm in telling me.'

The priest replied firmly: 'I would have to have indisputable proof of your good intentions.'

'I don't say,' murmured Sabot, 'I don't say but what we might come to an understanding.'

'You must take communion in public,' declared the priest, 'at High Mass next Sunday.'

The carpenter felt himself going pale, and without answering he asked: 'What about the pews? Are they to be done too?'

'Yes,' the priest replied firmly, 'but later.'

'I don't say,' Sabot answered, 'I don't say but what I might do it. I'm no atheist, I'm not; I've nothing against religion. It's the practice of it I don't like. But in a case like this I won't be stubborn.'

The two ladies of the Legion of Mary had got down from their chairs and hidden behind the altar. They were listening, pale with emotion.

The priest, seeing that he was victorious, suddenly adopted a good-natured, familiar attitude.

'Splendid!' he said. 'Splendid! That's very sensible of you, and you won't regret it. You'll see, you'll see.'

Sabot gave a wan smile and asked: 'Couldn't we put this communion off a bit?'

The priest resumed his stern expression.

'If this work is to be entrusted to you, I have to be convinced of your conversion.'

Then he went on more mildly: 'You'd better come to confession tomorrow, because I'll have to examine you at least twice.'

'Twice?' repeated Sabot.

'Yes,' said the priest, adding with a smile: 'You do realize, don't you, that you'll need a thorough spring-cleaning, a complete wash? So I'll expect you tomorrow.'

'Where do you do it?' the carpenter asked nervously.

'Why . . . in the confessional.'

'What? . . . In that box over there in the corner? Oh, no . . . I don't like that box of yours.'

'Why not?'

'Because . . . because I'm not used to it. And because I'm a bit hard of hearing too.'

The priest showed himself accommodating.

'All right,' he said. 'Come to my study in the presbytery. We'll do it there in private. Does that suit you?'

'Yes, that'll suit me all right, but not that box of yours.'

'Very well, I'll expect you tomorrow, after work, at six o'clock.'

'Right you are. See you tomorrow, Father. And damn the man who goes back on his word.'

He held out his big rough hand and the priest slapped his own into it with a loud smack.

The sound ran along the vaulted roof and died at the far end of the church, behind the organ pipes.

Throughout the following day Théodule Sabot felt nervous and uneasy. He suffered something akin to the apprehension one feels before going to have a tooth out. Again and again the thought would cross his mind: 'I've got to go to confession tonight.' And his troubled mind, the mind of a not very convinced atheist, was panicstricken by a vague and powerful dread of the divine mystery.

He set off for the presbytery as soon as he had finished his day's work. The priest was waiting for him in the garden, reading his breviary as he walked up and down a little path. He beamed at the carpenter and greeted him with a hearty laugh.

'Well, here we are! Come in, come in, Monsieur Sabot; nobody's going to eat you.'

Sabot went in first, stammering: 'If it's all the same to you, I'd like to get it over with straight away.'

'Just as you please,' said the priest. 'I've got my surplice here. One minute and I'll be ready for you.'

The carpenter, so nervous that he could scarcely think, watched him put on the white vestment with its pleated folds. The priest motioned to him.

'Kneel down on that hassock.'

Sabot remained standing, ashamed at having to kneel. He mumbled: 'What good does it do?'

The priest assumed a majestic air.

'Only on the knees,' he said, 'can a sinner approach the tribunal of penance.'

Sabot knelt down.

'Recite the *Confiteor*,' said the priest.

'What's that?' asked Sabot.

'The *Confiteor*. If you've forgotten it, then repeat the words I'm going to say one by one.'

And the priest pronounced the sacred prayer, saying each word slowly so that the carpenter could repeat it after him.

'Now, make your confession,' he said.

But Sabot said nothing, not knowing where to start.

The Abbé Maritime came to his rescue.

'My child, since you appear to be rather out of practice, I will ask you a few questions. We shall take God's commandments one by one. Listen to me and don't worry. Just answer my questions honestly and never be afraid of saying too much.

' "Thou shalt worship one God alone and love him with all thy heart." Have you loved anything or anybody as much as God? Have you loved him with all your heart, with all your soul, and with all your mind?'

Sabot started sweating with the effort of thinking.

'No,' he replied. 'Oh, no, Father, I love God as much as I can – yes, I love him all right. As for saying I don't love my kids – no, I can't say that. As for saying I'd choose God if I had to choose between him and them, I won't say I would. As for saying I'd lose a hundred francs for the love of God, I won't say that either. But I love him all right, I love him all the same.'

'You must love him more than anything,' the priest said solemnly.

And Sabot, full of good will, declared: 'I'll do my best, Father.'

The Abbé Maritime went on: ' "Thou shalt not take the name of the Lord in vain, nor swear by any other." Have you ever sworn any oaths?'

'Good heavens, no! I never swear, never. Sometimes, when I'm in a temper, I may say "God dammit". But I never swear.'

'But that *is* swearing!' exclaimed the priest. He added sternly: 'Don't do it any more. I'll continue. "Thou shalt keep the Sabbath holy and serve God devoutly." What do you do on Sundays?'

This time Sabot scratched his ear.

'Well, I serve God as best I can, Father. I serve him . . . at home. I work on Sundays . . .'

The priest magnanimously interrupted him to say: 'I know you'll behave better in the future. I'll pass over the next three commandments, as I'm sure you haven't broken the first two, and we'll take the sixth with the ninth. To proceed: "Thou shalt not take another's goods, nor keep them wittingly." Have you ever, in any way at all, taken something that didn't belong to you?'

'Oh, no!' said Théodule Sabot indignantly. 'Certainly not! I'm an honest man, Father, I swear I am. As for saying that I've never charged an extra hour or two to a customer who could pay, I won't say that. As for saying that I've never put a few centimes on to a bill – just a few centimes, mind – I won't say that either. But stealing – no, I've never done that.'

The priest went on sternly: 'Taking a single centime that doesn't belong to you constitutes a theft. Don't do it again. . . . "Thou shalt not bear false witness nor lie in any way." Have you told any lies?'

'No, certainly not. I'm no liar, I can tell you that. As for saying that I've never told a tall story, I won't say that. As for saying that I've never tried to pull the wool over another fellow's eyes when it suited me, I won't say that either. But I'm no liar, that I'm not.'

The priest said simply: 'Watch your tongue in future.'

Then he went on: '"Thou shalt not lust after the works of the flesh, save only in marriage." Have you ever desired or possessed any woman other than your own wife?'

'Oh, no, Father!' Sabot cried in tones of sincerity. 'Certainly not! Deceive my poor wife? No! No! Not so much as with the tip of my finger, and no more in thought than deed, I can tell you that.'

He paused for a few seconds, then went on in a lower voice, as if a sudden doubt had assailed him: 'As for saying that when I go to town I never go to a house – a bawdy-house, I mean – just to have a bit of fun and get a change of skin, I won't say that. . . . But I pay, Father. I always pay; and provided you pay, that's all right, isn't it?'

The priest did not press the point, and gave him absolution.

Théodule Sabot is working on the choir stalls and goes to communion every month.

# IN THE BEDROOM

A BIG fire was blazing in the hearth. The Japanese table was set for two and a teapot was steaming beside a sugar-bowl and a small carafe of rum.

The Comte de Sallure threw his hat, his gloves and his fur coat on to a chair while the Comtesse, after taking off her evening-wrap, smoothed her hair in front of the mirror. She smiled at her reflexion as she arranged the curls on her forehead with the tips of her jewelled fingers. Then she turned towards her husband, who had been looking at her for a few minutes as if hesitating to speak. Finally he said: 'Did you receive enough attention tonight?'

She looked him straight in the eye with a gleam of triumph and defiance in her gaze and replied: 'I should hope so.'

Then she sat down. He took a seat facing her, and, breaking a scone between his fingers, went on: 'It made me look . . . almost ridiculous.'

'Is this a scene?' she asked. 'Are you going to criticize my behaviour?'

'No, my dear, all I'm saying is that that Monsieur Burel's attitude towards you was almost indecent. If . . . if . . . if I had had any right to, I'd have called him to order.'

'Oh, come now, be honest. You've changed your ideas since last year, that's all. You didn't seem to care then whether anybody was paying me attentions or not. When I found out that you had a mistress, a mistress you were in love with, I told you, as you told me tonight, but with more reason, that I was distressed, that you were compromising Madame de Servy, that you were hurting me and making me look ridiculous. What did you reply? You made it clear to me that I was perfectly free, that marriage between two intelligent people was just a partnership, a social bond, but not a moral bond. Isn't that so? You gave me to understand that your mistress was infinitely more attractive than I, more captivating, more womanly. Yes, that's what you said: more womanly. Of course you said all this with the delicacy one would expect of a perfect gentleman, wrapping it up in compliments and expressing it with a tact to which I would be the first to pay tribute. The fact remains that I understood exactly what you meant.

'We agreed that we should go on living together, but quite independent of each other. We had a child who formed a link between us.

'You intimated to me that all that mattered to you was keeping up appearances, and that I could take a lover if I wished, provided that the liaison was kept secret. You spoke at some length, and very eloquently, about the skill and cleverness women showed in satisfying the proprieties, and so on and so forth.

'I understood, my dear, I understood perfectly. You were in love, deeply in love, with Madame de Servy at the time, and my lawful affection, my legitimate affection was a nuisance to you. I probably impaired your ardour to some extent. Since then we have lived separate lives. We go out together but each of us returns to his own quarters.

'Now, for the past month or two you have been behaving as if you were jealous. What is the reason for this?'

'My dear, I'm not jealous, but you are so young, so lively, so impetuous that I'm afraid of seeing you compromise your reputation.'

'If we are going to talk about reputations, I don't think that yours is exactly spotless.'

'Come now, this is no laughing matter. I'm talking to you seriously, as a friend. As for what you were saying just now, it was terribly exaggerated.'

'Not a bit of it. You admitted to me that you were having a liaison, and that was tantamount to giving me permission to imitate you. I haven't done so . . .'

'Allow me to. . . .'

'Please let me finish. I haven't done so. I have no lover, and I haven't had a lover . . . yet. I'm waiting and looking, but so far I haven't found one to suit me. He has to be very nice . . . nicer than you. . . . That's a compliment I'm paying you, but you don't seem to have noticed it.'

'My dear, all these jokes are completely uncalled for.'

'But I'm not joking at all. You talked to me about the eighteenth century and gave me to understand that you belonged to the Regency. I haven't forgotten a single word of what you said. And the day I choose to stop being as I am you will be unable to do anything about it, do you hear? Without even suspecting it, you will be a cuckold like so many others.'

'Oh, how can you use such words?'

'How can I use such words? . . . But you roared with laughter when Madame de Gers said that Monsieur de Servy looked like a cuckold hunting for his horns.'

'What may seem amusing coming from Madame de Gers is unseemly coming from you.'

'Not a bit of it. You just think the word "cuckold" is very funny when applied to Monsieur de Servy but not at all funny when applied to you. It all depends on your point of view. As a matter of fact I don't particularly care for that word: I used it simply to see if you were ripe.'

'Ripe? Ripe for what?'

'Why, for being deceived, of course. When a man gets angry when he hears that word, it means that . . . well, he's getting warm. In a couple of months you'll be the first to laugh when I mention . . . horns. Because when somebody's wearing horns he usually doesn't feel them.'

'You're talking in the most unseemly way tonight. I've never seen you like this before.'

'But then I've changed . . . for the worse. And that's your fault.'

'Look, my dear, let's talk seriously. I beg you, I implore you not to allow Monsieur Burel to pay the sort of improper attentions he paid you tonight.'

'You *are* jealous. I told you so.'

'No, no. I just don't like looking ridiculous. I don't intend to look ridiculous. And if I see that fellow breathing on your shoulders again – or rather down your bosom . . .'

'He was looking for an ear-trumpet.'

'I'll . . . I'll box his ears.'

'You aren't in love with me by any chance, are you?'

'I could do much worse.'

'Well, well! The trouble is that I'm not in love with you any more.'

The Comte stood up, walked around the little table and, going behind his wife, kissed her lightly on the back of the neck. She sprang up and, looking into his eyes, said: 'Let's have no more nonsense like that between us, if you don't mind. We are living apart. It's all over.'

'Come now, don't get angry. For some time now I've found you absolutely ravishing.'

'Then I've won. You too think that I'm . . . ripe.'

'I think that you're beautiful, my dear; your arms, your shoulders, your complexion . . .'

'Would captivate Monsieur Burel . . .'

'How cruel you are! But really, I've never seen a woman as beautiful as you.'

'You must have been fasting lately.'

'I beg your pardon?'

'I said you must have been fasting lately.'

'What do you mean?'

'When a man has been fasting, he's hungry, and when he's hungry he'll eat things he wouldn't like at any other time. I am the ... dish ... which used to be neglected but which you wouldn't mind getting your teeth into tonight.'

'Oh, Marguerite! Whoever taught you to talk like that?'

'Why *you* did! Look: since you broke with Madame de Servy you have had, to my knowledge, four mistresses, all of them cocottes, artists in their field. So how do you expect me to explain your ... fancy for me tonight, except by a temporary fast?'

'I'm going to be brutally frank with you, and come straight to the point. I've fallen in love with you again. Madly in love. There.'

'Well, well! So you'd like to ... begin again?'

'Yes, I would.'

'Tonight?'

'Oh, Marguerite!'

'There, you see? You're shocked again. Let's get this clear, shall we? We're nothing to each other any more, are we? I'm your wife, it's true, but a wife who is also a free agent. I was going to bestow my favours elsewhere, but you asked me to give you preference. Well, I'm prepared to do so ... at the same price.'

'I don't understand.'

'I'd better explain. Am I as attractive as your cocottes? Be honest with me.'

'A thousand times more attractive.'

'More than the most attractive of them?'

'A thousand times more.'

'Well, how much did the most attractive of them cost you in three months?'

'I don't follow you.'

'I said: how much did the most delightful of your mistresses cost you in three months, in money, jewels, suppers, dinners, theatres, and so on?'

'How do I know?'

'You must know. Come now, let's take a fairly modest figure. Five thousand francs a month: is that about right?'

'Yes . . . about that.'

'Well, my dear, give me five thousand francs straight away, and I'm yours for a month, starting tonight.'

'You must be mad.'

'If that's what you think – good night.'

The Comtesse left the room and went into her bedroom. The bed had been turned down. An indefinable perfume hung in the air, clinging to the curtains.

The Comte appeared in the doorway.

'It smells delightful in here,' he said.

'You think so? But I haven't changed my scent. I still use Peau d'Espagne.'

'Really? How odd. . . . It smells very nice.'

'Possibly. But now would you be good enough to go, because I want to go to bed.'

'Marguerite!'

'Go away!'

He came right in and sat down in an armchair.

'So that's how it is?' said the Comtesse. 'All right, so much the worse for you.'

She slowly took off her wrap, revealing her bare white arms. She raised them above her head to unpin her hair, and under a frothy cloud of lace a little pink flesh appeared at the edge of the black silk corset.

The Comte sprang to his feet and came over to her.

'Don't come any nearer,' said the Comtesse, 'or I'll get really angry!'

He clasped her in his arms and tried to kiss her. Leaning forward she seized a glass of scented water which was standing on her dressing-table and threw it over her shoulder into her husband's face.

He straightened up, dripping with water, and muttered: 'That was a stupid thing to do.'

'Maybe. . . . But you know my terms: five thousand francs.'

'But that would be ridiculous!'

'Why?'

'What do you mean, why? Whoever heard of a husband paying to go to bed with his wife . . .'

'What crude words you use!'

'Perhaps I do. But I repeat that the idea of a man paying for his wife is stupid.'

'It's not as stupid as going and paying a lot of cocottes when you have a wife of your own.'

'That may be, but I don't want to be ridiculous.'

The Comtesse sat down on a chaise longue and slowly took off her stockings, peeling them off like a snake's skin. Her pink legs emerged from the mauve silk sheaths, and she put her dainty feet one by one on the carpet.

The Comte came a little nearer and said in a tender voice: 'What an odd idea that was, Marguerite!'

'What idea?'

'Asking me for five thousand francs.'

'But nothing could be more natural. We are strangers to each other, aren't we? Well, you want me. You can't marry me because we are already married. So why shouldn't you buy me? After all, I might cost less than another woman.

'Think it over. Instead of going to some slut who would just squander it, your money will stay here, in your own home. Besides, for an intelligent man, could anything be more novel and amusing than paying for his own wife? Nobody really loves anything in the way of unlawful love unless it costs him a lot of money. By putting a price on our lawful love you'll give it a new value, a savour of debauchery, the spice of wickedness. Isn't that so?'

She stood up, almost naked, and walked towards her bathroom.

'Now, Monsieur, go away, or I shall ring for my maid.'

The Comte stood there looking at her, perplexed and annoyed, and suddenly tossed her his wallet.

'All right, you minx, there are five thousand. But let me tell you one thing...'

The Comtesse picked up the wallet, counted the money, and said in a slow drawl: 'What?'

'Don't expect to make a habit of it.'

She burst out laughing and, going towards him, said: 'Five thousand francs every month, Monsieur, or I'll send you back to your cocottes. Moreover if... if you're satisfied ... I'll ask for a rise.'

# REGRET

MONSIEUR SAVEL, who was known in Mantes as 'Old Savel', had just got up. It was raining. It was a sad autumn day; the leaves were falling. They were falling slowly in the rain, like rain of another kind, heavier and slower. Monsieur Savel was not in good spirits. He went from the fireplace to the window and from the window to the fireplace. Life had its dreary days. For him all its days would be dreary now, for he was sixty-two years old. He was alone in the world, an old bachelor, with nobody to share his life. How sad it was to die like that, all alone, without the comfort afforded by affection and devotion!

He thought about his barren, empty existence. He thought of the distant past, the past of his childhood, life at home with his parents; then school, the holidays, the period of his law studies in Paris. Then his father's illness and death.

He had come home to live with his mother. They had lived together very quietly, the young man and the old woman, wanting nothing more. She had died too. How sad a thing life was!

He had remained alone. And now it would soon be his turn to die. He would disappear, and it would be all over. There would be no Monsieur Paul Savel left on earth. What a dreadful thing to happen! Other people would live, would love, would laugh. Yes, they would enjoy themselves while he no longer existed! How strange it was that people could laugh, enjoy themselves, be merry and gay, when faced with the perpetual inevitability of death! If death were only a probability one could still entertain some hope; but no, it was inevitable, as inevitable as night after day.

It wouldn't be so terrible if only he had led a full life – if he had had adventures, exquisite pleasures, success or satisfaction of some sort or other. But he had had nothing. He had never done anything but get up, eat at the same hours, and go to bed again. And like that he had reached the age of sixty-two. He had not even got married, as other men did. Why not? Yes, why hadn't he got married? He could have done, for he was quite well off. Was it the opportunity which had been lacking? Perhaps. But then, that sort of opportunity had to be created. He was apathetic, that was the trouble. Apathy had been his great weakness, his failing, his vice. Some people spoiled their lives through apathy. It was so difficult for certain temperaments to get out of bed, to bustle about, to speak to people, to study problems.

He had never been loved. No woman had ever slept in his arms in the complete abandon of love. He knew nothing of the delicious anguish of waiting for a woman, the heavenly quivering of a hand clasped in his, the ecstasy of triumphant passion.

What superhuman happiness must fill the heart when two pairs of lips meet for the first time, when the embrace of four arms make a single creature, a supremely happy creature, of two creatures madly in love with each other!

Monsieur Savel had sat down in his dressing-gown, with his feet on the fender.

Admittedly his life had been a failure, an absolute failure. All the same, he had been in love. He had loved a woman secretly, painfully and apathetically, as he did everything else. Yes, he had loved his old friend Madame Sandres, the wife of his old companion Sandres. Oh, if only he had known her as a girl! But he had met her too late: she was already married. If she hadn't been, he would have proposed to her without the slightest doubt. Even so, he had loved her constantly, from the first day they had met.

He remembered how excited he had been every time he had seen her, how sad he had been every time he had left her, and the nights he had been unable to go to sleep for thinking of her.

In the morning he always woke up a little less in love with her than the night before. Why was that?

How pretty she had been in the old days, a dainty blonde, curly-haired and bubbling over with laughter! Sandres wasn't the man she ought to have married. Now she was fifty-eight. She seemed to be happy enough. Oh, if only she had loved him in the old days, if only she had loved him! And why shouldn't she have loved him, Savel, since he had been fond of her, Madame Sandres?

If only she had guessed his feelings! Hadn't she ever guessed anything, seen anything, understood anything? What would she have thought if she had? If he had spoken up, what would she have replied?

Savel asked himself a thousand other questions. He reviewed the whole of his life, trying to recapture a host of details.

He recalled all the long evenings spent playing cards at Sandres's house, when his friend's wife was young and charming.

He recalled things she had said to him, intonations her voice used to take on, silent little smiles which meant so much.

He recalled the walks the three of them had taken along the banks of the Seine and the picnics they had had on Sundays, for Sandres worked during the week at the sub-prefecture. And suddenly the distinct recollection came to him of an afternoon spent with her in a little wood by the river.

They had set out in the morning, taking their provisions with them wrapped in packets. It was a bright spring day, one of those days which make you feel quite light-headed. Everything smells good, everything seems happy, and the birds sing more gaily and dart about more swiftly. They had lunched on the grass under the willows, close to the water flowing lazily in the sunshine. The air was balmy, full of the smell of rising sap, and they breathed it in with delight. How good it was to be alive that day!

After lunch Sandres had stretched out on his back and gone to sleep. 'The best nap I've ever had,' he said when he woke up.

Madame Sandres had taken Savel's arm and the two of them had gone off along the river bank.

She leaned on his arm, laughing and saying: 'I'm drunk, my dear, absolutely drunk.'

He looked at her, his heart beating wildly. He felt himself turning pale, and was terrified that his eyes might be too bold, that the trembling of his hand might reveal his secret.

She had made herself a crown of leaves and water lilies, and had asked him: 'Do you like me like this?'

As he made no reply – for he could think of nothing to say and felt more like falling on his knees – she had burst out laughing with a sort of irritated laughter, saying: 'You big booby! You might at least say something!'

He felt close to tears, but he still couldn't find a single word to say.

All this came back to him now, as vividly as on the day it had happened. Why, he wondered, had she said to him: 'You big booby! You might at least say something'?

And he recalled how tenderly she had leaned on his arm. Passing under a bent tree, he had felt her ear against his cheek, and he had drawn back abruptly, for fear that she should think this contact was deliberate.

When he had said: 'Isn't it time we went back?' she had darted a strange glance at him. Yes, she had definitely looked at him in a peculiar way. It hadn't struck him at the time, but now he remembered it clearly.

'Just as you like. If you're feeling tired, let's go back.' And he had replied: 'It isn't that I'm feeling tired, but Sandres may be awake now.'

With a shrug of her shoulders she had said: 'If you're afraid my husband is awake, that's different. Let's go back.'

On the way back she remained silent and no longer leaned on his arm. Why?

He hadn't asked himself this question before. Now he had the impression he could glimpse something he had never understood before.

Was it possible?

Monsieur Savel felt himself blush and stood up, feeling as overwhelmed as if, thirty years before, he had heard Madame Sandres tell him: 'I love you.'

Was it possible? The suspicion which had just dawned upon him was sheer torture. Was it possible that he hadn't noticed, that he hadn't guessed?

Oh, if that was true, if he had come so close to such happiness without grasping it!

He said to himself: 'I must find out! I can't remain in this state of doubt! I must find out!'

And he got dressed hurriedly, throwing on his clothes. He thought to himself: 'I'm sixty-two and she's fifty-eight; there's no reason why I shouldn't ask her that.'

And he went out.

The Sandres house was on the other side of the street,

practically opposite his own. He went over to it and banged the knocker. The little maid opened the door.

She was astonished to see him so early in the day.

'You here already, Monsieur Savel?' she said. 'Has there been an accident?'

'No, my girl,' Savel replied. 'But go and tell your mistress that I would like to speak to her straight away.'

'The fact is, Madame is making her pear jam for the winter and she's busy over the stove, so she isn't dressed, you see.'

'Yes, but tell her it's about something very important.'

The little maid went off and Savel started pacing nervously up and down the drawing-room. Yet he didn't feel at all embarrassed. He was going to ask her his question as naturally as he would have asked her for a recipe. After all, he was sixty-two years old . . .

The door opened; she appeared. She was now a stout, round woman with full cheeks and a loud laugh. She came in holding her hands away from her body, with her sleeves rolled up and her bare arms sticky with a sugary juice. She asked anxiously: 'What's the matter? You aren't ill, are you?'

'No, my dear friend,' he replied; 'but I want to ask you about something very important to me which is tormenting me. Will you promise to answer me frankly?'

She smiled.

'I always speak frankly. Go on.'

'Well, the fact is, I've loved you since the first day I met you. Did you ever suspect?'

She burst out laughing and replied with something of her old intonation: 'You big booby! I knew from the very first day!'

Savel started trembling, and stammered: 'You knew? . . . But then . . .'

He fell silent.

'Then what?' she asked.

He went on: 'Then ... what did you think? ... What ... what ... what would you have replied?'

She laughed louder than ever. Drops of juice ran down her fingers and fell on to the floor.

'What would I have replied? But you didn't ask me anything. It wasn't for me to make a declaration.'

Then he took a step towards her.

'Tell me,' he said, 'tell me.... Do you remember the day Sandres went to sleep on the grass after lunch ... and we walked together as far as that bend in the river....'

He waited. She had stopped laughing and was looking him straight in the eyes.

'Yes, I remember it all right.'

Trembling slightly, he went on: 'Well ... that day ... if I had been ... if I had been enterprising ... what would you have done?'

She started smiling like a woman who has no regrets, and replied frankly in a voice tinged with irony: 'I would have yielded, my dear.'

Then she turned on her heels and went back to her jam.

Savel left the house utterly crushed, as if some disaster had just befallen him. He walked straight ahead towards the river, striding through the rain without thinking where he was going. When he reached the river he turned right and followed the bank. He walked for a long time, as if urged on by some instinct. His clothes were running with water and his hat, as limp and shapeless as a wet rag, was dripping like a roof. He walked on and on, straight ahead. And at last he came to the place where they had lunched on that distant day which he found so painful to remember.

Then he sat down under the leafless trees, and wept.

# THE DECORATION

SOME people are born with a predominant instinct, a sense of vocation or simply a desire which is aroused as soon as they begin to speak or think.

Ever since he was a child Monsieur Sacrement had had only one idea in his head – to be decorated. As a little boy he used to wear a zinc Cross of the Legion of Honour, just as other children wear a soldier's cap, and he took his mother's hand proudly in the street, puffing out his little chest decorated with the red ribbon and the metal star.

After an undistinguished career at school he failed in the Baccalauréat examination, and, not knowing what to do with himself, he married a pretty girl, for he had ample private means.

They lived in Paris like other well-to-do people of the upper middle class, mixing with people of their own set without going into society, proud of knowing a deputy who might one day become a minister, and numbering two permanent secretaries among their friends.

However, the idea which had entered Monsieur Sacrement's head during his formative years still haunted him, and he felt perpetually unhappy because he had not the right to wear a little coloured ribbon in his buttonhole.

Meeting people on the boulevard who were decorated was like a blow to the heart for him. He would eye them surreptitiously with a feeling of intense jealousy. Sometimes, during long afternoons when he had nothing to do, he would start counting them, saying to himself: 'Let's see how many I'll meet between the Madeleine and the Rue Drouot.'

He would walk along slowly, inspecting every coat with an eye practised in spotting the little patch of red. When he reached the end of his walk he was always astonished at the number he had counted: 'Eight officers and seventeen chevaliers. As many as that! It's ridiculous distributing crosses wholesale like that. Let's see if I meet as many on the way back.'

And he would slowly walk back the way he had come, upset when the crowd of hurrying passers-by interfered with his investigation and made it possible that he might miss somebody.

He knew the districts where the largest numbers were to be found. There were dozens of them in the Palais-Royal. There were not so many in the Avenue de l'Opéra as in the Rue de la Paix, while the right side of the boulevard was better patronized than the left.

They also seemed to prefer certain cafés and certain theatres. Whenever Monsieur Sacrement caught sight of a group of white-haired old gentlemen standing in the middle of the pavement, in everybody's way, he would say to himself: 'They must be officers of the Legion of Honour.' And he felt tempted to take off his hat to them.

He had often observed that the officers had a different bearing from mere chevaliers. They carried their heads higher. You could tell that they enjoyed greater official consideration and exercised wider influence.

Sometimes too Monsieur Sacrement was seized with a furious rage against everybody who was decorated; he felt a socialistic hatred for them.

Then, when he got home, as excited by the sight of so many crosses as a poor, starving wretch is after passing a big food shop, he would ask loudly: 'When are we going to be rid of this wretched government?'

His wife would ask in surprise: 'What's the matter with you today?'

'It makes me furious,' he would reply, 'to see all the injustices that are committed everywhere. Oh, the Communards were right, and no mistake!'

But after dinner he would leave the house again and go and look at the window displays of the shops which sold decorations. He would examine all the emblems of different shapes and various colours. He would have liked to possess them all, and to be able to walk at the head of a procession in a public ceremony, through a vast hall crowded with gaping people, with his opera-hat under his arm and his chest ablaze with decorations, rows of them in brochettes following the line of his ribs, shining like a star in the midst of admiring whispers and respectful murmurs.

Alas, he had done nothing to qualify for any decoration whatever.

'The Legion of Honour,' he told himself, 'is really too difficult for anybody to obtain unless he is a civil servant. But what if I tried to get appointed an Officer of the Academy?'

Unfortunately he had no idea how to set about it. He mentioned the problem to his wife, who was flabbergasted.

'An Officer of the Academy? What have you done to deserve that?'

'Try and understand what I'm saying!' he retorted angrily. 'What I want to know is how to set about it. Sometimes you really are too stupid for words.'

'You're quite right,' she answered with a smile. 'But I don't know what to suggest.'

An idea occurred to him.

'Suppose you had a word with Monsieur Rosselin,' he said. 'As a deputy he might be able to advise me what to do. You realize that I daren't broach the subject directly with him. It's rather delicate, rather difficult, but coming from you it would seem quite natural.'

Madame Sacrement did as he asked. Monsieur Rosselin promised to speak to the Minister about it. Then Sacrement started pestering him, and finally the deputy told him that he would have to make an official application and list his qualifications.

But what qualifications did he possess? That was the trouble. He didn't even have a Baccalauréat.

All the same, he set to work and began writing a pamphlet entitled *The People's Right to Education*. He was unable to finish it for want of ideas.

He looked for some easier subjects and tackled several in succession. The first was *Educating Children through the Eyes*. He suggested setting up free theatres in the poorer districts of Paris for the benefit of little children. Their parents would take them there when they were very young, and by means of a magic lantern they would be given some idea of every aspect of human knowledge. These visits would be regular lectures. The eyes would educate the mind, and the pictures would remain impressed on the memory, making knowledge visible, as it were. What could be simpler than teaching world history, geography, natural history, botany, zoology, anatomy and so on in that way?

He had this memoir printed and sent a copy to every deputy, ten to every minister, fifty to the President of the Republic, ten to every Parisian paper, and five to the provincial papers.

Then he dealt with the question of mobile lending libraries, suggesting that the State should arrange for little carts full of books to be drawn around the streets like orange carts. Every citizen would be entitled to borrow ten books a month in return for a subscription of one sou.

'The people,' wrote Monsieur Sacrement, 'will only put themselves out for the sake of their pleasures, and since they won't go in search of education, education must come to them.' And so on, and so forth.

These pamphlets failed to attract any notice, but he sent in his application all the same. He received a reply saying that the matter was receiving attention, that inquiries were being made. He felt sure of success and waited patiently. Nothing happened.

Then he made up his mind to take action on his own behalf. He asked for an interview with the Minister of Education, and was received by an official who was quite young but already solemn, even pompous, and who kept pressing a series of little white buttons, as if he were playing the piano, to summon ushers and messengers as well as subordinate officials. He assured the visitor that his application was going well and advised him to persevere with his admirable research.

Monsieur Sacrement accordingly set to work again.

Monsieur Rosselin, the deputy, now seemed to take a great interest in his success, and even gave him a lot of excellent practical advice. Incidentally, Monsieur Rosselin was decorated, although it was not known precisely what he had done to deserve such a distinction.

He suggested new subjects for Monsieur Sacrement to study and introduced him to learned societies which concerned themselves with especially obscure points of human knowledge in the hope of obtaining honour and recognition. He even recommended him to the Ministry.

One day when he was lunching at his friend's house (in the past few months he had become a frequent guest there) he whispered to him as he shook hands: 'I've just obtained a great favour for you. The Committee for Historical Studies has entrusted you with a commission. It's a question of research to be carried out in various libraries all over France.'

Sacrement was so excited by the news that he nearly fainted and could scarcely eat or drink. He set off a week later.

He went from town to town, studying catalogues, rummaging in lofts full of dusty old books, and earning the hatred of librarians.

One evening, happening to find himself in Rouen, he decided to drop in on his wife, whom he had not seen for a week; and he took the nine o'clock train which would get him home at midnight.

He had his latchkey with him, and he let himself into the house quietly, delighted at the idea of giving her a surprise. Unfortunately, he found that she had locked herself in her room. He shouted through the door: 'Jeanne, it's me!'

She was obviously very frightened, for he heard her jump out of bed, talking to herself as if she were dreaming. Then she dashed into her dressing-room, opened and closed the door, and ran round her bedroom several times in her bare feet, shaking the furniture so that the glass doors and ornaments rattled. Then at last she asked: 'Is it really you, Alexandre?'

'Of course it's me!' he replied. 'Open the door!'

The door was unlocked, and his wife threw herself into his arms, exclaiming: 'Oh, what a fright you gave me! What a surprise! What a joy!'

Then he started undressing carefully and methodically, as he did everything, and from a chair he picked up his overcoat, which he was in the habit of hanging in the hall. But suddenly he stopped in astonishment. There was a red ribbon in the buttonhole!

His wife rushed at him and tore the coat out of his hands.

'No!' she said. 'You've made a mistake. . . . Let me have it.'

But he hung on to it by one of the sleeves, refusing to let it go, and repeating in a kind of daze: 'Eh? . . . Why? . . . Just explain. . . . Whose is this overcoat? . . . It isn't mine, because it's got the Legion of Honour on it.'

She tried to pull it away from him in a panic, stammering: 'Listen . . . listen. . . . Let go of it. . . . It's a secret. . . . Listen to me.'

But he was growing angry and had turned pale.

'I want to know what this overcoat is doing here! It isn't mine!'

Then she shouted at him: 'Yes, it is! Listen to me. . . . Promise. . . . Well, the fact is, you've been decorated!'

He was so overcome that he let go of the overcoat and dropped into an armchair.

'I've been . . . you say I've been decorated? . . .'

'Yes. . . . But it's a secret, a great secret . . .'

She had put the glorious garment in a cupboard and came back to her husband, pale and trembling.

'Yes,' she went on, 'it's a new overcoat I've had made for you. But I promised I wouldn't say anything to you about it, because it won't be announced for a month or six weeks. You weren't supposed to know until your mission was over. It was Monsieur Rosselin who fixed it for you.'

'Rosselin!' stammered Sacrement, faint with delight. 'He got the decoration for me. . . . He. . . . Oh!'

And he was obliged to drink a glass of water.

A little piece of white pasteboard had fallen out of one of the pockets of the overcoat and was lying on the floor. Sacrement picked it up; it was a visiting card. He read out: 'Rosselin – Deputy.'

'You see?' said his wife.

And he started crying with joy.

A week later the *Officiel* announced that Monsieur Sacrement had been appointed a Chevalier of the Legion of Honour for exceptional services.

# THE PIECE OF STRING

On all the roads around Goderville the peasants and their wives were making their way towards the little town, for it was market day. The men were plodding along, their bodies leaning forward with every movement of their long bandy legs – legs deformed by hard work, by the pressure of the plough which also raises the left shoulder and twists the spine, by the spreading of the knees required to obtain a firm stance for reaping, and by all the slow, laborious tasks of country life. Their blue starched smocks, shining as if they were varnished, and decorated with a little pattern in white embroidery on the collar and cuffs, bellied out around their bony frames like balloons ready to fly away, with a head, two arms and two feet sticking out of each one.

Some were leading a cow or a calf by a rope, while their wives hurried the animal on by whipping its haunches with a leafy branch. The women carried large baskets on their arms from which protruded the heads of chickens or ducks. And they walked with a shorter, brisker step than their husbands, their gaunt, erect figures wrapped in skimpy little shawls pinned across their flat chests and their heads wrapped in tight-fitting white coifs topped with bonnets.

Then a cart went by, drawn at a trot by a small horse, with two men sitting side by side bumping up and down and a woman at the back holding on to the sides to lessen the jolts.

The square in Goderville was crowded with a confused mass of animals and human beings. The horns of the bullocks, the tall beaver hats of the well-to-do peasants, and the coifs of the peasant women stood out above the throng.

And the high-pitched, shrill, yapping voices made a wild, continuous din, dominated now and then by a great deep-throated roar of laughter from a jovial countryman or the long lowing of a cow tied to the wall of a house.

Everywhere was the smell of cowsheds and milk and manure, of hay and sweat, that sharp, unpleasant odour of men and animals which is peculiar to people who work on the land.

Maître Hauchecorne of Bréauté had just arrived in Goderville and was making his way towards the market square when he caught sight of a small piece of string on the ground. Maître Hauchecorne, a thrifty man like all true Normans, reflected that anything which might come in useful was worth picking up, so he bent down – though with some difficulty, for he suffered from rheumatism. He picked up the piece of thin cord and was about to roll it up carefully when he noticed Maître Malandain, the saddler, standing at his door watching him. They had had a quarrel some time before over a halter and they had remained on bad terms ever since, both of them being the sort to nurse a grudge. Maître Hauchecorne felt a little shamefaced at being seen by his enemy like this, picking a bit of string up out of the muck. He hurriedly concealed his find, first under his smock, then in his trouser pocket; then he pretended to go on looking for something on the ground which he couldn't find, before continuing on his way to the square, leaning forward, bent double by his rheumatism.

He was promptly lost in the noisy, slow-moving crowd, in which everyone was engaged in endless and excited bargaining. The peasants were prodding the cows, walking away and coming back in an agony of indecision, always afraid of being taken in and never daring to make up their minds, watching the vendor's eyes and perpetually trying to spot the man's trick and the animal's defect.

After putting their big baskets down at their feet, the women had taken out their fowls, which now lay on the ground, tied by their legs, their eyes terrified and their combs scarlet. They listened to the offers they were made and either stuck to their price, hard-faced and impassive, or else, suddenly deciding to accept the lower figure offered, shouted after the customer who was slowly walking away: 'All right, Maître Anthime, it's yours.'

Then, little by little, the crowd in the square thinned out, and as the Angelus rang for noon those who lived too far away to go home disappeared into the various inns.

At Jourdain's the main room was crowded with people eating, while the vast courtyard was full of vehicles of all sorts – carts, gigs, wagons, tilburies, and indescribable shandrydans, yellow with dung, broken down and patched together, raising their shafts to heaven like a pair of arms, or else heads down and bottoms up.

Close to the people sitting at table, the bright fire blazing in the huge fireplace was scorching the backs of the row on the right. Three spits were turning, carrying chickens, pigeons and legs of mutton; and a delicious smell of meat roasting and gravy trickling over browning flesh rose from the hearth, raising people's spirits and making their mouths water.

All the aristocracy of the plough took its meals at Maître Jourdain's. Innkeeper and horsedealer, he was a cunning rascal who had made his pile.

Dishes were brought in and emptied, as were the jugs of yellow cider. Everybody talked about the business he had done, what he had bought and sold. News and views were exchanged about the crops. The weather was good for the greens but rather damp for the wheat.

All of a sudden the roll of a drum sounded in the courtyard in front of the inn. Except for one or two who showed no interest everybody jumped up and ran to the door or windows with their mouths still full and their napkins in their hands.

After finishing his roll on the drum, the town crier made the following pronouncement, speaking in a jerky manner and pausing in the wrong places: 'Let it be known to the inhabitants of Goderville, and in general to all – persons present at the market that there was lost this morning, on the Beuzeville road, between – nine and ten o'clock, a black leather wallet containing five hundred francs and some business documents. Anybody finding the same is asked to bring it immediately – to the town hall or to return it to Maître Fortuné Houlbrèque of Manneville. There will be a reward of twenty francs.'

Then the man went away. The dull roll of the drum and the faint voice of the town crier could be heard once again in the distance.

Everybody began talking about the incident, estimating Maître Houlbrèque's chances of recovering or not recovering his wallet.

The meal came to an end.

They were finishing their coffee when the police sergeant appeared at the door and asked: 'Is Maître Hauchecorne of Bréauté here?'

Maître Hauchecorne, who was sitting at the far end of the table, replied: 'Yes, here I am.'

The sergeant went on: 'Maître Hauchecorne, will you be good enough to come with me to the town hall? The Mayor would like to have a word with you.'

The peasant, surprised and a little worried, tossed down his glass of brandy, stood up, and, even more bent than in the morning, for the first few steps after a rest were especially difficult, set off after the sergeant, repeating: 'Here I am, here I am.'

The Mayor was waiting for him, sitting in an armchair. He was the local notary, a stout, solemn individual, with a penchant for pompous phrases.

'Maître Hauchecorne,' he said, 'you were seen this morning, on the Beuzeville road, picking up the wallet lost by Maître Houlbrèque of Manneville.'

The peasant gazed in astonishment at the Mayor, already frightened by this suspicion which had fallen upon him, without understanding why.

'Me? I picked up the wallet?'

'Yes, you.'

'Honest, I don't know nothing about it.'

'You were seen.'

'I were seen? Who seen me?'

'Monsieur Malandain, the saddler.'

Then the old man remembered, understood, and flushed with anger.

'So he seen me, did he, the bastard! He seen me pick up this bit of string, Mayor – look!'

And rummaging in his pocket, he pulled out the little piece of string.

But the Mayor shook his head incredulously.

'You'll never persuade me, Maître Hauchecorne, that Monsieur Malandain, who is a man who can be trusted, mistook that piece of string for a wallet.'

The peasant angrily raised his hand and spat on the floor as proof of his good faith, repeating: 'But it's God's truth, honest it is! Not a word of it's a lie, so help me God!'

The Mayor went on: 'After picking up the object you even went on hunting about in the mud for some time to see whether some coin might not have fallen out.'

The old fellow was almost speechless with fear and indignation.

'Making up . . . making up . . . lies like that to damn an honest man! Making up lies like that!'

In spite of all his protestations the Mayor did not believe him.

He was confronted with Maître Malandain, who repeated and maintained his statement. They hurled insults at each other for an hour. Maître Hauchecorne was searched, at his own request. Nothing was found on him.

Finally the Mayor, not knowing what to think, sent him away, warning him that he was going to report the matter to the public prosecutor and ask for instructions.

The news had spread. As he left the town hall, the old man was surrounded by people who questioned him with a curiosity which was sometimes serious, sometimes ironical, but in which there was no indignation. He started telling the story of the piece of string. Nobody believed him. Everybody laughed.

As he walked along, other people stopped him, and he stopped his acquaintances, repeating his story and his protestations over and over again, and showing his pockets turned inside out to prove that he had got nothing.

Everybody said: 'Get along with you, you old rascal!'

And he lost his temper, irritated, angered and upset because nobody would believe him. Not knowing what to do, he simply went on repeating his story.

Darkness fell. It was time to go home. He set off with three of his neighbours to whom he pointed out the place where he had picked up the piece of string; and all the way home he talked of nothing else.

In the evening he took a turn round the village of Bréauté in order to tell everybody his story. He met with nothing but incredulity.

He felt ill all night as a result.

The next day, about one o'clock in the afternoon, Marius

Paumelle, a labourer on Maître Breton's farm at Ymauville, returned the wallet and its contents to Maître Houlbrèque of Manneville.

The man claimed to have found the object on the road; but, as he could not read, he had taken it home and given it to his employer.

The news spread round the neighbourhood and reached the ears of Maître Hauchecorne. He immediately went out and about repeating his story, this time with its sequel. He was triumphant.

'What really got my goat,' he said, 'wasn't so much the thing itself, if you see what I mean, but the lies. There's nothing worse than being blamed on account of a lie.'

He talked about his adventure all day; he told the story to people he met on the road, to people drinking in the inn, to people coming out of church the following Sunday. He stopped total strangers and told it to them. His mind was at rest now, and yet something still bothered him without his knowing exactly what it was. People seemed to be amused as they listened to him. They didn't appear to be convinced. He had the impression that remarks were being made behind his back.

The following Tuesday he went to the Goderville market, simply because he felt an urge to tell his story.

Malandain, standing at his door, burst out laughing when he saw him go by. Why?

He accosted a farmer from Criquetot, who didn't let him finish his story, but gave him a dig in the ribs and shouted at him: 'Go on, you old rogue!' Then he turned on his heels.

Maître Hauchecorne was taken aback and felt increasingly uneasy. Why had he been called an old rogue?

Once he had sat down at table in Jourdain's inn he started explaining the whole business all over again.

A horsedealer from Montivilliers called out to him: 'Get

along with you, you old rascal! I know your little game with the bit of string.'

Hauchecorne stammered: 'But they found the wallet!'

The other man retorted: 'Give over, Grandpa! Him as brings a thing back isn't always him as finds it. But mum's the word!'

The peasant was speechless. At last he understood. He was being accused of getting an accomplice to return the wallet.

He tried to protest, but the whole table burst out laughing.

He couldn't finish his meal, and went off in the midst of jeers and laughter.

He returned home ashamed and indignant, choking with anger and embarrassment, all the more upset in that he was quite capable, with his Norman cunning, of doing what he was accused of having done, and even of boasting of it as a clever trick. He dimly realized that, since his duplicity was widely known, it was impossible to prove his innocence. And the injustice of the suspicion cut him to the quick.

Then he began telling the story all over again, making it longer every day, adding fresh arguments at every telling, more energetic protestations, more solemn oaths, which he thought out and prepared in his hours of solitude, for he could think of nothing else but the incident of the piece of string. The more complicated his defence became, and the more subtle his arguments, the less people believed him.

'Them's a liar's arguments,' people used to say behind his back.

Realizing what was happening, he ate his heart out, exhausting himself in futile efforts.

He started visibly wasting away.

The local wags now used to get him to tell the story of the piece of string to amuse them, as people get an old soldier to talk about his battles. His mind, seriously affected, began to give way.

Towards the end of December he took to his bed.

He died early in January, and in the delirium of his death agony he kept on protesting his innocence, repeating over and over again: 'A bit of string . . . a little bit of string . . . look, Mayor, here it is . . .'

# THE MODEL

Curved like a crescent moon, the little town of Étretat, with its white cliffs, its white shingle and its blue sea, was dozing in the sunshine of a bright July day. At the two horns of the crescent the two gates jutted out into the calm water, the smaller on the right like a dwarf foot, the larger on the left like a giant leg; and the needle, broad at the base and tapering upwards almost to the height of the cliff, pointed its sharp tip towards the sky.

On the beach a crowd of people were sitting along the water's edge watching the bathers. On the Casino terrace another crowd was sitting or walking about under the cloudless sky, resembling a colourful garden with the ladies' bright dresses and the red and blue parasols embroidered with large silk flowers. And on the promenade at the end of the terrace some other people, the quiet, sedate members of the community, were sauntering up and down, far away from the elegant throng.

A young man called Jean Summer, well known as a painter of note, was walking glumly beside an invalid chair in which a young woman, his wife, was sitting. A manservant was slowly pushing the bathchair along, and the crippled woman was gazing sadly at the gay skies, the gay sunshine and the gay crowds.

They neither spoke nor looked at one another.

'Let's stop a minute,' said the woman.

They stopped, and the painter sat down on a folding stool which the manservant opened out for him.

The people passing behind the silent, motionless couple looked at them pityingly. Their devotion had become a local legend: he had married her in spite of her infirmity, touched by her love, people said.

Not far away two young men were sitting on a capstan, chatting and idly looking out to sea.

'No, it isn't true,' one of them said. 'I tell you I know Jean Summer very well.'

'Then why did he marry her? For she *was* already crippled at the time, wasn't she?'

'Yes, she was. He married her . . . he married her . . . for the reason men always marry, because he was a fool.'

'But there must have been some other reason . . .'

'Some other reason? My dear fellow, there's never any other reason. A man's a fool because he's a fool. Besides, as you know, painters make a speciality of ridiculous marriages. They nearly all marry models who have been their mistresses, damaged goods in every sense of the word. Why do they do it? Nobody knows. You would have thought that constant association with that breed of ninnies we call models would be bound to disgust them with that sort of female for good. But not a bit of it. They make them pose, and then they marry them. You ought to read that little book of Alphonse Daudet's, *Artists' Wives* – a wonderful book, so true to life and so cruel.

'In the case of the couple you see over there, it was a unique and terrible occurrence which brought about their marriage. The woman acted a comedy, or rather a terrifying drama. In fact she staked everything on a single throw. Was she sincere? Did she really love Jean? Who can tell in a case like that? Who can ever distinguish with any degree of precision between true and false in women's acts? They are always sincere, but their emotions are forever changing. They are passionate, criminal, devoted, admirable and ignoble, in response to fleeting emotions. They tell lies all the time, without meaning to, without knowing, and without understanding; yet with all this, and in spite of all this, they have an absolute honesty of emotion and feeling which they display in decisions which are violent, unexpected, incomprehensible and irrational, decisions which defeat all our reasoning, all our habits of caution, and all our selfish plans. And because their resolutions are so sudden and unexpected, they remain indecipherable riddles to us men. We are always asking ourselves: "Are they sincere, or are they being deceitful?"

'The fact is, my dear fellow, they are sincere and deceitful at one and the same time, because it is in their nature to be both to an extreme degree and yet to be neither.

'Look at the methods the most honest of women use to get what they want out of us. Those methods are both complicated and simple. So complicated that we never guess them in advance, yet so simple that after falling victim to them we can't help feeling surprised and saying to ourselves: "What! Did she fool me as easily as that?"

'And they always get their own way, old chap, especially when it's a question of getting us to marry them.

'But let me tell you Summer's story.

'The woman was a model, of course. She used to pose for him. She was a pretty girl, and elegant too, and by all accounts she had a wonderful figure. He fell in love with her, as a man tends to fall in love with any attractive woman he sees a lot of. He persuaded himself that he loved her with his whole heart and soul. That's a curious phenomenon, you know: as soon as a man wants a woman, he genuinely believes that he'll never be able to do without her for the rest of his life. He knows perfectly well that the same thing has happened to him before and that possession has always been followed by disgust; that to spend one's whole existence with another human being, one needs to feel, not a crude physical appetite, which is soon extinguished, but a kinship of soul, temperament and character. In the desire one feels, one has to be able to tell whether it is the result of physical beauty, a certain intoxication of the senses, or a profound intellectual attraction.

'Anyway, he imagined that he loved her; he swore fidelity to her a thousand times over; and he set up house with her.

'She was a sweet little thing, endowed with that charming silliness Paris girls acquire so easily. She chattered and babbled and said a lot of silly things which seemed witty because of the amusing way she put them. She was forever making some graceful gesture calculated to charm a painter's eye. Whenever she raised her arms, bent down, got into a carriage or offered you her hand, her movements were perfectly right and fitting.

'For three months Jean lived with her without seeing that she was really just like any other model.

'They rented a little house at Andressy for the summer.

'I was there, one evening, when the first doubts began to take shape in my friend's mind.

'As it was a glorious night, we decided to go for a walk by the river. The moon was pouring its radiance on to the shimmering waters, where its golden reflexions were broken up by the eddies and currents of the broad, slow-moving stream.

'We strolled along the river bank, a little intoxicated by that vague feeling of excitement which is often produced by a wonderful evening like that. We felt a longing to perform superhuman feats and fall in love with mysterious, delightfully poetic creatures. We could sense within us the stirring of strange ecstasies, desires and aspirations. And we said nothing, awed by the calm, living freshness of that delightful night, by the cool moonlight which seemed to go right through us, penetrating the body and steeping and scenting the soul in waves of bliss.

'All of a sudden Joséphine – for that's her name – cried out: "Oh! Did you see that big fish jump over there?"

'He replied without looking or thinking: "Yes, darling."

'She lost her temper.

' "No, you didn't," she said, "because you had your back to it."

' "You're right," he said with a smile. "It's such a wonderful night that I wasn't thinking of anything."

'She made no reply, but a minute later she felt an urge to talk, and she asked: "Are you going to Paris tomorrow?"

' "I've no idea," he replied.

'She got annoyed again.

' "If you think it's amusing," she said, "walking with somebody who never says a word! People talk unless they're absolutely stupid."

'He said nothing. Then, realizing with her perverse feminine intuition that it would exasperate him, she began singing that irritating song which has been dinned into our ears and driven us mad for the past two years: "I was looking in the air."

'He murmured: "Oh, do be quiet."

'She retorted furiously: "Why should I be quiet?"

'He replied: "You're spoiling the scenery for us."

'Then there was the inevitable scene, the usual stupid, hateful scene, with unexpected reproaches, tactless recriminations, and finally tears. She ran through the whole gamut. Then they went home. He had let her rant away without interruption, mesmerized by the beauty of the evening and dumbfounded by the woman's stupid reproaches.

'Three months later he was struggling frantically in the invisible, unbreakable bonds which a liaison like that weaves around us. She held him fast, tormenting him and making his life a martyrdom. They quarrelled from morning till night, hurling insults at each other and fighting like cat and dog.

'Finally he decided to put an end to it and break with her at all costs. He sold all his canvases, borrowed some money from his friends, raised twenty thousand francs – he had not made his name at the time – and left them on the mantelpiece one morning with a farewell letter.

'He took refuge at my place.

'About three o'clock in the afternoon the bell rang. I went and opened the door. A woman rushed at me, pushed me aside, and went straight into my studio: it was Joséphine.

'He stood up as soon as he saw her.

'She threw the envelope containing the banknotes at his feet with a truly noble gesture and said curtly: "There's your money. I don't want it."

'She was trembling and very pale, obviously ready to commit some act of folly. As for him, I saw him turn pale too, pale with anger and annoyance, ready perhaps to commit some act of violence.

'He asked: "What do you want?"

'She replied: "I don't want to be treated like a whore. You begged for me and you took me. I didn't ask for anything in return. Now keep me!"

'He stamped his foot.

' "No, this is too much!" he said. "If you think you're going to . . ."

'I had grabbed his arm.

' "Stop it, Jean. Leave this to me."

'I went over to her and gently, patiently, reasoned with her, putting forward all the usual arguments people use in such cases. She listened to me without moving, staring in front of her, silent and stubborn.

'Finally, not knowing what else to say, and seeing that things looked bad, I hit on a last argument. I said: "He still loves you, my dear; but his family wants him to get married, and ... you understand!"

'She gave a start.

' "Oh!... Now I understand ..."

'And turning towards him, she said: "So you're ... you're going to get married?"

'He replied bluntly: "Yes."

'She took a step forward.

' "If you get married, I'll kill myself.... Do you hear?"

'He shrugged his shoulders and retorted: "All right.... Kill yourself."

'Choking with anguish, she stammered: "You ... you ... you ... say that again."

'He repeated: "All right, kill yourself if you want to."

'Still looking alarmingly pale, she went on: "Don't dare me to do it. I'll throw myself out of the window."

'He started laughing, went over to the window, and opened it. Then, bowing like a man politely letting somebody go first, he said: "This way. After you!"

'She stared at him for a moment with a mad, terrible look in her eyes; then, taking a run as if she were going to jump over a hedge, she dashed past us both, cleared the balustrade, and disappeared.

'I shall never forget the effect that open window had on me after I had seen the falling body pass across it; it suddenly seemed as big as the sky and as empty as space. I stepped back instinctively, not daring to look down, as if I were going to fall out myself.

'Jean stood motionless, dazed with horror.

'The poor girl was carried in with both legs broken. She'll never walk again.

'Her lover, mad with remorse, and perhaps also feeling that he owed her something, took her back and married her.

'Well, that's the story, old chap.'

Dusk was falling. The young woman, feeling chilly, wanted to go home, and the servant began pushing the invalid chair back towards the village. The painter walked beside his wife; they had not said a single word to each other for an hour.

# THE HAND

A CIRCLE had formed round Monsieur Bermutier, the examining magistrate, who was giving his opinion about the mysterious Saint-Cloud affair, an inexplicable crime which had been the talk of Paris for a month. Nobody could make head or tail of it.

Standing with his back to the fireplace, Monsieur Bermutier talked on and on, marshalling the evidence, discussing the various theories, but coming to no conclusion.

Several ladies had left their chairs to come closer, and stood around him, their eyes fixed on the magistrate's clean-shaven lips uttering the weighty words. They shuddered and trembled, thrilled by that curious fear, that eager, insatiable longing for terror which haunts all women and tortures them like the pangs of hunger.

One of them, paler than the rest, broke a sudden silence to say: 'It's horrifying. There's something supernatural about it. We'll never know what really happened.'

The magistrate turned to her.

'Yes, Madame,' he said. 'We'll probably never know what really happened. But as for the word "supernatural" which you used just now, it has no place in this affair. We are dealing with a crime which was cleverly planned, ably carried out, and so wrapped in mystery that we cannot disengage it from the impenetrable circumstances surrounding it. But I once had to investigate a case which really seemed to have something weird about it. We had to abandon the investigation, as a matter of fact, for lack of evidence.'

Several ladies exclaimed with one voice: 'Oh, do tell us about it!'

Monsieur Bermutier gave a grave smile befitting an examining magistrate, and went on:

'At least do not imagine that even for a single moment I myself have ever considered that there was anything supernatural about the case in question. I believe only in natural causes. It would be much better if we used the word "inexplicable" instead of "supernatural" to describe things we do not understand. In any case, what really struck me in the affair I am going to tell you about was the circumstances leading up to and surrounding it. But now for the facts.

'At that time I was examining magistrate at Ajaccio, a little white town situated on the shore of a wonderful bay surrounded on all sides by high mountains.

'My chief task there was the investigation of vendettas. Some of those affairs are superb, ferocious, heroic, incredibly dramatic. They offer us the most splendid stories of revenge imaginable, age-old hatreds appeased for a while but never extinguished, abominable stratagems, murders which are really massacres, and wellnigh heroic feats. For two years I had heard about nothing but the price of blood, nothing but that terrible Corsican tradition which forces a man who has been wronged to wreak vengeance not only on the man who has wronged him, but also on his descendants and his relatives. I had known of old men, children and distant cousins who had had their throats slit, and my head was full of such stories.

'Well, one day I learned that an Englishman had just taken a lease for several years of a little villa at the far end of the bay. He had brought with him a French manservant whom he had taken into his service while passing through Marseilles.

'Before long everybody was talking about this strange individual, who lived alone in his house and never went out except to shoot and fish. He spoke to nobody, never came into the town, and practised for an hour or two every morning with a pistol and a carbine.

'Legends grew up about him. Some held that he was an eminent personage who had fled his country for political reasons, while others alleged that he was in hiding after committing an appalling crime of which they gave peculiarly gruesome details.

'In my capacity as examining magistrate I naturally tried to find out what I could about this man, but it proved impossible to discover anything except that he went by the name of Sir John Rowell.

'I had to be satisfied with keeping a close watch upon him, but nothing suspicious was reported to me about him.

'However, as the rumours about him continued, becoming more widespread as time went on, I decided to try and see this foreigner for myself, and I accordingly took to shooting regularly in the vicinity of his property.

'I had to wait a long time for the opportunity I needed. It came at last in the shape of a partridge which I shot under the Englishman's very nose. My dog brought me the dead bird, but I took it straight away to Sir John and asked him to accept it, apologizing at the same time for my bad manners.

'He was a big red-headed, red-bearded man, very tall and very broad, a sort of polite, easy-going Hercules. He had none of the traditional British stiffness, and, speaking with a pronounced English accent, he thanked me warmly for my courtesy. By the time a month had passed we had chatted together five or six times.

'One evening, as I was passing his door, I caught sight

of him sitting astride a chair in his garden, smoking his pipe. I greeted him, and he asked me in for a glass of beer. I didn't wait to be asked twice.

'He received me with all the punctilious courtesy of the English and spoke highly of both France and Corsica, declaring that he was very fond of that country and that particular stretch of coast.

'Proceeding very cautiously, and pretending a keen interest, I took the opportunity to question him about his life and his plans for the future. He answered readily enough, and told me that he had travelled a great deal in Africa, India and America. He added with a laugh: "Oh, yes, I've had plenty of adventures."

'Then I started talking about shooting, and he gave me the most curious details about hunting the hippopotamus, the tiger, the elephant and even the gorilla.

' "Those are all dangerous animals," I said.

' "Yes," he said with a smile, "but the worst of all is man."

'He suddenly burst out laughing, the laughter of a big, genial Englishman.

' "I've done a lot of man-hunting, too," he said.

'Then he talked about firearms and invited me into his house to show me guns of different types.

'The walls in his drawing-room were hung with black silk and embroidered in gold. Huge yellow flowers spread across the dark material, blazing like fire.

' "That's a Japanese fabric," he said.

'In the middle of the largest panel a strange object caught my eye. On a square of red velvet something black stood out clearly. I went closer: it was a hand, a human hand. Not the hand of a skeleton, white and clean, but a black, dried-up hand, with yellow nails. The muscles had been laid bare, and there were traces of dried blood like dirt on the bones, which had been cut clean through, as if with an axe, about the middle of the forearm.

'Round the wrist of this unclean member a heavy iron chain was riveted and soldered, fastening it to the wall by a ring strong enough to tether an elephant.

'"What's that?" I asked.

'"That was my worst enemy," the Englishman replied calmly. "He was an American. His hand was cut off with a sabre, skinned with a sharp stone, and dried in the sun for a week. That was a stroke of luck for me, and no mistake."

'I touched that human relic, which must have belonged to a giant of a man. The fingers were abnormally long and were joined together by huge sinews to which, in places, strips of skin were still adhering. That flayed hand was a terrible sight, suggesting some savage act of vengeance.

'"He must have been a very strong man," I said.

'"Oh yes," the Englishman replied quietly, "but I was stronger. I put that chain on to hold him fast."

'I thought he was joking and said: "There's no need for the chain now. The hand isn't going to run away."

'Sir John answered quite seriously: "It's always trying to get away. That chain is necessary."

'I shot a quick, inquiring look at him, wondering whether he was mad or just joking. But his face remained inscrutable, calm and benevolent. I changed the subject and admired his guns.

'However, I noticed that there were three loaded revolvers lying on various pieces of furniture, as if the man were living in constant fear of attack.

'I went to see him again several times. Then I stopped going. People had become accustomed to his presence and nobody took any interest in him any more.

'A whole year went by. Then, one morning towards the end of November, my servant woke me with the news that Sir John Rowell had been murdered during the night.

'Half an hour later I entered the Englishman's house with the superintendent of police and the captain of the local gendarmes. Sir John's valet was weeping outside the door, utterly distraught. At first I suspected him, but he was innocent. The murderer was never found.

'Going into the drawing-room, the first thing I saw was the corpse lying on its back in the middle of the floor.

'Sir John's waistcoat was torn and one sleeve of his coat had been practically torn off. There was every indication of a terrible struggle.

'The Englishman had been strangled. His black, swollen face was a horrible sight, and it bore an expression of appalling terror. His teeth were clenched on some object and in his neck which was covered with blood there were five holes which looked as if they had been made with iron spikes.

'We were joined by the doctor. He made a lengthy examination of the fingermarks in the flesh of the dead man's neck and then uttered these strange words: "It looks as if he had been strangled by a skeleton."

'A shiver ran down my spine, and I glanced at the wall where I had been accustomed to seeing the horrible flayed hand. The hand was no longer there. The chain had been broken and was hanging loose.

'Then I bent down to examine the corpse. Between its clenched teeth I found one of the fingers of the vanished hand, cut off, or rather bitten off, at the second joint.

'We proceeded to make a careful examination of the premises, but found nothing. No door or window had been forced, no piece of furniture broken into. The two watch-dogs had slept through the night undisturbed.

'This, in a few words, is the gist of the servant's evidence:

'For the past month, he told us, his master had seemed to be worried about something. He had received a great many letters, which he had burnt as soon as they arrived. Often he would take a horse-whip, and, in a fit of rage which looked like insanity, he would lash furiously at that withered hand which had been riveted to the wall and which, at the time of the crime, had mysteriously disappeared.

'He went to bed very late and carefully locked himself in his room. He always had firearms within reach. And during the night he could often be heard talking loudly as if he were quarrelling with somebody.

'On the night in question, however, he had made no sound, and it was only when his servant had come to open the windows the next morning that he had found Sir John murdered. He could think of nobody who might have committed the crime.

'I communicated everything I knew about the dead man to the magistrates and the police and a painstaking investigation was carried out throughout the island. It was all in vain.

'Well, one night, three months after the crime, I had a terrifying nightmare. I dreamed that I saw the hand, that horrible hand, running like a scorpion or a spider across my curtains and walls. Three times I woke up; three times I fell asleep again; three times I saw that hideous relic galloping round my room, using its fingers as legs.

'The next day it was brought to me. It had been found in the cemetery, on Sir John's grave – for he had been buried there after all attempts to trace his family had failed. The index finger was missing.

'That, ladies, is my story. That is all I know about the affair.'

The ladies were horrified, pale and trembling. One of them exclaimed: 'But that's no way to end a story! You haven't given us any explanation. We shall never be able to sleep unless you tell us your own theory as to what happened.'

The magistrate gave a grim smile.

'I'm afraid, ladies, that I'm going to spoil your terrifying dreams. My theory is simply that the rightful owner of the hand was not dead at all, and that he came looking for it with the hand he had left. But I have no idea how he managed it. The whole thing was a sort of vendetta.'

One of the ladies murmured: 'No, that can't be the explanation.'

And the magistrate, still smiling, concluded: 'I told you that you wouldn't like my theory.'

# IDYLL

THE train had just left Genoa on its way to Marseilles, and was following the long curves of the rocky coast, gliding like an iron snake between the sea and the mountains, creeping over the beaches of yellow sand edged with silver by the little waves, and plunging abruptly into the black-mouthed tunnels like an animal into its lair.

In the last carriage a stout woman and a young man sat facing each other, not saying a word, but glancing at each other now and then. She was about twenty-five, and sat next to the door, looking out at the scenery. She was a heavily built peasant woman from Piedmont, with dark eyes, a full bosom and fat cheeks. She had pushed several parcels under the wooden seat and was holding a basket on her knees.

The young man was about twenty. He was thin and sunburnt, with the dark complexion which comes from working in the fields in the blazing sun. Beside him, tied up in a kerchief, were his entire possessions: a pair of shoes, a shirt, a pair of breeches and a jacket. Under the seat he had hidden a pick and shovel tied together with a piece of rope. He was going to France to look for work.

The sun, rising in the sky, poured a rain of fire on to the coast. It was towards the end of May, and delightful odours were wafted into the railway carriages through the open windows. The orange-trees and lemon-trees were in flower, exhaling into the peaceful sky their sweet, heavy, disturbing scents, mingling them with the perfume of the roses which grew in profusion everywhere along the track, in the gardens of the rich, at the doors of tumbledown cottages, and in the open country too.

Roses are so very much at home along this coast! They fill the whole region with their light yet powerful fragrance and turn the very air into a delicacy, something tastier than wine and no less intoxicating.

The train was travelling slowly, as if to linger in this luxuriant garden. It kept stopping continually at little stations, in front of a few white houses, then set off again at a leisurely pace, after emitting a long whistle. Nobody ever got on. It was as if the whole world was dozing gently, reluctant to travel anywhere on that hot spring morning.

Every now and then the plump woman shut her eyes, only to open them suddenly whenever she felt her basket slipping off her lap. She would catch hold of it, look out of the window for a few minutes, then doze off again. Beads of sweat covered her forehead and she was breathing with difficulty, as if she were suffering from a painful constriction.

The young man had let his head fall forward on his chest and was sleeping the sound sleep of the countryman.

All of a sudden, as the train was leaving a little station, the peasant woman seemed to wake up; and, opening her basket, she took out a hunk of bread, some hard-boiled eggs, a flask of wine and some fine red plums. Then she started eating.

The man too had woken up suddenly and watched her eat, following every morsel as it travelled from her knees to her lips. He sat there hollow-cheeked, his arms folded, his eyes set, his lips pressed together.

The woman ate like a glutton, taking a swig of wine every now and then to wash down the eggs, and stopping occasionally to get her breath back.

Everything disappeared, the bread, the eggs, the plums,

the wine. As soon as she had finished her meal the man closed his eyes again. Then, feeling a little uncomfortable, she loosened her bodice, and the man suddenly looked at her again.

She took no notice but went on unbuttoning her dress. The pressure of her bosom stretched the material so that as the opening grew larger it revealed, between her breasts, a little white linen and a little flesh.

When she felt more comfortable the peasant woman said in Italian: 'It's so hot you can hardly breathe.'

The young man replied in the same language and with the same pronunciation: 'It's fine weather for travelling.'

'Do you come from Piedmont?' she asked.

'I'm from Asti.'

'And I'm from Casale.'

They were neighbours. They started chatting together.

They exchanged the long commonplace remarks which working people repeat over and over again and which are all-sufficient for their slow-moving and limited minds. They spoke of their homes and found that they had a number of common acquaintances. They quoted names, becoming friendlier every time they discovered another person they both knew. Rapid, hurried words with sonorous endings and the Italian intonation poured from their lips.

Then they talked about themselves. She was married and already had three children whom she had left with her sister, for she had found a situation as a wet-nurse, a good situation with a French lady in Marseilles.

He for his part was looking for work. He had been told that he would find some in Marseilles too, for they were doing a lot of building there.

Then they fell silent.

The heat was becoming terrible, beating down on the

roofs of the railway carriages. A cloud of dust rose in the air behind the train and came in through the windows; and the scent of the roses and orange-trees had become stronger, heavier and more penetrating.

The two travellers fell asleep once more.

They opened their eyes again almost at the same time. The sun was sinking towards the sea, pouring its light over the blue waters. It was cooler and the air seemed lighter.

The wet-nurse was panting for breath. Her dress was open, her cheeks looked flabby, and her eyes were dull.

'I haven't given milk since yesterday,' she said disconsolately. 'I feel as if I'm going to faint.'

He made no reply, not knowing what to say. She went on: 'When a woman's got as much milk as me, she's got to give it three times a day or she feels real bad. It's like a weight on my heart, it is; a weight that stops me breathing and makes me feel all limp. It's a terrible thing, having as much milk as that.'

'Yes,' he said. 'It must be very hard on you.'

She did indeed look quite ill, as if she were about to faint.

'I've only got to press on them,' she murmured, 'and the milk comes out like a fountain. It's a queer sight, and no mistake. You wouldn't believe it. At Casale all the neighbours used to come to watch.'

'Really?' he said.

'Yes, really. I wouldn't mind showing you, but it wouldn't do me any good. You can't make enough come out that way.'

And she fell silent.

The train stopped at a halt. Standing by a gate was a woman holding a crying infant in her arms. She was thin and dressed in rags.

'There's another woman I could help. And the baby

could help me too. Look here, I'm not well off, seeing as I'm leaving my home and family and my last little darling to go into service; but all the same, I'd willingly give five francs to have that baby for ten minutes so I could feed it. That would calm it down and me too. I think I'd feel a new woman.'

She fell silent once more. Then she passed her hot hand several times over her forehead, which was dripping with sweat, and groaned: 'I can't stand it any more. I feel as if I'm going to die.'

And with an unconscious gesture she opened her dress all the way.

The right breast appeared, huge and taut, with its brown nipple; and the poor woman moaned: 'Oh, dear! Oh, dear! What am I going to do?'

The train had moved off again and was continuing its journey amid the flowers which were giving off the pene-trating fragrance they exhale on warm evenings. Now and then a fishing boat came in sight which seemed to be asleep on the blue sea, with its motionless white sail reflected in the water as if another boat were there upside down.

The young man, looking very embarrassed, stammered: 'But ... Madame ... I might be able ... be able to help you.'

In a tired voice she replied: 'Yes, if you like. You'd be doing me a good turn, you would that. I can't stand it any more, really I can't.'

He knelt down in front of her, and she bent forward, pushing the dark tip of her breast towards his mouth as if he were a baby. In the movement she made to hold out her breast with both hands towards the man a drop of milk appeared on the nipple. He licked it up eagerly, gripped the heavy breast between his lips as if it had been a fruit, and began sucking regularly and greedily.

He had put his arms around the woman's waist to press her close to him; and he drunk slowly and steadily, with a movement of the neck like that of a baby.

Suddenly she said: 'That's enough for that one. Now take the other.'

And he obediently moved to the other breast.

She had placed both hands on the young man's back and was now breathing deeply and happily, enjoying the scent of the flowers mingled with the gusts of air blown into the carriages by the movement of the train.

'It smells nice round here,' she said.

He made no reply, but went on drinking at the fountain of her breast, closing his eyes as if to enjoy it better.

But then she gently pushed him away.

'That's enough, I feel better now. That's put new life into me.'

He had stood up, wiping his mouth with the back of his hand.

Pushing her breasts back inside her dress, she said: 'That was a real good turn you did me, Monsieur. Thank you very much.'

And he replied gratefully: 'It's me as has to thank you, Madame. I hadn't had a thing to eat for two days.'

# MOTHER SAVAGE

I HAD not been back to Virelogne for fifteen years. I returned there to do some shooting in the autumn, staying with my friend Serval, who had finally rebuilt his château, which had been destroyed by the Prussians.

I was terribly fond of that part of the country. There are some delightful places in this world which have a sensual charm for the eyes. One loves them with a physical love. We people who are attracted by the countryside cherish fond memories of certain springs, certain woods, certain ponds, certain hills, which have become familiar sights and can touch our hearts like happy events. Sometimes indeed the memory goes back towards a forest glade, or a spot on a river bank, or an orchard in blossom, glimpsed only once on a happy day, but preserved in our heart like those pictures of women seen in the street on a spring morning, wearing gay, flimsy dresses, and which leave in our soul and flesh an unappeased, unforgettable desire, the feeling that happiness has passed us by.

At Virelogne I loved the whole region, scattered with little woods and crossed by streams which ran through the ground like veins carrying blood to the earth. We fished in them for crayfish, trout and eels. What heavenly happiness we knew there! There were certain places where we could bathe, and we often found snipe in the tall grass which grew on the banks of those narrow brooks.

I walked along, as light-footed as a goat, watching my two dogs foraging ahead of me. Serval, a hundred yards to my right, was beating a field of lucerne. I went round the bushes which mark the edge of Saudres woods, and I noticed a cottage in ruins.

All of a sudden I remembered it as it had been the last time I had seen it, in 1869, neat, covered with vines, with chickens outside the door. What is sadder than a dead house, with nothing left standing but its skeleton, a sinister ruin?

I remembered too that a woman had given me a glass of wine inside the house, one day when I was very tired, and that afterwards Serval had told me the story of the occupants. The father, an old poacher, had been killed by the gendarmes. The son, whom I had seen before, was a tall, wiry fellow who was likewise supposed to be a ferocious killer of game. People called the family the Savages.

Was it a name or a nickname?

I called out to Serval. He came over to me with his long lanky stride. I asked him: 'What has become of the people who lived here?'

And he told me this story.

'When war was declared, the younger Savage, who was then thirty-three years old, enlisted, leaving his mother alone at home. People didn't feel too sorry for the old woman, though, because they knew she had money.

'So she stayed all alone in this isolated house, far away from the village, on the edge of the woods. But she wasn't afraid, because she was made of the same stuff as her men, a tough, tall, thin old woman, who didn't laugh very often and whom nobody joked with. Country women don't laugh much anyway. That's the men's business! They have sad, narrow souls, because they lead dull, dreary lives. The peasant learns a little noisy gaiety in the tavern, but his wife remains serious, forever wearing a stern expression.

The muscles of her face have never learnt the motions of laughter.

'Mother Savage continued to lead her usual life in her cottage, which was soon covered with snow. She came to the village once a week to get bread and a little meat; then she returned to her cottage. As there was talk of wolves in the region, she went out with a gun slung over her shoulder, her son's gun, which was rusty, with the butt worn down by the rubbing of the hand. She was a strange sight, the Savage woman, tall, rather bent, striding slowly through the snow, with the barrel of the gun showing above the tight black head-dress which imprisoned the white hair nobody had ever seen.

'One day the Prussians arrived. They were distributed among the local inhabitants according to the means and resources of each. The old woman, who was known to be well off, had four soldiers billeted on her.

'They were four big young fellows with fair skins, fair beards and blue eyes, who had remained quite plump in spite of the hardships they had already endured, and good-natured even though they were in conquered territory. Alone with that old woman, they showed her every consideration, sparing her fatigue and expense as best they could. All four were to be seen washing at the well every morning in their shirt-sleeves, splashing water, in the cold glare of the snow, over their pink and white flesh, the flesh of men of the north, while Mother Savage went to and fro, cooking their soup. They could then be seen cleaning the kitchen, polishing the floor, chopping wood, peeling potatoes, washing the linen, and doing all the household jobs, just like four good sons helping their mother.

'But the old woman kept thinking all the time about her own son, her tall thin boy with his hooked nose, his brown eyes, and the bushy moustache which covered his upper lip with a roll of black hair. Every day she asked each of the soldiers sitting around her hearth: "Do you know where the French regiment has gone – the Twenty-third Infantry? My boy is in it."

'They would reply: "No, we don't know. We have no idea."

'And, understanding her grief and anxiety, they, who had mothers of their own at home, performed countless little services for her. She for her part was quite fond of her four enemies, for peasants scarcely ever feel patriotic hatred: that is the prerogative of the upper classes. The humble, those who pay the most because they are poor and because every new burden weighs heavily on them, those who are killed in droves, who form the real cannon-fodder because they are the most numerous, who, in a word, suffer the most from the atrocious hardships of war because they are the weakest and most vulnerable, find it hard to understand those bellicose impulses, those touchy points of honour and those so-called political manoeuvres which exhaust two nations within six months, the victor as well as the vanquished.

'The people around here, speaking of Mother Savage's Germans, used to say: "Those four have found a cosy billet, and no mistake."

'Now, one morning, when the old woman was alone in the house, she caught sight of a man a long way off on the plain coming towards her home. Soon she recognized him: it was the man whose job it was to deliver letters. He handed her a folded piece of paper, and she took the spectacles she used for sewing out of their case. Then she read:

Madame Savage, this is to give you some sad news. Your son Victor was killed yesterday by a cannon-ball which pretty well cut him in two. I was very close, seeing as we were side by side in the company, and he had asked me to let you know if anything happened to him.

I took his watch out of his pocket to bring it back to you when the war is over.

Best regards.

CÉSAIRE RIVOT,<br>Private in the 23rd Infantry.

'The letter was dated three weeks earlier.

'She didn't cry. She stood stock still, so shocked and dazed that she didn't even feel any grief yet. She thought to herself: "Now it's Victor who's gone and got killed." Then, little by little, the tears came into her eyes and grief flooded into her heart. Ideas occurred to her one by one, horrible, agonizing ideas. She would never kiss him again, her big boy, never! The gendarmes had killed the father, the Prussians had killed the son. He had been cut in two by a cannon-ball. And it seemed to her that she could see the horrible thing happening: the head falling, the eyes wide open, while he was chewing the end of his bushy moustache as he always did when he was angry.

'What had they done with his body afterwards? If only they had sent her boy back to her, as they had sent back her husband, with the bullet in the middle of his forehead!

'But then she heard the sound of voices. It was the Prussians coming back from the village. She quickly hid the letter in her pocket and, having had time to wipe her eyes, greeted them calmly, looking her usual self.

'All four of them were laughing with delight, for they had brought back a fine rabbit, which had probably been stolen, and they made signs to the old woman that they were going to eat something good.

'She set to work straight away getting dinner ready, but when it came to killing the rabbit, her heart failed her.

269

And it wasn't the first by any means! One of the soldiers had to kill it with a punch behind the ears.

'Once the animal was dead she stripped the skin from the red body; but the sight of the blood which she was touching, which covered her hands, the warm blood which she could feel growing cold and congealing, made her tremble from head to foot; and she kept seeing her big boy cut in two and red all over, like the animal still quivering in her hands.

'She sat down to table with her Prussians, but she couldn't eat, not so much as a mouthful. They devoured the rabbit without bothering about her. She watched them on the sly, without speaking, thinking over an idea, her face so expressionless that they noticed nothing.

'Suddenly she said: "We've been together a whole month now and I don't even know your names."

'They understood, not without some difficulty, what she wanted, and gave her their names. But that wasn't enough: she got them to write them down for her on a piece of paper, with the addresses of their families; and, setting her spectacles on her big nose, she inspected the unfamiliar script and then folded the sheet of paper and put it in her pocket, with the letter which had told her of the death of her son.

'When the meal was over, she said to the men: "I'm going to do some work for you."

'And she started taking straw up to the loft in which they slept.

'They were puzzled by what she was doing. She explained to them that the straw would keep them warmer, and they gave her a helping hand. They piled the bundles of straw up to the roof and thus made themselves a sort of big, warm, sweet-smelling room with four walls of forage, where they would sleep wonderfully well.

'At supper one of them was upset to see that Mother Savage didn't eat anything again. She said that she was suffering from cramps. Then she lit a good fire to warm herself, and the four Germans climbed up to their room by the ladder which they used every evening.

'As soon as the trap-door was closed, the old woman took away the ladder. Then she quietly opened the outside door and went out to fetch some more bundles of straw with which she filled the kitchen. She walked barefoot in the snow, moving so quietly that the men heard nothing. Every now and then she listened to the loud, uneven snores of the four sleeping soldiers.

'When she decided her preparations were sufficient, she threw one of the bundles of straw into the hearth, and when it had caught fire she scattered it over the others. Then she went outside and watched.

'Within a few seconds a blinding glare lit up the whole inside of the cottage. Then it became a fearful brazier, a gigantic furnace, the light of which shone through the narrow window and fell on the snow in a dazzling ray.

'Then a great cry came from the top of the house, followed by a clamour of human screams, of heartrending shrieks of anguish and terror. Then, as the trap-door collapsed inside the cottage, a whirlwind of fire shot into the loft, pierced the thatched roof, and rose into the sky like the flame of a huge torch; and the whole cottage went up in flames.

'Nothing more could be heard inside but the crackling of the flames, the crumbling of the walls and the crashing of the beams. All of a sudden the roof fell in, and the glowing carcase of the house was hurled up into the air amid a cloud of smoke, a great fountain of sparks.

'The white countryside, lit up by fire, glistened like a cloth of silver tinted with red.

'In the distance a bell began ringing.

'Old Mother Savage remained standing in front of her burnt-out home, armed with her gun, her son's gun, for fear that one of the men should escape.

'When she saw that it was all over, she threw the weapon in the fire. An explosion rang out.

'People came running up, peasants and Prussians.

'They found the woman sitting on a tree trunk, calm and satisfied.

'A German officer, who spoke French like a Frenchman, asked her: "Where are your soldiers?"

'She stretched out her thin arm towards the red heap of the dying fire, and replied in a loud voice: "In there!"

'They crowded around her. The Prussian asked: "How did the fire break out?"

'"I started it," she said.

'They didn't believe her, thinking that the disaster had driven her mad all of a sudden. So, as everyone gathered around her to listen to her, she told the story from beginning to end, from the arrival of the letter to the last screams of the men who had been burnt with her house. She didn't leave out a single detail of what she had felt or of what she had done.

'When she had finished, she took two pieces of paper out of her pocket, and, in order to tell them apart, put on her spectacles again. Then, showing one of them, she said: "This one is Victor's death."

'Showing the other, and nodding in the direction of the red ruins, she added: "This one is their names so as you can write to their families."

'She calmly held out the white sheet of paper to the officer, who was holding her by the shoulders, and went on: "You must write to say what happened, and tell their parents that it was me that did it. Victoire Simon, the Savage woman! Don't forget."

'The officer shouted out some orders in German. She was seized and pushed against the walls of the house, which were still warm. Then twelve men lined up quickly facing her, at a distance of twenty yards. She didn't budge. She had understood, and stood there waiting.

'An order rang out, followed straight away by a long volley. A late shot went off by itself, after the others.

'The old woman didn't fall. She collapsed as if her legs had been chopped off.

'The Prussian officer came over to her. She had been practically cut in two, and in her hand she was clutching her letter soaked in blood.'

My friend Serval added: 'It was by way of a reprisal that the Germans destroyed the local château, which belonged to me.'

I for my part was thinking of the mothers of the four gentle boys burnt in there, and of the fearful heroism of that other mother, shot against that wall.

And I picked up a little stone, still blackened by the fire.

# GUILLEMOT ROCK

THIS is the guillemot season.

During the months of April and May, before the bathers arrive from Paris, one may observe, at the little seaside resort of Étretat, the sudden appearance of a few old gentlemen in high boots and tight-fitting shooting-coats. They spend four or five days at the Hôtel Hauville, disappear, come back three weeks later, then, after a second stay, go off for good.

They return the following spring.

These are the last hunters of the guillemot, the survivors of the hunters of bygone days; for thirty or forty years ago there were a score of these enthusiasts, but now there are only a few fanatical shots left.

The guillemot is an extremely rare migrant with curious habits. For nearly the whole of the year it lives in the neighbourhood of Newfoundland and the islands of Saint-Pierre and Miquelon; but at the mating season a band of emigrants cross the Atlantic every year and come to lay their eggs and hatch them out on the same spot, the rock known as Guillemot Rock, near Étretat. They are never to be found anywhere else. They have always come there, they have always been shot there, and still they come back; they will always come back. As soon as the young birds have been raised they set off again and disappear for another year.

Why do they never go anywhere else, choose some other point on that long white cliff which runs from Calais to Le Havre and which looks the same from one end to the other? What force, what irresistible instinct, what age-old habit drives these birds to return to this place? What initial emigration, what storm perhaps, cast their ancestors long ago on to this rock? And why have the children, the grand-children and all the descendants of the first-comers always returned there?

There are not many of them, a hundred at the most, as if only one family observed this tradition, performed this annual pilgrimage.

And every spring, as soon as the little wandering tribe is reinstalled on its rock, the same hunters likewise reappear in the village. Once the local people knew them as young men; now they are old, but they still keep the rendezvous they have been keeping for thirty or forty years.

They would not miss it for the world.

It was an April evening a few years ago. Three of the old guillemot hunters had just arrived; one was missing – Monsieur d'Arnelles.

He had written to nobody, given no news of himself. But he was not dead, like so many others, for they would have heard. At last, tired of waiting, the first-comers sat down at table: and dinner was nearly over when a carriage rolled into the yard of the inn where they were staying. Soon afterwards the late arrival came in.

He sat down happily, rubbing his hands, ate with a good appetite, and, when one of his companions expressed surprise at seeing him dressed in a frock coat, calmly replied: 'Yes, I didn't have time to change.'

All four went to bed as soon as they had left the table, for in order to surprise the birds it is necessary to set off before dawn.

Nothing could be more pleasant than these early morning expeditions.

At three in the morning the sailors wake the sportsmen by throwing sand at their window panes. In a few minutes they are ready and go down on to the shingle beach. Although there is no sign yet of the dawn, the stars have paled a little; the sea rattles the pebbles; and the breeze is so keen that the sportsmen shiver a little, in spite of their thick clothes.

Soon the two boats, pushed out by the sailors, rush down the slope of round pebbles with a noise like tearing canvas, and a moment later they are rocking gently on the first waves. The brown sails are hoisted, swell slightly, tremble, hesitate, and, bulging out again like round bellies, carry the tarred hulls out towards the wide opening down the river, which is dimly visible in the gloom.

The sky grows lighter; the darkness seems to melt away; the coast appears, still veiled in mist, the great white coast, as straight as a wall.

They go through the Manneporte, an enormous arch through which a ship could pass, round the headland of La Courtine, sail past the Vale of Antifer and the cape of the same name; and suddenly they see before them a beach on which hundreds of gulls are resting. Behind it is Guillemot Rock.

It is merely a little lump in the cliff wall; and on the narrow edge of the rock birds' heads appear, watching the boats.

They are there, motionless, waiting, not daring to fly off yet. A few of them, perched on the outer edges, look as if they are sitting on their rumps, upright like bottles, for their legs are so short that when they walk they seem to be gliding along on wheels; and when they want to take to the air they are unable to gather speed in a run and have to drop like stones, almost down as far as the men watching them.

They are aware of this weakness of theirs and the danger it entails, and are uncertain whether to decide to fly.

But the sailors start shouting and beating the gunwales with the wooden thole-pins, and the birds, taking fright, hurl themselves into space one by one and drop to the very surface of the waves; then, their wings beating rapidly, they gather speed and fly out to sea, unless a hail of shots brings them down first.

For an hour they are shot at like this, and forced to take flight one after another. Sometimes the females on their nests, completely absorbed in the business of hatching, refuse to fly off, and receive volley after volley. Their white plumage is splashed with spots of rosy blood, and the mother birds die without leaving their eggs.

On the first day Monsieur d'Arnelles shot with his usual enthusiasm; but when they set off on the way back about ten o'clock, beneath the high, bright sun which cast great triangles of light into the white clefts in the coast-line, he looked rather worried and occasionally seemed lost in thought, which was not like him.

As soon as they arrived back at the inn a manservant of some sort, dressed in black, came and whispered something to him. He seemed to reflect, hesitated, and then replied: 'No, tomorrow.'

The next day the shooting was resumed. This time Monsieur d'Arnelles often missed his birds even though they almost dropped on to the end of his gun barrel; and his friends jokingly asked him if he was in love, or if some secret anxiety was troubling his heart and mind. At last he admitted that this was the case.

'Yes, as a matter of fact I have to leave straight away, and it's very annoying.'

'What, you're going away? Why?'

'Oh, urgent business. I can't stay any longer.'

Then they talked about other things.

As soon as lunch was over, the servant in black re-appeared. Monsieur d'Arnelles ordered him to harness his horses, and the man was on the point of going out when the other three sportsmen intervened, urging and begging their friend to stay. In the end one of them said: 'Look here, this business of yours can't be so very urgent, since you've already waited two days!'

Monsieur d'Arnelles, thoroughly perplexed, reflected, visibly torn between pleasure and duty, unhappy and ill at ease.

After a long period of meditation he murmured hesitantly: 'The fact is ... the fact is ... I'm not alone here. I have my son-in-law with me.'

This brought a chorus of exclamations: 'Your son-in-law? ... But where is he?'

At that he suddenly looked embarrassed and blushed.

'What? Didn't you know? ... Why ... why ... he's in the stable. ... He's dead.'

There was a stupefied silence.

More and more embarrassed, Monsieur d'Arnelles went on: 'I had the misfortune to lose him; and as I was taking the body to my home at Briseville, I made a slight detour so as not to miss our rendezvous. But you will understand that I can't delay any longer.'

Then one of the sportsmen, bolder than the rest, said: 'But ... since he's dead ... it seems to me ... that he might as well wait one more day.'

The other two hesitated no longer.

'That's undeniable,' they said.

Monsieur d'Arnelles looked as if a great weight had been taken off his mind; but, still a little uneasy, he asked: 'You really think so?'

As one man the other three replied: 'Dammit all, my dear fellow, a couple of days more or less won't make any difference to him in his condition.'

At that, completely reassured, the father-in-law turned to the undertaker.

'In that case, my good man, make it the day after to-morrow.'

# IMPRUDENCE

BEFORE they were married they had loved each other chastely, up in the clouds. First there had been a charming encounter on a beach by the ocean. He had found her delightful, the rosy-cheeked girl he had seen passing by, with her gay parasols and her cool dresses, against the great horizon of the sea. He had fallen in love with her fair, delicate charm in that setting of blue waves and vast skies. And he had confused the tenderness which that girl on the threshold of womanhood aroused in him with the vague and powerful emotion which the clear salty air and the great seascape of sun and waves awakened in his soul, in his heart and in his blood.

She for her part had fallen in love with him because he courted her, and because he was young, quite wealthy, charming and attentive. She had fallen in love with him because it is natural for girls to fall in love with young men who say sweet nothings to them.

Then, for three months, they had lived side by side, holding hands, gazing into each other's eyes. The greetings they exchanged in the morning before going bathing, in the freshness of the new day, and their whispered good-byes in the evening on the sand under the stars, in the warmth of the calm night, already had a taste of kisses, although their lips had never met.

They dreamed of each other as soon as they fell asleep, thought of each other as soon as they awoke, and, without saying so as yet, called for and desired each other, body and soul.

After they were married they had worshipped each other

down on earth. First there had been a sort of tireless sensual frenzy, then an impassioned tenderness formed of palpable poetry, caresses which were already refined, and sweet, depraved inventions. All their glances had an impure significance, and all their gestures reminded them of the ardent intimacy of the night.

Now, without admitting it to each other, perhaps without realizing it yet, they were beginning to grow tired of each other. They were fond of each other, it is true, but they had nothing more to reveal to each other, nothing more to do that they had not done often, nothing more to learn from each other, not even a new word of love, an unexpected gesture, an intonation to lend more fire to an oft-repeated phrase.

They tried, however, to rekindle the feeble flame of their first embraces. Every day they devised some tender ruse, some simple or complicated game, in a series of desperate attempts to renew in their hearts the unquenchable ardour of the first days and in their veins the fire of the honeymoon.

Now and then they whipped up their desire enough to enjoy an hour of factitious excitement which was promptly followed by a disgusted weariness.

They had tried moonlight walks, strolls under the trees on balmy evenings, the poetry of river banks bathed in mist, the excitement of open-air dances.

Then, one morning, Henriette said to Paul: 'Will you take me out to dinner at a restaurant?'

'Why, of course, darling.'

'To a very fashionable restaurant?'

'Why, yes.'

He looked at her questioningly, realizing that she had something in mind which she did not want to put into words.

She went on: 'You know, a restaurant . . . how shall I put it? . . . a restaurant where people meet on the quiet.'

He smiled.

'I see what you mean. A private room in a fashionable restaurant?'

'That's it. But a restaurant where they know you, where you've already been to supper . . . no, to dinner . . . you know what I mean. . . . I'd like to . . . no, I daren't say it.'

'Go on, darling. Between the two of us, what does it matter? We're past the stage of having secrets from each other.'

'No, I daren't.'

'Come now, don't play the innocent. What were you going to say?'

'Well . . . all right. . . . I'd like . . . I'd like to be taken for your mistress . . . and I'd like the waiters, who don't know that you are married, to regard me as your mistress, and you too . . . for an hour or so, in that place which must have memories for you, I'd like you to believe that I'm your mistress. . . . There! . . . and I myself will believe that I'm your mistress. . . . I want to do something very wicked . . . I want to be unfaithful to you . . . with you. . . . There! . . . I know it's not nice, but it's what I'd like to do. . . . Don't make me blush. . . . I can feel myself blushing. . . . You can't imagine how much it would . . . excite me to have dinner with you like that in a place that's rather disreputable . . . in a private room where people make love every evening . . . every evening. . . . I know it's wicked of me. . . . I'm as red as a peony. Don't look at me. . . .'

He laughed, very much amused, and replied: 'Very well, this evening we'll go to a very smart place where they know me.'

About seven o'clock they were to be seen going up the

staircase of a big boulevard restaurant, he smiling triumphantly, she timid, veiled, overjoyed. As soon as they had been shown into a private room, furnished with four armchairs and a wide red velvet sofa, the head waiter came in, dressed in tails, to present the menu. Paul held it out to his wife.

'I've no idea – whatever people usually eat here.'

He read through the litany of dishes while taking off his overcoat, which he handed to a waiter. Then he said: 'A fairly substantial meal, I think. *Potage bisque, poulet à la diable, râble de lièvre, homard à l'américaine*, a highly seasoned salad, a dessert.'

The head waiter smiled as he looked at the young woman. He took back the menu, murmuring: 'What would Monsieur Paul like to drink?'

'Champagne, very dry.'

Henriette was pleased to find that this man knew her husband's name.

They sat down side by side on the sofa and started eating.

Ten candles lighted the room, reflected in a large mirror dulled by thousands of names which had been scratched on it with diamonds, covering the glass with a sort of vast cobweb.

Henriette drank glass after glass to put her into a gay mood, although she felt slightly giddy after the first few. Paul, excited by his memories, kept kissing his wife's hand. His eyes were shining brightly.

She felt strangely moved by this disreputable place, slightly sullied but happy and vibrant with excitement. Two solemn, silent waiters, accustomed to seeing everything and forgetting everything, to coming in only when necessary and to going out at moments of passion, came and went swiftly and softly.

By the time the dinner was half over, Henriette was completely tipsy, and Paul, who was in high spirits, squeezed her knee as hard as he could. She was chatting boldly now, her cheeks flushed, her eyes bright and moist.

'Come along, Paul, own up! I'd like to know everything, you know.'

'What do you mean, darling?'

'I don't dare say.'

'Go on.'

'Have you had any mistresses ... many mistresses ... before me?'

He hesitated, slightly perplexed, not knowing whether he should boast of his affairs or keep quiet about them.

'Oh, please tell me,' she went on. 'Have you had many?'

'A few.'

'How many?'

'Oh, I don't know. . . . Nobody knows that sort of thing.'

'You mean you didn't count them?'

'Why, no.'

'Then you must have had a lot?'

'I suppose so.'

'Roughly how many? Just roughly.'

'I've no idea, darling. There were some years when I had a lot, and some when I had only a few.'

'But how many a year?'

'Sometimes twenty or thirty, sometimes only four or five.'

'But that makes over a hundred women in all.'

'About that, yes.'

'Oh, how disgusting!'

'Why is it disgusting?'

'Because it's disgusting when you think about it ... all

those women . . . naked . . . and always . . . always the same thing. . . . Oh, yes, it's really disgusting, over a hundred women!'

He was shocked that she should consider that disgusting, and replied with that superior air which men assume to make women understand that they have said something foolish: 'Now that's ridiculous! If it's disgusting to have a hundred women, it's just as disgusting to have one.'

'Oh no, not at all!'

'Why not?'

'Because with one woman it's a liaison, it's a love which ties you to her, while with a hundred women it's dirty and immoral. I can't understand how a man can go to bed with all those prostitutes who are so dirty . . .'

'But they aren't dirty: they're very clean.'

'They can't be clean, carrying on that profession.'

'On the contrary, it's because of their profession that they're clean.'

'Get along with you! When you think that the previous night they were doing it with someone else! It's unspeakable!'

'It's no more unspeakable than drinking from this glass which heavens knows who drank from this morning, and which hasn't been washed half as carefully, you may be sure of that.'

'Oh, be quiet; you're revolting.'

'Then why did you ask me whether I've had any mistresses?'

'Tell me, were your mistresses all prostitutes? All hundred of them?'

'Why, no . . . no . . .'

'Then what were they?'

'Why, actresses ... working girls ... and a few society women.'

'How many society women?'

'Six.'

'Only six?'

'Yes.'

'Were they pretty?'

'Why, yes.'

'Prettier than the prostitutes?'

'No.'

'Which did you prefer, the prostitutes or the society women?'

'The prostitutes.'

'Oh, how disgusting you are! Why?'

'Because I don't care much for amateur talents.'

'Oh, you beast! You're really horrible, you know! But tell me, did you find it fun passing from one to another like that?'

'Why, yes.'

'Really?'

'Really.'

'What did you find enjoyable about it? Aren't they all the same?'

'Oh, no.'

'They don't resemble one another?'

'Not in the least.'

'In no way at all?'

'In no way at all.'

'How peculiar! In what respect are they different?'

'In every respect.'

'In body?'

'Yes, in body.'

'In the whole body?'

'Yes, in the whole body.'

'And in what else?'

'Why, in the way they . . . they kiss, the way they talk, the way they say the slightest thing.'

'I see. And is it fun changing?'

'Why, yes.'

'And are men different too?'

'That I don't know.'

'You don't know?'

'No.'

'They must be different.'

'Yes, I suppose so . . .'

She remained pensive, her glass of champagne in her hand. It was full, and she drank it at one draught; then, putting it down on the table, she threw both arms around her husband's neck and murmured into his mouth: 'Oh, darling, I love you so much!'

He clasped her in a passionate embrace. A waiter who was coming into the room drew back, closing the door, and the service was interrupted for about five minutes.

When the head waiter reappeared, looking grave and dignified, with the fruit for dessert, she was once again holding a full glass between her fingers; and, looking into the depths of the transparent yellow liquid, as if to see unknown, dreamed-of things, she was murmuring thoughtfully: 'Oh, yes, it must be fun all the same. . . .'

# THE SIGNAL

THE little Marquise de Rennedon was still asleep in her snug, scented bedroom. In her big, soft, low bed, between sheets of delicate cambric as fine as lace and as caressing as a kiss, she was sleeping in peaceful solitude the deep, happy sleep of a divorcee.

She was awakened by the sound of raised voices in the little blue drawing-room, and she recognized her dear friend the little Baronne de Grangerie, arguing with the maid who was refusing to allow her into her mistress's room.

The little Marquise got up, drew the bolts, turned the key, pulled back the door-curtain and showed her head, nothing but her head, half-hidden under a cloud of fair hair.

'What on earth brings you here at such an ungodly hour? It isn't nine o'clock yet.'

The little Baronne was looking very pale, nervous and excited.

'I've got to talk to you,' she replied. 'The most horrible thing has happened to me.'

'Come in, darling.'

Her friend went in and the two women exchanged kisses. Then the Marquise got back into bed while the maid opened the windows, letting in light and air. When she had left the room Madame de Rennedon said: 'Now tell me all about it.'

Madame de Grangerie started to cry, shedding those delightful limpid tears which add to a woman's charms. Taking care not to wipe her eyes, so as not to make them red, she stammered: 'Oh, my dear, what has happened to me is horrible, simply horrible. I didn't get a wink of sleep last night, not a wink. Just feel how my heart is beating.'

And taking her friend's hand, she put it on her breast, on that firm round covering of a woman's heart which the male often finds so satisfying that he makes no attempt to find what lies beneath it. Her heart was indeed beating very hard.

She went on: 'It happened yesterday... about four o'clock... or half past – I can't be sure. You know my flat, and you know that my little drawing-room, where I always sit, is on the first floor, overlooking the Rue Saint-Lazare. You also know that I have a mania for sitting at the window and watching people going by. That district around the station is so gay, so full of movement and life, I simply love it. Well, yesterday I was sitting in the low chair I have had placed in the window recess; the window was open, and I was thinking of nothing in particular, just breathing the fresh air. You remember how fine it was yesterday, don't you?

'All of a sudden I noticed that there was a woman on the other side of the street who was also sitting at her window, a woman in red. I was in mauve – you know my pretty mauve dress. I didn't know anything about the woman, except that she was a new tenant who had been there a month, and as it has been raining for a month I hadn't so much as set eyes on her. But I could tell straight away that she was a bad lot. At first I was rather shocked and disgusted that she should sit at her window like me, but gradually I began to find it amusing to watch her. She was leaning on her elbows, looking at the men in the street, and all the men, or nearly all of them, looked up at her. It was as if something told them of her presence when they got near the house, as if they could scent her as a dog scents game, for they would suddenly look up and exchange a swift glance with her, like a Masonic signal. Her look said: "Like to come up?" And theirs replied: "No time," or "Some other day," or "Broke," or else — in the case of respectable family men — "You shameless hussy!"

'You can't imagine what fun it was watching her playing her little game, or rather practising her profession.

'Every now and then she would suddenly shut the window and I would see a man going in. She had caught him like an angler landing a fish. Then I would look at my watch. They stayed there between twelve and twenty minutes, never any longer. In the end I began to be really fascinated by that spider-woman. Besides, she wasn't at all bad-looking.

'I began to wonder how she made her meaning clear so quickly and so completely. Did she use something more than a glance — a movement of the head, perhaps, or a gesture of the hand?

'I got my opera glasses to study her method. It was really very simple — first a glance, then a smile, and finally a tiny jerk of the head which meant: "Are you coming up?" But it was so slight, so casual, so discreet that it required a great deal of skill to carry it off as well as she did.

'I asked myself whether I could manage to do it — that little lift of the head which combined boldness and charm — because it really was very charming.

'So I went and tried it in front of my looking-glass. My dear, I did it better than she did, much better. I went back to the window feeling absolutely delighted.

'She wasn't catching anybody any more, poor girl, not a soul. She was really out of luck. When you come to think of it, it must be awful earning your living that way, but rather amusing at times, for after all some of the men you see in the street are quite good-looking.

'Now they were all walking on my side of the street, and not a soul on hers, because the sun had shifted. They came along one after another, young and old, dark and fair, grey-haired and white-haired.

'Some of them looked very nice – really very nice, my dear. Much better-looking than my husband, or yours – your *former* husband, I should say, now that you're divorced and can take your pick.

'I said to myself: If a respectable woman like myself signalled to them, would they understand? And I suddenly felt a mad longing to signal to them, a longing like the cravings pregnant women get, one of those terrible longings you can't possibly resist. I sometimes get urges like that, you know. It's silly, isn't it? I do believe that we women are just like monkeys. As a matter of fact, a doctor once told me that a monkey's brain is very like ours. We've always got to be imitating somebody – our husbands when we love them, during the first month after we've married them, and then our lovers, our women friends, or our confessors when they're nice. We adopt their attitudes, their tricks of speech, their words, their gestures, everything. It's all so ridiculous.

'Anyway, when I'm terribly tempted to do something I always do it.

'So I decided to try it out on one man, only one, just to see. After all, what could happen to me? Nothing at all. We'd exchange a smile and that would be all. I would never see him again. If I did, he wouldn't recognize me, and supposing he did, I'd simply deny it.

'I set about making my choice. I wanted somebody nice, really nice. All of a sudden I saw a tall, fair young man coming along. You know how I like fair men.

'I looked at him; he looked at me. I smiled; he smiled.

I gave the signal – oh, barely moving my head – and the next thing I knew, darling, he had come in through the front door.

'You can't imagine how I felt at that moment! I thought I was going to go mad, I was so frightened. Just think, he might say something to the servants – to Joseph, for instance, who's absolutely devoted to my husband! Joseph would be sure to think that I'd known the man for a long time.

'What on earth was I to do? At any moment he'd be ringing the bell, and then what would I do? I thought the best thing would be to run to the door, tell him he'd made a mistake, and beg him to go away. He would take pity on a woman, on a poor defenceless woman. So I rushed to the door and opened it just as he was reaching for the bell.

'I stammered in a panic: "Go away, Monsieur, go away, you're making a mistake. I'm a respectable married woman. It's all a mistake, a terrible mistake: I took you for a friend of mine – you look very like him. Have pity on me, Monsieur!"

'But he just burst out laughing, my dear, and answered: "Hello, my lovely. You know, I've heard that story before. You're married, so you want two louis instead of one. All right, you shall have them. Now show me the way."

'He pushed me in, shut the door, and as I stood there facing him, absolutely terrified, he kissed me. Then he put his arm round my waist and led me back into the drawing-room, the door of which I had left open.

'Then he started looking around, just like an auctioneer taking stock, and he went on: "You've got a smart little place here, and no mistake. You must be pretty hard up just now to go in for the window game!"

'So then I began pleading with him again. "Please go

away, Monsieur," I said. "My husband will be back any moment now. He always comes home about this time. I swear you've made a mistake!"

'He replied very calmly: "That's enough of that, my girl. If your husband does come back, I'll give him a few sous and he can go and have a drink across the way."

'Then he noticed Raoul's photograph on the mantelpiece and asked me: "Is that your husband?"

' "Yes," I said, "it is."

' "He looks a poor fish. And who's that? One of your girl friends?"

'He was pointing at the photograph of you, my dear — you know, the one in a ball dress. I didn't know what I was saying, and I stammered: "Yes, she's a friend of mine."

' "She's a good-looking girl. You must introduce me to her."

'Just then the clock struck five. Now Raoul always gets home at half past. Suppose he arrived before the other had gone! Then ... well, then I completely lost my head ... I thought ... I thought ... that the best thing was to get rid of that man as quickly as possible. ... The sooner it was over and done with ... you understand. ... Since I had to let him, my dear ... and there was no other way ... he wouldn't have gone otherwise ... I, well ... I shot the bolt on the drawing-room door ...'

The little Marquise de Rennedon had buried her head in her pillow and started laughing uproariously until the whole bed shook.

When she had calmed down slightly, she asked: 'And ... and ... you say he was a good-looking fellow?'

'Yes.'

'Then what are you complaining about?'

'But ... but ... you see, my dear ... the trouble is ... he said he'd come back tomorrow at the same time ... and I'm

terribly frightened. . . . You've no idea how stubborn he is
. . . or how determined. . . . Now what am I to do? . . .What
on earth am I to do?'

The little Marquise sat up in bed to think. Then she said
abruptly:

'Have him arrested.'

The little Baronne was dumbfounded. She stammered:
'What? What do you mean? Have him arrested? Whatever
for?'

'Oh, that's easy. You go to the police and tell them that
some man has been following you about for the last three
months, that he had the nerve to come up to your flat yesterday, that he threatened to come again tomorrow, and that
you want police protection. They'll send a couple of police-
men along who'll arrest him.'

'But, my dear, if he talks . . .'

'Why, they won't believe him, you silly, once you've told
your story to the police. But they'll believe you, because
you're a woman of the world and above suspicion.'

'Oh, I'd never dare.'

'You've got to dare, my dear, otherwise you're done for.'

'But just think . . . he'll say the most insulting things
about me when he's arrested.'

'Well, you'll have witnesses on your side, and he'll have
to pay up.'

'What do you mean, pay up?'

'He'll have to pay damages. In a case like this you've got
to be absolutely pitiless.'

'Oh, talking of damages . . . there's something else that's
worrying me dreadfully. . . . He left me . . . two louis . . . on
the mantelpiece.'

'Two louis?'

'Yes.'

'Is that all?'

'Yes.'

'Not much, is it? I would have felt humiliated if it had been me. Well?'

'Well, what should I do with the money?'

The little Marquise hesitated for a few seconds. Then she replied in a very serious voice: 'My dear, you must . . . you must buy your husband a little present. . . . It's the least you can do.'

# IN THE WOODS

THE Mayor was just going to sit down to lunch when he was told that the village policeman was waiting for him at the *mairie* with two prisoners.

He went over at once and, sure enough, found old Hochedur standing there keeping a stern eye on a middle-class couple of mature years.

The man, a stout old fellow with a red nose and white hair, seemed utterly dejected, while the woman, a round, plump little creature with shining cheeks, dressed up in her Sunday best, was glaring defiantly at the agent of the law who had arrested them.

'What's all this about, Hochedur?'

The village policeman made his report. He had gone out that morning at the usual time to patrol his beat from the edge of the Champioux woods to the boundaries of Argenteuil. He had not noticed anything unusual in the countryside, except that it was a fine day and that the corn was doing well, when young Bredel, who was hoeing his vineyard, had called out to him: 'Hey there, Pa Hochedur, go and take a look at the first thicket, on the edge of the woods, and you'll catch a pair of pigeons there who must be a hundred and thirty between them!'

He had set off in the direction young Bredel had indicated and had gone into the thicket. There he had heard words and sighs which made him suspect that a flagrant breach of morality was being committed.

He had accordingly advanced on his hands and knees, as if to surprise a poacher, and had apprehended this couple just as they were about to abandon themselves to their natural instincts.

The Mayor looked at the culprits in amazement, for the man was a good sixty years old and the woman fifty-five at least. He set about questioning them, beginning with the man, who answered in such a weak voice that he could scarcely be heard.

'What is your name?'

'Nicolas Beaurain.'

'Your occupation?'

'I'm a haberdasher in the Rue des Martyrs, in Paris.'

'What were you doing in the woods?'

The haberdasher remained silent, his head sunk on his fat stomach, his hands flat on his thighs. The Mayor went on: 'Do you deny what the agent of the municipal authorities has just stated?'

'No, Monsieur.'

'So you admit it?'

'Yes, Monsieur.'

'What have you to say in your defence?'

'Nothing, Monsieur.'

'Where did you meet your accomplice?'

'She's my wife, Monsieur.'

'Your wife?'

'Yes, Monsieur.'

'Then . . . then . . . you don't live together . . . in Paris?'

'I beg your pardon, Monsieur, but we *are* living together.'

'But in that case you're mad, absolutely mad, my dear sir, to let yourself get caught like this in the country at ten o'clock in the morning.'

The haberdasher looked as if he were ready to cry with shame. He murmured: 'It was her idea! I told her it was stupid, but when a woman's got an idea into her head, you can't move it anywhere else.'

The Mayor, who enjoyed a little bawdy humour, smiled and retorted: 'That isn't the trouble in your case. You wouldn't be here if she'd had the idea only in her head.'

Then Monsieur Beaurain flew into a temper, and turning to his wife he said: 'You see where you've landed us with your precious poetry? What a mess we're in! Now we'll have to appear in court, at our age, for an offence against public morality! And we'll have to shut up shop, sell our goodwill and move somewhere else! What a mess!'

Madame Beaurain stood up and, without looking at her husband, began to explain what had happened, without embarrassment, without futile modesty, almost without hesitation:

'Goodness knows, Monsieur, I realize we look ridiculous. But will you allow me to plead my case like a lawyer, or rather like a poor woman? Then I hope you'll be kind enough to send us home and spare us the disgrace of prosecution.

'A long time ago, when I was young, I met Monsieur Beaurain here one Sunday. He was an assistant in a haberdasher's, while I was a salesgirl in a dress shop. I remember it as if it was yesterday. I used to come and spend the odd Sunday here with a friend of mine, Rose Levêque, who lived with me in the Rue Pigalle. Rose had a sweetheart, but I didn't. He used to bring us here. One Saturday he told me with a laugh that he was going to bring a friend with him the next day. I knew what he wanted, of course, but I told him it was no use. You see, I was a good girl, Monsieur.

'The next day, then, we found Monsieur Beaurain waiting for us at the railway station. He was a good-looking man in those days. But I had made up my mind I wasn't going to give in to him, and no more did I.

'Well, eventually we arrived at Bezons. It was a lovely

day, the sort of day that sets your heart dancing. Even now, a fine day makes me lightheaded, and when I'm in the country I go quite mad. The green trees, the birds singing, the corn swaying in the wind, the swallows darting about, the smell of the grass, the poppies and daisies – all that sends me completely crazy. It's like champagne when you aren't used to it.

'Well, the weather was lovely, warm and bright, and you seemed to breathe it in through your mouth and drink it in with your eyes. Rose and Simon kept kissing each other every minute, and watching them really stirred me up inside. Monsieur Beaurain and I walked behind them without talking much, because when people don't know each other well they can't think of anything to say. He looked a shy young man, and I was pleased to see that he was rather bashful. Eventually we got to the little wood. It was as cool as anything in there and we all sat down on the grass. Rose and her sweetheart teased me because I looked so serious, but you can understand that I couldn't behave in any other way. Then they started kissing and cuddling again, just as if we hadn't been there, and then they whispered together, and then they got up and went off into the wood without saying a word. Well, you can imagine how I felt, all alone with that young fellow I'd never seen before. I felt so embarrassed at seeing them go off like that that I plucked up my courage and started to talk. I asked him what he did for a living and he told me he was a haberdasher's assistant, as I told you just now. So we chatted together for a few minutes and that gave him ideas, and he tried to take a few liberties, but I put him in his place and very sharp too. Isn't that so, Monsieur Beaurain?'

Monsieur Beaurain, who was looking at his feet in some embarrassment, made no reply, and she went on:

'Then he realized that I was a good girl and he started

courting me nicely, like a decent young fellow. From then on he came back every Sunday. He was very sweet on me, Monsieur. And I was very fond of him too, oh yes, I was very fond of him. He was a good-looking fellow in those days.

'To cut a long story short, he married me that September and we set up in business in the Rue des Martyrs.

'We had a hard time of it for several years, Monsieur. Business was bad, and we couldn't afford any outings in the country. In any case, we'd lost the habit. You've got other things to think about when you're in business, and the cashbox matters more than pretty speeches. We gradually grew older without noticing it, a quiet couple who didn't think much about love any more. But you don't miss a thing as long as you don't notice you've lost it.

'Eventually, Monsieur, business improved and we felt happier about the future. And then, well, I don't rightly know what happened inside me – no, I really don't know! But I started daydreaming like a little schoolgirl. The sight of the little carts full of flowers that you see pushed around the streets made me cry. The smell of violets came to me in my chair behind the cashdesk and made my heart start pounding wildly. Then I used to get up and go to the door and stand there looking at the blue sky between the roofs. When you look at the sky from a street in Paris it looks like a long river winding its way over the city, and the swallows move about in it like fishes. Oh, I know that it's silly thinking thoughts like that at my age! All the same, Monsieur, when you've worked all your life, there comes a time when you realize you could have done something else, and then you start having regrets. Oh yes, you really start having regrets! Just think, for twenty years I could have gone gathering kisses in the woods like other women! I used to think how nice it would be to lie under the trees loving somebody! And I thought about it every day and every night! I dreamed of moonlight on the water until I felt like drowning myself.

'I didn't dare talk to Monsieur Beaurain about all this at first. I knew that he'd laugh at me and send me back to my counter selling needles and thread. Besides, to tell the truth, Monsieur Beaurain didn't appeal to me very much any more; but when I looked at myself in the mirror I realized that I wasn't much of a beauty either.

'So one day I made up my mind and I suggested an outing in the country to the place where we first met. He agreed without suspecting anything, and we arrived here this morning about nine o'clock.

'It gave me quite a turn when I came across the corn-fields. A woman's heart never grows any older, you see. And you know, I didn't see my husband as he is now any more, but as he used to be. I swear he looked completely different, Monsieur. As true as I'm standing here now, I was drunk with love. I started kissing him, and he was more surprised than if I'd tried to murder him. He kept saying to me: "You're out of your head. You're completely mad. What's the matter with you?" I didn't listen to him, I didn't listen to anything but my heart. And I made him take me into the woods.... And that's what happened.... I've told you the truth, Monsieur, the whole truth.'

The Mayor had a nice sense of humour. He stood up, smiled, and said: 'Go in peace, Madame, and sin no more ... under the trees.'

# THE DEVIL

The peasant was standing opposite the doctor at the foot of the dying woman's bed. The old woman, calm, resigned and clear-headed, lay there looking at the two men and listening to their conversation. She was going to die: she accepted the fact. She was ninety-two, and her time had come.

Through the window and door, which were both open, the July sun streamed in, pouring its hot rays on the brown, uneven earth floor, which was beaten hard by the clogs of four generations of peasant folk. The smells of the fields came in too, wafted by the hot breeze, smells of grass, wheat and leaves scorched by the midday sun. The grasshoppers were chirping themselves hoarse, filling the countryside with their shrill song, like the noise made by the wooden rattles which are sold to children at fairs.

Raising his voice, the doctor said: 'Honoré, you can't leave your mother alone in this condition. She may die at any moment.'

The peasant replied miserably: 'All the same, I've got to get my wheat in. It's been lying out too long as it is. And the weather's just right now. What do you say, Mother?'

The dying woman, still in the grip of Norman avarice, nodded and blinked her assent, urging her son to get his wheat in and leave her to die all alone.

But the doctor stamped his foot angrily.

'You're a callous brute, I tell you, and I won't let you do it – is that clear? And if you've really got to get your wheat in today, then go and get Mother Rapet to watch over your mother, dammit! I insist – is that clear? And if you don't do as I say, I'll let you die like a dog when it's your turn to fall sick – is that clear?'

The peasant, a tall thin man with slow movements, tortured by indecision and torn between fear of the doctor and a violent passion for thrift, hesitated, calculated, and finally stammered: 'How much does Mother Rapet charge?'

'How should I know?' shouted the doctor. 'It depends on how long you need her. Dammit all, make your own arrangements with her. But I want her here an hour from now – is that clear?'

The man made up his mind: 'I'm going, I'm going. Don't take on, Doctor.'

And the doctor left, calling out as he went: 'Now you be careful, my man, because when I get my back up it's no laughing matter, believe me!'

As soon as he was alone with his mother the peasant turned to her and said in a resigned voice: 'I'm going to fetch Mother Rapet, seeing as Doctor says I must. Don't fret, now, till I'm back.'

And he too left the house.

Mother Rapet, an old woman who took in ironing, watched over the dead and dying in the village and the surrounding countryside. As soon as she had finished sewing up a customer in a sheet he would never cast aside, she would go back to ironing the linen of the living. As wrinkled as one of last year's apples, spiteful, envious, and incredibly tight-fisted, she was always bent double, as if she had broken her back constantly running the iron over her customers' linen. She also seemed to have a sort of monstrous, obscene passion for death-beds. Her only subjects of conversation were the people she had seen die and all the different sorts of death she had witnessed; and she described these death-agonies in great detail, never changing a single word, like a sportsman telling of his shooting exploits.

When Honoré Bontemps entered her house, he found her mixing some blue for the village girls' collars.

'Afternoon, Mother Rapet,' he said. 'How're you keeping?'

She turned her head to look at him.

'Middling, middling. And how's yourself?'

'Oh, I'm fine. It's my mother as isn't.'

'Your mother?'

'Yes, my mother.'

'What's wrong with your mother?'

'She's going to turn up her toes, that's what.'

The old woman took her hands out of the water, and the bluish, transparent drops ran down her fingers and fell back into the wash-tub.

She asked with sudden interest: 'Is she that bad?'

'Doctor says she won't last the afternoon.'

'She must be pretty bad, then.'

Honoré hesitated. He needed a few preliminary remarks to lead up to the proposal he had in mind; but as he could not think of anything to say he came straight to the point.

'How much do you want to watch over her till the end? I'm not well off, you know. I can't even afford a woman to look after the house. That's what's done for my poor old mother – too much worry, too much work. She's ninety-two, but she did the work of ten. They don't make 'em like that no more!'

Mother Rapet replied gravely: 'There's two rates. Two francs a day and three francs a night for the rich. One franc a day and two francs a night for the rest. You'll pay me one and two.'

The peasant thought this over. He knew his mother well. He knew her tenacity, her strength, her powers of resistance. She might last a week, in spite of the doctor's opinion.

He said firmly: 'No, I'd rather you gave me a fixed price for the whole job. That makes it a risk for both of us. Doctor says she'll go pretty soon. If she does, you win and I lose. But if she hangs on till tomorrow or longer, then I win and you lose.'

Mother Rapet looked at the man in surprise. She had never taken on a death for a fixed price before. She hesitated, tempted by the gamble involved. Then the suspicion occurred to her that he was trying to swindle her, and she replied: 'I can't say till I've seen your mother.'

'Then come and see her.'

She dried her hands and followed him straight away.

They did not speak to each other on the way. She walked fast, while he strode along as if he had to cross a stream with every step.

The cows lying in the fields, stupefied by the heat, sluggishly raised their heads and lowed feebly at these two people hurrying by, as if asking them for some fresh grass.

As they drew near to his house Honoré Bontemps murmured: 'Perhaps it's all over anyway.'

And his unconscious hope that this should be the case showed in his voice.

But the old woman was not dead. She was still lying on her back in her truckle-bed, with her hands on her purple calico counterpane – terribly thin, gnarled hands, like strange crab-like creatures, closed up by rheumatism, overwork, and all the tasks she had carried out for nearly a century.

Mother Rapet went up to the bed and inspected the dying woman. She felt her pulse, laid her hand on her chest, listened to her breathing, and asked her a few questions to hear the sound of her voice. Then, after studying her again for a long time, she left the house, followed by Honoré. She had come to the firm conclusion that the old woman would not last till nightfall.

'Well,' he asked.

Mother Rapet replied: 'Well, she'll last two days, maybe three. You'll give me six francs for the job, all in.'

'Six francs?' he cried. 'Six francs? Are you out of your mind? I tell you she'll last five or six hours, not a minute more!'

They haggled for a long time, each as stubborn as the other. But as Mother Rapet threatened to go home, time was passing, and the wheat wasn't going to get in by itself, he finally agreed to her terms.

'All right then, six francs, all in, till the body's taken away.'

'Six francs it is.'

He strode away to see to his wheat, which was lying on the ground under the hot harvest sun, while Mother Rapet went back into the house.

She had brought some work with her, for she sewed all the time she was watching over the dying and the dead, either for herself, or for the family which would pay her extra for the double job.

All of a sudden she asked: 'I suppose you've had the last sacraments, Mother Bontemps?'

The old woman shook her head, and Mother Rapet, who was very pious, jumped to her feet.

'Goodness gracious! You don't say! I'll go and fetch the priest.'

And she rushed off in the direction of the priest's house, running so fast that the little boys in the square thought there must have been an accident.

The priest came round straight away, wearing his surplice and preceded by a choirboy ringing a little bell to let people know that God was being carried through the quiet, scorching countryside. Men working in the distance took off their broad-brimmed hats and stood motionless until the white surplice had disappeared behind a farmhouse. Women gathering up the sheaves of wheat straightened up to make the sign of the cross. Some black hens scuttled in alarm along the ditches until they reached a well-known gap in the hedge through which they abruptly disappeared. A colt tethered in a meadow took fright at the sight of the surplice and started running around in circles at the end of its rope, kicking up its heels. The choirboy in his red cassock hurried along, and the priest, his head bent to one side and wearing his square biretta, followed him, murmuring prayers. Bringing up the rear came Mother Rapet, head down and bent double as if she were trying to prostrate herself as she walked, and with her hands folded as if in church.

Honoré saw them go by from a distance and asked: 'Where's our priest going?'

His farmhand, who was brighter than his master, replied: 'Why, he's taking your mother the last sacraments, of course!'

The peasant showed no surprise.

'Like enough it is,' he said, and went back to his work.

Mother Bontemps made her confession, received absolution and took communion; and the priest went away, leaving the two women alone in the stifling cottage.

Then Mother Rapet began looking at the dying woman, wondering if she would take a long time to go.

The daylight was fading. The cooler air was blowing into the house in stronger puffs, making a cheap print fastened to the wall with two pins flap up and down. The little curtains at the window, once white but now yellow and fly-blown, looked as if they were trying to fly off, struggling to get away, like the old woman's soul.

Motionless, her eyes open, she seemed to be waiting calmly for the death which was so near but so slow in coming. Her quick breathing was making a slight whistling sound in her congested throat. It would stop before long, and there would be one woman less in the world, whom nobody would miss.

At nightfall Honoré returned. Going up to the bed, he saw that his mother was still alive.

'How're you feeling?' he asked, as he used to do whenever she was out of sorts.

Then he sent Mother Rapet away, telling her: 'Five o'clock tomorrow, without fail.'

She replied: 'Five o'clock tomorrow it is.'

Sure enough, she arrived at daybreak.

Honoré was eating his soup, which he had made himself, before going out into the fields.

'Well, is your mother dead?' asked Mother Rapet.

With a mischievous twinkle in his eyes he replied: 'She's a bit better if anything.'

And off he went.

Mother Rapet suddenly felt uneasy. She went over to the dying woman, who was still in the same condition, short of breath and impassive, her eyes open and her hands clenched on the counterpane.

The nurse realized that things could go on like this for two days, four days, even a week, and fear gripped her miserly heart, while she felt a rush of anger against the cunning fellow who had tricked her and against this woman who refused to die.

All the same, she set to work and waited, her eyes fixed on Mother Bontemps's wrinkled face.

Honoré came in for his dinner. He seemed pleased with himself, almost jovial. Then he went off again. He was certainly getting in his wheat under excellent conditions.

Mother Rapet was becoming more and more exasperated; every minute that went by now seemed to her so much stolen time and stolen money. She felt a longing, a mad longing, to seize this stubborn, obstinate, pig-headed old fool by the throat, and with a little squeeze stop the short, quick breathing which was robbing her of her time and money.

Then she reflected that this would be a dangerous thing to do. Another idea occurred to her, and she went over to the bed.

'Have you seen the Devil yet?' she asked.

Mother Bontemps murmured: 'No.'

Then Mother Rapet started talking, telling stories calculated to fill the dying woman's feeble mind with terror.

A few minutes before death, she said, the Devil always appeared to the dying. He had a broom in his hand and a cooking-pot on his head, and he uttered loud shrieks. Once you had seen him, it was all over, you had only a few moments to live. And she listed all the people to whom the Devil had appeared that year in her presence: Joséphine Loisel, Eulalie Ratier, Sophie Padagnau, Séraphine Grospied.

These stories eventually affected Mother Bontemps, who stirred uneasily, moving her hands about, and trying to turn her head to see the far end of the room.

Suddenly Mother Rapet disappeared behind the foot of the bed. She took a sheet out of the wardrobe and wrapped herself in it; on her head she put the cooking-pot, whose three short curved feet stuck up like three horns; in her right hand she seized a broom and in her left a tin bucket, which she tossed into the air so that it fell with a clatter.

It made a terrible noise as it hit the ground. Then, clambering on to a chair, Mother Rapet raised the curtain at the foot of the bed and appeared there, gesticulating, uttering shrill cries inside the iron pot which hid her face, and, like the Devil in a Punch and Judy show, shaking her broom at the dying woman.

Utterly terrified, her eyes wide with panic, the old peasant woman made a superhuman effort to get up and run away. She actually managed to raise her shoulders and the upper part of her body; then she fell back with a great sigh. It was all over.

Mother Rapet calmly put everything back in its place: the broom in the corner by the wardrobe, the sheet inside the cooking-pot in the hearth, the bucket on the shelf and the chair against the wall. Then, with the ritual gestures of her trade, she closed the dead woman's staring eyes, put a plate on the bed, filled it from the holy-water basin, dipped the sprig of boxwood in it which was nailed up above the chest of drawers, and, kneeling down, started fervently reciting the prayers for the dead which she knew by heart as part of her calling.

When Honoré came home at nightfall he found her praying, and he promptly calculated that she had made a whole franc out of him, for she had spent only three days and one night watching over his mother, which came to five francs, whereas he owed her six.

# THE HORLA

*8 May*.  What a glorious day! I spent the whole morning stretched out in the grass in front of my house, under the huge plane tree which covers it completely, giving it shelter and shade.

I love this part of the country and I love living here because it is here that I have my roots, those deep and delicate roots which bind a man to the soil where his forefathers were born and died, bind him to ways of thinking and eating, to local customs, dishes, turns of phrase, to the intonations of the peasants' voices, to the smells of the villages, of the earth, of the very air.

I love this house of mine where I grew up. From my windows I can see the Seine flowing alongside my garden, beyond the main road, almost through my house, the great, wide Seine which goes from Rouen to Le Havre, covered with passing boats.

Over to the left is Rouen, a vast city of blue roofs lying beneath a bristling host of Gothic belfries. They are beyond number, these belfries, slender or sturdy, dominated by the cathedral's iron steeple, and filled with bells which ring out in the limpid air of fine mornings, sending me the sweet, distant hum of their iron tongues, a brazen song borne to me by the breeze, louder or fainter as it swells or dies away.

How delightful everything was this morning!

About eleven o'clock a long line of boats passed my gate, drawn by a pint-sized tug which panted with the effort and vomited thick clouds of smoke.

After a couple of English schooners, their red flags

fluttering against the sky, came a splendid Brazilian three-master, all white and gleaming and spotlessly clean. The sight of this boat gave me such pleasure that for some unknown reason I saluted her.

*12 May.* I have had a touch of fever for the last few days; I feel unwell, or rather I feel sad.

Where do they come from, these mysterious influences which turn our happiness into gloom and our self-assurance into distress? It is as if the air, the invisible air, were full of unfathomable powers, whose mysterious proximity affects us. I wake up full of high spirits, with a longing to sing bubbling up in my throat. Why? I go for a stroll by the river, and after walking a little way, I suddenly turn back feeling miserable, as if some misfortune were waiting for me at home. Why? Has some cold shiver, passing over my skin, shaken my nerves and saddened my soul? Has the shape of the clouds or the colour of the day, that ever-changing colour of things, troubled my thoughts as it passed through my eyes? Who can tell? Everything about us, everything we see without looking at it, everything we brush past without knowing it, everything we touch without feeling it, everything we meet without noticing it, has swift, surprising and inexplicable effects on us, on our senses, and through them on our ideas, on our very hearts.

How profound it is, that mystery of the Invisible; We cannot fathom it with our wretched senses; with our eyes which can perceive neither what is too small nor what is too big, neither what is too close nor what is too distant, neither the inhabitants of a star nor the inhabitants of a drop of water.... Or with our ears which deceive us by transmitting the vibrations of the air to us as sonorous notes, for they are fairies which work the miracle of changing that movement into sound, and through that metamorphosis give birth to music, which turns the mute agitation of Nature into song.... Or with our sense of smell, which is feebler than that of any dog.... Or with our taste, which can barely detect the age of a wine.

Oh, if only we had other senses which could work other miracles on our behalf, how many more things we could discover around us!

*16 May.* I am ill: that's certain! I have a fever, an atrocious fever, or rather a feverish weakness which afflicts my mind just as much as my body. All the time I have this terrible feeling of imminent danger, this apprehension of impending misfortune or approaching death, this presentiment which is doubtless the first sign of some disease, as yet unknown, germinating in my blood and my flesh.

*18 May.* I have just been to see my doctor for I could not sleep any more. He found that my pulse was rapid, my pupils dilated, and my nerves on edge, but that I had no symptoms of an alarming nature. I have to take showers and drink bromide of potassium.

*25 May.* No change. My condition is really very strange. As evening draws on an incomprehensible uneasiness comes over me, as if the darkness held some dreadful threat for me. I dine hurriedly, then try to read; but I cannot understand the words; I can scarcely make out the letters. So then I pace up and down my drawing-room in the grip of a vague and irresistible fear, fear of sleep and fear of my bed.

About two o'clock I go up to my room. I am no sooner inside than I double-lock the door and shoot the bolts. I am afraid ... but of what? ... I was never afraid of anything before. ... I open my wardrobes, I look under my bed, and I listen. ... I listen to what? ... Isn't it strange that a slight indisposition, a disorder of the circulation perhaps, an irritation of the nerves, a little congestion, a small disturbance in the delicate, imperfect functioning of the human machine, can make a melancholic of the happiest of men and a coward of the bravest? Then I go to bed and wait for sleep as if I were waiting for the executioner. I wait for it in terror of its coming, with my heart pounding and my legs trembling. My whole body shivers in the warmth of the bedclothes, till the moment when I suddenly fall asleep like a man falling into a chasm full of stagnant water to drown. Nowadays I no longer feel the approach of this perfidious sleep, lurking near me, watching me, waiting to seize me by the head, close my eyes, annihilate me.

I sleep for a long time — two or three hours; then a dream — no, a nightmare — takes hold of me. I am fully aware that I am in bed and asleep ... I feel it and know it ... and I also feel somebody approach me, look at me, touch me, climb on to my bed, touch me, kneel on my chest, take my neck between his hands and squeeze ... squeeze ... with all his strength, trying to strangle me.

I for my part struggle madly, hampered by that terrible helplessness which paralyses us in dreams. I try to cry out – I can't; I try to move – I can't; gasping for breath and making frantic efforts, I try to turn over, to throw off this creature who is crushing me and choking me – I can't!

And suddenly I wake up panic-stricken, bathed in sweat. I light a candle. I am alone.

After this nightmare, which is repeated every night, I finally fall into a peaceful sleep which lasts until dawn.

2 *June*. My condition has grown worse than ever. What can be the matter with me? The bromide is useless, the showers are useless. Just now, to tire out a body already

exhausted enough, I went for a walk in Roumare Forest. At first I thought that the fresh air, the clear mild air, full of the scent of leaves and grass, was pouring new blood into my veins, new energy into my heart. I set off down a broad avenue, then turned towards La Bouille down a narrow walk between two ranks of tremendously tall trees, which stretched a thick roof of an almost black green between the sky and me.

A shiver suddenly ran through me, not a shiver of cold but a strange shiver of fear.

I quickened my pace, uneasy at being alone in this wood, foolishly frightened for no reason by the profound solitude. All of a sudden it seemed to me that I was being followed, that somebody was hard on my heels, very close, near enough to touch me.

I swung round. I was alone. I could see nothing behind me but the long, straight walk, empty, high, terrifyingly empty; and in front of me too it stretched away as far as the eyes could see, the same in every way, and just as frightening.

I shut my eyes; I don't know why. And I started spinning around on one heel, very fast, like a top. I almost fell; I opened my eyes again; the trees were dancing; the earth was swaying; I was forced to sit down. But now I didn't know which way I had come! How odd! How very odd! I had absolutely no idea. I set off towards the right and eventually found myself back in the avenue which had taken me into the middle of the forest.

*3 June*.   Last night was terrible. I am going to go away for a few weeks. A short holiday will probably put me right.

*2 July*.   Home again. I am completely cured. What is

more, I have had a delightful holiday. I visited Mont Saint-Michel, which I had never seen before.

What a splendid sight meets your eyes when you arrive at Avranches, as I did, about dusk! The town stands on a hill, and I was taken into the municipal park on the outskirts. I uttered a cry of astonishment. An immense bay stretched out before me as far as the eye could see, between two widely separated coasts which disappeared into far-off mists; and in the middle of this vast yellow bay under a pale golden sky, a strange hill, dark and pointed, rose up from the sands. The sun had just disappeared, and silhouetted against a horizon still ablaze with fire was that fantastic rock, bearing a no less fantastic monument on its summit.

At dawn I went out to see it. The tide was out, as it had been the previous evening, and I saw the astonishing abbey grow in height before my eyes as I drew closer to it. After walking for several hours I reached the huge pile of rocks which bears the little city dominated by the great church. Climbing the steep, narrow street, I entered the most wonderful Gothic dwelling made for God on this earth, a building as vast as a town, full of low rooms under oppressive ceilings, and lofty galleries supported by frail pillars. I entered that gigantic granite jewel, which is as delicate as a piece of lacework, thronged with towers and slender belfries pierced by spiral staircases, towers and belfries which thrust into the blue sky of day and the black sky of night their strange heads bristling with chimeras, devils, fantastic beasts and monstrous flowers, and which are linked together by carved arches of intricate design.

When I reached the top I said to the monk accompanying me: 'Father, what a wonderful place this is!'

'The winds are very strong,' he replied, and we started

chatting together as we watched the tide coming in, sweeping across the sands and covering them with steel armour.

The monk told me a great many stories, all the stories of that place, legends, more legends and still more legends. One of them impressed me enormously. The local inhabitants, the people who live on the mount, claim to hear voices at night on the sands, followed by the sound of two goats, one bleating loudly, the other softly. Sceptics insist that what they hear is the screeching of the gulls, which sometimes sounds like bleating and sometimes like the wail of human voices; but fishermen returning late at night swear that between one tide and the next, near the little town cut off from the world, they have met an old shepherd wandering on the dunes. Nobody has ever seen his head, which is hidden by his cloak, but he leads behind him a goat with the face of a man and a she-goat with the face of a woman, both of them with long white hair and constantly talking, quarrelling in an unknown tongue, then suddenly breaking off to bleat at the tops of their voices.

'Do you believe that story?' I asked the monk.

'I don't know,' he murmured.

'If,' I went on, 'there existed on this earth creatures other than ourselves, how could we have failed to know of their existence long ago? Why haven't you seen them? Why haven't I seen them myself?'

He replied: 'Do we see a hundred-thousandth part of all that exists? Take the wind, for instance, the greatest force in Nature, which knocks down men, blows down buildings, uproots trees, whips up the sea into watery mountains, destroys cliffs and hurls great ships on to the reefs; the wind which kills, whistles, groans and roars – have you seen it, can you see it? And yet it exists.'

In the face of this simple reasoning I fell silent. This man was either a sage or a fool. I could not have said which, but I held my peace. For what he had just said, I had often thought.

*3 July.* I slept badly last night. There must be a feverish influence at work here, for my coachman is suffering from the same trouble as myself. Coming home yesterday, I noticed his curious pallor.

'What's the matter with you, Jean?' I asked.

'I can't get a good night's sleep any more, Monsieur. My nights just eat into my days. Since you went away, Monsieur, it's been like that all the time.'

The other servants are all right, however, but I am terrified of its taking hold of me again.

*4 July.* It has taken hold of me again all right. My old nightmares have come back. Last night I felt somebody squatting on top of me, pressing his mouth against mine and drinking my life through my lips. Yes, he was draining it out of my throat like a leech. Then he got off me, sated, and I woke up so bruised and battered and exhausted that I couldn't move. If this goes on for many more days I shall certainly go away again.

*5 July.* Have I lost my reason? What happened last night is so peculiar that my head reels just to think of it.

I had locked my door, as I do now every evening; then, feeling thirsty, I drank half a glass of water, and I happened to notice that my carafe was full right up to the crystal stopper.

After that I went to bed, falling into one of my dreadful slumbers from which I was roused about two hours later by a shock more frightful than any I had experienced before.

Imagine a man who is stabbed to death in his sleep and who wakes up with a knife in his lung, with a death-rattle in his throat, covered with blood, unable to breathe, on the point of death, and incapable of understanding what has happened to him – and there you have what I felt.

When I had finally come to my senses I felt thirsty again; I lit a candle and went over to the table on which my carafe was standing. I picked it up and tipped it over my glass; nothing came out. It was empty! It was completely empty! At first I was utterly mystified; then, all of a sudden, such a terrible feeling swept over me that I had to sit down, or rather, that I collapsed into a chair. Then I jumped to my feet to look around me. After that I sat down again, frantic with fear and surprise in face of the transparent carafe. I gazed at it with a fixed stare, trying to find an answer to the riddle. My hands were trembling. Somebody must have drunk the water, but who? I myself perhaps? Yes, it could only have been myself! In that case I was a sleepwalker; unknown to myself I was living that mysterious double life which makes us wonder whether there are two creatures in us or whether, when our mind is asleep, some alien being, invisible and unknowable, takes control of our captive body, which obeys that other being as it obeys us, or even more readily than it obeys us.

Oh, who can ever understand my dreadful anguish? Who can understand the feelings of a sane-minded, wide-awake, thoroughly rational man as he gazes in horror into a glass carafe, looking for a little water which has disappeared during his sleep? I stayed there until daybreak, not daring to go back to bed.

*6 July*.  I am going mad. All the water in my carafe was drunk again last night; or rather, I drank it.

But did I? Was it I? Who else could it be? Who? Oh, God, I am going mad! Who can save me?

*10 July*.  I have been carrying out some astonishing experiments. I am definitely insane! And yet . . .

On 6 July, before going to bed, I set out on my table some wine, milk, water, bread and strawberries.

Somebody drank – I drank – all the water and a little milk. The wine was left untouched, as were the strawberries and the bread.

On 7 July I carried out the same experiment, with the same result.

On 8 July I cut out the water and the milk. Nothing was touched.

Finally, on 9 July, I put out the water and the milk again, but by themselves, taking care to wrap the carafes in white muslin cloths and to tie down the stoppers. Then I rubbed my lips, my beard and my hands with black lead, and went to bed.

The same irresistible sleep took hold of me, followed shortly afterwards by the same horrible awakening. I had not stirred; the sheets themselves were unmarked. I rushed over to my table. The cloths wrapped around the carafes were still spotless. I untied the strings, quivering with fear. All the water had been drunk! All the milk had been drunk! God Almighty!

I am leaving in a few minutes for Paris.

*12 July*.  Paris. I obviously lost my head these last few days. I must have been the plaything of my fevered imagination, unless I really am a sleepwalker, or unless I have fallen under one of those well authenticated but so far inexplicable influences known as suggestions. In any case my terror bordered on madness, and twenty-four hours in Paris have been enough to restore my mental equilibrium.

Yesterday, after doing some shopping and paying a few calls, which put fresh life and spirit into me, I ended the day at the Théâtre-Français. They were presenting a play by the younger Dumas, and his lively, powerful mind completed my cure. There can be no doubt that solitude is dangerous for active minds. We need to be surrounded by men who think and talk. When we are alone for any length of time we people the void with phantoms.

I returned to my hotel in high spirits, walking along the boulevards. Amid the jostling of the crowd I thought, somewhat contemptuously, about my fears and suppositions of last week, when I believed, yes, believed, that an invisible being was living in my house. How weak our minds are, and how easily they are shaken and troubled as soon as they are confronted with a tiny incomprehensible fact!

Instead of coming to the simple conclusion: 'I don't understand because the cause escapes me', we promptly imagine terrifying mysteries and supernatural powers.

*14 July*. Bastille Day. I went for a stroll through the streets. The fireworks and flags filled me with a childish pleasure. Yet it is really very silly to be happy on a set day, by order of the government. The nation is a stupid herd, alternating between imbecile acceptance and savage rebellion. You say to it: 'Enjoy yourself.' It enjoys itself. You say to it: 'Go and fight your neighbour.' It goes to fight. You say to it: 'Vote for the Emperor.' It votes for the Emperor. Then you say to it: 'Vote for the Republic.' And it votes for the Republic.

Its rulers are just as stupid; but instead of obeying men they obey principles, which can only be ridiculous, sterile and false, by reason of the very fact that they are principles, that is to say ideas which are regarded as certain and immutable, in this world where nobody can be sure of anything, since light and sound are both illusions.

*16 July.* Yesterday I saw some things which have deeply disturbed me.

I was dining with my cousin, Madame Sablé, whose husband is in command of the 76th Light Horse at Limoges. At her house I found myself sitting with two young women, one of whom is married to a doctor, Doctor Parent, who devotes a great deal of his time to nervous illnesses and the extraordinary phenomena produced by recent experiments in hypnotism and suggestion.

He gave us a lengthy account of the astonishing results obtained by English scientists and the doctors of the Nancy school.

The facts he put forward struck me as so peculiar that I confessed that I was a complete sceptic.

'We are,' he maintained, 'on the point of discovering one of Nature's most important secrets on this earth, for she undoubtedly has far more important secrets out there among the stars. Ever since man began to think, ever since he learned how to express and record his thoughts, he has been aware of the existence close beside him of a mystery impervious to his crude, imperfect senses and he has tried to compensate for his physical incapacity by the strength of his intelligence. As long as his intelligence remained in a rudimentary state this obsession with invisible phenomena took crude and simple forms. That is the explanation of the popular notions of the supernatural, the legends of wandering spirits, fairies, gnomes, ghosts – I would even say the legend of God as well, for our concepts of the artificer-creator, from whatever religion they come to us, are really the most uninspired, stupid, unacceptable inventions ever devised by a terrified brain. Nothing could be truer than Voltaire's dictum: "God made man in his own image, but man has taken his revenge in kind."

'However, for just over a century now, we seem to have had glimpses of something new. Mesmer and a few others have set our feet on a new path and, especially in the last four or five years, we have obtained some astonishing results.'

My cousin, who like myself was very sceptical, smiled. Doctor Parent asked her: 'Shall I try to put you to sleep, Madame?'

'Yes, if you wish.'

She sat down in an armchair and he fixed her with a hypnotic stare. I for my part felt suddenly uneasy, my heart pounding wildly and my throat contracted. I saw Madame Sablé's eyes grow drowsy, her lips tighten, her breasts rise and fall.

Within ten minutes she was asleep.

'Go behind her,' said the doctor.

I sat down behind her. He put a visiting card in her hands and said: 'This is a mirror: what can you see in it?'

'I can see my cousin,' she replied.

'What is he doing?'

'He's twisting his moustache.'

'And now?'

'He's taking a photograph out of his pocket.'

'Whose photograph is it?'

'A photograph of himself.'

She was right! And that photograph had just been delivered to me, that very evening, at my hotel.

'What is he doing in the photograph?'

'He's standing with his hat in his hand.'

She could obviously see things in that card, in that piece

of white cardboard, as she would have seen them in a mirror. The young women cried out in horror: 'Enough! That's enough!'

But the doctor said in an authoritative tone of voice: 'You will get up tomorrow at eight o'clock. Then you will go to see your cousin at his hotel and beg him to lend you five thousand francs which your husband has asked you to obtain and will ask you for on his next leave.'

Then he woke her up.

On my way back to the hotel I thought about this curious séance, and I was assailed by doubts, not as to the absolute, unquestionable good faith of my cousin, whom I had known like a sister since my childhood, but as to the possibility of a trick on the part of the doctor. Might he not have had a mirror concealed in his hand which he had shown the young woman at the same time as his visiting card? Professional conjurors do much stranger things than that.

As soon as I got back to the hotel I went to bed.

Well, this morning, about half past eight, I was awoken by my man who said to me: 'Madame Sablé is here, Monsieur, asking to see you straight away.'

I dressed hurriedly and had her shown in.

She sat down, looking extremely agitated, her eyes downcast, and, without raising her veil, said: 'My dear cousin, I have a great favour to ask you.'

'What is it, cousin?'

'I find it very embarrassing to tell you, and yet I must. I need five thousand francs desperately.'

'*You* need five thousand francs? Oh, come now!'

'Yes, I do. Or rather my husband does, and he has told me to get them.'

I was so astonished that I stammered as I spoke to her. I wondered whether she and Doctor Parent might not be making fun of me, and whether this might not be just a comedy planned in advance and very well acted.

But when I looked closely at her, all my doubts vanished. This request for money was so distasteful to her that she was trembling with anguish, and I could see that she was choking back sobs.

I knew that she was extremely rich, and I went on: 'What! Do you mean to say that your husband can't lay his hands on five thousand francs? Come now, think. Are you sure that he told you to ask me for them?'

She hesitated for a few moments as if she were making a great effort to search her memory. Then she replied: 'Yes ... yes ... I'm sure he did.'

'Did he tell you in a letter?'

She hesitated again, thinking over my question. I guessed at the agonizing torment of her mind. She didn't know. All that she knew was that she had to borrow five thousand francs from me for her husband. So she plucked up enough courage to lie.

'Yes, he told me in a letter.'

'But when did he write to you? You didn't say anything to me about it yesterday.'

'I got his letter this morning.'

'Can you let me see it?'

'No ... no ... no ... it was very private ... too personal ... I've ... I've burnt it.'

'So your husband is in debt, is he?'

She hesitated again, then murmured: 'I don't know.'

I told her curtly: 'The fact is, my dear cousin, I can't lay my hands on the five thousand francs just now.'

She let out a sort of anguished cry.

'Oh, please, please get the money for me ...'

She grew more and more excited, clasping her hands together as if she were praying to me. The tone of her voice changed as she spoke; she wept and stammered, harassed and dominated by the irresistible order she had received.

'Oh, I beg you, I implore you. . . . If you only knew how unhappy I am. . . . I have to have the money today.'

I took pity on her.

'You shall have it later today, I promise you.'

'Oh, thank you, thank you!' she cried. 'How kind you are!'

'Do you remember,' I went on, 'what happened at your house yesterday?'

'Yes.'

'Do you remember that Doctor Parent put you to sleep?'

'Yes.'

'Well, he ordered you to come and borrow five thousand francs from me this morning, and you are now obeying that order.'

She thought this over for a few moments and replied: 'Because my husband wants the money.'

For a whole hour I tried to convince her, but all in vain.

After she had left I ran to the doctor's house. He was just going out, and he listened to me with a smile. Then he said: 'Now do you believe?'

'I have no alternative.'

'Let's go to see your cousin.'

She was already dozing on a chaise longue, utterly worn out. The doctor felt her pulse and gazed at her for some time, with one hand pointing at her eyes, which she gradually closed under the irresistible influence of that magnetic force.

When she had been put to sleep he told her:

'Your husband no longer needs those five thousand francs. You will therefore forget that you asked your cousin to lend them to you, and, if he mentions it to you, you will not understand.'

Then he woke her up. I took a wallet out of my pocket.

'Here, my dear cousin,' I said, 'is what you asked me for this morning.'

She was so astonished that I did not dare to press the point. All the same, I tried to stir her memory, but she denied everything fiercely, thought I was making fun of her, and in the end nearly lost her temper.

I have just got back to the hotel and been unable to eat any lunch because this experience has disturbed me so profoundly.

*19 July.* A lot of people I have told about this adventure have made fun of me. I don't know what to think about it now. The wise man says: Perhaps?

*21 July.* I dined today at Bougival, then spent the evening at the rowing-club dance. There can be no doubt that everything depends on places and settings. To believe in the supernatural on the island of La Grenouillère would be the height of folly. . . . But at the top of Mont Saint-Michel? . . . Or in India? We fall irresistibly under the influence of our surroundings. I am going home next week.

*30 July.* I arrived home yesterday. All is well.

*2 August.* Nothing new. The weather is glorious. I spend my days watching the Seine flow by.

*4 August.* My servants are quarrelling among themselves. They maintain that somebody keeps breaking the glasses in the cupboards at night. My man blames the cook, who blames the linen-maid, who blames the other two. Which of them is the culprit? It would take a clever man to find out.

*6 August.* This time I'm not mad. I've seen it . . . I've seen it . . . I've seen it ! . . . I still feel cold right down to my fingertips . . . I still feel chilled to the marrow . . . I've seen it !

At two o'clock, in broad daylight, I was strolling in my rose-garden . . . among the autumn roses which are just beginning to come out.

As I stopped to look at a *Géant des Batailles* which bore three magnificent flowers, I saw, distinctly saw, right in front of me, the stem of one of those roses bend as if an invisible hand had twisted it, then break as if that same hand had plucked it. Then the flower swept upwards, describing the curve an arm would have made carrying it towards a mouth, and remained suspended in the limpid air, all alone, motionless, a terrifying splash of red three paces from my eyes.

I rushed madly at it to grasp it. There was nothing there: it had disappeared. Then I was filled with a furious rage against myself, for a sane, serious-minded man doesn't have hallucinations like that.

But was it really an hallucination? I turned round to look for the stem, and I found it straight away on the bush, newly broken, between the other two roses which still remained on the branch.

Then I came back into the house utterly appalled, for I am certain now, as certain as I am that night follows day, that an invisible creature exists beside me which feeds on milk and water, which can touch things, pick them up and move them about, which is therefore endowed with a material nature, imperceptible though it may be to our senses, and which is living like myself beneath my roof . . .

7 *August*.  I had a peaceful night. He drank the water in my carafe, but he did not disturb my sleep.

I wonder if I am mad. While I was walking along the river bank just now, in the blazing sunshine, I was afflicted with doubts as to my sanity, not vague doubts such as I have had before, but detailed, well-founded doubts. I have seen some madmen in my time; I have known some who remained intelligent, lucid, even clear-headed, about everything in life except one single point. They would talk clearly, easily and profoundly about everything, until all of a sudden their mind ran aground on the reef of their madness and was torn to pieces, scattered to the winds and sunk without trace in that fearful raging sea, full of surging waves, fogs and squalls, which we call 'insanity'.

I would certainly think that I was utterly and completely mad if I were not in full possession of my faculties, if I were not perfectly aware of my state of mind, if I were not able to sound it and analyse it with absolute lucidity. I would therefore seem to be just suffering from hallucinations while remaining perfectly sane. Some unknown disturbance must have taken place in my brain, one of those disturbances which modern physiologists are trying to examine and elucidate; and this disturbance has presumably opened up a deep chasm in my mind, in the logical order of my ideas. Similar phenomena occur in dreams when they take us through the most improbable phantasmagoria without our feeling any surprise, because the mechanism of checking and verification is asleep, while the imaginative faculty is awake and working. May not the explanation be that one of the imperceptible keys of my cerebral keyboard is jammed? Sometimes, after an accident, a man loses his memory for proper names, or verbs, or figures, or simply dates. The localization of all the various divisions of the mind has now been conclusively established. It is scarcely a matter for surprise, therefore, that my ability to verify the unreality of certain hallucinations should be impaired just now.

Such were my thoughts as I strolled along beside the water. The sunshine covered the river with light, made the earth a place of beauty, and filled my heart with a feeling of love for life, for the swallows whose swift flight rejoices my eyes, for the riverside grasses whose whispering charms my ears.

Little by little, however, an inexplicable uneasiness came stealing over me. Some force, it seemed to me, some occult force was slowing me down, stopping me, preventing me from going any farther, calling me back. I felt that distressing impulse to turn back which takes hold of you when you have left someone you love at home ill and you have a presentiment that the illness has taken a turn for the worse.

So, in spite of myself, I turned back, convinced that I would find bad news at home, a letter or a telegram. There was nothing, and I was left feeling more puzzled and more uneasy than if I had had another fantastic vision.

*8 August.* Yesterday I had a terrible evening. He no longer shows himself but I can feel him near me, spying on me, watching me, penetrating me, dominating me, and more to be feared when he hides in this way than if he revealed his constant invisible presence by supernatural phenomena.

I slept well all the same.

*9 August.* Nothing, but I am afraid.

*10 August.* Nothing; what will happen tomorrow?

*11 August.* Still nothing; I cannot stay at home any longer with this fear and these thoughts in my mind; I shall go away.

*12 August.* Ten o'clock at night. All day I have wanted to go away; I couldn't do it. All day I have wanted to perform that easy, simple act, which would have given me my freedom – to go outside and get into my carriage and drive to Rouen; I couldn't do it. Why?

*13 August.* When certain illnesses affect you, all the springs in your physical being seem broken, all your energy exhausted, all your muscles as soft as flesh and your flesh as liquid as water. In a strange, distressing way, I feel as if all this had happened to my spiritual being. I no longer have any strength, any courage, any control over myself, even any power to set my will in motion. I can no longer will anything; but someone wills things for me – and I obey.

*14 August.* I am done for! Someone is in possession of my mind and controlling it! Someone is directing my every act, my every movement, my every thought. I no longer count for anything within myself; I am nothing but a terrified, captive spectator of all the things I do. I want to go out. I cannot. He does not want to; and I remain, trembling and panic-stricken in the armchair where he keeps me seated. I want no more than to stand up, to rise from my seat so that I may believe that I am still my own master. I cannot! I am riveted to my chair, and my chair cleaves to the floor, so that no power on earth could possibly lift us.

Then, all of a sudden, I must, must, must go to the bottom of my garden to pick some strawberries and eat them. And I go. I pick some strawberries and I eat them! Oh, God! God! God! Is there a God? If there is, then deliver me! Save me! Help me! Forgive me! Take pity on me! Have mercy on me! Save me! Oh, what suffering! What torment! What terror!

*15 August.* This is exactly how my poor cousin was possessed and dominated when she came to borrow five thousand francs from me. She was in the power of an alien will which had entered into her, like another soul, a parasitic, tyrannical soul. Is the world coming to an end?

But what is this being who dominates me, this unknowable creature, this invisible wanderer of a supernatural race?

So the Invisible Ones exist! Then why, since the world began, have they never manifested themselves as clearly as they have to me? I have never read of anything like the things that have happened in my house. Oh, if only I could leave it, if only I could go away, flee and never return! I should be saved, but I can't do it.

*16 August.* Today I managed to escape for two hours, like a prisoner who finds the door of his dungeon accidentally left open. I felt that I was free all of a sudden, and that he was far away. I ordered the horses to be harnessed as quickly as possible, and I drove to Rouen. Oh, what a joy it was to be able to tell a man: 'Drive to Rouen,' and to be obeyed.

I stopped at the library and asked them to lend me Doctor Hermann Herestauss's great treatise on the unknown inhabitants of the ancient and modern worlds.

Then, just as I was getting back into my carriage, I meant to say: 'Drive to the station,' but instead I shouted – I didn't say, I shouted – in such a loud voice that the passers-by turned round: 'Drive home,' and I fell back on the cushions of my carriage, utterly panic-stricken. He had come back and taken possession of me once more.

*17 August.* Oh, what a night! What a night! Yet it seems to me that I ought to feel pleased. I read until one o'clock in the morning. Hermann Herestauss, a doctor of philosophy and theology, has written a book on the history and manifestation of all the invisible beings who haunt mankind or have been invented by men's minds. He describes their origins, their domain, their powers. But none of them is at all like the one who is haunting me. It is as if ever since man has been capable of thought he has had a fearful presentiment of some new being, more powerful than himself, his successor in this world, and, feeling the proximity of this master, but unable to guess at its nature, he has created in his terror the whole fantastic host of occult beings, vague phantoms born of fear.

Well, after reading until one o'clock in the morning, I went and sat down by my open window to cool my head and refresh my mind in the gentle night air.

It was fine and warm. How I would have enjoyed that night in former days!

No moon. The stars shimmered and twinkled in the depths of the dark sky. Who lives in those worlds? What forms of life, what living creatures, what animals, what plants exist out there? What do the thinking creatures in those distant worlds know that is outside our knowledge? What can they do that is beyond our power? What can they see that we do not know? Will not one of them, sooner or later, on his way through space, appear on our earth to conquer it, just as the Normans once crossed the seas to subjugate weaker peoples?

For we humans are so weak, so defenceless, so ignorant, so small on this speck of dust spinning around in a drop of water!

I dozed off, dreaming like this in the fresh night air.

After sleeping for about forty minutes I opened my eyes

without moving, awakened by some strange, vague emotion. At first I saw nothing; then, all of a sudden, I had the impression that a page of the book lying open on my table had turned over by itself. Yet not a breath of air had come in through my window. Surprised, I waited and watched. After about four minutes I saw – yes, I saw with my own eyes – another page rise in the air and fall on the preceding one, as if a finger had turned it over. My armchair was empty, seemed empty; but I realized that *he* was there, sitting in my place, reading. With one wild bound, like the bound of a maddened animal about to tear its trainer to pieces, I sprang across the room to seize him, throttle him, kill him. . . . But before I reached it my chair tipped over as if someone had fled from me, my table rocked, my lamp fell over and went out, and my window closed as if some thief, caught in the act, had jumped out into the night, slamming it shut behind him.

So he had run away; he had been frightened, frightened of me!

In that case . . . in that case . . . tomorrow . . . or the day after . . . or some day in the future, I shall be able to seize him between my hands and force him to the ground! Don't dogs sometimes bite their masters and fly at their throats?

*18 August.* I have been thinking all day. Oh, yes, I shall obey him, follow his impulses, carry out all his wishes, make myself humble, servile, submissive. He has the upper hand. But a time will come . . .

*19 August.* I know . . . I know . . . I know everything! I have just read this in the *Revue du Monde Scientifique*:

A curious item of news has reached us from Rio de Janeiro. An epidemic of madness, comparable to those waves of collective insanity which affected the peoples of Europe in the

Middle Ages, is raging just now in the province of Sao Paulo. The frenzied inhabitants leave their houses, desert their villages and abandon their fields, saying that they are pursued, possessed, and dominated like human cattle by invisible though tangible beings, vampires of some kind who feed on their vitality during their sleep and also drink water and milk without apparently touching any other form of food.

Professor Don Pedro Henriquez, accompanied by several leading doctors, has left for the province of Sao Paulo, to study on the spot the causes and symptoms of this extraordinary madness, and to recommend to the Emperor those measures which he considers most likely to restore the delirious inhabitants to sanity.

Ah, now I remember the splendid Brazilian three-master which sailed past my windows on 8 May, on her way up the Seine! I thought her so pretty, so white, so gay! But the Being was on board, having come all the way from that far-off land where his race was born! And he saw me! He saw my white house too; and he jumped ashore from the ship. Oh, God!

Now I know, I understand. Man's reign on earth is over.

He has come, he whom the primitive peoples dreaded in their early fears, who was exorcized by anxious priests and summoned on dark nights by sorcerers who never even saw him. He whom the presentiments of the world's temporary masters endowed with the monstrous or pleasing forms of gnomes, spirits, genii, fairies and hobgoblins. After the crude concepts of primitive fears men of greater perspicacity came to see him more clearly. Mesmer guessed at his essential character, and it is already ten years since the doctors discovered the precise nature of his power before he exercised it himself. They have played with this weapon of the new Lord, the imposition of a mysterious will upon the enslaved minds of man. They call it magnetism, hypnotism, suggestion . . . heaven knows what else. I have seen them toying with this terrible force like foolish children. Woe to us! Woe to man! He has come, the . . . the . . . what is his name? . . . the . . . it is as if he were shouting his name in my ear, and I cannot hear it . . . the . . . yes . . . he *is* shouting it . . . I am listening . . . I cannot . . . say it again . . . the . . . Horla . . . I heard it . . . the Horla . . . it is he . . . the Horla. . . . He has come!

Oh, the vulture has eaten the dove, and the wolf has eaten the lamb; the lion has devoured the sharp-horned buffalo, and man has killed the lion with arrow, sword and gun; but the Horla is going to make of man what we have made of the horse and the ox: his chattel, his servant and his food, by the mere exercise of his will. Woe to us!

Yet sometimes the animal rebels and kills its trainer. . . . I too want . . . I could . . . but I must recognize him, touch him, see him! Scientists say that an animal's eye is different from ours and cannot see as ours does. . . . And my eye cannot make out this newcomer who is oppressing me.

Why not? Oh, now I remember the words of the monk on Mont Saint-Michel: 'Do we see a hundred-thousandth part of all that exists? Take the wind, for instance, the greatest force in Nature, which knocks down men, blows down buildings, uproots trees, whips up the sea into watery mountains, destroys cliffs and hurls great ships on to the reefs, the wind which kills, whistles, groans and roars – have you seen it, can you see it? And yet it exists.'

And I thought too: my eyes are so weak, so imperfect that they cannot even make out solid objects if they are transparent like glass. If a sheet of plate glass bars my way I hurl myself against it as a bird which has flown into a room beats its head against the window panes. Countless other things deceive and mislead my eyes – so it is small wonder that they should be unable to distinguish a new object which allows light to pass through it.

A new being! Why not? Such a being was bound to come, for why should we be the last? Why are we unable to see him, as we can see all other beings created before us? Because his constitution is more perfect, his body more delicate and complete than ours – ours which is so weak, so clumsily conceived, encumbered with organs that are always tired and strained like an over-complicated mechanism; ours which lives like a plant or an animal, feeding laboriously on air, grass and meat, a living machine subject to disease, deformity and decay, short-winded, ill-regulated, simple and complex, ingeniously ill-made, crudely and delicately constructed, a rough model of a being which might become intelligent and impressive.

There have been so few different creatures in this world, from the oyster to man. Why not one more, once we have reached the end of the interval between the successive appearances of the various species?

Why not one more? Why not other trees as well, bearing huge bright flowers filling whole regions with their scent? Why not other elements than fire, air, earth and water? There are only four of them, only four of those sources of life and strength! What a pitiful number! Why not forty, four hundred, four thousand? How poor, mean and wretched everything is, grudgingly given, poorly designed, clumsily made. Think of the grace of the elephant and the hippopotamus! Think of the elegance of the camel!

But what about that winged flower, the butterfly? you will say. I can imagine one as big as a hundred worlds, with wings whose shape, beauty, colour and movement I cannot find words to describe. But I can see it going from star to star, refreshing and perfuming them with the gentle, harmonious breath of its passage. And the peoples of the universe watch it going by, in an ecstasy of delight.

But what is the matter with me? It is he, he, the Horla, who is haunting me, filling my head with these mad ideas! He is in me; he is taking possession of my soul; I shall kill him!

*19 August.* I shall kill him! I have seen him! I sat down yesterday evening at my table and made a great show of concentrating on writing. I knew very well that he would come and prowl around me, very close to me, so close that I might perhaps be able to touch him, to seize him! And then!... Then I should have the strength of a desperate man; I should have my hands, my knees, my chest, my forehead, my teeth, to strangle him, crush him, bite him, tear him to pieces.

I watched for him with all my senses on the alert.

I had lit both my lamps and the eight candles on my mantelpiece, as if I thought that all this light would help me to make him out.

In front of me was my bed, an old oak four-poster; on my right, the fireplace; on my left, the door, which I had carefully shut after leaving it open long enough to attract him; and behind me, a very tall wardrobe with a mirror front, which I use every day for shaving and dressing and in which I used to inspect myself from head to foot every time I passed in front of it.

So there I was, pretending to be busy writing in order to deceive him, for he was watching me too; and suddenly I felt, I was certain, that he was reading over my shoulder, that he was there, brushing against my ear.

I jumped up with both hands outstretched, spinning round so fast that I almost fell. Well?... It was as bright as day, but I could not see myself in the mirror! It was empty and bright, and full of light to the very depths. My reflection was nowhere to be seen, yet I was standing right in front of it! I could see the whole limpid piece of glass from top to bottom. I stared at it with panic-stricken eyes, unable to take a single step, to make the slightest movement, knowing that he was there, that his invisible body had swallowed up my reflection, but aware that he was going to escape me yet again.

How frightened I was! Then, all of a sudden, I began to see myself in a mist at the back of the mirror, as if I were looking through a sheet of water; and it seemed to me that this water was slowly gliding from left to right, so that my reflection was becoming clearer every moment. It was like the last stage of an eclipse. What was hiding me did not seem to have clearly defined outlines, but a sort of opaque transparency, growing gradually lighter.

Finally I was able to see myself completely, as I do every day when I look in the mirror.

I had seen him! The horror of it lingers with me still, making me shudder when I think of it.

*20 August.* I must kill him, but how, seeing that I cannot touch him? Poison? But he would see me putting it in the water; and besides, would our poisons have any effect on an invisible body? No, almost certainly not. . . . Then how? . . . How?

*21 August.* I have sent for a locksmith from Rouen and asked him to fit my room with iron shutters, such as certain private houses in Paris have on the ground floor to keep out burglars. He is also making me a door to match. I have got myself the reputation of a coward, but what do I care?

*10 September.* Rouen, Hôtel Continental. It is done . . . it is done. . . . But is he dead? I am still badly shaken by what I have seen.

Yesterday, after the locksmith had put up my iron shutters and my iron door, I left everything open until midnight, even though it was beginning to get cold.

All of a sudden I felt that he was there, and I was filled with joy, an insane feeling of joy. I stood up slowly and strolled up and down the room for a long time, so that he should suspect nothing; then I took off my shoes and casually put on my slippers; then I closed my iron shutters, and, sauntering back to the door, I closed that too, double-locking it. Returning to the window, I secured it with a padlock, putting the key in my pocket.

Suddenly I realized that he was circling excitedly around me, that he in his turn was afraid, that he was ordering me to open the door and let him out. I almost gave way, but held fast in the end. Instead, standing with my back to the door, I opened it a little way, just far enough for me to slip out backwards; and as I am very tall, my head touched the lintel. I was sure that he could not have escaped, and I locked him in by himself, all by himself. How wonderful! I had him! Then I ran downstairs; in the drawing-room, which is directly underneath my bedroom, I picked up my two lamps and emptied all the oil on to the carpet, the furniture, everything; then I set fire to it and fled, after carefully double-locking the big front door.

I went and hid at the bottom of my garden, in a clump of laurels. What a time it took! What a long time! Everything was dark, silent, still; not a breath of air, not a single star; just mountainous clouds which I could not see, but which lay heavily, oh, so heavily, on my soul.

I watched my house and waited. What a long time it took! I was beginning to think that the fire had gone out by itself, or that *he* had put it out, when one of the ground floor windows fell out under the pressure of the fire, and a flame, a great red and yellow flame, a long, soft, caressing flame, licked its way up the white wall to the roof. A glow of light poured out over the trees, the branches, the leaves, and a shudder of fear ran through them too. The birds awoke; a dog started howling; it seemed as if dawn were breaking. Then two more windows exploded and I saw that the entire ground floor of my house was now just a raging furnace. Then a cry, a terrible cry, the heartrending cry of a woman rang out through the night, and two dormer windows were flung open! I had forgotten my servants! I saw their terrified faces and their waving arms...

Then, frantic with horror, I started running towards the village, shouting: 'Help! Help! Fire! Fire!' I met people already on their way to the fire, and I turned back with them to watch.

By now the house was no more than a horrible, awe-inspiring funeral pyre, a monstrous pyre in which human beings were burning, and *he* was burning too, he, my prisoner, the new Being, the new master, the Horla!

Suddenly the entire roof fell in, and a volcano of flames shot up towards the sky.

Through every window opening into the furnace I could see the fiery cauldron, and I thought to myself that he was there, in that oven, dead...

Dead? Perhaps. Or perhaps that body of his, through which the light of day could pass, was impervious to the means of destruction which kill our bodies?

Suppose he was not dead?... Perhaps only time alone has power over that Invisible and Fearful Being. Why should he possess that transparent, unknowable body, that spiritual body, if he too must fear sickness, injury, infirmity, premature destruction?

Premature destruction? That is the source of all human

dread. After man, the Horla. After him who can die any day, any hour, any minute, from any sort of accident, there has come he who shall die only at his appointed day, hour and minute, because he has reached the limit of his existence.

No ... no ... I know beyond a doubt that he is not dead. ... In that case ... in that case ... I shall have to kill — myself.

# THE MASK

THERE was a fancy-dress ball at the Élysée-Montmartre that evening to celebrate Mid-Lent, and the crowd was pouring into the brightly lit passage that led to the dance-hall like water into a lock. The overwhelming clamour of the orchestra was bursting through the walls and the roof like a musical storm, to spread throughout the neighbourhood, arousing in the streets and even in the depths of the nearby houses that irresistible desire to jump about, keep warm, and have fun which slumbers deep in the human animal.

The regular frequenters of the place were arriving from all parts of Paris, people from all classes of society who enjoyed vulgar, noisy fun which was a little squalid and slightly depraved. There were clerks, pimps and tarts — tarts of every sort, from those in common cotton to those in the finest batiste, rich tarts, old and bejewelled, and poor tarts of sixteen eager to paint the town red, go with men and spend money. There were men of the world in evening dress prowling about in the sweating crowd, in search of young flesh, fruit with the bloom rubbed off but still tasty, their eyes skinned and their noses following the scent. And there were masked dancers who seemed chiefly inspired by the desire to have a good time.

Groups of people had already gathered around the famous quadrilles to watch their capers. The swaying hedge, the quivering mass of men and women encircling the four dancers, coiled itself round like a snake, advancing and withdrawing in response to the movements of the four performers. The two women, whose thighs seemed to be joined to their bodies with indiarubber springs, executed amazing acrobatics with their legs. They kicked them up in the air so violently that their limbs seemed about to fly off, and then, suddenly parting them as if they were split up to the navel, with one in front and one behind, they touched the floor with the centre of their bodies in a rapid scissor movement which was both comic and revolting.

Their male partners leapt into the air, performing rapid motions with their legs, flapping their arms like the stumps of featherless wings, and obviously panting for breath under their masks.

One of them, who was performing in the most famous of the quadrilles in place of a celebrated dancer, the handsome Songe-au-Gosse, and doing his best to keep up with the indefatigable Arête-de-Veau, was executing some peculiar solo steps which the onlookers were greeting with ironic laughter.

He was a thin man, dressed as a dandy, and wearing a handsome varnished mask with a fair moustache and a curly wig.

He looked rather like a wax dummy from the Musée Grévin, a curious caricature of the charming young man in the fashion plates, and he was dancing with an earnest but awkward energy, a comical frenzy. He seemed rusty in comparison with the others, as he tried to imitate their capers, as stiff and clumsy as a mongrel playing with greyhounds. Sarcastic cheers egged him on, and, drunk with enthusiasm, he leaped about so frantically that all of a sudden, carried away by a wild rush, he ran straight at the wall of onlookers, which opened to let him through, then closed again around the dancer's motionless body, lying flat on his face.

Some men picked him up and carried him away. There were shouts for a doctor. A gentleman came forward, young and elegant, wearing evening dress with large pearls in his shirtfront. 'I am a professor in the medical school,' he said in a modest voice. Everyone made way for him, and in a little room full of files like a business-man's office he found the dancer, still unconscious, being laid across a couple of chairs. The first thing the doctor did was to try to remove the mask, but he discovered that it was fastened in a complicated way by a multitude of thin wires which ingeniously attached it to the edges of the wig and enclosed the entire head in a rigid framework; only somebody familiar with the fastenings could undo them. Even the man's neck was encased from the chin down in a false skin, and this glove-like sheath, painted to look like human flesh, reached as far as the shirt collar.

A pair of strong scissors was brought along, and when the doctor had made a cut in this astonishing contraption from shoulder to temple he opened up the carapace. Inside he found the face of an old man, pale, worn-out, thin and wrinkled. The shock to those who had carried in the curly-headed young dancer was so great that nobody laughed and nobody said a word.

They stared at his body stretched out on the straw-bottomed chairs, at the tired face with its closed eyes and its sprinkling of white hairs – some of them long hairs hanging over the forehead, the others a stubbly growth on the cheeks and chin – and beside this poor head the small, handsome, varnished mask, the youthful mask which was still smiling.

After a long period of unconsciousness the man came to, but he still seemed so weak and ill that the doctor feared some dangerous complication.

'Where do you live?' he asked.

The old dancer seemed to rack his brains before he remembered, and then he gave the name of a street which none of the people there knew. He had to be asked for further details of the neighbourhood, and he had the greatest difficulty providing these, speaking with a slowness and indecision which revealed the disturbed condition of his mind.

'I'll take you home myself,' said the doctor.

He felt a sudden curiosity to find out who this strange dancer was, to see where this curious mountebank lived.

Before long a cab was carrying the two of them to the far side of the Butte Montmartre.

The address they drove to was a tall, shabby building with a slimy staircase, one of those buildings riddled with windows which always look unfinished and stand between two patches of waste land, squalid warrens inhabited by wretched creatures in rags.

The doctor, hanging on to the banister rail, a winding wooden rail to which his hand kept sticking, helped the dazed old man, whose strength seemed to be coming back, up to the fourth floor.

The door they knocked on opened and a woman appeared, old like the dancer, and neatly dressed, with a white nightcap framing a bony, strong-featured face, one of those broad, kindly, coarse faces typical of hard-working, dependable working-class women.

'Heavens!' she exclaimed. 'What's happened to him?'

When the matter had been briefly explained to her she calmed down, and reassured the doctor himself, telling him that this was by no means the first time this sort of thing had happened.

'All he needs, Monsieur, is to be put to bed. He'll have a good night's sleep, and tomorrow he'll be as right as rain.'

'But he can scarcely speak,' said the doctor.

'Oh, it's nothing, he's just had a drop too much. He ate

no dinner so as to be light and nimble, and then he drank a couple of absinthes to perk himself up. Absinthe revives his legs, you see, but it takes away his wits and his tongue. He's too old to go dancing the way he does. But I've lost all hope of getting him to see sense.'

The doctor, surprised by what she had said, pressed the point.

'But why does he dance like that at his age?'

She shrugged her shoulders, flushed by the anger slowly building up in her.

'Why indeed? If you must know, it's so that people will think he's young under his mask, so that women will still take him for a gay dog and whisper dirty things in his ear, so that he can rub up against them and smell their scent and their paint and powder.... Oh, it makes me sick! I've had a fine life of it, I can tell you, Monsieur, for the forty years it's been going on.... But I've got to get him to bed before he takes bad. Would it be asking too much for you to give me a hand? When he's like this, it's a real job for me on my own.'

The old man was sitting on his bed with a drunken look in his eyes, his long white hair hanging over his face.

His companion looked at him with anger and pity in her eyes. She went on: 'Look what a handsome face he's got for his age. And he's got to go and doll himself up so that people'll think he's young. A crying shame, that's what it is. Don't you agree he's got a handsome face, Monsieur? Wait a minute and I'll show you before we put him to bed.'

She went over to a table which had a jug and basin, a tablet of soap, and a brush and comb on it. She picked up the brush, went back to the bed, and pulled the drunkard's tangled hair back from his forehead. Within a few moments she had given him the face of an artist's model, with long curls falling around his neck. Then, stepping back to contemplate him, she asked: 'Don't you think he's good-looking for his age?'

'He is indeed,' declared the doctor, who was beginning to enjoy himself.

'If you'd only known him when he was twenty-five!' she went on. 'But we've got to get him to bed, or his absinthes will go bad on him. Look, Monsieur, will you pull at his sleeve?... Higher up.... That's it.... Now his trousers. ... Wait a minute, and I'll take off his shoes.... That's right.... Now hold him up while I turn the bed down.... There.... Into bed with him.... If you think he'll move up later on to make room for me, you can think again. I'll have to find room for myself, and he doesn't care where. There now, you gay dog!'

As soon as he felt himself lying between the sheets the old fellow shut his eyes, opened them, and shut them again, his whole face expressing contentment and a resolute determination to go to sleep.

Examining him with growing interest, the doctor asked: 'So he plays the young man at fancy-dress balls, does he?'

'At every one of them, Monsieur, and you wouldn't believe the state he's in when he gets back here in the morning. It's regret that drives him to it, you see, and makes him put a cardboard face over his own. Yes, regret at not being what he was, and not having the success he used to have with women.'

He was asleep now, and beginning to snore. She looked at him with pity in her eyes, and went on: 'Oh, he had his successes in the old days all right! More than you'd imagine, Monsieur – more than all the fine gentlemen in the world, and all the singers and generals.'

'Really? Then what did he do for a living?'

'Oh, that probably surprises you, seeing that you didn't

know him when he was on top of the world. When I met him it was a ball like tonight, for he's always been a great one for dancing. I fell for him the moment I saw him, hook, line and sinker. He was a lovely man, Monsieur – just to look at him made you want to cry – dark as a crow, with curly hair and eyes as big as windows. Oh, yes, he was a lovely man! He picked me up that night, and I've never left him since, not a single day, in spite of everything! And he's given me some hard times, I can tell you that.'

'You're married?' asked the doctor.

She answered simply: 'Yes, Monsieur . . . otherwise he'd have ditched me like the others. I've been his wife and his housekeeper, and everything else, anything he wanted. . . . Oh, the times he's made me cry . . . though I never let him see! . . . Because he used to tell me all about his affairs . . . me, Monsieur . . . never thinking how it hurt me to listen . . .'

'But you still haven't said what he did for a living.'

'So I haven't . . . I clean forgot to tell you. . . . He was the chief assistant at Martel's, but an assistant like they'd never had before . . . an artist earning ten francs an hour on an average . . .'

'Martel's. . . . What was that?'

'The hairdresser's, Monsieur, the big hairdresser's near the Opera where all the actresses used to go. Yes, all the smartest actresses had their hair done by Ambroise, and gave him a fortune in tips. Oh, women are all the same, Monsieur, every one of them. When a man takes their fancy, they offer themselves to him. It's all so easy . . . and so hard to hear about. Because he told me everything . . . he couldn't keep quiet about it, just couldn't keep quiet about it. Those things do so please a man . . . maybe talking about them even more than doing them.

'When I saw him come home at night looking a little

pale, with shining eyes and a satisfied look on his face, I'd say to myself: "He's had another one. I bet he's had another one." Then I'd feel a longing to question him, a longing that burnt me up inside, but at the same time I had a longing not to know, an urge to stop him talking if he started. So we'd just sit there looking at each other.

'I knew perfectly well that he'd never keep quiet, that he'd come out with it in the end. I could tell that from the way he looked and the way he laughed, just to let me know what had happened. "I've had a good day today, Madeleine," he'd say. I'd pretend I hadn't noticed, I hadn't guessed. I'd just lay the table, bring the soup, and sit down facing him.

'At times like that, Monsieur, it was like somebody'd crushed all my feeling for him with a stone. It hurt, it hurt something awful. But he didn't realize that, he didn't know. He just had to tell somebody about it, to brag about it, to show how the ladies loved him . . . and I was the only one he could tell . . . the only one. . . . So I had to listen to him and drink it all up like poison.

'He'd start on his soup, and then he'd say: "Another one today, Madeleine."

'And I'd think: "Here we go! Heavens, what a man! Why did I ever have to meet him?"

'Then off he'd go: "Another one today, and a real beauty this time." It'd be a girl from the Vaudeville, or a little thing from the Variétés, or maybe a leading lady, one of the real top-liners. He'd tell me their names, what their rooms were like, and everything about them, yes, everything, Monsieur. . . . Details that tore my heart out. And he'd come back to it and start his story all over again, so pleased with himself that I'd pretend to laugh so he wouldn't be cross with me.

'Maybe what he told me wasn't all true. He was such a

boaster he was quite capable of making it up! On the other hand, maybe it was true. On those nights he made a great show of being tired, and said he wanted to go to bed straight after supper. We used to have our supper at eleven, Monsieur, because he never came home sooner than that, on account of the jobs he did in the evening.

'When he'd finished telling me about his latest affair, he'd walk up and down the bedroom smoking cigarettes. He'd look so handsome with his moustache and his curly hair that I'd think: "It must be true after all. Seeing that I'm mad about the man, why shouldn't other women be just as crazy about him?" Then I'd feel like crying, or screaming, or running away, or throwing myself out of the window, but I'd just clear the supper things away while he went on smoking. He'd give a big yawn, opening his mouth wide, and before going to bed he'd say two or three times: "Lord, I bet I sleep well tonight!"

'I don't hold it against him because he didn't know how much he hurt me. He just couldn't know. He loved boasting about women like a peacock spreading its tail out. He'd got to the point of thinking that they all looked at him and wanted him.

'He had a hard time when he started showing his age.

'Oh, Monsieur, when I saw his first grey hair I got such a shock it fair took my breath away. Then I had a thrill of joy – nasty, cruel joy, but a tremendous feeling all the same! I said to myself: "It's all over ... it's all over ..." I felt like I was going to be let out of prison. I was going to have him all to myself, because the others wouldn't want him any more.

'It was one morning, in our bed. He was still asleep, and I was bending over him to wake him with a kiss, when I spotted a little thread shining like silver in the curls on his temples. Such a surprise it was! I'd never have thought it possible. At first I thought of pulling it out so he wouldn't see: but when I looked closer I spotted another one higher up. Grey hairs! His hair was going grey! My heart was pounding and my skin was all moist, but deep down I felt really happy.

'It's not very nice thinking like that, but I did my housework that morning with a light heart, leaving him to go on sleeping; and when he woke up by himself I said: "Do you know what I found while you were asleep?"

"No," he said.

'"I found you've got some grey hairs."

'He was so annoyed he sat up with a start as if I'd tickled him, and he glared at me and said: "You're lying!"

'"No, I'm not. You've got four on your left temple."

'He jumped out of bed and ran to the mirror, but he couldn't find them. So I showed him the first one I'd spotted, the one lowest down, the little curly one, and I said: "It's not surprising, seeing the life you lead. Two years from now you'll be finished."

'Well, Monsieur, I never spoke a truer word. Two years later, you wouldn't have recognized him. How quickly a man changes! He was still a good-looking fellow, but he was losing his freshness and the women weren't running after him any more. Oh, I had a hard time of it, I did, in those days – he really put me through it. I couldn't do a thing right, not a thing. He left his trade for the hat business and lost a pile of money. Then he tried being an actor, but he wasn't any good at that. And then he started going to dance-halls. Luckily he'd had enough sense to put a bit of money aside, and that's what we live on. It's enough, but it's not much. And to think that at one time he had a small fortune!

'Now you've seen what he gets up to. It's like a frenzy

that's got hold of him. He's got to be young, he's got to dance with women smelling of scent and powder. The poor old dear!'

Deeply touched, and on the verge of tears, she looked at her snoring husband. Then, tiptoeing over to him, she planted a kiss on his hair. The doctor had stood up and was getting ready to go. He had nothing more to say to this strange couple.

As he was leaving, the woman said: 'Would you mind giving me your address? If he gets worse, I'll come and fetch you.'

# MOUCHE

## *Reminiscences of a Rowing Man*

THIS is what he told us:

'I saw some funny things and some funny girls in those days, when I used to go boating on the river. Many's the time I've felt like writing a little book called *On the Seine*, describing that carefree athletic life, a life of poverty and gaiety, of noisy, rollicking fun, that I led in my twenties.

'I was a penniless clerk at the time; now I'm a successful man who can throw away huge sums to gratify a passing whim. I had a thousand modest, unattainable desires in my heart which gilded my existence with fantastic hopes. Today, I really can't think of anything that would induce me to get out of the armchair where I sit dozing. Though life could be hard, how simple and enjoyable it was to live like that, between the office in Paris and the river at Argenteuil. For ten years my great, my only, my absorbing passion was the Seine, that lovely, calm, varied, stinking river, full of mirages and filth. I think I loved it so much because it gave me the feeling of being alive. Oh, those strolls along the flower-covered banks, with my friends the frogs dreamily cooling their bellies on water-lily leaves, and the frail, dainty lilies among the tall grasses, which parted suddenly to reveal a scene from a Japanese album as a kingfisher darted past me like a blue flame! How I loved all that, with an instinctive passion of the eyes which spread through my whole body in a feeling of deep and natural joy!

'Just as others remember nights of passion, I cherish memories of sunrises on misty mornings, with floating, drifting vapours, white as ghosts before the dawn, and then, as the first ray of sunshine touched the meadows, lit with a lovely rosy glow; and I cherish memories too of the moon silvering the rippling surface of the water with a radiance which brought all my dreams to life.

'And all that, that symbol of everlasting illusion, was born for me on the foul water which swept all the refuse of Paris down to the sea.

'Besides, what a gay life we led! There were five of us, a small group of friends who are pillars of the community today. As none of us had any money we had set up an indescribable sort of club in a frightful pothouse at Argenteuil, renting a single dormitory bedroom where I spent what were the maddest nights of my life. We thought about nothing but having fun and rowing, for all of us, with one exception, regarded rowing as a religion. I remember adventures those five rascals had, and pranks they thought up, which were so fantastic that nobody could possibly believe them today. Nobody behaves like that any more, even on the Seine, because the crazy fun which was the breath of life to us means nothing to people nowadays.

'The five of us owned a single boat between us, which had cost us enormous trouble to buy and which gave us more fun than we shall ever have again. It was a yawl, broad in the beam and rather heavy, but solid, roomy and comfortable. I won't try to describe my friends to you. One of them was a mischievous little chap nicknamed Petit Bleu, and another a tall, wild-looking fellow with grey eyes and black hair whom we called Tomahawk. Then there was a lazy, witty character we nicknamed La Tôque, the only one who never touched an oar, on the pretext that he would be sure to capsize the boat; a slim, elegant, very well-groomed fellow we called N'a-qu'un-Oeil after a recently published novel by Cladel, and also because he

wore a monocle; and lastly myself, whom the others had
baptized Joseph Prunier. We lived in perfect harmony,
our only regret being that we hadn't a girl to take the
tiller. A woman is an indispensable adjunct to a boat like
ours – indispensable because she keeps minds and hearts
awake, because she provides excitement, amusement and
distraction, and because she gives a spice to life and, with
a red parasol gliding past green banks, decoration too. But
an ordinary coxwoman was no use to us five, who could
scarcely be described as ordinary people. We needed somebody unusual, odd, ready for anything, in short almost
impossible to find. We had tried a good many without
success – girls who just played at being helmswomen,
stupid creatures who were more interested in the light
wine that went to their heads than in the water that kept
them afloat. We kept them for a single Sunday and then
sent them packing in disgust.

'But then one Saturday evening N'a-qu'un-Oeil brought
along a lively, skinny little thing who was always hopping
and skipping around, a young tease who was full of that
skittishness which passes for wit among the street arabs of
both sexes who have grown up on the pavements of Paris.
She was a sweet girl but not really pretty, a rough sketch
of a woman with a little of everything in her, one of those
silhouettes which artists draw in three strokes on the table-
cloth in a café after dinner, between a glass of brandy and
a cigarette. Nature sometimes turns out creatures like that.

'On that first evening she astonished and amused us,
and was so unpredictable that none of us could make up
our minds about her. Landing in the midst of a bunch of
men who were ready to get up to any kind of prank, she
was soon in command of the situation, and by the next day
she had conquered us completely.

'She was absolutely crazy into the bargain. She told us

that she had been born with a glass of absinthe in her belly, which her mother had drunk just before giving birth to her, and she had never sobered up since, because, she said, her nurse used to keep her strength up with tots of rum. She herself always called the bottles lined up on bar-room shelves "my Holy Family".

'I don't know which of us christened her "Mouche", nor why that name was given her. But it suited her perfectly, and it stuck to her. So every week our yawl, which was called *Feuille-à-l'Envers*, would travel along the Seine between Asnières and Maisons-Laffitte with a load of five light-hearted strapping young fellows, steered by a lively, scatter-brained creature under a parasol of painted paper, who treated us as if we were slaves charged with the duty of taking her for a row, and whom we all adored.

'We adored her, first of all for a variety of reasons, and then for one in particular. She was a sort of little word-mill in the stern of our boat, chatting away in the wind blowing over the water. She babbled incessantly with the continuous sound of those winged toys that spin in the breeze, trotting out the most unexpected, amusing and astonishing things. In that mind of hers, which seemed like a patchwork of rags of all kinds and colours, not sewn together but only tacked, there was fairy-tale fantasy, bawdy, immodesty, impudence, jokes and surprises, and a sense of fresh air and scenery such as you would get travelling in a balloon.

'We used to ask her questions just to hear the far-fetched answers she would produce. The one we fired at her most often was: "Why are you called Mouche?"

'She thought up such fantastic reasons that we would stop rowing to laugh at them.

'She appealed to us as a woman too and La Tôque, who never did any rowing but spent the whole day sitting beside her in the helmsman's seat, once said in reply to the traditional question "Why are you called Mouche?": "Because she's a little Spanish fly."

'And that is exactly what she was: a little buzzing, exciting Spanish fly, not the classic poisonous cantharides, shiny and hooded, but a little red-winged Spanish fly who was beginning to have an oddly disturbing effect on the whole crew of the *Feuille-à-l'Envers*.

'What stupid jokes we made about that Leaf on which our Fly had alighted!

'Ever since Mouche had joined our crew N'a-qu'un-Oeil had taken up a superior, preponderant role among us, the role of a gentleman who has a woman, compared with four others who have none. He sometimes abused this privilege to the point of exasperating us by kissing Mouche in front of us, perching her on his knees after meals, and assuming all kinds of humiliating and irritating prerogatives.

'We had fitted up a curtain in the dormitory to isolate them from the rest of us.

'But I soon noticed that my companions were thinking along the same lines as myself, and asking themselves: "Why, under what exceptional law, by virtue of what inadmissible principle, should Mouche, who seems uninhibited by any principles, be faithful to her lover when women of higher social standing are not faithful to their husbands?"

'Our assessment of the situation was accurate, as we soon discovered. Our only regret was that we hadn't made it earlier and so wasted precious time. Mouche was unfaithful to N'a-qu'un-Oeil with all the other sailors of the *Feuille-à-l'Envers*.

'She did this without any difficulty, without any resistance, the first time each of us asked.

'Heavens, how shocking prudish folk are going to find this! But why? Is there a single fashionable courtesan without a dozen lovers, and is there a single one of those lovers stupid enough not to know it? Isn't it the done thing to have a regular evening with some famous, much-sought-after woman, just as one has a regular evening at the Opera, the Théâtre-Français, or the Odéon, now that they are putting on the minor classics? A dozen men club together to keep a cocotte who finds it difficult to make a fair distribution of her time, just as a dozen men will club together to buy a racehorse ridden by a single jockey – the perfect symbol of the real lover.

'For reasons of delicacy we left Mouche to N'a-qu'un-Oeil from Saturday evening to Monday morning. The days on the river were his. We deceived him only during the week, in Paris, far from the Seine, which for boating men like us was almost tantamount to not deceiving him at all.

'The odd thing about the situation was that the four men filching Mouche's favours knew all about the sharing of those favours, talked about it among themselves, and even made veiled allusions to it in her presence which made her roar with laughter. Only N'a-qu'un-Oeil seemed to know nothing about it, and his ignorance of the situation produced a sort of awkwardness between him and us; it seemed to set him apart, isolate him, and destroy our former trust and intimacy. It gave him in our eyes a difficult and rather ridiculous part to play, the part of a deceived lover, almost that of a husband.

'However, as he was extremely intelligent, and had a dry sense of humour, we sometimes wondered, rather uneasily, whether he might not have his suspicions.

'He took care to enlighten us in a way which was painful for us. We were on our way to Bougival for lunch and we were rowing hard when La Tôque, who had the triumphant look of a contented man that morning, and, seated beside the helmswoman, seemed to be pressing up against her rather too freely for our liking, suddenly called out: "Stop!"

'The eight oars rose out of the water.

'Then, turning to his neighbour, he asked: "Why are you called Mouche?"

'Before she could answer, N'a-qu'un-Oeil, who was sitting in the bows, said drily: "Because she settles on all sorts of carrion."

'At first there was an embarrassed silence, followed by a general inclination to laugh. Even Mouche was dumbfounded.

'Then La Tôque gave the order: "All together."

'The boat moved forward again.

'The matter was closed, the mystery cleared up.

'This little incident changed nothing in our habits. Its only result was to restore cordial relations between N'a-qu'un-Oeil and ourselves. He became once more the privileged possessor of Mouche from Saturday evening until Monday morning, his superiority over the rest of us having been firmly established by this definition, which incidentally put a stop to all questions about the name Mouche. From then on we contented ourselves with the secondary role of grateful and attentive friends who took discreet advantage of weekdays without there being any sense of rivalry between us.

'Everything went very well for about three months. Then, all of a sudden, Mouche began to behave strangely with us all. She was less high-spirited and became edgy, ill-at-ease, almost irritable.

'We kept asking her: "What's the matter with you?"

'She would answer: "Nothing, leave me alone."

'We learned the truth from N'a-qu'un-Oeil one Saturday evening. We had just sat down at table in the little dining-room which Barbichon, the proprietor of our pothouse, reserved for us in his establishment, and after finishing our soup we were waiting for the fried fish when our friend, who also looked a little worried, took Mouche's hand and then began speaking.

'"My dear friends," he said, "I have something very serious to tell you which may lead to some lengthy discussion. But we'll have time for that between courses. Poor Mouche has given me a disastrous piece of news which she has asked me to pass on to you.

'"She is pregnant.

'"I have only two things to add. This is no time to leave her in the lurch, and any attempt to find out who's the father is forbidden."

'The first effect of this news was utter amazement, a sense of disaster. We looked at one another as if we wanted to accuse somebody. But whom? Yes, whom? I have never felt as keenly as I did at that moment the unfairness of that cruel jest of Nature's which never allows a man to know for certain whether he is the father of his child.

'Then, little by little, we came to experience a comforting sense of consolation, born, oddly enough, of a vague feeling of solidarity.

'Tomahawk, who hardly ever spoke, expressed this growing serenity in the following words: "Well, it can't be helped, and union is strength."

'A boy came in from the kitchen with the gudgeon. We didn't pitch into it as we usually did, because when all was said and done we were rather upset.

'N'a-qu-un-Oeil went on: "In these circumstances she has been good enough to make a full confession to me. We are all equally guilty. Let's shake hands on it and adopt the child."

'This proposal was unanimously accepted. We raised our arms above the dish of fried fish and swore a solemn oath: "We'll adopt it."

'Then, suddenly realizing that she was saved, and relieved of the horrible weight of anxiety which had been burdening her for a month, that sweet, crazy victim of love exclaimed: "Oh, my dear friends! You're so kind, so very, very kind. . . . Thank you all!"

'And for the first time in our presence she burst into tears.

'From then on we would talk about the child in the boat as if it had already been born, and each of us showed an exaggerated degree of interest in the slow but regular swelling of our helmswoman's waist.

'We would stop rowing and ask: "Mouche?"

'She would reply: "Present!"

'"Boy or girl?"

'"Boy."

'"What will he be?"

'Then she would give free rein to her imagination in the most fantastic way, telling us endless stories, astonishing accounts of the child's life from the day of his birth to his final triumph. He was everything, that child, in the innocent, passionate, touching dreams of that extraordinary little creature who now lived chastely among the five men she called her "five papas". She saw and described him as a sailor discovering a new world bigger than America; as a general winning back Alsace and Lorraine for France; as an emperor founding a dynasty of wise and generous sovereigns who would give our country lasting happiness; as a scientist finding first the secret of making gold and then that of eternal life; and as an aeronaut devising a method of travelling to the stars and turning the infinite reaches of space into a vast promenade for mankind – thus making all men's most improbable and magnificent dreams come true.

'Heavens, how sweet and amusing the poor thing was until the end of that summer!

'It was on the twentieth of September that her dream was destroyed. We were rowing back after lunch at Maisons-Laffitte, and we were passing Saint-Germain when she said that she was thirsty and asked us to stop at Le Pecq.

'For some time past she had been growing heavy and this annoyed her dreadfully. She could no longer skip around as before, or leap from the boat to the bank as she was used to doing. But she still tried to, in spite of all we said or did to stop her, and she would have fallen a score of times if our arms had not been waiting to catch her.

'That day she was rash enough to try to leave the boat while it was still moving, in one of those displays of bravado which sometimes prove fatal to sick or tired athletes.

'Just as we were coming alongside, before we could guess what she was going to do or stop her, she stood up, took a spring, and tried to jump on to the quay.

'But she was not strong enough to reach it and just touched the stone edging with one foot. She slipped, struck her belly against the sharp corner, and with a loud cry disappeared into the water.

'All five of us dived in together, and brought out a poor fainting creature, deathly pale and already suffering terrible pain.

'We carried her as quickly as we could to the nearest inn and then sent for a doctor.

'During the ten hours her miscarriage lasted she bore

the appalling agony with heroic courage. We stood around miserably, sick with worry and fear.

'Finally she was delivered of a dead child, and for a few more days we had serious fears for her life.

'At last the doctor told us one morning: "I think she's over the worst. That girl must be made of iron!" And we all went into her room together, our hearts bursting with relief.

'Speaking for us all, N'a-qu'un-Oeil said to her: "You're out of danger, Mouche dear, and we're all delighted!"

'Then for the second time we saw her cry. With her eyes swimming with tears, she stammered: "Oh, if you only knew, if you only knew.... I'm so unhappy, so unhappy. ... I'll never get over it."

'"Over what, Mouche dear?"

'"Killing him, of course, for I did kill him! Oh, I know I didn't mean to, but I'm so unhappy all the same...."

'She burst out sobbing. We stood around her, deeply moved, not knowing what to say.

'She went on: "Did you see him?"

'With one voice we answered: "Yes."

'"It was a boy, wasn't it?"

'"Yes."

'"And beautiful?"

'We hesitated. Petit-Bleu, who had fewer scruples than the rest of us, made up his mind what to say.

'"Very beautiful."

'This was unwise of him, for she started moaning, almost howling with despair.

'Then N'a-qu'un-Oeil, who perhaps loved her more than any of us, hit on a wonderful idea to calm her down. Kissing her tear-dimmed eyes, he said: "Cheer up, Mouche dear, cheer up. We'll make you another one."

'The sense of humour which was in her very bones

suddenly came alive, and half convinced, half laughing, with tears still in her eyes and her heart full of pain, she looked around at us all and asked: "Honest?"

'And we answered as one man: "Honest."'